When the Games

FROZE

NANA IS A WOMAN FROM GHANA WHO ENDEAVORS TO FORM A FOUNDATION
AGAINST FEMALE GENITAL MUTILATION.

A.M. PEABODY

When The Games Froze
Copyright © 2024 by A.M. Peabody

All rights reserved. No part of this publication may be reproduced, distributed, or transmitted in any form or by any means, including photocopying, recording, or other electronic or mechanical methods, without the prior written permission of the author, except in the case of brief quotations embodied in critical reviews and certain other non-commercial uses permitted by copyright law.

ISBN
978-1-964488-02-8 (Paperback)
978-1-964488-03-5 (eBook)
978-1-964488-01-1 (Hardcover)

When the Games
FROZE

Table of Contents

Chapter 1	A Memorable Thanksgiving	1
Chapter 2	A December Friday	16
Chapter 3	The Campaign	24
Chapter 4	Disaster Strikes	31
Chapter 5	The Tours	51
Chapter 6	The Surprise	67
Chapter 7	Road to the Stadium	76
Chapter 8	Long Healing	89
Chapter 9	Then there were Two	97
Chapter 10	Nana Returns to the Job Force	108
Chapter 11	The Samaritan	124
Chapter 12	A Twist of Life	149
Chapter 13	A Step toward the Stars and Stripes	175
Chapter 14	Nana's Adventures	222
Chapter 15	The Unspeakable	257

Chapter One

A MEMORABLE THANKSGIVING

How wonderful and pleasant it is when brothers live in harmony! – Psalm 133:1 (NLT)

On the eve of Thanksgiving, Shirley and Nana busied themselves in their eat-in kitchen. Shirley seasoned the turkey, while Nana chopped celery, tomato, onion, fennel and garlic. A southern American girl from Georgia, Shirley was an excellent cook, and she enjoyed cooking the traditional Thanksgiving dinner. "I'm going to make this bird really tasty with all the spices we have." Shirley bragged to Nana as she washed her hands in the kitchen sink.

"I have no doubt about that." Nana continued to chop vegetables and spices. "I witness it every year without eating any of it." They laughed, knowing that Nana was a vegetarian, and she had never had the pleasure of tasting Shirley's traditional Thanksgiving turkey. Nana had a large dish of tofu loaf. Shirley seasoned the tofu loaf for Nana. Thanksgiving was the only day of the year that Nana did not enjoy Shirley's fabulous cooking.

The front door opened, and Jean-Claude entered in his Europa Airlines flight attendant uniform. "The French Prince is home!" He teased as the girls ran to greet him as they always did.

"Is that what happened in the last three weeks since you've been away?" Shirley smartly asked. "Who crowned you prince?" She hugged him. "Welcome home, we missed you."

"Welcome home dear." Nana gave him a hug and looked him over. "You are looking great, French Prince." The three laughed, as he raced down to his basement apartment to unload his luggage and get comfortable.

"So, how many people are we having over tomorrow?" Jean-Claude returned and sat on the bar stool as he regarded the amount of food the girls had. "Is it an Army?"

"Didn't you hear? The whole French army arrives tomorrow." They laughed at Shirley's smart retort. She had indoctrinated her two foreign roommates into the celebration of the biggest American holiday of the year.

"Frank is coming." Nana explained. "Is Paula still coming?" She asked Jean-Claude.

He nodded. "She said she would. She will be in Washington until Sunday." Paula Braun was Jean-Claude's girlfriend of three years.

"That's your army right there." Shirley snapped her fingers. "Frank alone needs a turkey all to himself." Frank had a hearty appetite, and Shirley always teased him about it.

The girls continued to work in the kitchen late into the night. Jean-Claude excused himself and took a nap for about two hours. He later found them still busy in the kitchen. They wanted to have most of the preparations done before Thanksgiving morning. "You need your rest ladies." He reminded them.

"Well, it's good to see somebody's getting enough rest for all of us." Shirley smiled at him.

"Remember what we have to do tomorrow morning." Nana explained to Jean-Claude. "We adopted a family again this year." Each year, the three roommates had a Thanksgiving tradition. They adopted a random family in Washington, D.C. and delivered a full Thanksgiving dinner to the chosen family. The family was always chosen through a local charity organization.

"We have a special surprise this year. Frank will join us." Shirley beamed with pride. "He's going to give an autographed football to the ten-year-old boy in our adopted family."

"Wow! We get better every year." Jean-Claude exclaimed with excitement. They took a box of toys to the children, in addition to the thanksgiving dinner the year before. Their little charity donation was Nana's idea five years earlier. Now, it was a tradition.

"I am on the do-good committee at the office this year." Nana told them. "I need ideas for our Children's Holiday Fund."

Shirley chuckled, "They have more committees going on at her job than the government." They laughed. "They have a committee for everything."

"How is work, by the way?" Jean-Claude asked Nana. "Anymore abuse from your clients?"

"You mean the verbal lynching?" Nana replied as she began to put away the food that was on the kitchen counter. "We have one client who believes that we are slaves on his grandfather's plantation." Shirley and Jean-Claude laughed at her analogy. "He called to speak with one of my colleagues. He was told that Gerald was on vacation for a week. Do you know what he asked?" Shirley and Jean-Claude waited with eager ears for Nana's continuation, as she shook her head in disbelief. "He asked, 'why do they allow you people to take vacations anyway?'"

"Unbelievable!" Shirley remarked as Jean-Claude's brown eyes became larger than life. "He said what?"

"Another client returned from her trip." Nana continued. "She wrote a bad customer service report about me. She complained that I reminded her of the multiple revisions to her itinerary prior to her leaving." The three took delight in exchanging stories about their clients when they reunited. Nana felt that she fitted well in that office because the clientele and co-workers were predominantly international. The International Financial Trust (IFT) was an international lending organization, servicing mostly developing countries. "Do you recall the big snow blizzard?" Nana asked while her two roommates nodded. "Our client, Mr. Nicopoulos criticized Proficiency Travel for closing the office for one day."

"Is he the same client that said Proficiency Travel should not allow the employees to take lunch breaks?" Jean-Claude inquired.

"He's the same one." Nana chuckled and shook her head in disgust. "He said it prevented him from reaching us when he wanted to reach us."

"Somebody needs to inform your Mr. Nicopoulos that the emancipation was signed in 1869." Shirley fitted more things in the refrigerator as she talked. "He must think Proficiency is running a slave plantation." They laughed. "I have some crazy clients, but Nana's clients win all of the awards." They laughed harder. Their interlude was the typical reunion. The three roommates referred to the sessions as their "therapy". Their jobs entailed service to the public and they knew how stressful those jobs were. They had agreed a long time before to serve as support for each other.

"Well, you know we have some crazy clients as well." Jean-Claude assured them. "We had one passenger on the flight to Dulles who had one too many cocktails. He decided that the seat was not comfortable enough for him. So, he sprawled out on the floor in the aisle."

"Now that's a winner!" Shirley remarked as they laughed. "So, what did you do?"

Jean-Claude shrugged. "Four flight attendants, including yours truly had to lift him back onto his seat." Jean-Claude's body motions made his stories even funnier. "This passenger was far from lightweight, believe me." Nana and Shirley laughed hysterically.

"Well, a lady came to the salon this week with green hair!" Shirley stopped laughing long enough to tell a story about her own client. "She tried to color her hair at home. She realized that she was not a professional after all."

"So, it was Shirley to the rescue." Nana remarked.

"Yes, it was." Shirley continued. "Poor lady – she wore a hat when she came in. I worked for hours to strip the green from her hair, and then I applied the correct color she wanted."

"That is scary. I think I will keep my brown hair." Jean-Claude ran his fingers through his crew cut.

Nana went over to where he sat and ruffled his hair. "Shirley, don't you think he would look great with purple highlights?" They laughed as the girls tidied the kitchen.

"I will call Proficiency Travel to tell them that you want to work with Mr. Nicopoulos exclusively." Jean-Claude threatened revenge, but Nana knew that his jokes were as far as he would go.

"Mr. Nicopoulos does not deserve my polite service. I think he crawled from under a sewage system." Nana replied.

"Ooh! Girl, you need to finish your hit play. You need to stage it. Your Mr. Nicopoulos really gets under your skin." Shirley reminded her. Nana majored in English Literature and minored in theatrics. She aspired to become a playwright someday, but she paid the bills from her travel agent salary. Her parents insisted that she studied one of the sciences, but she did what she enjoyed.

"How is that project going by the way?" Jean-Claude wanted to know. He had read several of Nana's plays in the past, but she was not successful in a big way. She had staged a couple of them in school theaters but nothing beyond that.

"I am working hard on it – every spare moment of the day." She spent more than a year writing and re-writing that play. She and her roommates hoped that the latest one would get her in one of the big theaters in Washington.

"Think about it. A big break for you would get you out of the reins of Mr. Nicopoulos, the IFT, even Proficiency Travel." Jean-Claude reminded her.

"You are absolutely right." Nana thought for a moment. "I have always dreamed of success. I would take good care of you two."

"You have such a kind heart, Nana." Shirley blinked to hide her emotions. "I hope you make it. Most people dream of success, only a few of them work to get it. You are one of those few." She patted Nana on the back. "I wish you all the best, kiddo."

"Well, you might only need to support one of us." Jean-Claude teased. "We just need to get our buddy, Frank to marry Shirley. They can support the two of us." The three laughed. Jean-Claude and Nana were responsible for the football star's and Shirley's relationship. He called her every night from San Antonio.

"I am capable of supporting myself, thank you very much." Shirley blushed and strutted over to the living room with her roommates in tow. She loved Frank and enjoyed his company, but she was unsure about giving up her present life. She liked the Washington, D.C. area and aspired to someday open her own cosmetology business. Her father wanted her to graduate from college and become a mortician or a pathologist. Shirley's father was second generation in the embalming business. His father owned a funeral home in Georgia, and he followed in his footsteps. He expected both Shirley and her brother, Wayne to assume the family tradition. Wayne did exactly as his father expected, while Shirley wanted no part of it. She told her father in no uncertain terms, "Pop, I don't want to mess with no dead bodies." Jimmy Marshall was stern with her. "Let me remind you young lady. You would not have the life you have now if it were not for those many dead bodies that I, as you put it, messed with." Shirley went to Spellman College upon her father's persistence, but she did not graduate. She dropped out after two years, attended cosmetology school and did well. She was encouraged by a schoolmate from Washington, D.C. to move to the area. Her schoolmate knew someone who owned a salon in the District of Columbia. There, Shirley landed her first job as a shampoo girl, and later was given her very own booth. Her father did not succeed in getting her to become a mortician or pathologist, but he was proud of her independence. After all, Shirley's brother, Wayne was a successful mortician, who ran the family's business. "You know I would jump to Frank's proposal for marriage, but I don't know if I'm ready to move to San Antonio." Shirley smiled at her roommates.

"Why not live here and commute on weekends?" Jean-Claude thought of everything. He liked the couple together and wanted to see them make a lifetime of it.

"Shirley, you have a good point. Uprooting yourself for a man is not a wise decision." Jean-Claude was about to interrupt Nana, but she held up her hand and continued. "The difference is that Frank is a decent man. We trust him with you."

"I trust me with him." Shirley teased. "You guys are getting too serious on me. The man has not breathed about the 'M' word." The three laughed at themselves. "This reminds me of something. Nana, what happened to Mr. Heavy Mustache?" In the past, Nana always went out with a few men, but she terminated each relationship after a couple of dates.

Nana displayed her dimpled smile. "Shirley, you are full of it." She shifted in her seat.

Jean-Claude became excited. "Wait a minute! I've been gone for too long. Who is Mr. Heavy Mustache?" He turned to Nana with a demanding smile. "I want all the dirt."

"I have no dirt for you, my dear." Nana reached over and patted Jean-Claude's shoulder. "His name is Lami Khanami. He is an economist at the IFT. I had lunch with him twice, then dinner twice."

"That's it?" Jean-Claude was anxious.

"Yes." Nana nervously scratched her head. "I do not wish to see him further."

"What is wrong with him, Nana?" Jean-Claude and Shirley inquired in unison.

"He is no different from the others. After a couple of dinners or movies..." She waved her hand. "They want to jump in the bed." Her roommates laughed but Nana remained serious.

"Two consenting adults usually do become intimate." Jean-Claude advised.

"You just pointed out the problem." Nana told him. "You said two consenting adults. This adult did not consent."

"Nana, these days, nobody waits for a proposal before getting intimate." Shirley added. "I know you follow your African traditions and all but…"

Nana interrupted her. "I will sleep with a man when the right one comes." She seemed irritated. Her roommates had been concerned for a long time about Nana's social life. Jean-Claude recalled the rumor that was around their campus during their school years. Some students thought that Nana was a not a real woman. He quickly dispelled that gossip, knowing she was indeed a real woman. They laughed about it and Nana remarked, "When you don't jump into bed with every man you meet, they call you names."

Shirley teased her roommate. "Girl, you have got to be the only thirty-year old virgin in the whole world."

Nana was quick to respond. "I guess we had better contact the world book of records." The two girls laughed while Jean-Claude almost choked on his drink.

"I missed our little interludes while I was away." Jean-Claude told them. "These moments keep me smiling while I am in flight for hours on end."

"I thought your moments with someone else did that." Shirley was unable to resist.

Jean-Claude flashed his large brown eyes at Shirley and blushed. "Those too do that." His roommates knew that Paula was the special person in his life, but he never openly discussed his sex life. He and Paula Braun met when Europa Airlines sent him to an in-flight safety seminar in London. Paula's employer, Alignment Airlines, conducted the seminar. Paula was one of five pilots who were guest speakers, and she was the only female pilot at the seminar. Though Paula was a born American, she spoke fluent French and German. They went to lunch on the second day of the seminar, followed by the London nightlife. They returned to the States as great friends. Shirley and Nana were happy that he had a friend. "Seriously, I missed you two a whole lot." Jean-Claude chuckled. "My mother used to think that I was in love with Nana. I think she knows different now."

Nana snapped her fingers and teased. "Just think I could have had this handsome hunk." The three laughed as Nana glanced up at the clock on the mantle. "That is it guys, I am off to my bed." She stood and yawned. "We have a long day tomorrow."

Shirley joined in. "I need bag less eyes tomorrow for Frank." They laughed at Shirley's remark and retired, each to her room and Jean-Claude to his.

Thanksgiving Day

"You ladies really took Thanksgiving to another level this year." Paula remarked after she took in the dining room table. Shirley and Nana decorated the table with fresh flowers and scented candles. The décor added ambiance to the aroma from the gourmet style dishes. Everyone was in a pleasant mood at dinner, and they ate heartily, especially Frank whose plate was piled high with enough for five.

"I passed on lunch today just for this meal." Frank said between mouthfuls.

"Looks like you skipped the last week of eating, Buddy." Jean-Claude cracked a joke with his former schoolmate and friend.

"I wonder where the food goes though." Shirley stopped laughing long enough to make her point. "He has no stomach, no bulges, just muscles." Frank was indeed a fit football player. His well-built body was difficult to escape. Women marveled and admired him.

Frank looked at the beauty that sat next to him. "How can you wonder that babe?" He gave her one of his sexy grins. "I leave most of the food on the football field." They laughed at his remark. Frank was one of the best quarterbacks in the football association. At thirty, he had already led the San Antonio Gorillas to two consecutive Big Bowls and won both. He had appeared on the cover of every sport magazine and every talk and magazine program. He was a well-rounded quarterback, who refused to be classified as a running or in-the-pocket quarterback. The defense of the opposition was never able to predict his moves. He stayed in the pocket and threw the ball at times, or he tricked them and ran with the ball. His football statistics for touchdown passes were the highest. He had scored a few touchdowns himself.

"So Frank, who do you play on Sunday?" Paula wanted to know.

"We play the Manhattan Greyhounds on Sunday in San Antonio." Frank slowly shook his head. "That stadium will be packed – we got to give the fans a big win."

"I have no doubt about that." Jean-Claude chuckled. "Paula should have asked which team you are going to beat." The Gorillas had won nine out of their ten games played. They lost early in the season to the same Manhattan Greyhounds. Frank missed that game, due to a bad case of the flu.

"Speaking of games, we should catch the last quarter of the Leopards and Unicorns." Frank reminded them as he leaned over and planted a kiss on Shirley's lips. Everyone transferred to the living room to watch the game. "Wow! The Unicorns are getting their butts spanked." Frank exclaimed as he gave Nana a high five. The Unicorns were in the same division as the Gorillas, Frank's team.

"Baby, don't you play the Unicorns next week?" Shirley asked.

He pulled Shirley onto his lap and hugged her snugly. "You bet, babe." Frank was in a great mood. "It looks like they will be getting two butt spankings in a row." He was confident about his work but was far from being arrogant. Frank had every right to be confident, not only about his work but his appearance as well. His entire 230-pound frame stood at 6feet 4 inches tall.

"I hear you man." Jean-Claude had a habit of speaking 'hip', as he called it, when he and Frank got together.

The game was at its end, and the Ann Arbor Leopards had defeated the Alexandria Unicorns. The final score was 35 to 14. Earlier that day, Frank, Shirley, Jean-Claude, and Nana went to the home of the family they adopted for Thanksgiving. They gave the family two turkeys; two honey baked hams, several cans of cranberry sauce, four apple pies, four pumpkin pies and five pounds of fresh green beans. Frank gave an autographed football to each of the three sons in the family and a Gorillas sweatshirt to each of the four daughters. He promised to pay for a football summer camp for the three boys the following year. The single mother was grateful for their generosity. She cried as the children jumped around with glee.

They told Paula about their morning, and she was impressed. "I will definitely join you next year." Paula's blue eyes showed excitement. "Your annual ritual could grow into a far bigger event." Her Midwestern accent became more noticeable when she was excited. "The three of us could get the travel industry involved as sponsors." She indicated Jean-Claude, Nana, and herself. "Frank can engage the football association, while Shirley can get the cosmetology industry."

"We are a real productive group. Aren't we?" Shirley added her approval.

"I'd say. If we take this to the next level, it meets my approval." Nana let them know. Everyone agreed that they would seek sponsorship and expand their charity project to more families each year. They used their own resources each year, but they were only able to afford to adopt one family a year.

"I realize that our jobs require most of our time – yet we make the time for other things that are important to us." Frank looked at his friends. "We can make time for the kids." He knew that he had the most money among all of his friends, and he was prepared to take on most of the financial expenses. He enjoyed giving back to the community. "When I see those kids' eyes light up, it kind of reminds me of when Tommie and I were that age."

"I don't think it was that long ago. Was it?" Shirley tried to get him out of the serious mode, and they laughed.

Frank kissed the back of her neck. "It was long enough to have you in my life, babe."

"Would you like us to leave the room, Frank?" Nana teased.

"Can a man show his lady a little bit of affection, Nana?" Frank grinned.

Shirley stood and took Frank by the hand. "Nana's right. I think we will call it a night."

"Go ahead, Shirley." Nana smiled, knowing that her friends were eager to get to other business. "I will turn on the dishwasher while I clean up." Shirley's duty was to take care of the dishes.

"Thanks girl, you're the best." Shirley threw Nana a kiss.

"Flattery will get you back in the kitchen." Nana reminded her.

"It's got me going to bed early." Shirley teased.

"Frank, take her away before I change my mind." Nana teased back.

"We'll make breakfast for everybody in the morning." Frank tried to make up for their early exit.

"We won't count on it." Nana knew that Shirley liked to linger in bed, especially when Frank visited. She prepared to load the dishwasher.

"We can help you with that." Paula told Nana, indicating her and Jean-Claude.

"No Paula, you flew in from L.A. this morning." She smiled shyly. "I know you are really fit to be tired." She glanced at Jean-Claude. "So is my brother here. He has been a sport at hanging with us since he returned." She knew that the two had not been fortunate to spend time together often. Jean-Claude worked the flights between Washington Dulles Airport and Paris Charles de Gaulle, and sometimes the flight between Paris and Ouagadougou, Burkina Faso in West Africa. He enjoyed going to Ouagadougou, and he always brought back artifacts for Nana. He knew how much she appreciated her African art. Paula flew planes between the West Coast and the South Pacific corridor. Her trips back to the East Coast were primarily intended for time with Jean-Claude.

"Are you sure about that?" Jean-Claude felt bad, leaving her to clean up alone.

Nana was persistent. "Of course, I am sure." She stopped for a moment and faced her roommate. "Have you ever known me to say what I did not mean?"

"Hmmm…." Jean-Claude pretended to ponder with his hand under his chin.

Nana and Paula laughed. "Paula, do you see what I endure from him?"

Jean-Claude kissed her on the cheek. "Goodnight kid, but don't stay up too late."

"Goodnight, I promise not to." She smiled. "Pleasant dreams to you." She and Paula exchanged goodnights and she found herself all alone in the kitchen.

Later that night in her bedroom, Nana lay in bed and listened to the laughter from Shirley's bedroom. She had the master bedroom and Shirley occupied the second room. Jean-Claude had the basement apartment, which gave him the privacy he needed. They had the third bedroom set up with fitness equipment. She heard the familiar noises from Shirley's room and Nana smiled quietly. She remembered the first time that Frank spent the night at their house. Jean-Claude and Nana kept a late night in their living room as they enjoyed drinks and a chat. They heard a scream from Shirley's room and they both raced up the stairs. Jean-Claude banged on the door and demanded to know if Shirley was okay in his French accent. "What in the world is going on in there, Frank?" Jean-Claude and Nana were embarrassed when Shirley and Frank chuckled at Jean-Claude's question. Shirley apologized the next morning. Nana smiled, as she reflected on the incident. She still was unable to understand why

Shirley allowed herself to get out of control. Shirley claimed that she was unable to restrain herself.

She was glad that Shirley was crazy about Frank and so was he about Shirley. Nana was willing to succumb to celibacy than to risk being hurt. She was unsure whether it was the physical hurt or the emotional hurt that frightened her more. She struggled with her secret fear, of which her roommates were unaware. She felt lonely at times, like that particular night, but those times were short lived. After all, Frank and Paula did not visit often. She knew that Jean-Claude and Paula enjoyed each other's company. There Nana lay, wide-awake, haunted by her secret fear, yet she yearned for the day when she would overcome that fear. She glanced at the clock radio on her nightstand. The time registered 3:45am. She rolled over, covered her head with the sheet and drifted to where she wanted to be – in her dreams.

Friday after Thanksgiving

A couple from Ghana with whom Nana was acquainted gave a party at their home in Reston. They invited Nana, her roommates, and their guests. Frank hired a limo, and everyone piled in and headed for the party. The limo was equipped with beer, wine, and champagne that Frank had ordered. They were already in the party mood by the time they arrived at the elaborate three-story home in Reston. Nana had visited the couple's home in the past, but the house was impressive to the others. She made the introductions, and her friends were welcomed to the house and the party.

"Any friends of Nana's are friends of ours." Mr. Nkruma told them. The couple was the only Ghanaians that Nana knew when she came to the States. The couple were long-time friends and neighbors of her parents. Mr. Nkruma served as Counsel General at the Ghanaian Embassy in Washington, D.C. The walls in their house bore only African art from throughout the continent.

The evening was far more enjoyable than Nana's friends imagined. Though many of the male guests recognized Frank from television, they were respectful of his privacy. One guest asked him for his autograph. He wanted to take it to his ten-year old son who suffered from leukemia. Frank took the man's address and promised to send his son an autographed football. Frank believed in making children's dreams come true.

The five friends danced to the beat of African rhythms until late. They enjoyed the taste of fine West African cuisine and marveled at the luxurious African eveningwear. Most of the men wore kente robes thrown across one shoulder. The women wore gowns of beautiful African prints with matching head wraps. Nana explained about the kente cloth to her friends. "The kente is a ceremonial cloth in Ghana. We wear it only on special occasions, such as receptions and weddings. The kente is equivalent to the western tuxedo."

"We don't even know that here in the States. I see people wearing kente for no special occasion whatsoever." Frank remarked.

"Sweetheart, from what Nana told me, what you see everyday is not the real kente." Shirley told Frank.

"The authentic kente is hard to obtain. Some people in Ghana work most of their lives to get their first kente." Nana told them. "We have professional kente weavers in Ghana."

"Well, we learned a lot tonight about your country, Nana." Paula told her as she sipped champagne.

"We should all plan a trip to Ghana." Jean-Claude suggested. He had seen much of West Africa, and he enjoyed his trips to the continent.

"I would like that; I can be your tour guide." Nana spoke before she thought about why she had never been back since she left for school in the States. The reason was part of her secret fear, but she would not dare tell her friends.

"Sounds like a plan to me. Let's make it after football season, that's all." Frank added and put his arm about Shirley's shoulders. "Want to go to Africa, babe?"

"Does a bird fly?" Shirley replied. "Can we go tomorrow?" They laughed at her response. They finally left the party in the limo that Frank hired.

"Hey Frank, thanks for the ride." Paula said as she reached over and shook Frank's hand. "I like hanging out with you."

"It is not everyday that we get to attend a party with foreign dignitaries." Frank glanced over at Nana. "I figured we should at least arrive in the style for the occasion."

"My clients would want my head if I forgot to request their complimentary limo to the airport." Nana told them.

"Why is it complimentary?" Frank wanted to know.

"Europa Wings Airlines, my employer has a contract with the International Financial Trust. We offer their travelers free limo rides to the airport or from the airport." Jean-Claude explained to Frank.

"One of the many incentives the IFT enjoys from the airlines." Nana added. "Even though it is complimentary, they still demand it."

"Are they that bad?" Frank asked.

"Anything free gets their attention." Nana told them. "We held a welcome event in September for our clients at the IFT to come to our office. It was a meet and greet event." She paused and chuckled. "You should have seen how some of them behaved over the give-away items. One lady insisted that I give her a tin of mints that was on my desk. I tried to explain that the mints were not a give-away item, but I had to let her have them anyway."

"Were they your personal item?" Shirley asked as she laughed.

Nana nodded. "Indeed it was my personal mints. Would you believe that?"

"Unbelievable!" Jean-Claude laughed.

They arrived back at the townhouse in Herndon, and everyone headed for bed. They danced and enjoyed themselves at the party. Back in her bedroom, Nana thought about the evening as she prepared for bed. She usually went through her rituals of the evening before she retired. She flossed and brushed and cleaned her face, and then she had a quiet time of meditation. She finally lay in her bed and thought about many things. She missed her parents and missed the life in Ghana. She had a different life in Virginia. Nana had her biological family in Ghana, but she considered Jean-Claude, Shirley, Frank, Tommie and Paula her family. They looked out for her and understood her better than her own parents did. She enjoyed the time she spent with them. She wondered what she would do without her friends. She knew that they would all someday go their separate ways. Frank would probably marry Shirley and Jean-Claude would eventually marry Paula or move to a place of his own with Paula. She wanted to be prepared for that. Perhaps she would devote her time to her career as a playwright. She wanted to pursue that and eventually leave Proficiency Travel and the IFT. Nana drifted off with her thoughts far from where she really was.

The holiday weekend progressed quickly for the roommates and their friends. Their last full day together was special, and they wanted to make the best of it. They decided to formally establish their foundation, "The Friends Foundation". They elected their officers and drafted the bylaws of the foundation. The day was a productive one for them. "The Friends Foundation" would continue their thanksgiving charity meals but they would increase the number of recipient families to ten families. In addition, the foundation would run a book and toy drive during the Christmas holidays for needy children. Their future goal was to set up a "Friends Foundation College Scholarship" fund and have indigent students apply for the fund. The student with the highest-grade point average would be the recipient. They were pleased with their work by the time the plan was completed.

Chapter Two

A DECEMBER FRIDAY

I look up to the mountains – does my help come from there? – Psalm 121:1 (NLT)

The phones rang with persistence at Proficiency Travel. They had not stopped ringing since that morning. The travel office was located at the client site, the International Financial Trust (IFT) in downtown Washington, D.C.

Nana Nkuku's fingers bounced about her computer keyboard in rapid motions. She was a great typist, an attribute she acquired from her high school years. Her father persisted that his daughter learned typing at an early age. "You will need it in preparing your college term papers. You just never know what direction your life will take. Treat typing like you would mathematics or science." Kofi Nkuku told his daughter. Her father's words turned out to be true. Nana worked as a travel agent, a job that called for a great deal of typing.

"Thank you for calling Proficiency Travel, this is Nana." She continued to type as she answered the phone. Nana had just completed another call when the next one came in. She wore a headset attached to the phone.

"No need to get professional on me – it's just me." Shirley chuckled at the other end of the phone.

Nana laughed. "I am so glad to hear your voice! I thought it was another client." They laughed at her relief. "These phones have been ringing non-stop since I came in. You would think that the entire IFT has decided to travel."

Proficiency Travel serviced the International Financial Trust (IFT) in an exclusive contract. Nana was not allowed to even issue tickets for her friends or relatives. She and her co-workers were allowed to prepare tickets only for themselves, with permission from the transportation department of the IFT. Proficiency Travel reported directly to the IFT transportation department.

"So what's up Miss Marshall?" Nana was grateful for the break. She put her phone in the 'break mode' that Proficiency allowed them.

"After you left this morning, Jean-Claude called from his flight."

"Is he abusing Europa Wings Airlines' phone again?" They both laughed at Nana's assumption about Jean-Claude.

"He called to let us know that he will arrive this afternoon." Shirley explained.

"Great! I am glad that he will make it for the weekend."

"I know- he had me worried for a while there." Shirley was excited but she heard the strain in her other roommate's voice. "Girl, you're letting those IFT clients stress you out again?"

"What's a girl to do, Shirley?" Nana shrugged at the other end.

"A girl can move on by finding another job!" Shirley was outgoing and outspoken. She did not conceal her feelings. "Do you think that if you fell sick or died, those clients would even care?" She grunted and continued. "They would express sympathy and move on to work with another one of your co-workers. Proficiency might send flowers."

Nana heard the familiar lecture many times. "I know but I work for the largest travel company in the world. No other travel agency will offer the benefits or the salary I get from Proficiency." She sighed. "I have my favorite clients who are nice to me. Then I encounter somebody like Ms. Foo Young this morning."

"What is her problem?" Shirley wanted Nana to talk about the problem and put it behind her.

"She asked to be booked on a smaller airline. I tried to talk her into flying on a more reputable airline. She protested and said that her husband was on the smaller airline, and she had to be on the same flight." Nana explained with strain in her voice. "I had already issued her ticket on the smaller airline when that carrier threatened to strike. She emailed me and complained about the ensuing strike, so I voided out her ticket and rebooked her on the more reputable airline." Nana kept her voice at a low tone in the office. "Do you think that made her happy?"

"But that is what she wanted." Shirley interjected.

"She lodged a complaint against me to my supervisor and to the head of the IFT transportation."

"Does she realize what bearing her complaint can have on your job?"

"She does not care. They are spoiled people, who must have things their way at any cost."

"I have some crazy clients but at least I enjoy what I do."

"Let's not go there." Nana did not want to discuss it further. She had no privacy in her cubicle, and her calls were subject to being monitored.

"Just reminding you that if I'm going to deal with difficult clients, I should enjoy what I do, that's all." Shirley did not know when to stop. She worried about the stress under which her roommate was. Nana always insisted on leaving Proficiency Travel with dignity. She did not want to leave and go to another travel job. She wanted to leave the travel industry for her playwright career. Nana also knew that the bills had to be paid.

"Change will come in due time, Shirley." Nana sighed.

"I know, I know." Shirley chose not to pressure her friend any further but was not quite done. "I just like to remind you that you have options."

"I do know that." Nana whispered into the phone. "I had better run. I am getting nasty looks from Jessica." Jessica Reinbird, Nana's supervisor did not care much for her. She was convinced that Jessica possessed a passionate dislike for her.

"I don't want you to get in trouble." Shirley whispered back. "Bye."

"I will see you this evening." Nana ended her personal call and proceeded to take another call from a client. She knew that one of her options was to return to Ghana. With her English Literature degree, a teaching job would come easy in Ghana. She knew that the possibility existed for her to open her own school for children. She even thought about opening a school for the arts in Ghana. Nana fancied the idea of giving back to her country. The question that continued to nag her was whether or not she wanted to return to Ghana and settle. Her thought was interrupted by another client's call. "Thank you for calling Proficiency Travel, this is Nana. May I help you?"

"Yes Nana, I certainly hope you can help me." The voice on the phone was unfriendly, but polite. "I just received my itinerary from your office. Why am I leaving Detroit one hour after I am scheduled to arrive in Chicago?" Nana attempted to explain but the client continued. "I am catching an international flight from Chicago, and I do not want to miss that flight."

"May I have your name please?" Nana remained calm while the client rambled.

"Grace Dodd." She continued. "I am an IFT contractor out of Michigan."

"Ms. Dodd, I have your itinerary displayed. Your itinerary shows you departing Detroit's Metro Airport at 1:30p.m., Eastern Time. You will arrive in Chicago's O'Hare Airport at 1:45p.m., Central Time."

"Oh, the one-hour time difference! I should have guessed. Sorry to have troubled you." Grace Dodd calmed down, while Nana suppressed her laughter.

"No trouble at all, Ms. Dodd. Thanks for checking. Have a safe and pleasant trip." Nana wore a smile on her face as she ended the call. She gathered from the call, that Ms. Dodd was not an experienced traveler. Her final destination on her itinerary was Osaka, Japan. Nana told herself that she did not want to be a flight attendant on Ms. Dodd's international flight.

Though she did not enjoy the work she did, Nana found that there was never a dull moment in her day. She was guaranteed an irate client; one that annoyed her or one that amused her. But there were kind and special clients. There were not many, however, she appreciated them. Her favorite clients were Mr. Nilsson from Norway; Mr. Karlsson from Iceland; Brit from Sweden; Adele from Cameroon and Mr. Von Boomos from Belgium. They took her to lunch and brought her gifts from various parts of the world. Mr. Nilsson flirted with her a few times, but she insisted on keeping the relationship at a business level.

When one of her favorite clients called, Nana dropped everything to take care of their needs. She knew that those were relationships she wanted to last a lifetime. The clients were likely to move to their countries of origin after they retired or to another assigned country. She vowed to remain in touch with them. Her grandmother told her and her cousins when they were children that an acquaintance was only a passing encounter, but a relationship was something one built to last a lifetime. She thought of her grandmother's analogy from decades before and decided that Jessica Reinbird was definitely an acquaintance.

Herndon, Virginia, U.S.A.

The three-bedroom townhouse was brightly lit and buzzed with anticipation. Nana was relieved to be home after a busy Friday at Proficiency Travel. She and Shirley planned a restful weekend, but they were unsure of how restful it would be with Jean-Claude's arrival. The girls anticipated his arrival two weeks prior, but he called to postpone it. They both enjoyed their roommate's company to the degree that they did not mind giving up a restful weekend.

Nana was in the kitchen; she prepared a tofu loaf for dinner, while Shirley placed chicken pieces in the oven. Though Shirley and Jean-Claude were not vegetarians like Nana, they still enjoyed the taste of her vegetarian dishes that she prepared. "You either convert to vegetarianism or cease enjoying the food when I cook it." Nana never failed to tease them.

"Hey ladies, I'm home!" Jean-Claude interrupted them as he entered the kitchen. The girls dropped what they were doing and raced to hug and welcome him. The three had been roommates for more than a decade.

"Welcome home sugar plum." Shirley landed a kiss on his cheek.

"I missed you a lot, my brother." Nana looked him over. "You look great. The trip must have been worth it." The three laughed.

They never failed to mention to others how fate had brought them together. Jean-Claude Girard, a thirty-year old flight attendant from Nice, France immigrated to the United States. His father died when he was only seven years old. He won a student exchange contest to study in the American state of Virginia when he was sixteen. Jean-Claude was taken by the life in the United States and decided to attend college at the University of Maryland, where he obtained a degree in Finance.

Jean-Claude was at the University of Maryland when he met a bright student, Nana Nkuku from Accra, Ghana. They both belonged to the Foreign Student Association at the university. Nana came to the States to further her education. Her father, a proud Ghanaian sacrificed all of his savings for his only child to obtain a sound college education. Nana, with no family in the States, found common ground with Jean-Claude, who was also in America without family. His celebrated arrival was long awaited. He had just spent two weeks in Nice, France with his mother and another week working a flight between West Africa and Paris. The girls bombarded him with questions.

"Did you get to rest, or did you have to work the flight to Dulles?" Shirley inquired.

He shook his head. "No rest for me. I flight attended today." He indicated his uniform, as he joined them in the kitchen. "I will get changed, and then come back up to help." He offered in his French accent.

"You park yourself right on that stool." Shirley pointed to the breakfast bar. "Now tell us all about your trip." Although Nana and Jean-Claude knew each other long before they met Shirley, he was just as close to Shirley as he was to Nana. Shirley Marshall, a cosmetologist, was a volunteer at the Universal Cancer Association when Nana met her. Shirley worked with cancer survivors, where she advised them on wig styling as part of their rehabilitation. Nana was just out of the University of Maryland and had been eager to enter a volunteer program, when she went to work with the Universal Cancer Association (UCA). She and Shirley established a bond and began a lasting relationship. Jean-Claude and Nana maintained their close friendship after graduation. When Nana invited Shirley to have dinner at her apartment with Jean-Claude, it was not surprising that the three young people found common interests.

"Yes mother." Jean-Claude joked as he straddled the stool.

"No, you left her in Nice." Shirley responded with one hand on her hip.

Jean-Claude looked over at Nana and shook his head. They were used to Shirley's constant jokes and remarks. "I had a great time with my mother, by the way. I think she tried to over-feed me. I assured her that the two of you do a good job of that already." They laughed. "She sent something for each of you with her love." He flashed them his boyish smile. Jean-Claude was a great sight to behold. He possessed the physique of a fashion model with flat abs, broad shoulders and stood at five feet, eleven inches. He wore his brown hair in a short crew-cut style that accented his large brown eyes and heavy eyelashes. His angelic facial features and full ripe lips made him look younger than his thirty years. Although he had lived in the United States since he was sixteen, Jean-Claude maintained his fashionable European way of dressing. "So what do you ladies have planned for the weekend?"

"We have nothing eventful, just hanging out here. I have to work tomorrow at the salon." Shirley made a funny face.

"I am trying to finish my latest play." Nana remarked. "But we could do something to welcome you back."

"I hate to tell you this, but this is a short trip. I am back in the air on Sunday, headed for Paris, then to Ouagadougou." Shirley chuckled, as she always did when her roommates mentioned the name, Ouagadougou. "From Burkina Faso, I will stop in Bamako, Mali, then Dakar and back to Paris. I will take a peek at my mother for a day, then make it is back here for Christmas."

"I am jetlagged just listening to you." Shirley sighed. "Well, you have to be here for Christmas so we will excuse you for running off after being here for only two nights."

"Work, Shirley. I am hardly running off." Jean-Claude assured them.

A December Sunday Morning

The weekend quickly slipped by, and it was time for Jean-Claude to get back to work. Shirley worked all Saturday, while Jean-Claude and Nana went to Washington and visited museums and memorials. The two friends enjoyed hopping around to museums and memorials in Washington.

"Well ladies, it is that time again where saying goodbye does not come easy for me." Jean-Claude placed his bags beside the front door, ready to leave, as Shirley answered the ringing phone.

"Hi sweetheart." Shirley displayed her even white teeth. "He's still here but only for a minute." She beckoned Jean-Claude to get the phone. "It's Frank; he wants to talk to you." Shirley's grin was wide as she handed the phone to Jean-Claude.

"Hey buddy, what's up man?" Jean-Claude's roommates took delight in hearing him speak like an American in his French accent. "I only came for a breather but will be back later this month for Christmas."

"Sorry I didn't call earlier but I am busy working. We have a crucial division game this afternoon." Frank Thurston explained on the other end of the phone. Frank was the third of the trio from the University of Maryland. Nana, Jean-Claude, and Frank were inseparable at the university. Frank was one of the most popular students on campus. He was the starting quarterback for the football team. Frank was an all-around student who excelled in his academics as well as athletics. He went to the University of Maryland on a football scholarship, but he was eligible for an academic scholarship as well. Frank's former schoolmates had introduced him to their roommate; he fell in love with the shapely southern girl. They were closer than any girlfriend he had dated in high school or college.

"Who in your division do you play today?" Jean-Claude inquired. He was familiar with the teams in Frank's division and knew their records.

"We play the Birds. I'm calling from Harrisburg, where we'll play later today." The Harrisburg Birds always played a competitive game against the San Antonio Gorillas. Frank was the quarterback for the Gorillas, and every team in the league wanted to beat them. Both Frank and his younger brother, Tommie Thurston played for the San Antonio Gorillas. Although Tommie played as a quarterback at Virginia Tech on a football scholarship, he was drafted as a running back by San Antonio.

Their single mother, Amelia, brought up Frank and Tommie after their father abandoned them when Frank was only eight and Tommie was six. Amelia Thurston was devastated and found herself going out to work to support her boys. She taught them from an early age that there was nothing in life that they were unable to do if they had determination and perseverance. Both boys took their mother's advice and did well in school. They had no contact with their father; he ran off with a younger woman and got in trouble with the law and went to prison. The boys were teenagers at the time and never heard any more from their father. Amelia never remarried. She devoted her time to raising her sons and working as a secretary in a Washington, D.C. law firm. Her career in a law firm influenced Frank, who majored in Criminal Justice at the University of Maryland but chose a career in football instead.

"Well buddy, it is a tough one for you, but I have no doubt that Tommie and you are going to pull it off like you always do. Too bad I will not be here to see the game. My flight is in three hours." Jean-Claude glanced at his watch. "I will see you at Christmas I suppose. Peace man." He handed the phone back to Shirley, as he picked up his bags.

Shirley continued her conversation with Frank, after she wished Jean-Claude a safe trip and gave him a hug. Nana drove him to the airport, as she usually did.

Chapter Three

THE CAMPAIGN

The Lord is my Shepherd; I have all that I need. – Psalm 23:1 (NLT)

The roommates and their friends sat in the living room of their townhouse relaxed in conversation and excited about their foundation. They watched a news program on television. Nana returned from the kitchen with drinks in her hand when everyone in the room became silent. Their attention was drawn to the story that was told by the host of the show. He interviewed a twelve-year old girl from a country in East Africa, who wept as she spoke. The girl had escaped from her native country to the United States with the assistance of an American expatriate. Her family attempted to perform something called female circumcision on her, but they were unsuccessful. She escaped and took refuge at the home of the American expatriate. The American lady brought her to the United States without her parents' consent. The United States Immigration denied the girl's application for asylum and her story became public knowledge. She sent out an appeal to the immigration officials to grant her asylum based on the fact that her human rights would be violated if she returned to her native country in East Africa.

As they watched the girl tell her story, they were as dumbfounded as was the host of the show. What really grabbed their attention was when Nana began to sob and gasp between breaths. She appeared as though she was having a heart attack; and they rushed over to where she stood. She was suddenly mute, and her friends were unable to figure out what had happened to her. They wondered if she knew the girl or if her reaction was done only in sympathy for the girl. Frank led her to the recliner while Shirley rushed to the kitchen for a glass of water.

"Sip on this Nana, it will make you feel better." Shirley held the glass to her roommate's lips with trembling hands. She had never seen Nana in such a condition as long as she knew her. Nana finally took sips of the water, while Jean-Claude wiped her face with a damp washcloth. "Nana, what is going on?" Shirley asked. "Are you feeling sorry for the girl that much?"

Nana spoke slowly through sobs. She struggled with her words. The moment seemed as though time had frozen when her friends heard Nana's first sentence. "I have no vagina…" Her voice faded into more sobs.

"Is this some sort of joke, Nana?" Shirley was the first to react.

"Babe, she's not joking, she's crying. I know when Nana's joking." Frank's face was serious.

"Well, what do you have then?" Shirley was emotional while Jean-Claude and Paula remained quiet. The two looked like they had just heard the worse news of their lives.

Nana sniffed and wiped her eyes with a tissue that Frank handed her. "Well, I did have one, but it was taken away when I was eight years old."

"You are making no sense Nana. Talk to us, girl!" Shirley was close to hysterics, while Paula and the two men sat stunned and speechless.

Nana continued. "When I was eight years old, my mother along with five other mothers in our village took us to the bush. They had us circumcised." Her sobs told her friends that she had just unloaded the burden she had carried since she was a child. No one spoke, not even Shirley. Nana proceeded to give them the vivid picture in her words that they would never have imagined. She told of the elderly lady who performed the circumcision. The woman did not use anesthesia, neither did she use sterilized blades. She used the same blade on all five of them. Nana was the fourth girl. She experienced the trauma of watching her three playmates get mutilated before it was her turn. "I was so frightened when I saw Leila pass out before the lady was done with her. The blade was quick, as she chopped off Leila's clitoris. I recall Leila in a pool of blood on the ground, while her mother cried out for her little girl." She paused and took two deep breaths before she continued. "The old woman then took a rough rope, with which she stitched up the vulva of Leila's vagina. She left only a tiny opening to accommodate urination."

Nana told them how she fainted when it was her turn. She remembered the vicious stabs of pain, as she slipped in and out of consciousness. Her mother held her while the old woman performed the brutal act on her. "They called it female circumcision back then, but it is now referred to as female genital mutilation." She recalled throwing up several times, as she lost total control of her bowels. Nothing stopped the old lady from carrying out her duty.

Her friends remained quiet as she recounted the details. Frank finally broke his silence. "How in the world could a mother sit there and allow an old woman to mutilate her eight-year-old baby?"

"Our mothers had no choice in the matter. They follow the traditions. They would have faced serious ramifications had they refused to have it done to us. A woman just did not speak out against such traditions." Nana wiped a tear that trickled down her cheek. "The same was done to our mothers as well as to their mothers."

"Yes, but it has to stop at some point." Frank spoke again. "It's not a great tradition to pass down from generation to generation, Nana."

"But it has been that way for centuries. I agree that it should be outlawed but how and when will that happen?" Nana responded with tears in her eyes.

Shirley found herself lost for words for the first time in her life. She wept for her dear friend, as she listened to Nana's account. Paula and Jean-Claude were quiet, but they had fury in their eyes, especially Jean-Claude. He loved Nana like his own sister and wanted to fly to Ghana and beat up her parents to a pulp.

"The next day, we heard that Leila and Gotie were dead. They hemorrhaged to death. A week later, Doni died from a serious infection, which led to high fever and convulsions." Nana told them everything as she cried and still remembered like it happened the day before. "Kiddi and I are the only two from my group that are alive today." She told them that Kiddi Afambo had left Ghana as a teenager and never returned. Unlike Nana, Kiddi never forgave her parents or the people in their village. She wanted nothing to do with her roots.

"Do you know where Kiddi is now?" Frank asked.

"She lives in England. We exchange birthday cards every year but nothing further." Nana paused and stared at her hands on her lap. "We vowed to keep that part of our lives a secret." Shirley went over to where Nana sat and comforted her.

"Why did you decide to divulge your secret now?" Jean-Claude finally broke his silence. He was outraged.

"Because when I saw that little girl tonight, everything overcame me. I had flashbacks. I want to expose what goes on in those countries. I want our foundation to address it. I want to save the little girls that are being born as we speak. I want to save the little girls that are about to turn five or eight."

"The Friends Foundation will go after them with a vengeance." Jean-Claude told her. He took Nana's hand and gently kissed the back of it. "You must know that your life will change when we go public with this. We need you and Kiddi to be the spokespersons for our cause."

Nana shook her head. "Kiddi will never do it. She will cut me off once I go public with my story."

"We can give it a try. If she refuses, we will go forward with only you." Jean-Claude persisted.

What was to become the biggest controversial topic in the world, they began to plan and strategize right in the Herndon townhouse. The five friends sprang into action. Frank made phone calls to his coach and other football players. His younger brother, Tommie Thurston was a rookie that year in the Football Association. Tommie was outraged when Frank told him. He solicited players from their team as well as other teams in the Association. Frank and Tommie played for the same team, something that rarely happened with brothers.

Paula and Jean-Claude got other pilots and flight attendants involved. They planned a fundraising dinner in Washington, D.C. at the World Intercontinental Hotel. Everyone and every organization that they approached was receptive to their cause. They found it difficult to believe that such a brutal and barbaric act was still practiced in the world at that time.

Nana wrote a long letter to her childhood playmate, Kiddi Afambo. She told her what she had done and how it helped her mental state of mind, by the revelation of their secret. She asked her to join her to go public with what they had hidden all of their adult lives. Kiddi wrote back and wanted no part of it but Nana did not relent. She wrote to her three more times. She stressed the desperate need to end the vicious act on little girls. She wrote, "Nobody wants to talk about it and each day that goes by, five more eight-year-old girls will suffer or die at the hands of a female genital mutilator. We must stop it." The next time Nana heard from Kiddi, she agreed to fly to Washington, D.C. to attend the first fundraising dinner at "The Friends Foundation".

Friends against Female Genital Mutilation

On a cool and windy Saturday evening in April, "The Friends Foundation" introduced their newly named organization, "Friends against Female Genital Mutilation." (FAFGM) The ballroom at the Washington, D.C. World Intercontinental Hotel was packed with donors from all over the United States. Coaches, players, and owners represented every football team in the Association. Several airlines and hotels in the travel industry were present to pledge their financial and moral support. Proficiency Travel and the International Financial Trust (IFT) made their presence known that night in support of Nana, their employee.

Both Nana and Kiddi spoke that night. Nana stood tall and faced hundreds of their guests, as she told them what female genital mutilation (FGM) was. "Good evening. My name is Nana Nkuku from the Republic of Ghana. I was a victim of female genital mutilation at the age of eight." She told the crowd how she had suffered indescribable pain with every urination and monthly menstrual period.

Kiddi spoke after Nana and revealed that she had finally been able to experience sexual intercourse and normal urination, only after she underwent corrective surgery. "But how many girls are financially able to have the surgery?" Kiddi asked but made a statement. "How many girls are able to escape like the girl whom Nana saw on television?" She was emotional as she delivered her words from the heart. "Sixty percent of girls who undergo the procedure of female genital mutilation barely survive or not at all. They die from infection, convulsions, high fever, or HIV/AIDS. Many of them become mentally disable because they never recover from the trauma of the act." Kiddi wiped her brow, as she struggled with the truth of their secret of many years. "Nana and I ask you tonight, ladies and gentlemen to please help us in ending this senseless barbaric tradition in the world."

The entire room applauded with emotion, as they gave Nana and Kiddi a standing ovation. Kiddi walked back to her seat and fell into Nana's waiting arms. Jean-Claude, Frank, Paula, and Shirley followed and embraced their newly found friend. That night, "Friends against Female Genital Mutilation" (FAFGM) raised a hundred thousand dollars to help fight the nations that still allowed the practice of FGM. Their goal was to have the act outlawed and proclaimed illegal in countries throughout the world.

"Friends against Female Genital Mutilation" wrote to the United Nations to have their member nations vote in favor of making FGM illegal in their countries. All of the western nations voted in favor of the bill, including the United States and Canada. Several African nations voted in favor of the bill, which included Cameroon, Egypt, Senegal, Ghana, and South Africa. However, many voted against the bill, much to Nana's and Kiddi's disappointment. Nana's father called and told her that she was no longer his daughter, since she had brought disgrace to him, his family, and his country. He told her that he would never be able to walk with his head up in public again. She told her father that he should have been ashamed to hold his head high from the day he sent his eight-year-old little girl to be mutilated and marked for life. "Papa, how would you like it, if someone took a blade and cut off the tip of your penis, then stitched it with a rope where you urinate?" She did not believe that she actually spoke in that manner to her father, something she had never done before. "That is what you had them do to me." She began to cry when she heard her father say, "Goodbye" and the line went dead.

"Friends against Female Genital Mutilation" grew into an actual large foundation. It became bigger than they had ever imagined. They continued to adopt needy families each Thanksgiving and Christmas. "Friends against Female Genital Mutilation" became a non-profit organization with several players and coaches from the Football League as members. FAFGM, as the foundation was more commonly known, became far more controversial than just helping needy families during the holidays. They raised funds to send students to college. They paid the rent and mortgage for two random workers in celebration of each Labor Day. The foundation spoke out against any known civil rights violation by large corporations. Nana found it hard to believe that her little charity idea five years earlier had blossomed into a large and well-funded organization.

Everyone wondered how the friends continued to maintain their jobs with the hard work they did for the foundation. They always responded,

"The foundation is not hard work, it is something that we enjoy doing." They refused to pay themselves from the foundation funds. Their jobs paid their bills. Kiddi joined the four friends and spoke at universities and to women organizations around Europe. Nana made the time to speak at the University of Maryland, her former school, and other universities in the United States.

"You should see how many speaking engagements I have lined up!" Nana told Shirley one night as they had dinner. Jean-Claude and Paula were back on the road working their flight routes and Frank was in training camp, in preparation for the upcoming football season.

"Isn't it wonderful how everyone just volunteers to help out once they hear what our cause is?" Shirley bit on a piece of chicken. "I'm so proud of us!" They laughed at Shirley's expression, but Nana knew that Shirley was right. They had every right to be proud of themselves for what they had done in the world and continued to do. They caused a stir in the world and made some nations add a new law to their constitutions, while others developed a dislike for their organization. She had lost communication with her father, but she had no regrets.

Nana smiled at Shirley. "Yes, I too am proud of us." They slapped high five and finished their dinner.

Chapter Four

DISASTER STRIKES

I took my troubles to the Lord; I cried out to him, and he answered my prayer. – Psalm 120:1 (NLT)

"Friends against Female Genital Mutilation" planned their usual annual fundraising dinner. They always held it in April because it was convenient with the football season over, and the Washington, D.C. area was beautiful during that time of year. The cherry blossoms sprouted, and the vegetation was green. Tourists flocked in from all over the world to visit museums, monuments, the White House and photograph the cherry blossoms. For anyone who liked to visit Washington, it was the best time to do it.

Frank was already in Washington for the event. He decided to arrive a few days earlier to spend some quality time with Shirley. He knew that the girls would need him to take care of any loose ends before their big night. They had already held a total of three fundraising dinners since the launch of their foundation. They knew the routine well.

Jean-Claude called from Nice, where he had spent a week with his mother. He was scheduled to arrive two days before the dinner. He wanted to be in Washington when Paula arrived. He knew that Paula was scheduled to fly from Hawaii to Los Angeles and then to Washington, D.C.

Kiddi phoned Nana with her flight itinerary. She informed them that her husband and son would be joining her on the trip. The World Intercontinental in Washington, D.C. had blocked off a certain number of rooms to accommodate the guests of the foundation. Kiddi and her family planned to stay in the city to take in the sights of Washington, D.C. Nana was full of excitement. She had not seen Kiddi since dinner the year before. They went from communicating through greeting cards once a year to seeing each other every year.

❁

Nana left to pick up Jean-Claude from the airport. Shirley and Frank sat in the living room as they watched television. "Do you notice how different Nana is these days?" Shirley mentioned to Frank. "She is like a new person."

"All those years we thought we knew everything about her." Frank pondered. "We took it for granted that she was keeping guys off because of her culture. You know the virgin thing and all."

"Yes, it was because of her culture or tradition but not the way we imagined." Shirley said. "I can't imagine the pain she went through, keeping such a secret all those years."

Frank looked pensive and shook his head. "I wish she had told us a long time before."

"I wonder how long she would have carried that secret around on her shoulders, if that girl had not appeared on that program." Shirley thought out aloud.

"It could have been forever. Remember she and Kiddi had that agreement, never to disclose their secret." Frank crossed his long legs. "God has a way of bringing things out at the right time babe."

"I asked her why they cut the clitoris off the girls. She told me that the girls are not considered marriageable without that done to them." Shirley frowned. "I have never heard such nonsense before."

"I know. I have done research on it since we began the campaign against it. If you ask me, it is a male thing babe. The men want to make sure that their women don't have sexual desires. The fathers want to make sure that their daughters remain virgins until they are married." He put his arm around Shirley's shoulders. "There is a lot involved in that."

"Nana said that they have been doing it in Africa for over two thousand years." She placed her head on Frank's shoulder. "She said that most men over there believe that a woman's body was not intended for sexual pleasure, only for childbearing."

"That is an archaic way of thinking. I find it hard to believe that people still think that way today."

The front door to the Herndon townhouse opened and Nana entered with Jean-Claude in tow. "Well, well, well! I'm home." Jean-Claude proclaimed as he walked through the door. "Hey Frank buddy, it is good to see you again." He and Frank embraced and gave each other a handshake.

"Welcome back to State side man." Frank was glad to see his old college friend again.

"And how is my other girl?" Jean-Claude stretched his arms out to receive Shirley, as she fell into them. "Has my buddy here been treating you good?" He indicated Frank.

"Yes, he has been, really good." Shirley blushed and returned to Frank's side.

Jean-Claude chuckled and winked at Shirley. "I'm just checking to make sure that everyone behaved while I was away." They laughed. "So are we ready for the dinner?" Dinner was only two nights away. Nana had briefed him on a few things on the way from the airport.

"Paula called early this morning." Shirley told him. "She had just touched down in Honolulu. She will be arriving in L.A. late tonight."

"Great!" Jean-Claude appeared relieved that Paula was going to make dinner. With Paula's schedule, he had not been sure whether or not she would make it. "I suppose she will catch a red eye to Dulles." His statement was more of a thought.

"You know what that means." Nana grinned. "No sleep for you."

"Either that or she will take a taxi from the airport." Jean-Claude ran his fingers through his hair. "I am not tired. I did not work the flight over."

"Good for you buddy." Frank leaned over and shook Jean-Claude's hand. "It must be good to be served for a change."

"You bet." Jean-Claude responded, as the two men laughed in agreement.

A few hours later, the friends were still up and about in the townhouse. The television was on in the living room, as they listened more than they watched. They heard a sudden familiar voice coming from the television. Everyone was quiet and attentive to the big screen plasma set that was mounted on the wall. The voice was that of Frank Thurston. He did his first public service announcement for "Friends against Female Genital Mutilation". The announcement was brief: *"Hi I'm Frank Thurston, a football quarterback of the San Antonio Gorillas- and I am against female genital mutilation."* They applauded after the announcement, including Frank himself.

"I have not had the pleasure of seeing your announcement before." Shirley told Frank. "You look good sweetheart." She leaned over and kissed him lightly on the lips.

"Thanks." Frank blushed. "Have you seen some of the others though?" The girls nodded to his question. Several announcements were run by most of the major networks throughout the country. "My head coach and offensive coordinator also did announcements. So has Tommie."

"You should see Paula's announcement." Nana told them. "Shirley and I saw it last week. She is so serious on it."

"Well, it is a serious topic, Nana." Jean-Claude reminded her. "So how did Paula say it?" He was excited to see that the campaign had progressed into televised public announcements. They started with radio only, and it was a few football players that initially agreed to participate. Within the previous months, they saw airline pilots; including Paula, flight attendants, football coaches; players and owners deliver public service announcements on both radio and television.

"The same thing that Frank said but she says: *'I'm Paula Braun, an airline pilot and I am against female genital mutilation.'*" Nana mocked. "She was dressed in her pilot uniform."

"We are on our way guys!" Jean-Claude was excited. "Friends against Female Genital Mutilation finally have a voice." He took off his flight attendant jacket and threw it over his left arm. "We are telling them, no more of that brutal act!" He looked thoughtful. "Have you seen some of the international papers lately? While I was over in Senegal last month, I was careful not to disclose my identity."

"I read an article in an international magazine recently. It had asserted that some folks in high places in the world are not too pleased with what we are doing." Nana remarked. "But why would you not want to disclose your identity?"

"You just said it." Jean-Claude pointed out. "I travel over there a great deal. I don't want to go waving attention to myself or anything." He chuckled. "The last thing I want is to end up in some prison over there."

"Jean-Claude, you are getting way ahead of yourself now." Shirley laughed. "Why would they put you in prison over there? You are exercising your first amendment rights."

"Shirley, there are no first amendment rights over there." Nana pointed out. "You can end up in prison for no reason whatsoever." She waved her hand in dismissal. "In any case, too many eyes are on them about female genital mutilation. We are safe."

"Of course we are. I have seen articles here and there about it." Shirley said. "What is that new women's magazine that ran so many articles on it?" She pondered.

"*Global Woman Magazine* ran several articles about it. They have requested an interview with me and Kiddi." Nana reminded her. "A Christian organization is active in creating public awareness in Egypt as well. The owned by the high fashion model, who was an actual victim of the practice, continues to speak out about it throughout Europe and Africa. She authored several books about it."

"We have also received statements of support from a U.N. supported organization." Shirley added. Various women's organizations joined in the fight against FGM. The media in the United States was on target with reports on the subject. Many in North America had not heard of FGM, and while they were appalled by what they learned, they wondered if anyone practiced it within their own society. Neighborhoods had become so diverse in the United States, that the public expressed concern. Many foreign residents stayed close to their traditions and customs, even though they made a home in the States. Letters came in from all parts of the United States, bearing questions about FGM.

Nana and Kiddi set up a special email address to where the public wrote with questions. Both of them had access to the box and answered the questions as they came in. "Friends against Female Genital Mutilation" set up a website, www.fafgm.com with a blog page. They registered up to a thousand hits a day. Nana took out her laptop and they all gathered around where she sat as she shared with them the many questions that came in and what she and Kiddi wrote on their blog.

Questions came in everyday to them. The most frequently asked question was "What is FGM?" Kiddi responded, "FGM is the acronym for Female Genital Mutilation, and is sometimes called FGC for Female Genital Cutting."

The two friends, Nana and Kiddi took turns in responding to the questions. "What is the real meaning of Female Genital Mutilation or Cutting then?" The same person wrote back. Kiddi explained, "Female genital mutilation (FGM) or cutting, more commonly known as Female Circumcision is the intentional removal of the external parts of the female genitalia, for non-medical reasons." She elaborated further, "There are three different related types of procedures," they wrote. The first type is the Traditional Circumcision, known as Sunna Circumcision, consists of the removal of the prepuce, which is the retractable fold of the skin and the tip of the clitoris. The second type is Clitoridectomy, which is the removal of the entire clitoris (prepuce and glands) and the removal of the adjacent labia. The third type is Infibulation, known as the pharonic circumcision, where the Clitoridectomy is performed, including the removal of all or part of the labia minora and the labia majora. In this type, whatever skin is left, it is stitched up, allowing only a small hole to accommodate urine and menstrual blood flow. In Africa, 85% of FGM cases consist of Clitoridectomy and 15% of Infibulation."

"What was the purpose of FGM and why is it practiced?" Wrote to a lady from Los Angeles, and Nana responded. "Most FGM societies feel that unless a girl has had the procedure done, she is not a woman and is not marriageable. They believe that she is unclean. In some societies, it is believed that the procedure will reduce a woman's desire for sex and in doing so, will reduce the chance of sex prior to marriage. In other societies, the clitoris and labia are viewed as male parts on the female body, thus the removal of those parts enhances the femininity of the girl. Then there are those societies that believe that if the clitoris touches the baby's head during birth, the baby will die and the mother's milk will be poisonous, while some believe that an unmutilated female cannot conceive."

Nana and Kiddi communicated through emails each day and discussed the questions and answers on their message board. They blogged about FGM and tried to educate the people in the western world about the practice. They wanted to raise awareness in every way they knew.

Nana continued her blog, "These are only some of the many myths that have steered and influenced grandparents and parents for centuries, to have the procedure performed on little girls. The primary reason, in my opinion is due to the insecurities of a highly male-dominated society. They believe that an intact clitoris will generate sexual arousal in women and such societies believe that the woman's body was only intended for reproductive purposes and not for the enjoyment of sexual intercourse."

Someone wanted to know if FGM was a religious practice and Kiddi blogged about it on her page the following day. She wrote, "No, FGM has nothing to do with religion. It is a cultural practice, which dates back more than 2000 years. Some might justify their actions by hiding behind religion, but the act has absolutely nothing to do with religion, according to Christianity, Islam, Judaism, Buddhism or Hinduism."

She continued, "The practice is performed by a woman who might be a midwife in her village, with no formal medical training. She is referred to in some countries as the Gypsy Woman, and in other countries, as the Medicine or Zoe Woman. The word Zoe has something to do with secret society in some West African cultures."

A woman from Miami, Florida wanted to know if Kiddi's child was adopted or if he was her biological child. Kiddi decided to tell them the truth. "I underwent corrective surgery and was able to enjoy normal urination, sexual intercourse and a normal childbirth." She continued, "Some of the girls on whom the act is performed are able to engage in sexual intercourse and conceive children, provided they survive the practice or later, survive the pain of their first sexual encounter."

Several people wanted to know why the girls took so long to come forward about what had happened to them during their childhood. Nana explained to them how they vowed, not disclose their secret about what had happened to them. She told them about the emotional experience she encountered when she saw the girl on television, as she told her own story and how she escaped from FGM.

Kiddi wrote about the dangers and the health problems that FGM poses. "FGM can cause a range of health problems, both short-term and long-term. The kinds of problems that develop depend upon the degree of the cutting and the cleanliness of the tools used to perform the cutting. In most countries, FGM is performed in unclean conditions where unsterilized scissors, razor blades or knives are used. A young lady recalled at 5 years old, the Gypsy Woman in her village in Somalia, took out a blood-stained, sawed-off razor blade from her apron pocket, spat on it, wiped it on her apron and used it to cut her." Kiddi continued with her blog, "Some of the results of FGM are the initial severe pain; the shock; severe hemorrhaging, possibly resulting in death; urine retention; infection resulting in convulsions and possibly death; contraction of HIV/AIDS due to non-sterilized instruments in multiple cuttings; cysts; damage to the urethra resulting in urinary incontinence; painful sexual intercourse; sexual dysfunction and difficulties with childbirth." Her fingers bounced about the keyboard of her laptop, "Many of the girls who undergo female genital mutilation never recover psychologically. Some result in suicide because they are unable to live through the mental trauma."

The flow of emails and the volume that came in both to their email box and the message board compelled Nana to take an extended leave of absence from Proficiency Travel at the International Financial Trust (IFT). She scheduled several speaking engagements around the country and became the official spokesperson against FGM in the States. Kiddi did the same in Europe and England. Both ladies raised money just from their appearances for their organization. The campaign was indeed in full force.

Nana, Shirley, and Frank briefed Jean-Claude on everything that he missed while he was in Africa and Europe. "You guys have been busy!" Jean-Claude was pleased with the reports and looked forward to another fundraising dinner within the next two nights. "So Frank what is going on in the world of football these days?"

"As you know, I made the Post Bowl. So did Tommie." Frank furrowed his brow. "The big news now is Milton Dude. He got himself arrested. He was just in the wrong place at the wrong time during the Big Bowl."

"No, I have not seen much State side news." Jean-Claude was surprised. He had watched Milton Dude, a running back play since his rookie year. "What happened?"

"He went out partying the night after the Big Bowl. He had some guys in his car that were not clean." Frank frowned. "They had drugs on them with guns. The police officers pulled them over for a random check. Milton was driving the car, so he went to jail with the rest of his friends."

"What a way to celebrate his Big Bowl victory." Nana remarked. Frank's team made it to the playoffs but did not make it to the Big Bowl that year. "Frank, you know what I have always wondered?"

"What Nana?"

"When do you guys use the bathroom during the games?" Everyone, including Nana laughed. "No, because other than when you return to the locker room at half time, I never see anyone leave the field for that purpose. I see them leave if there is a severe injury, but never for anything else."

"You are right. We are dressed appropriately to accommodate anything that needs to be expelled during the game." He smiled. "We appreciate half time, which is all I can say."

"Wow! That is messy." Nana exclaimed.

"If they didn't do that, the game would stop each time a player needed to use the facility." Frank explained without embarrassment. "I have never needed to do number two during regulation though."

"Thank goodness for that!" Jean-Claude exclaimed between chuckles. "That would be a great way to avoid being sacked." They laughed at his comments. Jean-Claude glanced at the clock on the mantel. "Do you realize that we have not slept at all?"

"It is already four in the morning." Nana added. "Paula should be landing at Dulles within an hour."

"You are right." Jean-Claude pondered. "I wonder why she didn't call when she arrived in Los Angeles."

"The flight might have been delayed out of Honolulu." Frank saw the look of concern on Jean-Claude's face and tried to reassure him that everything was well. "Anyone for tea or coffee while we wait for Paula's arrival?"

"Coffee sounds like a great idea." Nana and Shirley chimed in, as they followed Frank to the kitchen with Jean-Claude in tow.

They sipped on coffee and tea and snacked on slices of strawberry shortcake while they waited to hear from Paula. Jean-Claude's mobile phone rang at about quarter to five. "It has to be Paula now. Hallo." Everyone saw the look on Jean-Claude's face as he listened to the caller. "Impossible! Are you sure?" He sat back down on the bar stool next to Nana. "Thanks for the call."

"What happened?" Shirley shouted when she noticed that Jean-Claude had put down his phone, but tears streamed down his face. He was motionless. His three friends rushed to his side.

He finally spoke after he regained his composure. "That was Duane Garrison, a pilot from Alignment Airlines." Jean-Claude's voice cracked. "Paula's plane never made it to L.A." His shoulders shook as he wept. "The plane exploded over the Pacific Ocean." Paula had been a pilot with Alignment Airlines for fifteen years.

"Noooooo!" Both Shirley and Nana wailed in unison as a dark cloud overcame the Virginia townhouse. The girls wept with grave emotion while Frank led Jean-Claude back to the living room.

"I had a bad feeling when she did not call us because she always calls between flights." Jean-Claude said through tears. "I should give her parents a call, but they are still asleep in the mid-west."

Frank was quiet since Duane Garrison's phone call to Jean-Claude. "Paula was such an experienced pilot. This is unimaginable." He finally spoke with a shaky voice.

Jean-Claude slowly rose from the sofa. "Listen guys, I just need to be alone for a little bit." His voice broke again as he waved to them and disappeared to his basement apartment.

Though the friends had not slept the entire night and it was already past six in the morning, they were unable to find sleep. Shirley, Frank and Nana remained in the living room in periodic silence. During intervals, someone made a remark about Paula's character.

"Why did it have to be Paula's plane?" Nana sobbed. "She was in such great spirits the last time she called to say she was on her way." She sniffed. "She was so vigilant about our campaign."

"She was anxious to get back here to solicit more pilots in the union to join the campaign." Shirley pointed out. "She told me that she had even persuaded pilots in Australia to commit to the campaign."

"What are we going to do about the dinner tomorrow night?" Frank asked the girls. "How can we cancel it?"

"Let's wait for Jean-Claude to decide." Nana said between sniffles. "Let it be his decision." Both Frank and Shirley nodded in agreement.

Somber Reports

The day following the plane explosion, the friends found little time to sit and mourn their loss. Jean-Claude decided that they should not cancel the annual fundraising dinner. Instead, they would dedicate the evening to Paula Braun. "I know that is exactly what Paula would have wanted." Jean-Claude had persisted.

They stayed up the entire night before, while they consoled each other, including Jean-Claude. He called Paula's parents at six that morning, Mountain Time, to give them the news. He knew that they were early risers and he wanted to be the first to tell them. Paula's mother fainted when he told her, and her father's voice was shaky as he spoke to Jean-Claude. "Thanks for calling to tell us. I imagine that Alignment Airlines will be calling later this morning to notify us." Mr. Braun told Jean-Claude.

Jean-Claude sat in the middle of his bed, his body in the shape of an upright fetus. He hugged his knees as he rocked back and forth. He did not know how prolific his tear gland was until his loss. The tears flooded his cheeks while the mucous escaped from his nostrils. He wondered how this tragedy had happened. Paula was one of the best and most experienced pilots Alignment Airlines had on their staff. She always took her job seriously. She never regarded flying as a job. "Flying for me is a career, it is what I enjoy doing." Paula had told them many times before. Jean-Claude was anxious for the FAA to come back with the report from the black box. He wondered if they would find the box. Duane Garrison said that it was an explosion. He thought about the fun times that he had spent with Paula. She was not just a lover; she was a dear friend. He would never forget the day that they met in London at the in-flight seminar. Paula was eloquent in her presentation. He continued to rock and weep until a knock at the door brought him back to the present.

"Jean-Claude, Kiddi is upstairs. She wants to see you." It was Nana at the door.

"I will be up shortly." He slowly left his bed, cleaned up his face and put on a shirt. He knew that he needed to show strength for the girls and then there was the dinner that night. He needed to focus on the work they had ahead. Paula felt strongly about the foundation, and they would honor her by moving forward with their plans. He made his way swiftly up the stairs to where Kiddi and his friends congregated in the living room. "Kiddi, how are you? Just as lovely as the last time I saw you." He tried to make light of their reunion.

Kiddi hugged him. She whimpered as they held their embrace. "I am so very sorry." She whispered as she let go of him. "What a shocking tragedy this is!" She remarked as she took her seat.

"I think you should know that the reports are not promising." Nana said to Jean-Claude as they watched the news.

"Well, I am not surprised. What are they saying?" Jean-Claude walked to the kitchen and got a bottle of water out of the refrigerator.

"That the aircraft disintegrated, there is no reason to send out a rescue crew because there are no survivors." Frank explained. "Everything in the plane incinerated before it hit the ocean."

"I figured as much." Jean-Claude's lips quivered as he spoke, but he restrained himself from releasing tears in the presence of his friends. "Let's talk about tonight's affair. Do we have everything in order?" He changed the subject and they understood.

"Everything is ready as was planned before the news." Shirley told him. "Will you be able to read a tribute to Paula or do you prefer if Frank or Nana read it?"

"I would prefer if Frank or Nana read it." Jean-Claude looked over at Frank and Nana. "Do you mind?"

"Since Nana and Kiddi are making their usual presentations, I will take care of that, J.C." Frank assured him. "I got it."

"Thanks Frank." Jean-Claude nodded. "Really appreciate it."

"Kiddi, we would like you to come over tomorrow for lunch after you have rested from tonight." Shirley told her. "I will prepare lots of food tomorrow."

"Are you sure you are up to it, babe?" Frank asked Shirley.

"Positive. Nana told me that when someone passes away in West Africa, they cook a lot of food as folks come to pay their respects." Shirley spoke with pride as she exhibited her knowledge of West African culture. "She said that visitors also bring food."

"Is that how you mourn?" Jean-Claude asked. "I like that idea of mourning it helps to take away the sadness."

"We sit on the mat, weep and mourn but we dance and sing in celebration of the life that the deceased lived." Nana told them. "Tonight, we must celebrate Paula's life. She was a wonderful person; she would not want to see us sad."

"You are absolutely right Nana." Jean-Claude stood. "I will go downstairs to prepare myself for a night of celebration." He smiled for the first time since the tragic news, and everyone echoed his suggestion.

Kiddi brought her change of clothes so that she would get dressed at their house. "Nana, you do not mind if I shared your room?"

"Of course you may, Kiddi." Everyone disappeared to where they would get dressed for the dinner.

The Foundation Dinner

The dinner was a big success. The friends celebrated the day after dinner at the Herndon townhouse. They were joined by Tommie Thurston, Frank's younger brother and Kiddi with her family and Amelia Thurston. Shirley and Nana prepared an assortment of dishes. Jean-Claude, Frank and Tommie supplied a case of champagne. They invited a few of Nana's colleagues from Proficiency and a couple of Shirley's clients.

"Did you see the papers this morning?" Tommie asked as he held up the "Style" section of the local Sunday paper. *"The most spectacular event for charity in this decade…"* He read to them.

The dinner was indeed spectacular. The Foundation was able to pique the interest of several of Hollywood's celebrities and Washington's politicians. The CFA was fully represented. Retired players from the year prior made their appearances in support of FAFGM. The dinner looked more like a combination of the Academy Awards and the Hall of Fame that night. The program began with a moment of silence in memory of Paula, the crew and the passengers on board the aircraft. Paula was honored that night by the foundation to which she was so dedicated. She had lost her life on her way to dinner.

The friends were popular and controversial. FGM was no longer an unfamiliar incident that only happened in far away places. The world was now educated by FAFGM, and the majority of the world wanted to see it eradicated.

Nana told the crowd that night, "The response FAFGM has received, tells us that the world is now smaller." She paused until after the applause. "The smaller the world becomes, the louder it speaks out against the inhumane acts on its inhabitants." She was interrupted again by the applause.

Kiddi spoke with emotion. "We will no longer sit by quietly while little defenseless girls are brutally cut." She paused with a smirk on her face. "They want us to call it cutting, not mutilation." The sound of groans filled the room as she continued. "We cannot find any word to sugar-coat this despicable act. Whether it is called circumcision, cutting or mutilation, it is wrong. FAFGM will continue to speak out against it."

Frank's tribute to Paula caused many sniffles. "Paula Braun was a pilot; a dear friend; a respectable American; a loving daughter and a devoted member of FAFGM." Frank fought to hold back his emotions. "Tonight we celebrate our friend Paula Braun's short but meaningful life. Paula was on her way here to Washington, D.C. to participate in our third annual fundraising dinner for FAFGM." He hung his head in thought; his tall frame slumped at the podium. "Paula must always be remembered as the great pilot who got the airlines involved in the plight to eradicate FGM."

The dinner was a black-tie affair. The World Intercontinental Hotel in Washington hosted it every year. It was their contribution to the Foundation. Nana placed many of her international clients at that hotel in the past. She approached their sales office with reluctance about sponsoring the event the first year. Once the manager learned what FGM was, they readily agreed to host the event.

"So what's next for FAFGM?" Tommie asked.

"We continue to move ahead with our plans." Frank looked over at Jean-Claude for approval. "I think it is what Paula would want us to do."

"Absolutely," Jean-Claude concurred, his large brown eyes stretched. "We now move ahead louder than ever."

"I fully agree to that." Kiddi took a sip of her champagne as she nodded with vigor. "We have sounded the trumpet. The world has listened in agreement." She took another sip. "Now we go after the wretched bastards." Her English accent was profound as she expressed her feelings.

"I drink to that." Nana raised her glass and clicked glasses with Kiddi and Shirley. "With the United Nations' support against FGM, we should be able to get them to end this thing."

They knew that it was only half of their task. They vowed to educate the American people about the practice, to the point where they wrote to their individual congresspeople, and senators for help.

FAFGM collected over two million signatures through the internet from around the world. Their website had over a thousand visitors a day. They hired a lobbyist in Washington, D.C. to help them with the United States Congress. They pondered if they should ask the U.S. Congress to impose sanctions on the nations that allowed the practice of FGM to continue without outlawing it, but they realized that sanctions would affect the innocent more than it would the perpetrators. Their goal was to have the nations in Africa and other parts of the world declare the practice of FGM unlawful. The foundation wanted it to be a written decree on the law books of each nation in Africa and other places where it was practiced. They knew the gravity of the request, but it was possible.

"The resistance from some men in those countries is stronger though." Shirley pointed out. "We have received serious anonymous letters, urging us to discontinue our push."

Shirley was right. The foundation had indeed received such letters. Some of them were threatening but the letters did not stop them. Meanwhile, they had not received any recent letters. Jean-Claude and Frank concluded that those letters were only pranks.

"They can resist all they want, "Frank remarked. "No number of letters will stop us."

"Frank is right. We must not forget the reason we have come this far." Jean-Claude stood as he looked at their visitors in the living room. "All of this is not about the fanfare. It is not about the glamour, nor the glitter." He took a few steps to where Nana and Kiddi sat. "It is about what Nana and Kiddi suffered many years ago; what girls suffer today." He returned to his seat with a distant look on his face.

"So is everyone attending the memorial service on Tuesday?" Nana asked. Paula's parents had planned a memorial service to be held in Minnesota for their daughter. They invited Jean-Claude and his friends. Frank and Tommie were granted excuse from football practice so that they would attend the service in Minnesota.

"Absolutely Nana," Kiddi spoke with certainty. "I had my return flight to London changed just to be in attendance."

"Thanks Kiddi." Jean-Claude told her. "Paula would be pleased to see everyone there."

"It is the least I can do to pay my last respect to Paula, a dear friend and supporter." Kiddi told them.

Farewell to Paula

St. Paul, Minnesota

Two days later, the friends gathered in Minnesota at an Episcopal church to say a final farewell to their friend. Her parents had attended that church since Paula was a child. She was a girl acolyte in the church during her formative years. The church was not surprised when she became a pilot; she always did things differently from the other girls. She lost touch with the church after high school. Paula moved to Michigan to attend the University of Michigan. After college, she went to Florida to aviation school. She rarely made it back to her roots except for special occasions.

The Brauns noticed that their daughter was somewhat of a tom boy during her childhood. Paula attended her high school prom with the boy whom everyone knew as her boyfriend. Andrew Gephardt was a handsome young man. He and Paula had been an item throughout high school. Everyone assumed that the relationship between the two would result in an eventual marriage. Both the Brauns and Andrew's parents had entertained that same assumption. Paula and Andrew drifted apart after their first-year college year. Andrew remained in Minnesota and got married to Nicole Crimson, another local girl. Like Andrew, Nicole had remained in Minnesota for college. Andrew waited two years for Paula, but she showed less interest in him during her visits home from school.

Then the rumors began to spread around their small town that Paula was interested in someone else. Andrew was adamant about dismissing the rumor. He made it clear that Paula would never entertain the thought of seeing someone else. Andrew was crushed when Paula came home on one of her visits and told him the truth. He took her to dinner that night. They caught up on their activities at school. Andrew felt confident that night that Paula would accept his proposal. He had selected the ring with much care. While they joked with each other, Andrew shared with Paula the rumor.

"Would you believe the false statements that some of our own friends have said about you?" He sipped his drink with a smile. "I told them that they are only jealous because you will be going to aviation school to become a great pilot."

"Don't make any enemies for yourself on my account." She looked away from Andrew. "Remember you have to live in this town, I don't."

"Well, if we're together, you will be wherever I am Paula." He seemed surprised by her reaction to the rumor. "They're saying that you're seeing someone else Paula." He stared her straight in the eye, but Paula avoided his stare.

"I have something important to tell you." She looked down at her hands as she searched for the words. "I came home to tell you something important."

"I'm not sure I know where this is going." Andrew interrupted her.

"Please let me finish." She held both hands up. "Just hear me out." He nodded in agreement as she continued. "I love you, Andrew. I have always loved you." He nodded and stared at her. "My life has taken on a different twist." She sighed as though her body was on the verge of an explosion. "I am not the same Paula that you knew back in high school."

He saw that she struggled to say it. "Paula, are you really seeing someone else?" She shook her head with vigor, but she stared down at her hands in her lap. "Damn it Paula, if you are not, then why not fight for your good name?" He kept his voice low. "I have waited for you…" He fought back the tears as he interrupted her.

"I don't have anything to prove to anyone, Andrew, not even to you." She finally spoke. "I have no struggle with my reputation." Her lips quivered. "I wanted to stay here and marry you and have a family. It would have been the right thing to do, I thought, but it is not what I really want for me." A tear escaped from her eye, but Andrew was too upset to notice. "I just want to focus on my studies and my career. That is all I can tell you at this time." She dabbed her eyes with a tissue she took from her purse and looked Andrew in the eye. "I cannot make any promises to you right now as far as marriage or a commitment. I just want to be the best pilot – not the best female pilot but the best pilot there is."

Andrew was crushed. "So because you're going to be this big-time pilot, you want nothing to do with me?"

Paula's heart went out for him, but she did not want the distraction from her studies. "Andrew, I am leaving it up to you." She sighed. "If you want to wait for me until I finish my studies, then that is fine with me. I am not going to run into another man's arms in the meantime." She shrugged her shoulders. "I just don't want to hold you up, that's all."

Andrew reached across the table and slapped Paula on the face. He threw some money on the table to take care of the drinks, since they had not yet ordered dinner, and he ran out of the restaurant. He hailed a taxi and went home. Andrew mourned for several days. He made it clear to his parents and to Paula that he never wanted to see or speak to her again. Paula left her hometown with the rumor unconfirmed and still lurking that she had dumped Andrew because she wanted to be with someone else.

Her parents expressed their disappointment in her. She exchanged harsh words with her parents and took an early flight back to Michigan. Her father told her, "If the rumor is true, then you need to be honest with Andrew. He is a nice young man."

Paula stormed out of the house when she heard her father draw conclusions about her. Her mother screamed in repeated hysterics.

The years slipped by, and Paula excelled in her studies. She did remarkable work at the University of Michigan and obtained a scholarship to aviation school, but her parents did not attend her college graduation. They were still angry because she had not married Andrew and given them grandchildren.

Andrew Gephardt did not trust another woman with his heart until Nicole Crimson invited him to her party and insisted that she would not take no for an answer. He accepted her invitation and enjoyed the party and Nicole's company. After that night, followed several more dates and walks in the park. Nicole did not hesitate to accept Andrew's marriage proposal after they had dated for a year.

He found it in his heart to forgive Paula after his marriage to Nicole. They made peace with each other, and Paula was grateful. Paula made peace with her parents long before and brought Jean-Claude to meet and visit them on several occasions. During one of those visits, she ran into Andrew and Nicole, and they met Jean-Claude. Andrew saw that Paula was happy with Jean-Claude and her new life. She traveled the world. He knew that she would not have the time for a husband and children. Andrew knew that Paula had specific goals to keep.

Now seated at the memorial service in the back of the church were Andrew and Nicole, along with several of Paula's high schoolmates. Andrew wept during the entire service, but it was Nicole Crimson who delivered an emotional tribute on behalf of Paula's classmates.

Jean-Claude's tribute was the most moving of all the tributes. He spoke about the type of friend that Paula had been to many and about Paula, the humanitarian. He told them about the loving daughter that Paula was and about the dedicated employee she was. He told them that he had loved Paula from the day they met, and he had decent intentions toward her. "Paula was loved by the many lives that she touched during her brief life here on earth." He told them, "FAFGM was dear to her heart." Jean-Claude paused as he fought back the tears. "She was on her way to Washington, D.C. for that purpose when she met her untimely death." His lips trembled as he allowed the tears to escape from his eyes.

Nana, Shirley and Kiddi cried while Frank and Tommie sat with shock on their faces. After the service, Mrs. Braun cried harder when she saw the FAFGM friends. "The last time Paula visited she told me that FAFGM was her extended family." Her tears flowed as she spoke. "My husband and I will always support FAFGM in her memory. We want you all to stay connected with us."

Alignment Airlines was fully represented, Paula's immediate boss, along with the General Manager of Alignment, several flight attendants, and pilots.

The Brauns did not warm up to the fact that their daughter had opted to be with a French man, instead of an all-American Mid-Western boy. Mary Braun told her husband a long time ago, "She is our only child. She is not going to change her mind about her choice of companion. We either accept her for who she is or lose our daughter for good." She was stern with her husband. "I will not lose my child." Jean-Claude visited the Brauns in St. Paul a few times. The charmer that he was, they had given in and taken to Jean-Claude. His own mother sent flowers to the Brauns when she learned of Paula's death.

Nana and Shirley found themselves back in Herndon, with Jean-Claude back on his usual route, and Kiddi back in London. Jean-Claude felt that getting back to work was what he needed. They all tried to get back to their daily routine, but they did so with difficulty.

"If we are having this much difficulty, what do you think poor Jean-Claude is encountering without us." Nana mentioned Shirley.

"I know, he tries to act strong, but I know how much he's hurting inside." She shook her head with a sad expression. "Life is so complicated."

Chapter Five

THE TOURS

But I will call on God, and the Lord will rescue me. – Psalm 55:16 (NLT)

With only two months left of Nana's leave of absence from Proficiency, she and Kiddi busied themselves with speaking engagements. Frank was busy with football and was having the season of his career. He was named quarterback of the year in the CFA and the San Antonio Gorillas were assured of another trip to the playoffs, their third since Frank Thurston had been their quarterback. Shirley agreed to handle administrative duties for the foundation while Nana and Kiddi were on the road. Jean-Claude took Paula's death harder than the friends realized but he was back and forth between France, Washington, and West Africa. He took time off and spent two weeks with his mother in the South of France, but he returned to his flight attendant duties.

Carnegie Hall, New York City

The Foundation hired a public relations firm to handle their promotional affairs. Don& Day Public Relations booked a full scheduled tour for Kiddi and Nana, covering states in certain regions of the United States. Kiddi took time away from her son and husband in England to tour with Nana. Their first stop on the tour was New York City, where they spoke to a crowd of mostly women at Carnegie Hall.

Kiddi spoke first and told the crowd her personal story. "Many women have written to me, wanting to know about my personal life." The crowd roared as she paused until they were quiet. "Well, I have decided to tell it all." She was interrupted again by the applause. "The first eight years of my life could not have been happier." The room was quiet as she continued.

"Then the day that I call *Brutal Day* happened. I was eight years old when the *Medicine Woman* stripped me of my womanhood." She shifted from one foot to the other. Each time she spoke about it, she relived *Brutal Day*. "My mother held me down while the *Medicine Woman* cut off my clitoris and labia." Kiddi did not notice the faces of the crowd, but Nana did. Some wore total shock while others groaned with imaginary pain as Kiddi continued. "She then stitched up the remaining skin where my labia had been, leaving a tiny opening to accommodate urination." Kiddi paused as she fought back tears. "All of this was done with no sterilized instruments." She bit hard on her bottom lip. "I recall suffering from nightmares for years following *Brutal Day*. Fever ripped through my body in the days that followed, leading to convulsions. Thankfully, my father was acquainted with a physician who treated the fever." She paused. "He treated the fever and convulsions, but the worse scar still remains with me." The crowd moaned. "Yes, I grew up; I was able to obtain a scholarship to study nursing in England after secondary school. I knew that I would never return to my native land once I was out of there. My father tried to marry me off to an old man, but I told him I would kill myself if he did." She composed herself. "I think he really believed that I would, but it saved me." The crowd chuckled along with her. "I became a surgical registered nurse and landed a job in a hospital. It was there that I met my husband, a surgical intern at the time." She finally smiled. "He performed corrective surgery on me before I was able to have sexual intercourse and eventually, have my son." The room was quiet. "There you have it. Thanks for listening, you have been great." She waved to the audience and left the stage.

Nana was introduced after the applause dissipated. "Since Kiddi and I faced the dreadful *Medicine Woman* on the same *Brutal Day*, I will not bore you with the same story." She smiled, and then her smile faded into a serious glare. "What I am here to tell you is what happens to the little girls' lives following *Brutal Day*." The audience was quiet once again. "Kiddi and I survived, however far too many of the girls do not. They either die from severe infection, which causes convulsions and later death, or they live a life full of nightmares. Some of them never recover mentally or emotionally. They become mentally or emotionally unstable. Most are forced into marriage with a man as old as their fathers, for a wedding night of rape." The audience listened in shock. "I call it rape because most of the girls, at twelve years old do not want to be married to a sixty-year-old man." The audience reacted. "If she does not willingly succumb to his sexual advances, her husband rapes her." Nana waited for silence before she spoke again. "What Kiddi did not tell you is that the tiny opening which the Medicine Woman leaves after stitching is so tiny that a girl can take up to half an hour to urinate at a time." The audience was baffled. "Imagine feeling the rush of wanting to urinate but instead of the steady flow that normal urination has, you sit for half an hour, releasing one drop at a time. Imagine the pain."

The women in New York became so angry at what they heard from Kiddi and Nana that they decided to do something about it. They began a petition for signatures to appeal to their congress people and senators for help. They wanted the brutality of girls in those countries to stop.

Philadelphia, Boston & Atlanta

Their next stop was Philadelphia. The Mayor of the city met with them the morning prior to their town hall meeting at the convention center. He assured them of his support and the support from the city of Philadelphia. He had heard of the rousing welcome they received in New York and he and the people of Philadelphia were not going to be overshadowed. He arranged for a tour of the city for Kiddi and Nana in a convertible with streamers that read, *"End Female Genital Mutilation"* A crowd of women and girls lined the sidewalks cheering and waving as the convertible slowly made its way across the city. Don& Day Public Relations did an excellent job of alerting the media and city authorities in most of the cities that Nana and Kiddi visited, so that they received a great welcome.

Female Genital Mutilation was the most popular phrase in Philadelphia among people alike, and by the time Nana and Kiddi left for Boston, they had left an impact on the women of that city.

Their itinerary for Boston was done differently than those of New York and Philadelphia. They visited universities in the area and spoke to a large student body of women at each school. They repeated much of their previous speeches in Boston, as they spoke at Harvard and Radcliffe in Cambridge, Mount Ida College and Boston College in Newton, Bentley in Waltham, Wellesley, and Northeastern in Boston. They covered a great deal of territory while in Boston and the students received them as though they were celebrities.

In one of Nana's speeches in Boston, she elaborated more on the dangers of the practice. Don and Day realized that the dangers left a greater impact on the audiences' minds. Nana spoke about short-term health problems. "FGM can cause a range of health problems. Some of the short-term problems are bleeding or hemorrhaging, and if the bleeding is severe, the girls will likely die. Infection from the wound can develop into an abscess. Girls have been known to get high fever, go into convulsions and shock, like what happened to Kiddi." She paused to control her emotions. "In most convulsion cases, the girls die, if the infection is left untreated." The audience was riveted. "The girls are routinely cut without first being numbed or having anesthesia, so the worst pain tends to occur the day after, when they have to urinate onto the wound." She frowned as she relived her own pain from many years earlier. "The trauma the girls suffer, from being held down during the procedure, which can be physically or psychologically traumatic."

Kiddi took the stage at the podium and told them about the long-term health problems. "There are major problems using the bathroom. Since the girls are left with only a small opening for urination and menstrual bleeding, this can slow or strain the normal flow of urine, which can cause infections, as Nana pointed out." She paused for composure. "Not being able to have sex normally because the procedure leaves women with scars that cover most of their vagina. This makes sex very painful. These scars can also develop into cysts or thickened scars that can be uncomfortable. The girls have painful menstruation and may not be able to pass all of their menstrual blood, which leads to repeated infections. It is difficult for a healthcare professional to examine a woman's reproductive organs, if she has been mutilated or cut." She took a sip of water from the glass on the podium. "There is increased risk of sexually transmitted infections, since in most cases the same tool is used for several procedures without sterilization, as in our case. There has been a growing concern that these conditions increase the chance of spreading life-threatening infections, such as hepatitis and HIV." As Kiddi spoke, she placed emphasis on her words to make the point. "The psychological and emotional stress rate is extremely high, since some girls do not understand what is being done to them and why. The girls are taken to the Bush without an explanation. In most cases, they are incredibly young and are barbarically cut while their mothers or grandmothers hold them down blindfolded, as in Nana's and my case." The audience saw the toll it took on her to relive the experience. "There are major problems becoming pregnant, during pregnancy and childbirth. The infertility rates among women who have had FGM are as high as 25% to 30% and are mostly related to problems with being able to achieve sexual intercourse enjoyment. The scar that covers the vagina makes it very difficult. Most healthcare professionals recommend cesarean section. With rising numbers of young women coming to the United States and to Europe, doctors have begun caring for increased patients who have been cut and are facing some of these challenges." She continued, "Based on a study done, cesarean section, post-partum hemorrhage, extended hospital stays, the need for infant resuscitation, and death are only some of the results of FGM." Kiddi took several sips of water and ended her speech. "Thank you, ladies and gentlemen. You have been great – we appreciate your support."

The flight from Boston to Atlanta was not long enough for Nana and Kiddi. They already felt fatigue after the third leg of their tour. "You know something, though we are exhausted, it is a wonderful feeling of exhaustion." Nana told Kiddi as she reclined her seat in the economy class cabin.

"Absolutely, it is amazing how well we have been received so far." Kiddi agreed with Nana and chuckled. "I was taken aback when a couple of young ladies asked us for our autographs."

"So was I." Nana made a face. "I really don't want to turn this into a Nana and Kiddi celebration." She looked at Kiddi for agreement. "I want them to listen to the message and understand why we are appealing to them."

"I know it is all about stopping FGM and making sure that little girls are spared from what you and I endured."

They landed amidst a bad thunderstorm in Atlanta but Nana and Kiddi were not about to allow the storm to dampen their trip to the south. Neither of them had ever been to Atlanta and they looked forward to it. "This city is referred to as the Hollywood of the south, while others call it the New York of the south." Nana told Kiddi as they disembarked the plane.

"Is that true?" Kiddi had visited both New York and Hollywood and was curious.

"Well we are about to find out." Nana responded and laughed.

The sedan driver held up a sign with their names printed on it as they made their way toward him. He took possession of their bags as he led them to the waiting sedan. They stayed at a hotel in Atlanta, convenient to most places. By the time they checked into their room, it was already dinner time.

"Let's order room service and call it a night if that meets your approval." Kiddi suggested.

"I was just about to suggest the same." Nana reached for the menu on the desk in their room. She selected grilled portabella mushroom on a bed of baby spinach and Kiddi chose grilled salmon with baked potato and a salad. They had not eaten since lunch in Boston. "I am starved." Nana exclaimed.

The two ladies were quickly asleep once they ate dinner and showered. They did not engage in conversation and fell asleep with the television on. They knew that their schedule the following day was full of engagements.

The first speaking engagement was at Spelman College, an all-woman school. They received a great deal of interest at Spelman. The women at Spelman had several questions about FGM while both Nana and Kiddi carefully explained the procedure and why and where it is done.

Kiddi and Nana took questions from the audience. "Where is FGM practiced?" A student asked.

Nana answered, "FGM is practiced in Western, Eastern and North-Eastern Africa, Middle East, Near East and Southeast Asia. With the influx of immigrants to the United States and Europe in recent years, isolated cases of the procedure have been reported in such cities as Seattle, Atlanta, London, Paris and others. Five years ago, a Nigerian father was arrested in a city here in America after he took scissors that were not sterilized and cut off the clitoris of his 3-year-old daughter. He rushed her to the emergency, as she hemorrhaged into unconsciousness."

"Do you know specific countries in Africa where it is practiced?" Another student inquired.

"The question should be where it is not practiced." Kiddi said. "Currently there are only two countries in Africa where the practice has been outlawed. The first country was Egypt, where a Christian organization was instrumental in that. The second country to have it outlawed was Senegal. There again, another organization used an educational approach to have it outlawed. The third country on the continent to declare it illegal was Cameroon, thanks to a woman judge, who used her influence and position to have the illegality passed into law." The audience applauded.

"On whom is it performed generally?" A first-year student asked.

Nana answered, "Depending on the country and culture, it can be performed from a week old to 15 years old. In some countries like Liberia in West Africa, it is performed on the girl between 8 to 12 years old, prior to puberty. The girl remains in the Bush until she reaches puberty, and when she is sent back into society, her parents prepare her to become a wife. In most cases, her husband will be a man 3 times her age."

Nana and Kiddi felt positive when they left Spelman; the crowd applauded and gave them a standing ovation. "I think they liked us, and I like the questions they asked us. Kiddi told her childhood friend.

As they spoke across the country, a representative from Don and Day Public Relations, Cynthia Platt took signatures in support. From Spelman, they made an appearance at another all-woman school, Agnes Scott College in Decatur. They found the same questions there as they had at Spelman.

Durham, Charlotte, Nashville, San Antonio

Nana and Kiddi flew from Atlanta to Durham. They were like two little girls, full of excitement and anticipation. As the plane landed at Raleigh-Durham Airport, the girls had their foreheads pinned against the windows. They began a game in which they analyzed each visiting city by the appearance of the airport.

The ladies enjoyed a quiet dinner after arrival, in the hotel restaurant where they checked in hours earlier. Cynthia Platt from Don and Day Public Relations joined them for dinner. They went over their schedule for the next day. Kiddi and Nana only had one appearance in Durham the next day before they got on the road to their next visiting city, Charlotte, North Carolina.

The following day, Nana and Kiddi found themselves standing before a full auditorium at Duke University. The students were curious and eager to learn more about what had become one of the hottest topics of the decade.

Nana and Kiddi both made their usual speeches, which brought tears to the eyes of most of the women in the auditorium. They answered many questions that were asked by the attendees.

"Why did your mothers not protest against cutting you?" A student inquired in her southern accent.

Kiddi smiled at the young lady before she responded. She thought her accent was cute. "You must keep in mind that our mothers loved us very much." Kiddi told the young lady in her own British accent. "The procedure had been done to our mothers, as it had been done to their own mothers. It was what they knew at the time."

"When it is the only way one knows, one believes that it is the right way." Nana chimed in to help Kiddi.

Nana and Kiddi spent an additional hour shaking hands with the students, as they answered additional questions and signed autographs. They were impressed by the reception at Duke University.

"They were really interested in what we had to say." Nana said to Kiddi as they sat next to each other in the back seat of the comfortable sports utility vehicle (SUV). Cynthia sat in the front passenger seat. The driver pointed out some of the sights of the countryside as they drove along the highway.

As they entered Charlotte, they observed a different kind of city. Durham gave them the impression of a university atmosphere, while Charlotte appeared to be fast developing into a metropolitan city.

"Well ladies, I suggest you get yourselves a very restful evening." Cynthia told them. "You have another busy day ahead. You may want to order dinner to your room." She smiled at them. "Relax and enjoy your evening. See you in the morning."

Nana and Kiddi were excited and bright eyed the next morning. They looked forward to a day of activities. They were scheduled to speak to a church congregation, early that morning. Later, they had an invitation to witness the local football team play in Charlotte.

That morning at the church service, the ladies shared their experiences with the congregation at church. The pastor did not open the floor for questions, in order not to disrupt the continuity of the service.

"Today's entire offering is donated to the Friends against FGM." The Pastor told his congregation. "We are blessed in America to be isolated from such atrocious acts." He continued as groans of agreement filled the sanctuary. "Sisters Nkuku and Afambo have devoted their time to fighting this dreadful practice that is done to helpless little girls."

The choir bellowed a beautiful gospel selection that had even Nana and Kiddi rocking where they sat. They thanked the pastor and quickly left for the hotel. The ladies changed from church attire to sporting outfits. Nana wore a green and yellow sweat suit and a matching baseball cap. Kiddi wore a red and green sweat suit with a matching sweat band around her head. Both ladies wore sneakers. Kiddi wanted to wear a pair of flat dress shoes at first.

"Sweats just do not go with dress shoes." Nana told her through laughter.

"Says who, Miss America?" Kiddi shot back in a joke.

"The fashion police standing before you said so." Nana responded, still laughing.

"Well pardon me, Miss Fashion Police for calling you Miss America." Kiddi teased. "Now let's go learn about American Football."

"You will be learning about American Football today, my dear friend." Nana pointed her finger at Kiddi as they walked out of the hotel lobby to their rented SUV. Cynthia had already checked them out of their rooms and had their luggage sent to the vehicle. "I already know the game." Nana bragged to Kiddi.

Nana, Kiddi and Cynthia sat in the owner's box to watch the game. The Football Association had pledged its support to FAFGM. Every team in the association invited FAFGM to attend their games. They accepted some of the invitations, but they were unable to attend all of the games.

Nana, the team owner, and his wife explained the game to Kiddi, who looked confused. "What was it that just happened?" Kiddi inquired as the stadium was at its loudest.

"That was a touchdown by the home team." Nana told her. "Remember when the player reaches the end zone where the goal posts are, it is a touchdown, which is worth six points."

"Is it the equivalent of a goal in soccer?" Kiddi asked.

"Except that in soccer, a goal is only worth one point." The owner remarked. "Now the kicker just kicked the ball through the goal posts to score an extra point."

"You know, you call it soccer, but we call it football." Kiddi told the team owner and his wife.

"Then what do you call this?" The owner's wife asked, indicating the game that was being played.

Kiddi shrugged her shoulders. "We just call it American Football." Everyone in the owner's box laughed at the way in which Kiddi answered.

The game was enjoyable, and the home team walked away in victory. They thanked their hosts and departed Charlotte for Nashville.

Their visit to Nashville was scheduled for an appearance. They had an appointment with singer and actress Diane Parsons. She heard about their foundation and the tour.

The letter of invitation from Ms. Parsons read, "I understand that Nashville is not on your itinerary, but I am extending an invitation to speak with you at your convenience."

"It is no way that we can turn Ms. Diane Parsons down." Shirley told her friends after they read the letter. It was two weeks before their tour. Now they found themselves only a few hours away from meeting the great Diane Parsons.

One thing the two Ghanaian beauties had discovered was that each city they visited was different from the other. Nana recalled the remark she always heard people say, "once you have seen one U.S. city, you have seen them all." She knew that the statement was untrue. She found each city to have a special attraction.

Diane Parsons was hospitable in the old southern way to Nana and Kiddi. She met them in her hotel suite, where she ordered dinner for them.

"Thanks for coming and taking the time out of your busy schedule to meet with me." Diane told them.

"It is our pleasure." They chimed in.

"Since I heard about FAFGM, I have been reading materials on the practice that was done to you." Diane told the ladies, as she searched for the right words. "I applaud you for going public. I know it was not an easy decision for you."

"Thank you." Both girls smiled at Diane.

"I asked you here to let you know of my commitment to your cause." Nana and Kiddi exchanged a glance and smile as Diane continued. "I will hold a concert right here in Nashville at the Grand Ole Opry." The girls were baffled, as was Cynthia. "I will invite some of my friends, such as Rhea McKinley and Keith Regent to join me. We will stage a good old down home country music concert."

"Would you do that for us?" Nana asked.

"I most certainly will, honey." Diane told them. "We will raise enough money to support your foundation."

"Ms Parsons, we want to build support centers throughout Africa for victims of FGM." Kiddi told Diane. "The project will cost a great deal of money."

"Your gesture will help us get the first support center underway." Nana added.

Diane promised her full commitment over a scrumptious dinner and later the two friends left for their room. They had an early flight to San Antonio the next morning.

Frank and Shirley were at San Antonio Airport to meet Kiddi and Nana. Shirley was like an eager child as she greeted her two friends.

"What's up girl?" Shirley asked Nana as she gave her a big hug. "I missed you." She had been alone at the townhouse since Nana and Kiddi left on tour. Jean-Claude had not been back since his last break.

"I miss you too." Nana put her arm about Shirley's shoulder. "I only wish you had joined us earlier." Though they spoke by phone every day, Shirley still asked several questions about the tour and Nana briefed both Frank and her on their meeting with Diane Parsons.

A limousine took them to their hotel where Shirley had a room for herself. In the lobby, Frank parted company with them.

"So I will see you after the game tonight." He told them.

"You mean after the 'win' tonight, honey." Shirley corrected him.

"Babe I'm going into this game tonight with two of my starting offensive linesmen out." He shrugged. "Not to mention, Chuck and Dick are both out on defense with injuries." He kissed Shirley lightly on the lips. "In any case, enjoy the game, ladies. Your box seats are reserved. Jimmy will be waiting for you in his suite." He glanced at his watch. "Gotta run – be on time."

Jimmy Jeffries was the owner of the San Antonio Gorillas, the team for which both Frank and his brother, Tommie played. Jimmy had many years before made a name for himself and his team. The Gorillas were thought of as the team with which Americans identified. Frank and Tommie looked up to Jimmy Jeffries like a father figure. Jimmy liked to see his team win and the Thurston brothers always delivered a win. He liked the two brothers and would do almost anything for them. They stayed out of trouble and came to practice early and performed well at the games. Amelia Thurston trusted her sons with Jimmy Jeffries.

Nana, Shirley, Kiddi and Cynthia were escorted through a security entrance of the San Antonio Gorillas Stadium.

"Good evening, ladies." A smiling Jimmy Jeffries welcomed them to his private suite, as he shook hands with each lady. He repeated their names as they introduced themselves to him. "Thank you for joining me tonight. Please call me Jimmy." He told them so because the women addressed him as 'Mr. Jeffries'.

"We want to thank you for inviting us to watch the game in your fabulous facility." Nana told Jimmy.

"It is my pleasure – my pleasure." Jimmy smiled. "So which of you ladies is a Gorilla fan?" Jimmy wanted to figure out which one of the women was Frank's girlfriend, without being pointed.

"All of us are." Shirley spoke quickly, while the others concurred. Jimmy had his answer by the special light in Shirley's eyes. He saw why she had won Frank's heart. He wanted to scrutinize Shirley. He had a sudden parental protective urge.

Nana and Shirley were in disbelief that they were actually seated in his private suite with the great football owner, Jimmy Jeffries. They watched Jimmy many Sundays while he sat in that very suite to watch his beloved Gorillas play. He appeared to be much taller than he seemed on television.

The ladies noticed how Jimmy became serious as the national anthem was played and the coin was tossed to decide which team's offense would first take the field. The whistle blew and the game began.

The stadium went wild when the Gorillas' defense stopped the Alexandria Unicorns offense on a third downplay. Jimmy Jeffries was positive that Shirley was Frank's girlfriend when she jumped out of her seat as Frank threw his first pass of the night and completed it.

The Gorillas scored three touchdowns against the Unicorns before half time. Two of those were touchdown passes thrown by Frank. Nana and her friends saw the pleasure in Jimmy's demeanor.

Nana, Kiddi and Shirley were interviewed at half time by a reporter. The commentators mentioned during the game that Jimmy had special guests in his suite. The camera picked up Jimmy in celebration with his guests after one of Frank's touchdown passes. They mentioned Frank's involvement with Shirley, Nana, and Jean-Claude.

"We do understand the need for your foundation. But tell us how football fits into FGM." The reporter asked Nana.

"Had it not been football it would have been theatre, film, literature, anything." Nana explained. "FGM is something that fits in with any issue or anyone. It has to do with interest, empathy, passion and most importantly, the individual."

"It is not about football or anything else – it is about individuals as Nana mentioned." Kiddi joined the conversation. "It is about Jimmy Jeffries, Diane Parsons and so many others from the Football Association and the arts, who have committed their support."

"For instance, Frank Thurston has pledged $500 to FAFGM for each touchdown the Gorillas score this season." Shirley informed the reporter. "It is about individuals caring."

"And I am pledging $5,000 for each touchdown Frank passes this season." Jimmy told the reporter and the girls.

The girls were equally touched and surprised. They thanked Jimmy with glee. Frank threw two more touchdown passes that night, including the one that gave the Gorillas the victory.

The girls were escorted back to their limo where they waited for Frank. He had every reporter's microphone before him during the post game show. He was patient as he answered each question.

"The pledge that Jimmy made tonight is the best incentive I could ever be given." Frank referred to the pledge of $5,000 from Jimmy earlier. "It is my duty to uphold his pledge." He told the reporters.

Later, Tommie joined the friends and his older brother at the hotel. He was happy to see the girls after so long. Tommie himself performed well in the game as a running back. They celebrated until late into the night.

The next morning, Kiddi, Nana and Cynthia said goodbye to Shirley, Tommie and Frank. They boarded a flight to Dallas-Fort Worth Airport, where they connected to an international flight to London. Kiddi and Nana had completed their tour of the United States. They looked forward to doing the same work in Europe. The girls believed that they would have a success in Europe, judging by their great success in the States.

The girls made an appearance at Oxford University, where they addressed another full auditorium. They attended a soccer game between Manchester United and Leeds, two of England's popular teams. Cynthia had not been to London before. Nana and Kiddi played tour guide, as they took her to Big Ben, Hyde Park, Buckingham Palace and Harrods Department store.

Their success at Oxford was overwhelming. Now the women prepared themselves to have fun. They had the pleasure of meeting Kiddi's husband and son, along with several of her close friends.

"Kiddi, you have a very lovely home." Nana told her childhood friend.

"Thank you. I like living here." Kiddi smiled. She felt fortunate and blessed to have a loving and understanding husband and a beautiful healthy child. She never failed to thank God for her blessings.

The final stop on the tour was Paris. The girls took the train from London to Paris, where they met Jean-Claude. He and Nana behaved like two children who had not seen each other for years. Jean-Claude wanted to hear the details of the entire tour in the U.S. Nana and Kiddi brought him up to date, as they checked in at the front desk of their hotel.

The girls spoke at an international center, attended by more than two hundred women and men. Cynthia was able to have everyone at the international center sign the petition toward the eradication of FGM.

The friends decided to enjoy France, since their work was done. Jean-Claude scheduled a few things for them to do. They took the train to Nice to visit his mother.

Jean-Claude's mother, Madam Marie Girard, was glad to finally meet his dearest friends. She had met Nana many years before at their college graduation. Madam Girard went out of her way to prepare for their visit. She was an excellent cook and prepared an assortment of delicious French food. The girls ate heartily, which made Madam Girard happy.

"Madam Girard, these are the tastiest pastries I have ever eaten." Cynthia complimented the petite French woman.

"Merci, Mademoiselle Cynthia." Jean-Claude knew that his mother understood and spoke good English, but she insisted on speaking French to anyone from the States. "Parley vous Francais?" Madam Girard smiled at Cynthia.

"Mama, non." Jean-Claude interrupted his mother before Cynthia answered. "She does not speak French." He turned to Cynthia, "I'm sorry – pardon my mother.

Jean-Claude took his friends to where he attended primary school. They visited the cathedral where he and his mother attended mass when he was a child. They took photographs at his school as well as the cathedral.

Later that evening, they took the train back to Paris, after they said a warm farewell to Madam Girard.

The following day, Jean-Claude joined his friends on the Europa Wings flight from Paris to Washington Dulles Airport.

"It certainly feels good to be a passenger for a change." Jean-Claude reclined his seat after take-off. "I intend to enjoy this ride." He told Nana who was seated next to him. "It is not everyday that a flight attendant has this pleasure."

Jean-Claude took leave from his duties so that he would appear before the U.S. Congress to testify against FGM with his friends. While in Nice, they were notified that their lobbyist had just received confirmation for the testimony of FAFGM.

Capitol Hill, Washington, DC

"My name is Nana Nkuku. I was born in Accra, Ghana. My first eight years were the happiest any girl at that age could wish for. Then one day, my mother took me to the bush to see the Medicine Woman." Nana sat poised before suited men who were twice her age and addressed them.

She wore a pin-striped navy suit, accented by a pale blue shirt with French cuffs. She sat next to Kiddi at the end of the bench. Jean-Claude and Shirley sat on the other side of Kiddi with Frank on the other end. Tommie and Cynthia were in the back, only as observers. Each of the friends had an opportunity to testify.

The faces of the members of Congress wore the look of terror, as they listened to Nana's and Kiddi's testimonies. Then they heard from Jean-Claude, Shirley and Frank about how they made the discovery of FGM and founded FAFGM.

Following the testimonies, the friends exchanged handshakes with the congressional members. The friends gave them more than enough to absorb. They were well educated on female genital mutilation/cutting after the friends' appearance.

"We will review your testimonies and the document you have presented to us." The Chair of the Human Rights Congressional Committee told the friends. "I personally find this practice appalling and unimaginable." He shook his head in disbelief. "When we have made our decision, we will notify your representative." He slammed down his gavel and they adjourned the hearing.

On the steps of the U.S. Capitol, the friends took a photograph together.

"We did it." Frank said to the others. "The bill which will impose sanctions on practicing countries is now before the U.S. Congress."

"Who would have believed that we would be standing here today?" Jean-Claude said. They all joined hands and had a moment of silence in Paula's memory.

"You know that the sanction thing is only to serve as a threat to the countries, but we really do not want them to impose sanctions, because the innocent women and children will suffer more than the main individuals who deserve to suffer." Nana told her friends.

"Whatever works for the little girls is fine with us." Frank responded.

Chapter Six

THE SURPRISE

The Lord is my light and my salvation – so why should I be afraid? The Lord is my fortress, protecting me from danger, so why should I tremble? – Psalm 27:1 (NLT)

The alarm sounded from the surround-sound system on the mantle in Nana's bedroom. She was scheduled to return to her job at the International Finance Trust (IFT) that morning. She rolled over in her queen-sized four-poster bed, stretched and turned on the lamp beside the bed. She wondered why she was returning to work. Their foundation had raised a great deal of money since they began. She was celebrated on television, radio and in the print media. She wondered how her co-workers would behave toward her now. How much more awful her supervisor would be to her.

Nana did her usual morning meditation. She then prepared to leave for downtown Washington, D.C., where the IFT was located. She had not ridden the Metro for three months. Nana realized that nothing had changed with the Metro, except that the fares were higher.

She settled in a window seat and began to read the morning paper. She looked up from the paper and noticed that people stared at her.

"I think I saw you on Football Night recently." A male passenger in the train smiled and said to her.

She smiled at the man with a pang of embarrassment, and simply nodded. She was grateful that the next stop was hers.

"Welcome back." Her co-workers said in unison as Nana walked in the 10th floor office of the IFT building.

"Thank you." She had a hug for each of them. Everyone gathered around her cubicle to ask questions and to hear all about her time off.

"So you're a big star now." Nana's supervisor, Jessica remarked with sarcasm in her voice.

"No I am hardly a star. It is not about me." Nana responded without looking at Jessica.

"I'm glad to hear that. We don't need any controversy here." Jessica shot back in a stern tone.

Nana ignored Jessica's remark and continued to clean her desk and arrange her belongings in the cubicle. She wanted to be ready for the phones when the calls began to come in.

Nana's first day back was a busy one. Her clients were pleased to hear her voice again, as she answered the phone. She looked around her little cubicle and assessed her co-workers. Everyone talked on the phone, as they arranged travel itineraries for clients at the IFT. She wondered why she had returned to the job. Though she never played the lottery, Nana always said that if she ever won the lottery, she would continue to work. Now she questioned her decision to return to work. She felt out of place.

Two months after Nana returned to her job, she decided about her future. She planned the rest of her life in a document. She listed everything she always wanted to do and dated each item in a timeline. The completion of her play was at the top of the list. She called the document, "The blueprint of my life".

Nana was back to her job for over six months. Kiddi returned to her role as wife and mother. Jean-Claude was still on the Paris-Dakar and Paris-Abidjan as well as Paris-Ouagadougou route for Europa Wings. He called every week to check up on his friends and to get updates on the foundation. Shirley talked more about opening her Just-for-Men salon. Frank's career in the Football Association soared that season.

Nana and Shirley threw ideas around to plan Shirley's salon.

"Why does it have to be only for men?" Nana asked Shirley.

"I want that because I want something different." Shirley smiled as she explained. "I don't just want a salon; I want one with a specific niche."

"I suppose you are right." Nana remarked. "You could offer haircuts, shampoos and conditioners on the men." She was excited at the idea.

"That is exactly what I am talking about." Shirley seemed pensive. "But you know, men usually just get their hair cuts and keep going. I'm not sure they will like being pampered like that."

"Are you kidding me?" She looked at Shirley through stretched eyes. "Your appointment book would be full – more than you could handle if your service pampers men."

"You do have an idea there." She thought for a moment. "A service that offers special scalp massages for an extra charge." She got on her blackberry phone to input notes. "I'm going to put a price tag on each service."

"Now that's my friend." They exchanged smiles as the phone in Shirley's hand rang.

Shirley was on the phone for only a moment, and she was off. She turned to Nana with a curious expression. "That was Frank. He wants to see me this weekend."

"See you? Since when he called to set an appointment to see you?" Nana puzzled. She wondered what her friend had in mind.

"This weekend is the Gorillas' bye-week so he will come up for the weekend." Both Nana and Shirley were equally puzzled by the call and the sudden visit.

"Well, there is no harm in a man coming to visit his love." Nana assured her friend. She patted Shirley on the back. "No worries when it comes to Frank."

The Weekend

Shirley and Frank had the townhouse to themselves on Saturday. Nana was gone to their company luncheon in Southern Maryland. The luncheon was scheduled from noon until four in the afternoon. The drive from Herndon to the luncheon location was approximately an hour and a half.

Frank arrived at Dulles Airport at noon. He picked up his rental vehicle and headed for the townhouse in Herndon. His anticipation of seeing Shirley again caused his heart to skip a beat, as he drove on the toll road and took the Herndon exit.

Shirley prepared Frank's favorite meal; stir-fry strips of steak with mushroom and a lot of onion. She had steamed greens and jasmine rice. A bottle of red wine was placed on the dining room table with two wine glasses and a place setting for two.

"Something smells good." Frank said as he walked in and lifted Shirley up off the floor in a hug. He gently kissed her on the lips and placed her back onto her feet.

"I hope you're hungry." She managed to respond after she caught her breath.

The couple sat down to eat the lunch which Shirley had so carefully prepared.

"This is the best meal I have ever had." Frank told his girlfriend. "A lot of love must have gone into this meal."

She smiled from ear to ear and blushed. "Glad you like it."

After lunch, Frank helped Shirley load the dishes in the dishwasher. Then they retreated to the living room with their glasses of wine.

As Shirley sat and sipped her wine, Frank stood and stared at her with a gleam in his eyes. She looked up at him from where she sat. "What?" She smiled.

Frank got down on his right knee. He pulled out a little blue velvet box. He wore a serious expression on his face. He then took Shirley's slender hand in his large one. He looked her in the eye and spoke with confidence. "Will you be my wife for the rest of my life?" He displayed a beautiful 2-carat diamond ring from the little box.

Shirley began to cry as the tears escaped down her blushed cheeks. She still had not answered Frank and he wondered if he would be rejected. "Yes," she said almost in a whisper.

He jumped off his knee, picked her up and spun her around in his arms. Once they sat down again and clicked their glasses in a toast, Frank spoke. "I promise you, babe that I will keep you happy for the rest of your life."

Shirley still cried but her tears were joyful ones. Frank took her by surprise. She wondered if Nana knew about it.

Nana arrived home just as Frank and Shirley were on their way out to dinner. As she walked in, Shirley stood beside the door, with her left hand extended. Nana ignored her hand and rushed over to her former classmate, Frank, and embraced him.

"Welcome back to Virginia, buddy. So you decided to grace us with your presence during your bye-week." She continued as she shed her coat and walked to the coat closest to hang it.

Frank smiled. "Yes, indeed buddy." He indicated Shirley who had moved away from the door. She figured that Nana knew nothing about the surprise after all. "I almost gave your friend a heart attack today."

"Why what happened?" She rushed over to Shirley. As she got closer, she noticed the rock of a stone on her friend's hand. "I am so excited for you, Shirley." Nana exclaimed and grabbed Shirley. The friends hugged and wept tears of joy together.

Frank watched the two women. He knew what a good friend Nana was to both him and Shirley. "Ladies pull yourselves together."

The girls broke up their teary episode and finally spoke.

"We have to call Jean-Claude." Nana said with excitement. "Have you called your parents yet?" She gave Frank another hug. "Congratulations buddy." They exchanged high-five. "It's about time." The three laughed.

"I called my parents and Frank called his mom." Shirley wore a glow. "Mom cried – pop said what you said." She laughed. "That it was about time." They laughed again. "We are going out to celebrate. Are you coming?"

"Please do join us." Frank added.

"Oh, no I cannot tag along." She looked from Frank to Shirley. "You should not have me along with you for your special night."

"Are you sure?" Shirley asked. "If it had not been for you and Jean-Claude, I would have never met Frank."

"I am positive." Nana waved her hand toward the door. "Get out of here – go have yourselves a great time."

Nana had a reason for her decision to remain at home. She wanted to follow the list of goals she had set. She retreated to her bedroom after the couple left and opened her laptop to resume work on her play. Hours later, she heard them return but she continued to write until the early hours of the morning.

Six weeks later, Nana completed her play. She had worked on the play for several years, but she was always interrupted and was not able to complete it before.

"Now that you have finished the play, what is the next step?" Shirley asked Nana as they sat in the living room one evening.

She shrugged. "I am just happy to finish it at the moment." She pondered for a minute. "I would like to see it staged."

"Then we will get it staged." Shirley was enthusiastic. "We can do it."

"But we have to first plan your wedding." She smiled at Shirley.

Frank and Shirley set their wedding date for after the football season. It was evident that his team would make it to the post season. He did not want the distraction of the wedding with the Gorillas' post season.

"My mother has that covered." Shirley waved her hand in the air. "Her sisters and all her friends have made a career out of planning my wedding."

"We also have the benefit dinner coming up in a couple of weeks." Nana reminded her. They always held their annual benefit dinner the first week of each January. The foundation had made enough money to afford to hire an event planner to handle the planning and logistics of the dinner. The foundation had come a long way from its first benefit dinner. They had come an even longer way from when they took Thanksgiving dinner to a needy family each year. The foundation continued the Thanksgiving tradition, but they gave to more than just one family each year. A great deal of time had passed. Nana thought of Paula and how long it was since they put her to rest.

Another Benefit Dinner

The townhouse in Herndon, Virginia was fully occupied again. Kiddi was back in the States to attend the tenth annual benefit dinner of FAFGM.

Jean-Claude was at home. He had not been back for a long time. His schedule to West Africa kept him away from the States a great deal.

Since the Gorillas won home field advantage in the playoffs and were the winner of their division, Frank and Tommie were allowed to attend the dinner.

The friends were interviewed that morning by a television station and a live radio broadcast about the success of the foundation.

Nana wore a lovely red velvet gown, trimmed with her native kente material. The gown was designed and made by a Ghanaian designer in London. Kiddi brought the gown with her. Since she and Nana were the same size, the designer fitted the gown on her. Kiddi wore a black gown, made similarly to Nana's gown but it was trimmed with solid red fabric. Shirley wore a navy chiffon gown, with short sleeves and a flair shirt that accented her small waist. The three ladies looked dazzling.

Jean-Claude whistled. "Oh my, you ladies look like you should own Hollywood." Everyone laughed at his remark. The men all wore black evening dinner jackets since it was a black-tie evening.

The dinner was a great success. The foundation raised a million dollars that night. Kiddi's husband flew in that afternoon of dinner to support her. Amelia Thurston, Frank's, and Tommie's mother was in attendance. Jimmy Jeffries, the owner of the Gorillas, and his wife were seated at the table with Amelia and Tommie. Singer Diane Parsons performed at the dinner. She had long before upheld her promise to hold a concert to raise funds for the foundation. The Ghanaian Ambassador and his wife made an appearance at the dinner. Singer Alena Keene performed and some of the other big names in attendance were Billionaire Shirlene Joshua, Philanthropist Melanie Gaines, Actor and movie Producer, Tyrone Peal and Billionaire Wesley Butler. Frank's and Tommie's coach and several individuals from the Football Association attended. That dinner was the largest and most successful of all of them.

A tribute was made to Paula. Her parents were there to receive the trophy in her memory. Jean-Claude's mother, Madam Girard came in from Nice to attend the dinner. She had not visited the States since Jean-Claude's graduation from the university. Shirley's parents traveled from Atlanta for dinner.

The foundation announced that night at the dinner that they had already purchased land in three countries in Africa to construct support centers for victims of FGM. In addition, they leased space in buildings in the Middle East and Southeast Asia, where they planned to open more centers.

"We are close to our goal." Frank told their guests in the grand ballroom of the World Intercontinental Hotel. "Our goal is to have support centers on every continent where FGM is practiced." Applause filled the room as Frank paused. "We were only a group of friends who set out to help others, more than fifteen years ago." The applause interrupted him again. "On behalf of my friends, I thank each of you in the room for your support of our foundation. We intend to make a difference in thousands of little girls' lives. The rest of the friends of the foundation then joined him on the stage, as they waved to their guests and said that they would see them the following year. The evening was recorded for television later that month.

Making the Big Bowl

With the successful benefit dinner behind them, the friends began to plan a trip to Africa. They planned to visit the three countries where they had purchased the land for their centers.

The trip was postponed, after the Gorillas became the winner of the championship game that won them a trip to the Big Bowl later that month. The Gorillas were scheduled to host the Big Bowl that year at their stadium.

Frank was in the sporting news everyday since the championship game. He was on the cover of such magazines as *Sports Outline*, *Dark*, *Timeline*, *Talkweek*, *Gentlemen Monthly* and the *San Antonio*. Shirley and Nana purchased a copy of each magazine. Shirley began to worry if she would be able to cope with such a life.

"Of course you will." Nana assured her friend. "All you have to do is hold your head high – keep your dignity at all times and be there for Frank."

"You make it sound so simple."

"It is simple. Frank is going to play for another five years at the most before he retires." Nana patted her on the shoulder. "His face will not be plastered on the cover of every magazine once he retires. Beside it is only because of the Big Bowl this year."

"So do you want to go to the Big Bowl?"

"Was I born in Ghana? Do I eat fufu?" They laughed.

"Frank wanted to know. He's trying to get Jean-Claude to make it to the Big Bowl, but he isn't sure yet."

"I know Kiddi cannot make it." Nana pointed out. "She has been away from her family a lot lately."

"Then there is the trip to Africa; she plans to join us there."

The friends had a full schedule ahead. The Big Bowl was first, then the trip to Africa. Not long after the trip to Africa, Frank's and Shirley's wedding would take place. After the honeymoon, it would be the time for Frank and Tommie to report to training camp again.

"So are you going to find a new roommate after I get married?"

"No. Jean-Claude and I have discussed it. We do not want to break in a new person." She made a face and they laughed. "Your room will be a guest room so when Kiddi visits, she will have her own room."

"What about your play?"

"What about it?"

"Diane Parsons said she would show the script to a friend of hers in Atlanta."

"That is good. In the meantime, I have made a decision about Proficiency Travel." Nana smiled at Shirley and raised her eyebrows. "I wrote my letter of resignation last night. I will turn it in to them on Monday morning. I gave them two weeks." Shirley gave her a hug and high five.

Nana felt ready to make that crucial move. Her days at Proficiency began to feel meaningless. She felt like a fixture in the travel industry. She just did not want to sell airline tickets for the rest of her life. She knew that there was a lot more to Nana Nkuku than being a travel agent, not that being a travel agent was wrong; it just was not for her. She saw the years slip by and her age went up by twelve months with each birthday. Shirley was about to get married; Jean-Claude was hardly at home. He had become a workaholic since Paula's death. She needed a turn in her own life. Monday would begin that turn for her.

Chapter Seven

ROAD TO THE STADIUM

God is our refuge and strength, always ready to help in times of trouble. – Psalm 46:1 (NLT)

The friends came together for another holiday weekend. Most of the weekend was spent working together on their foundation and the trip to Africa. They were pleased with the direction in which their organization was headed. The long holiday weekend in January came to an end for the four friends at the Herndon townhouse. Frank left on an early Saturday morning flight for San Antonio, where he would join his team for the Big Bowl. He looked forward to their big day. He was most likely to be named the most valuable player of the year. Shirley drove him to Dulles Airport that morning with teary eyes. She knew that with the upcoming game and later the Post Bowl game, she would see little of Frank. He hated to leave, as he always did. They hung on to each other until the final boarding was called. "I hate to leave you with those sad eyes, babe." Frank held her close to him and kissed her gently on the lips. Then he kissed her hard.

Shirley caught her breath. "You kissed me like it's your last kiss." She teased him.

"In a way it is, babe. I don't know when I'll be back here in D.C. with you." He sighed. "You need to stop working so hard. Come to the Post Bowl as your vacation." He thought for a minute. "If we win the Big Bowl, you can come with me to Florida." She promised him she would, and he disappeared through the gate with a thrown kiss.

Though Jean-Claude came on his break for the holiday weekend, he was unable to remain in the States for the Big Bowl. He wished Frank all the success and predicted his score, San Antonio Gorillas 21 – Sacramento Cheetahs 14.

On the Sunday of the Big Bowl, Nana and Shirley drove Jean-Claude to the airport. He was on his way back to his regular route to Paris. "I know you'll be back in a few weeks." Shirley said to him at the airport.

"You are correct my dear. It is Dulles to Paris, then to Dakar." Jean-Claude told them as he had a kiss on the cheek for each roommate. "Behave yourselves until Papa gets back." He teased them in his French accent.

"Papa is the one who needs to behave." They all laughed at Shirley's remark, and he went to his gate.

Shirley and Nana returned to their Herndon home and found that they missed the two men who had just left. The house seemed quiet and empty. Jean-Claude always brought a lot of life to the house when he was at home. Frank brought extra treat of excitement to them.

Nana was a free woman. She left her job the week before with a warm send off. Her co-workers took her out to dinner on her last day. They wanted to have a send-off party in the office, but Jessica would not hear of it. She was invited to the dinner, but she declined. Jessica just did not like Nana at all. She held disdain for her, while Nana went about the office and was not bothered by her supervisor's behavior. She knew that she had done nothing to deserve the treatment Jessica gave her. Her co-workers told her that Jessica was just envious of her, but it was a problem that Nana was unable to fix.

Frank's and Tommie's Big Day

Shirley and Nana were saddened by the news that all flights to San Antonio were full for more than six months. They were unable to obtain seats to the Big Bowl to see Frank and Tommie play in person. Though they had seen them play in person before, this game was the big one and they wanted to be there. Jimmy Jeffries even invited them to sit in his suite with him and his family. Amelia Thurston declined Jimmy's invitation. She said that she preferred to watch the game from the comfort of her home; she got to see more from home than when she attended their games. She assured Jimmy that she would be there in spirit.

"Shirley what time does the game begin?" Nana asked as she doubled her feet under her on the sofa and switched on the television in the living room.

Shirley reclined in the black leather recliner in the corner from where Nana sat. "The actual game starts in twenty minutes. This is the pre-game show." She smiled with dreamy eyes. "Frank is dressed by now; probably getting his boys all fired up." She did not quite finish her statement when Frank appeared on the screen with Halid Kamal, the sports sideline reporter.

"Now Frank, you're coming into this game with a seventeen and one season record, having won all of your post season games. What do you think the Gorillas need to do tonight to stop Daryl Garrett?" Halid Kamal asked him.

"Well, the Cheetahs are a tough team. Our defense will have to step up to stop Daryl. He's fast; everybody knows that, but our defense will be able to handle him." Frank spoke with confidence, smiled, and accepted the well wishes from Halid.

Not long after the pre-game show, the National Anthem was sung by singer Alena Keene and the coin was tossed. The Gorillas received the ball with special teams. "Yes!" Shirley exclaimed and gave Nana a high five. Sylvester Johns of special teams ran the ball all the way to the fifty-yard line, just shy of the Cheetah's territory on the field. The stadium was exuberant.

Quarterback Frank Thurston and his offense strolled out onto the field. Running back Thomson caught Frank's first pass and landed at the ten-yard line of the Cheetahs. The stadium patrons were on their feet and Nana and Shirley were beside themselves. From the huddle, Frank did a trick play, which the Cheetahs' defense did not expect. He handed off the ball to Thomson but before the Cheetahs could emerge on Thomson, Frank repossessed it and sneaked in the end zone. The officials signaled a touchdown, as Frank was smoldered by his fellow players. Nana and Shirley did their usual victory dance. Nana had taught Shirley a special victory dance from Ghana, and they never failed to do the dance when the Gorillas played well.

The Gorillas scored early on their first drive of the game, but the Cheetahs were unable to answer with a score. They punted the ball off to the Gorillas, who marched down the field as Tommie caught a touchdown pass from his brother.

The game was late in the second quarter with the score at 35 to 6. The Gorillas held the Cheetahs to only two field goals, while the offense dominated almost the entire first half of the game. Frank was four for six; he threw six passes and got four touchdowns plus the one he ran in himself. The stadium was so loud, "one is unable to hear oneself", the commentator remarked.

At half time, Frank was interviewed about his unstoppable performance in the game. They asked him about his engagement and his involvement with the foundation. He was articulate and sincere. Nana and Shirley enjoyed the halftime show but were eager to see the rest of the game.

After halftime, the girls were just about to pop open a bottle of wine in an early celebration of the game, when the unthinkable happened. The Cheetahs had the ball on their own forty-yard line. Nana and Shirley did not believe what they saw. The stadium was in smoke; the field appeared to be in darkness. The girls screamed and did not stop their screams. Similar screams were heard throughout the neighborhood in Herndon.

The television screen went black and within seconds, the station returned with an emergency warning at the top of the screen. The stadium was just attacked with a bomb and there was chaos everywhere. The news reporter said that a bomb exploded in the stands, and they did not know any more until communications were restored. Chaos broke out throughout the country. No one knew the casualties on the ground, but the media speculated that everyone on the field survived.

Shirley screamed as she and Nana hung onto each other. "Where is Frank; where is my baby?"

"They still don't know of any casualties down on the field." Nana tried to console her though she needed consolation herself. She wanted to know that Frank was safe; that through a miracle, he and Tommie were able to get out.

Just then, the special announcement came on the television. "The nation has been attacked by terrorists; one of the worse terrorist attacks on American soil. Since the September 11th attacks in 2001, the United States has not suffered such blatant and outrageous attack. We now have confirmation that there are survivors, but names will not be released until families have been notified."

"Oh my God, Nana, what has happened?" Shirley screamed as Nana rocked back and forth in her seat. They tried to listen to the rest of the broadcast but the worst was yet to come.

"We just received breaking news that some of the players on the sideline may have survived but they are in critical condition. Medics are short; hospitals are calling for all medical personnel, including volunteers to report to the nearest medical facility here in San Antonio." The report continued.

"I pray that Frank and Tommie survived. Those guys are my brothers; they are not just friends to me." Nana stressed the word brother, as her eyes filled with tears.

Shirley put her arm around Nana's shoulders. "We must know that we have each other in this. We must pray and ask for the best." Shirley and Nana tried to call Frank's mother in Potomac, Maryland but the phone line was dead. Shirley was frantic as she pounded the button on the phone receiver and tears poured down her face. "I got to know; I got to know Nana."

Nana walked over and removed the phone from Shirley's grip. She took her in her arms and rocked her as she wept in silence for her friends. "We will find out; we will get through by cell phone; the phones are bound to come back on." She spoke through sobs.

Nana and Shirley sat in solitude as they watched the reports with close attention. The only sound in the Herndon townhouse was from the television. The news was their only source of knowledge. They were unable to remove their attention from the television – they felt lifeless attempting anything else. The ladies did not speak for more than two hours but tears continued to flow down their faces.

The newscaster came on after a commercial break. "The nation has been placed at a stand-still; the biggest sports day in this country has been stopped in time – the biggest game has been frozen…" Then he announced that the President of the Competitive Football Association (CFA) was about to make a statement.

"…we are appalled by what has befallen us today." The CFA President told the football fans with tears in his eyes and anger in his voice. "On behalf of the CFA, I extend profound regrets to all of the families – in fact, to all of the fans." He paused to clear his throat. "I don't believe that there is a family that is not affected by this monstrous act." He paused again for composure. "I assure you that the CFA will do everything we can to cooperate with the American government to bring the perpetrators to justice." As he continued his announcement, he revealed that they still did not know of survivors or casualties. He told the public that the CFA had suspended any further football activities until further notice.

Nana and Shirley sat in silence as the CFA President finished his statement. The television station returned to the news coverage of the attack, but Nana and Shirley had no drive left in them to continue. They retreated to their bedrooms, though they knew that sleep was something far in the distance.

Four Weeks Later

The rescue workers dug under concrete at the stadium that was hit. They discovered many bodies and parts of bodies. The CFA set up volunteer teams to receive phone calls from families and friends – a condolence team was formed to visit the families of players and team personnel. The individual football clubs collaborated with the CFA to provide special services to the victims and their families.

Frank was found in a hospital in San Antonio, Texas. The phone service was restored twenty-four hours after that dreadful Sunday. Shirley and Nana were able to reach Frank's mother and she was distraught. Mrs. Thurston was hit two folds. Her younger son, Tommie Thurston was found as one of the casualties.

Mrs. Thurston sat in her large family room and held her sons' photographs. She wept to Nana and Shirley. "Oh God, why would this happen to my boys – why? My boys were good boys – they never hurt anyone." She blew her nose into a tissue that Nana handed her. "They never got into any trouble at all." She continued to cry.

Amelia Thurston had indeed done a remarkable job with her two sons. John Thurston, her husband, had walked out of their lives when Frank and Tommie were little boys. He ran off with another woman, and left Amelia devastated and heartbroken. She vowed not to trust another man. She promised her boys that they would always have her wholeheartedly, with no distractions. Amelia made sure that her sons received the best education that she could afford. She gave them all the love a mother could give, yet she governed her home like an army general. She set rules and ensured that the boys followed them. Amelia taught her sons values and academics — self respect and respect for others — honesty and spirituality. She gave them books to read about the facts of life, when they came of age. She taught them to be gentlemen to ladies. She told them when they began to date, "if you are man enough to ask a girl out for a date, you had better be man enough to pay for that date." Frank had even quoted his mother's words to Shirley when she once offered to go fifty-fifty on a dinner tab.

Amelia sent her boys to Archbishop Stephen High School in Washington, D.C. She worked two jobs to pay their tuition. She took advantage of the offer that the school had, which was two children for full tuition on the first child and the second child went for half the tuition. Though both boys played football in high school, she instilled in them that academics took priority.

Frank graduated and went to the University of Maryland on a football scholarship. Two years later, Tommie went to Virginia Tech on a full football scholarship. Both Frank and Tommie did well at their universities and graduated with no problem. Frank was drafted as a rookie quarterback and two years later, Tommie was drafted as a running back. The boys purchased a fabulous home in Potomac, Maryland for their mother. Amelia, a humble woman was reluctant to move out of her two-bedroom row house in Northeast Washington.

"I don't see why we just can't renovate the house and stay right here." Amelia argued with her sons.

"We want to do this for you, Ma." Tommie told her with plea in his eyes.

"I know, baby; but it will be the same if you fix up the house where you boys grew up." She smiled at Tommie. "The people in this neighborhood are our family now."

"You can come back to visit them anytime, Ma." Frank reminded her. "We will not live at home with you – we are in San Antonio. We want you to have this house, that's all." They were able to convince a resistant Amelia to give up her neighborhood and move to Potomac. She adjusted to the new house and the new life, but she continued to visit her old neighborhood in Northeast Washington.

Six Weeks Later

The FAA restored air service and the sky was again invaded by planes in all directions. Air service had been suspended since that Sunday of the attack on the Stadium; the authorities wanted to take no chances, as they had not forgotten September 11, 2001. Family members flew to hospitals from all cities to locate or visit their wounded relatives.

Amelia Thurston flew to San Antonio to identify Tommie's body; Tommie was burned beyond recognition. Shirley was glad that she accompanied Amelia for support to the morgue; she collapsed when she saw her son's charred remains. They met with Trevor, Tommie's and Frank's agent at their hotel. "I want my son's body to go directly to Brown's Funeral Home in Washington, D.C." Amelia told Trevor. "They will take good care of Tommie – I know." She paused and groaned as though she carried the world on her shoulders. "I will put my son away in the manner he deserves."

Trevor nodded and attempted to console her. "Mrs. Thurston, you can't imagine how distraught we all are. I'm so sorry about Tommie – he was a great kid. He was easy to manage – he never gave any problems." He patted her folded hands on her lap. "I want you to brace yourself when you see Frank. Mr. Jeffries will see you tomorrow – I spoke with him this morning." They stood as he shook her hand. "I will see you in Washington at the funeral. He also shook Shirley's hand before he left them.

"Thank you for everything." Amelia said in a frail voice. Trevor was one of the survivors with minor wounds. They lost two coaches from the Gorillas, but the Cheetahs lost several players and three coaches, including their lead quarterback.

Though Trevor had prepared them for Frank's appearance, they never imagined that he was that injured. He was in the intensive care unit where they placed many of the survivors. Frank suffered third degree burns on his entire body. His left arm was broken and so were his jaw and nose. He had a fractured skull and four broken ribs. "We have two positive factors here, Mrs. Thurston." Dr. Alec Vanderhurst told Amelia. "Frank is right-handed – his right hand is not broken, and he is not comatose."

"I guess we must be thankful for the positive things." Amelia responded in her soft-spoken voice.

Frank was conscious as they entered his room in ICU. He heard and understood everything around him but was unable to speak. He was able to respond to his physicians and everyone else. His eyes lit up when he saw his mother and Shirley. They were asked not to cry in Frank's presence.

Amelia bit hard on her bottom lip before she spoke to her son. "Hi Frankie- I'm here now baby. Everything will be all right." She took a deep breath as she stroked his bandaged arm. "You're in God's hands – you will be better." She did not tell him that his brother was dead. She would tell him in time.

Shirley smiled and moved closer to the bed. She took his right hand that had no bandage; she lifted it on a slant and bend down to kiss it. "Hi sweetheart – I miss you a lot." Her lips trembled. "You know that I'm here for you, no matter what…" Her voice faded as she lowered her lips to his bandaged forehead. "Nana sends her love – she's planning to visit you soon." She noticed a flicker in his eyes at the mention of Nana's name. "If you understand everything I said, move your right fingers." He responded and moved his fingers over her hand.

Shirley and Amelia remained in Texas for the rest of the week. They stayed in a hotel near the hospital, but they spent most of their time at the hospital. Frank showed improvement but it was a slow one. Shirley wanted him back to normal, but she had no idea how normal Frank would ever be. She had given her heart to Frank Thurston, and she wanted it to stay with him. She had never felt so strongly about any man the way she felt about him. She smiled in her hotel room as she remembered her mother's words when she first took Frank to meet her parents.

"A good-looking man with brains – has lots of money and crazy about you." Her mother chuckled. "A woman can't ask for more in a man."

Shirley continued to smile as she thought to herself. "Mama left out one attribute of Frank's that only I would know. He is a fantastic lover." She laughed out aloud, and closed her eyes to reminisce about their great moments of the past. She hoped that Frank would recover and lose none of his stamina. She thought about the way he loved her – the day he proposed; it made in cry and smile at the same time.

Amelia and Shirley returned from Texas and Amelia wasted no time with the preparations of Tommie's funeral. Nana and Shirley were helpful to assist her with the arrangements. They ran errands for her and played secretary to her. They sent out announcements to the newspapers and the rest of the media.

The day Tommie was put to rest was a bright, sunny, and chilly February day. Amelia looked out the limo window and thought of her younger son. "Tommie's attitude in life was for everything to always be bright and to shine." She told Shirley, Jean-Claude, Kiddi and Nana who rode with her to the service. "Today's weather is an example of how he viewed life."

"He had a good teacher, Mrs. T." Shirley told Amelia as she patted her hand. She always called Amelia Mrs. T and so did Nana and Jean-Claude.

Amelia did not cry at the funeral. She had shed all of her tears earlier, and she knew that she would never stop mourning her son. She wanted to put Tommie to rest and focus on Frank's recovery. She sat tall and looked straight ahead as friends of hers, Tommie's and Frank's stepped up to the microphone to speak about Tommie's life.

The President of the CFA spoke highly of Tommie, "Tommie Thurston was one of the best kids the CFA ever drafted. He will be missed dearly." He addressed Amelia directly, "Mrs. Thurston, I wish you had raised all of the players in the CFA. Your sons have been an asset to our association." His remark put a smile on Amelia's face.

Jimmy Jeffries, the owner of the San Antonio Gorillas delivered a eulogy that had every eye in the church moist with tears. He told of his fatherly relationship with the Thurston boys and how Tommie would never be replaced in his heart.

The church in Northeast Washington was crowded with sympathizers from the CFA, from Tommie's high school and Virginia Tech. The entire Northeast neighborhood in Washington where the boys grew up turned out for Tommie's home-going. Mounted on his casket was a large football with his name printed on it.

Nana cried more than Shirley. Frank had tried in the past to get his brother and Nana together, but she always backed out of each date. Her little secret did not allow her to go out with Tommie at the time. She was hesitant to begin a relationship with him and have it end on a sour note. The last thing she wanted was to ruin her relationship with Frank and his family. Tommie teased her each time he saw her and called her 'the girl that could have been his'. She thought of the devastation she would have suffered, had Tommie been her boyfriend. She already suffered regrets, but it was too late. She knew that Tommie Thurston could have had his pick of women, but he liked her. She recalled how he bombarded her with questions about Ghana when they first met.

"Why didn't the Ghanaians kick out the Brits long before they did?" Tommie asked Nana.

"Such things took time back then. The old folks were much more conservative in their actions." She explained. She smiled as she thought about his curiosity and honesty. They had just returned from the grave site, where Tommie was put to rest. She and Shirley knew that they had more on their minds than they could handle. Shirley wanted to be in Texas at Frank's bedside. Nana wanted to visit her classmate as well. Jean-Claude was eager to see Frank.

Amelia held Tommie's repast at a hotel ballroom in Washington, D.C. Although she did not want a celebration, she knew that Tommie would have wanted it. Jimmy Jeffries urged her to give Tommie a homegoing that he deserved. The entire funeral service was televised live on the football channel and portions of the repast were given coverage.

Jean-Claude, Nana, Shirley and Kiddi sat at the family table with Amelia, Tommie's agent, Trevor and Jimmy and his wife. Several of Amelia's friends from both her old and new neighborhoods got up and paid tribute to Tommie at the repast. They told those who had gathered what an exemplary upbringing Amelia had given her sons.

"Tommie used to come everyday to walk my dog for me when he was a little boy." One lady from Amelia's old neighborhood said.

"He shoveled our snow in the neighborhood for $10.00 a house. We used to call him our little businessman." Another said.

"He was more than a player on my team – he was a son to me." Jimmy Jeffries told them. "Mrs. Thurston Ma'am, even though your son's life was shortened by an unexplained act, he leaves you with something you ought to be proud of – an honorable memory."

Tommie's friends from Virginia Tech and friends from Archbishop Stephen paid tributes to him. Each one of them told the guests what a pleasure it was to have got to known Tommie. "He never forgot his old friends and the old neighborhood even though he had become a big football star and all." A high school classmate said.

Jean-Claude spoke on behalf of the foundation. Nana spoke at the church service. She lost control in the middle of her tribute. She presented a wreath from the foundation. Now, she sat and listened to Jean-Claude pay his tribute. "Tommie was always the life of the party – he told the jokes but when it was time for business, he was dependable."

Nana dabbed her eyes with a tissue as she listened to Jean-Claude. She wondered why the terrorists had targeted the football stadium during the Big Bowl. After all, the Football Association had nothing to do with politics. She felt that the Football Association made a difference in countless of young men's lives, not only American young men but several Africans played in the CFA from various West African countries. She wondered what most of those players' lives would have been like, had it not been for the Football Association. Many of them came from under-privileged families. The Football Association made it possible for those young men to obtain college education and a career. Nana wondered why anyone would want to destroy an organization that did so much for young men. She hoped that they would find the degenerates who were responsible for the attack. Nana recalled the time when someone at Proficiency Travel asked her why she liked football so much; when she was not born in America and did not grow up there either. She answered the person with pleasure. "Like soccer, American Football has about 11 players on the field. What I like about this game is the unity that brings the players together. The only time I have seen all races of men embrace each other and show affection is on the field. It reminds me of the World Cup in soccer."

"You look like your thoughts are far away. Are you ready to go?" Jean-Claude's question brought her back to the present moment. She was so engaged in her thoughts that she did not realize that the repast was over.

"Yes, I am ready." She stood as they said goodbye to Jimmy and everyone at their table. They all had a kiss for Amelia, as they saw her in the limo before they left for Herndon.

In less than four years, the foundation suffered the loss of two loved ones. They wondered what went wrong. They drove home in silence that evening.

Chapter Eight

LONG HEALING

Those who live in the shelter of the Most High will find rest in the shadow of the almighty – Psalm 91:1 (NLT)

Shirley sat next to Frank's hospital bed and held his hand. He made tremendous improvement. He spoke clearer and healed better than the doctors expected.

Shirley was beside his bed everyday since after Tommie's funeral. She, Nana, Jean-Claude and Kiddi flew to San Antonio to visit Frank after the funeral. The friends stayed for two days with Shirley. Kiddi and Jean-Claude left and returned to Europe. Kiddi went back to London and Jean-Claude to his job. Nana remained with Shirley and Amelia for two weeks. She returned to Virginia to check on their residence. Shirley and Amelia took turns at the hospital.

"Hi babe, you shouldn't have let me sleep so long." Frank woke up from a two-hour sleep. Shirley did not take her eyes off him the entire time.

"Hey, you sleepy head, you needed your rest." She flashed a smile at him that made him want to take her in his arms. "How are you?"

He shifted in the bed. "I'm okay as long as you're here." He half smiled at her. "I love you, Shirley Marshall." He took her hand in his. "Do you still want to marry this broken up man?"

She threw her head back and laughed. "You're not broken up." She leaned over and her lips found his parched ones. "Nothing has changed – I don't want to marry anybody else, Mr. Thurston."

"Do you realize that this is the most we have spent together since we met?" Frank asked her. "Sometimes God does things that seem negative to us, but we later see the positive from them." Frank was always on the road during football seasons. His off seasons were brief; he spent most of the time on the practice field with his quarterback coach.

"Only you would find a positive from such devastation."

"We have to do that." He stared in her eyes. "It helps me keep my sanity." They laughed.

Frank and Shirley spent many more days and weeks together at the hospital. She watched his condition improve each day. She informed all of her clients that she would be away for an indefinite period. She hoped that she would not lose her clients but if she did, then it was what it was. Frank was going to be her husband; he and his mother needed her. Shirley and Amelia stayed at Frank's house while they were in San Antonio. Amelia wanted to have him transferred to a hospital in the Washington, D.C. area but Jimmy Jeffries insisted that Frank remained in San Antonio. Frank owned a beautiful six-bedroom home on the outskirts of San Antonio.

Frank underwent five different surgeries and Jimmy Jeffries ensured that he had only the best physicians. His surgeon, Dr. Alec Vanderhurst was the best in the Southwest area of the United States and one of the best in the country. He was born in England and had grown up there. Alec was offered the job as Chief of Surgeons at the hospital in San Antonio. He accepted the offer and moved to the States. He was one of the best reconstructive surgeons in the world.

"So how are we coming along today?" Dr. Vanderhurst inquired as he walked in Frank's room. He picked up the chart and studied it.

"Hi Dr. V. We are making progress." Shirley told him. She had come to know him and the other doctors as well as the nurses quite well.

"Glad to hear that." The doctor checked Frank's blood pressure, his legs, feet, arms, neck and all of his vital signs. "Everything looks great. We have scheduled you for physical therapy."

"When do I begin, Doc?" Frank actually looked forward to physical therapy. The doctor's news told him that he was better enough to begin physical exercise. He did not mention to Shirley and his mother but Frank wanted to get back on the football field.

"You begin tomorrow morning. Your therapist will be here at 8:00." Dr. Vanderhurst smiled. "I wish you all the best. I will see you tomorrow."

Frank had therapy the next morning and several mornings after that. Dr. Robert Reeves, his therapist, reported Frank's improvement each day to Dr. Vanderhurst.

Therapy was a challenge for Frank, but he was determined to heal. Shirley attended therapy with him every morning, even though it hurt to watch him struggle through his first set of therapy sessions. She was pleased to see Frank improve in his sessions.

"At the rate you're going, you will be out of here sooner than you imagine." Dr. Reeves told him.

It was what Frank wanted to hear. "Thanks Doc."

It was four months since the attack on the football stadium, but the investigation had not determined who took the bomb into the stadium. They did not establish a motive either. Meanwhile, the reports showed that there were five hundred casualties, two hundred were left critical and two thousand suffered minor injuries. Others walked away with mere scratches here and there, such as Jimmy Jeffries and others in the Football Association. The people on the side lines were hit the hardest; the ones higher in the stands fared better as survivors than those in the lower stands and on the actual field.

Frank was not told about his brother's death until he showed improvement. Amelia and the physicians felt that he was not ready for the news. He continued to inquire about his brother's well-being. Amelia knew that she could not continue to conceal Tommie's death from him.

"Baby, I need to tell you about Tommie." Amelia paused for composure, as she bit down on her bottom lip. "Tommie didn't survive the stadium attack." She held onto his hand for equal support. "We had his funeral already."

Frank wept like a child; he and his brother were close. They were never apart until they left for college. "Why was it Tommie, Ma? Why was it my little brother?" He continued to repeat Tommie's name through sobs as he held onto his mother.

What Amelia did not tell Frank is that he too would have been a casualty, had he not been in the locker room at the time of the bombing. The back-up quarterback for their team was killed along with Tommie. Frank searched his soul and asked God to help him move forward and understand what had happened. He wanted his football career back as much as he wanted his brother back on the field with him. He came to terms with himself; he knew that his life was spared for a reason, and he was determined to live each day with a meaning.

FGM in the United States

Nana sat in the living room of their townhouse alone. She went over her stage play five times. She had already contacted Diane Parsons and told her that the play was completed. Diane urged her to send the completed script to her; she intended to forward it to a stage producer friend in Atlanta. Nana ensured that the script was perfect before she submitted it to professionals.

She took a break from the script and switched on the television to watch the national news. The first news item left Nana baffled.

"A West African father was arrested and detained earlier today in Tulsa, Oklahoma. The father took a pair of scissors and clipped his three-year old daughter's private part." The news anchor delivered the story, as Nana turned up the volume. "The father rushed his daughter to the emergency room only after the child was unconscious. The child is reported in critical condition." The news anchor continued to explain. "The hospital administrator has confirmed that it is a case of Female genital mutilation, which is a cultural practice in parts of Africa, Asia and the Middle East. Last year, an organization founded in the United States called Friends against Female Genital Mutilation presented a bill to Congress. That bill is still before Congress. In other news…"

Nana sat without motion for half an hour. The sound of the phone brought her back to where her mind was. "Hello."

"Have you seen the news?" Shirley shouted in the phone. "Frank is outraged – I feel like getting my hands on that father."

"I saw the story." Nana spoke for the first time. Her voice told Shirley that her friend was in tears. "I think FAFGM needs to issue a statement to the press about this."

"I absolutely agree." She took deep breaths to calm herself down. "Frank too wants us to do that."

"Good – I will contact Cynthia and have her prepare a statement."

"I'll let Frank know."

"How is he?"

"He's doing great. Dr. V said he should be ready to go home soon."

"That is wonderful news. Give him my warm regards."

The next day Cynthia released a statement to the Media from FAFGM. She called a press conference and Nana read the statement on behalf of the foundation. She had not made a public appearance since Tommie's funeral. She wished that her friends were there with her. Jean-Claude was at work in Africa and Kiddi was with her family in England.

She wore a summer turquoise suit and cream pumps. Nana stood at the podium with Cynthia and another representative from Don& Day Public Relations.

"FAFGM is equally saddened and outraged over the heinous act committed on the three-year-old little girl a few days ago." Nana read the statement to the press and the public. "We are absolutely appalled by the fact that this can happen right here on American soil. This is a message to the world that the defiance continues in spite of our appeal to end this practice." She continued to appeal to Congress to pass the bill that was already before them.

After Nana's appearance, she was bombarded with phone calls. Television networks wanted to interview her; women wanted to know how they could help; others offered to write letters to their Congress representatives and ask that they pass the bill.

Nana made several appearances on television after that appeal. She represented the foundation well. Both Jean-Claude and Kiddi called to express their appreciation for her representation.

The trial of the West African father became one of the most controversial cases in Tulsa. The little girl remained in a coma since the day her father cut her. He was held without bond. Nana called each week to check on the condition of the girl. The nurses had come to know who she was. She sent flowers on behalf of the foundation. Frank and Shirley sent stuffed animals. Thimbi, the little girl had no idea of the attention that her condition had caused. Her hospital room was full of balloons, flowers and stuffed animals from all over the country. Her photograph was the poster face of FGM in America.

Another organization called Mothers of Daughters came forward and denounced FGM; it was one of many other organizations that had denounced the practiced. Mothers of Daughters offered to partner with FAFGM.

After her last television interview, Nana sat alone in her bedroom and reflected on her parents. Her father had long since reunited with her from the time he cut her off. Her mother continued to keep in touch with her, even when Mr. Nkuku forbade her to do so.

"What mother turns her back on her child especially when she has done nothing to shame us?" Mrs. Nkuku argued with her husband.

Nana forgave her parents for having cut her off. She knew that they loved her, but they acted out an old cultural tradition over which they had no control. At least they thought at the time that they had no control. She wondered why her father did not just rebel against public sentiment. She knew that at the time, he would not have rebelled. Nana respected her father for the time he came out and denounced FGM. He apologized to her for the decision they had made when she was their little girl. It was something that Kiddi's father did not do before he died. She vowed to work so that other girls in the future would not sit and reflect on a similar past.

Dr. Vanderhurst walked in Frank's room with a broad smile on his face. "Good morning Q.B." He held the chart under his arm; his stethoscope hung over his neck. He nicknamed Frank Q.B. for the position he played in football. "Are you ready to go home today?"

Frank's eyes lit up. "I'm ready as I'm ever going to be Doc."

"Your mother and Shirley are on their way to take you home."

"Thanks Doc. I really appreciate everything you've done for me."

"It is my pleasure." He exchanged a handshake with Frank. "Take care of yourself." He walked toward the door. "I'll see a couple of patients, but I'll be out front to see you off."

Frank did not expect what greeted him in front of the hospital. The hospital lawn swarmed with reporters and photographers. He walked out between Shirley and Amelia. Jimmy Jeffries walked next to Amelia and Dr. Vanderhurst was next to Shirley. Frank insisted that he did not need a wheelchair. They stood behind the podium that was set up for the surprise press conference.

"How do you feel after such a lengthy stay in the hospital?" One reporter asked.

"I feel great." Frank responded. He wore a pair of blue jeans with a navy sport jacket over a sport shirt. On his head was a San Antonio Gorilla baseball cap.

"Are you well enough to play ball again?" Another reporter inquired.

"I will ask my Doc to answer that question." He turned to Dr. Vanderhurst.

Alec moved closer to the microphone. "Mr. Thurston is released today with a clean bill of health. He has been given clearance to lead his life as he wishes."

"Jimmy, you have stayed by Frank's side through this tragedy. Does he still have his job as quarterback?" A reporter from the back asked.

"I have never given anyone the impression that Frank Thurston would not have his job next season. The Football Association has been stricken with the worse tragedy in its history. My only concern has been Frank's well-being, not only his physical well being but his emotional one as well. We have all suffered a great loss." Jimmy responded in his profound Texas accent.

"Frank, do you plan to continue the work with your foundation on FGM?" A female reporter asked.

"I absolutely do intend to continue. The foundation is the strongest it has ever been. I always get to the finish line in anything I do." They all laughed at Frank's statement.

"Frank, what will it feel like to play without your brother on the field with you?" Another reporter asked.

"Since I've not been on the field yet, I guess I will not know until it happens." He did not like the question and neither did Jimmy.

"Okay, thanks for coming. My quarterback is anxious to get home with his family." With that last statement from Jimmy, he, Frank, Amelia and Shirley disappeared into the stretch limo that waited in the front of the hospital, after they thanked Alec and said goodbye.

Frank did enjoy being back in his own bed, and not a hospital bed. He asked Amelia and Shirley to remain in San Antonio a little longer. Nana called to welcome him home as did Jean-Claude from France. Jean-Claude told him how great he looked at the press conference. He had caught it on the international news channel in France.

Nana was accustomed to being alone in the townhouse. Shirley was gone for such a long time and so had Jean-Claude. She figured that it prepared her for the day when Shirley would get married and move out. As her thoughts drifted from one item to the other, the phone interrupted her daydream.

"Hello."

"Nana, we've got it – it passed Nana." The voice at the other end of the phone was Chuck, the lobbyist for the foundation.

"Did the bill get passed? Oh my goodness, Chuck. Thank you so much." Nana jumped around the kitchen with glee.

"Watch the evening news. Your phone will begin to ring for comments so be prepared."

"I will tell them what a great lobbyist we have." She and Chuck laughed at her statement and excitement. "I have to call my friends. Thank you."

Nana called Frank and Shirley first. The three celebrated on the phone. Then she placed a call to Jean-Claude; it was late in France, but she wanted him to know. He was elated as he let out a shout-out into the phone. She did not want to disturb Kiddi's family; instead of a call, she sent her an email and a text with the great news.

Later that evening, Nana watched the news as the networks ran the story. Congress had passed the bill to impose sanctions on any country that allowed the practice of female genital mutilation. The bill read that the practice should be banned and declared an illegal act against humanity. Anyone who practiced FGM in the fifty United States would be subject to ten years imprisonment and/or deportation if the perpetrator was not a U.S. citizen. The sanctions included: no foreign aid; no free trade between such countries and the U.S.; government officials of such practicing countries would be placed on a "no fly" list.

Nana told herself that even though the sanctions were harsh, but so was FGM. Little Thimbi in Tulsa never came out of the coma. She died before her father's trial. He was tried for first degree manslaughter. He was sentenced to serve ten years in the state penitentiary. Nana thought of the old Medicine Woman who had cut Kiddi and her so many years before. If she was already dead, she wondered what her sentence was like on her final day on earth. She imagined that it was a much harsher sentence.

Chapter Nine

THEN THERE WERE TWO

O Lord, I have come to you for protection; don't let me be disgraced. Save me, for you do what is right. – Psalm 31:1 (NLT)

Frank was out of the hospital for a month. He continued his rehabilitation regimen with Dr. Reeves, three times a week. He did well in therapy and Dr. Reeves cleared him for football camp.

Frank and Shirley rescheduled their wedding date. He told Shirley and his mother that while he was in the coma, he experienced a type of vision; the vision told him to make his marriage to Shirley a priority. He knew that his life would not be complete without her. He wanted to keep his promise to marry her from his vision. He saw how devoted Shirley was to him during his tragedy and grief. They set the date for August 9th of that year.

The Football Association announced that the training camp for that year was delayed by a month. Jimmy Jeffries built a state-of-the-art stadium to replace the one that was bombed.

Frank figured that the delay would give him enough time to get married and honeymoon before he needed to report to camp. Shirley and Amelia returned to Washington. Mrs. Marshall and her planning committee resumed their duties with the plans of Shirley's wedding. Mrs. Marshall told Nana to schedule the shower without delay.

Nana sent out invitations to all of Shirley's closest friends in Atlanta and Washington, D.C. The shower was scheduled to be held at a hotel in Fairfax, Virginia. Since the wedding was only a week after the shower, Kiddi arrived a week early to attend the shower. Her husband and son were scheduled to follow a week later to attend the wedding.

The shower was successful and enjoyable. It was well attended by Shirley's high school mates, cousins, aunts, her mother, Frank's mother,

Kiddi, Nana and several of her female clients. She received about a hundred gifts at the shower. The women played games, sang Shirley's favorite songs and ate as though there was not a day left in their lives.

Unlike the usual male stripper surprise at showers, Nana and Kiddi thought that a different surprise would please Shirley a lot better than a male stripper. Beside Frank had asked Nana to omit a male stripper from their plans. The reason he claimed was because Shirley's mother and aunts and his own mother would be present. Nana felt that it was a good enough reason.

Shirley stood beside the door as she talked to one of her cousins at the shower, when Nana took the microphone and announced that a surprise gift was in store for Shirley.

"If this is a male stripper, you will be in a lot of trouble, Nana." Shirley raised her voice from across the room, as everyone laughed.

"Now just why on earth you're going to think that I'm a male stripper?" Every woman in the room turned in surprise to see Diane Parsons walk in. She made that statement in her usual Tennessee accent. Diane took the microphone from Nana and began to sing one of Shirley's favorite songs. She walked over to Shirley and continued to sing to her. Everyone applauded, sang along and rocked, as Shirley wiped the corners of her eyes.

Shirley was busy as she packed after the shower. "I did not realize how much stuff I had accumulated over the years." She told Nana and Kiddi.

"Especially when you buy everything you see." Nana teased her.

"That is not true." Shirley laughed. She knew that Nana teased her, but she also knew that she did more shopping than she needed things.

All of her shower gifts were shipped to her new home in San Antonio, which was Frank's house. The wedding gifts were shipped directly from the stores where they were registered to San Antonio.

Shirley had eight trash bags of clothing for the goodwill, they were scheduled to be picked up the next day.

The night before the wedding, Shirley spent hours with Nana, Kiddi and her female relatives. Her relatives all came from Atlanta to attend the wedding.

"So are you nervous yet about tomorrow?" Kiddi asked Shirley.

"I'm only nervous a little." She stopped and placed the pants in her hand on the bed. "I just want to make sure that I can be the best wife to Frank. I realize that he could have married any woman he wanted; he chose me."

"Do not forget that it goes both ways." Nana told her friend. "You could have had any man you wanted as well."

"That is why you're my best friend. You always look out for me, even though you knew Frank first."

Nana went over to Shirley and gave her a hug. "I will miss you a lot but I'm happy for you.

The Wedding Day

Nana took her role as Maid of Honor seriously. She did research to know all of the duties of a maid of honor. She arranged and planned the bridal shower with care. She ensured that all of Shirley's belongings were shipped to San Antonio. Nana made a check list and by the day of the wedding, everything on her list was checked off.

"You look lovely baby." Shirley's mother told her as they fussed over her in her bedroom. She did look beautiful in the off-white wedding gown. The gown was straight and fitted with sequence of beads from the shoulders to the tail. The dress showed off Shirley's figure. The trail was attached to the dress by snaps. Her head dress was a little off-white hat that was positioned on the top of her head with white beads that dangled from the hat. The beads replaced what would have been a veil. Her satin off-white pumps had a cluster of beads on the top.

The six flower girls marched in first, locked in the arms of six ring bearers. The little girls all wore pink dresses, pink anklets and white shoes. They dropped petals as they marched in the church. The little boys wore black tuxedos with bow ties.

Five bridesmaids marched in, one after the other, all dressed in pink with white pumps. Their dresses were simple spaghetti straps and straight skirts to correspond with Shirley's gown. Nana followed the five bridesmaids and took her place across from Jean-Claude, who was the Bestman. Frank and the other men wore black tuxedos and white shirts.

Then it was time for Shirley to enter with her father. The church was quiet except for the sound of the organ. She and her father made their way down the aisle at a slow pace, as everyone stood. Frank did not take his eyes off Shirley during her entire journey down the aisle. By the time she arrived at the Alter, it felt like an eternity to him.

Nana and Jean-Claude were partners in the wedding, in their roles as Maid of Honor and Bestman. Had Tommie been alive, he would have been her partner. Shirley's two cousins were bridesmaids, as were Kiddi and her two friends from high school. Beside Jean-Claude, Frank had two of his teammates, Wayne Marshall, Shirley's older brother, Alec Vanderhurst and Sean Jeffries, Jimmy's son.

The ceremony went as expected. They exchanged conventional vows. "I, Shirley take you Frank to be my lawful husband – to have and to hold – in sickness and in health, until death parts us." A few joyful tears escaped her eyes, as she recited the vows.

Frank repeated his vows, the rings were exchanged, and the officiating clergyman pronounced them man and wife. Frank waited to hear the words, "You may kiss your bride." He took Shirley in his arms like he had never before and kissed her until the guests began to applaud. Shirley was Mrs. Shirley Marshall-Thurston. She was in a daze of disbelief.

"I am married now." She said to Nana just before they marched out of the church.

Shirley and Frank enjoyed the reception. Many couples do not enjoy their wedding, but they did. They danced the electric slide with their friends and relatives; they danced the waltz with the wedding party. Frank danced with Amelia and Shirley's mother. Shirley danced with her father and cousins. She was a happy bride.

Nana and Jean-Claude danced and had a great time. Frank attempted to introduce Nana to Alec Vanderhurst during the reception. "We met at the rehearsal dinner." Nana told Frank, as she exchanged a handshake with the doctor. She did not realize that Frank's plan was to play match maker. Alec was single and available. Frank knew him well; they had met in Frank's rookie year in San Antonio through Jimmy.

Alec asked Nana to dance and an hour later, they had already danced several selections and talked a great deal. At the end of the evening, they felt comfortable with each other. Both Frank and Shirley were pleased when they observed the fun that Nana and Alec had at their wedding.

As Nana sat and talked to Alec, she watched the little flower girls in pink as they danced around the floor. She thought of how great it would be to have all of the little girls in Africa, Asia and the Middle East as safe as those little flower girls appeared to be. She wondered how many little girls were being cut at that very moment in the world while those little girls in America danced around in pretty pink dresses.

Frank and Shirley left early the next morning for their honeymoon. Most of the guests left for their respective homes the Sunday that followed the wedding. The couple flew to the island of Kauai in Hawaii for their week-long honeymoon.

Kiddi and her family left the same day. Jean-Claude left the Monday after the wedding. Nana was grateful for an extra day of his company. Jean-Claude and Nana had a heart-to-heart conversation before he left for his work.

"It is these occasions that are the most difficult for me." Jean-Claude told Nana. "I cannot stop missing Paula." He seemed distant. "If you meet someone you really like, do not procrastinate."

"Where is all of this coming from, my brother?" Nana regarded him closely. "This is not like you. You are always so resilient."

"I know, but this situation is different." He looked at Nana and slowly shook his head. "When I think about what Paula and I could have had, I don't want you to let FGM keep you from experiencing love."

"No worries, my brother." She smiled. "If I ever meet that right person, I promise not to let him get away." She ruffled his hair, which was one of her favorite things to do to him. "Do you want to join me for tea in the kitchen?"

"I'll have coffee – you can have tea." He responded as he followed her to the kitchen, where they talked late into the night. "You know, since we lost Paula, I have changed my outlook on life. I think more of what happens to us when we leave this earth. My mother taught me that there is heaven and there is hell. If you live well on earth and follow God's laws, you will go to heaven. If you do not follow his laws, you will burn in hell. I only pray that Paula is in heaven. That is where I want to go when I'm no longer here."

"Do you really believe that?"

"Now I do but when I was younger, I did not believe all of that."

"I know that there must be a God because someone is responsible for the universe. Scientists want us to believe that it is not so." Nana was changed in her beliefs after the attack on the stadium and the loss of Tommie. More importantly, she saw how God spared her buddy, Frank's life. She was more curious about religion, especially Christianity. She did research on it and was more interested. She asked a lot of questions whenever she was with Mrs. Thurston.

Jean-Claude left the next morning for his usual route.

Kauai, Hawaii

Frank and Shirley arrived in Kauai after a long trip. On the way, they connected in Dallas from San Antonio to a non-stop flight to Honolulu. They spent an hour in transit at Honolulu Airport before they took a local flight to Kauai. Although they were tired, neither of them wanted to rest. Frank had been to Honolulu a couple of times for the post bowl game, but never to Kauai. Shirley had never been off the mainland at all. A limo took them to their hotel, where they stayed in the honeymoon suite, equipped with an oversized Jacuzzi, a private sauna, a den, a separate large bedroom and a dining room. They were pleased with the accommodations.

"Babe, we don't need to go anywhere – I just want to stay in here with you the entire week." Frank told Shirley as he took her in his arms and held her close.

"I want to do the same, but we've got to eat." She looked up at him.

"That is precisely why they invented room service." He kissed her lightly on the lips.

That night they did order room service for dinner. They enjoyed a quiet evening together in the Jacuzzi, made passionate love and then ate dinner.

"So Mrs. Thurston, what do you want to do with the rest of your life?"

"I want to love you until the day I die." She wondered what he had in mind. They sat at the dining room table in their suite.

"I know that – it goes without saying." He looked at her from his dinner plate. "You've always dreamed of having your own salon."

"I still do – Nana and I discussed that a couple of months ago. I want to have a full-service salon for men." She looked at him for reaction, but he wanted to hear more. "A man would be able to get his haircut, shampoo and conditioner. He would have the choice of a manicure, a pedicure and a shave."

"That is a great idea, babe." He pulled back his chair from the table and helped her up from hers. "It is settled – you can have your salon. You can begin to plan it when we get home. That is my wedding gift to you"

She simply smiled but she danced inside. "Thanks sweetheart." She said a secret 'thank you' to God for having sent her Frank. Shirley knew that Frank would make her the happiest woman in the world. She knew that she could not have asked for better. He had good looks; he was smart; he was wealthy, and he loved her.

The next day they took a helicopter ride all over the island. Shirley sat between the pilot and Frank. She realized that a helicopter ride was quite different from that of a jet. They flew deep in the valley and high over the mountains, then close to the ocean as though they would land in the water. She was nervous but she did not show it. Frank videotaped the scenery with his camcorder. He taped Shirley as she boarded the helicopter and did the same as she disembarked.

They snorkeled with the dolphins one day and went on an historical tour of the island on another day. They took a boat ride around the island and watched the whales. Frank videotaped the baby dolphins danced before the boat. Shirley was excited and had a great time each day. They wined and dined and took in the sights during the day; at night they wrapped themselves around each other, as they allowed the inner soles of their bodies to bond as one.

Herndon, Virginia

While Frank and Shirley honeymooned in Hawaii, Nana formed a beautiful friendship back on the mainland. She was eager to tell the couple, but she vowed not to disturb them while they were on their honeymoon.

Dr. Alec Vanderhurst called her every day after the wedding. Though he lived in San Antonio, he enjoyed long phone conversations with his newfound friend. They exchanged information about each other, while they became more familiar. They wanted to know their favorite foods, their birthdays, their hobbies and even favorite places in the world.

Nana had never engaged in that type of relationship with a man in her life. In the past, all of the men she met and dated wanted to move to sex after two or three dates. Alec did not allude to that topic in any of their conversations. He wanted to know her; her likes and dislikes. She felt like she had found a welcome friend.

Alec learned about the foundation through his friendship with Frank and Sean Jeffries. He even once sent in a donation; but they received so many donations, that Nana did not specifically remember his. He was careful when he discussed the foundation and FGM with Nana. He did not push her for information about her own experience with FGM.

"How are you now Nana?" Alec asked in one of their conversations.

"I'm fine – what happened was a long time ago." She wondered if she wanted to revisit it; but she felt like she revisited it with each speech she made. "Kiddi and I have gotten past our devastation – it is the little girls of today whom I worry about." She sighed. "As we speak, many little girls are being cut this very hour."

"Through your foundation and your public appearance, you make a difference for those little girls."

They held several conversations like that; they did not realize how close those conversations brought them together. Alec told her of his trip to Africa with his parents when he was only a teenager. "Sorry we did not visit any countries in West Africa – we went on Safari in both Kenya and Tanzania. I had a great time in Mombassa."

Frank and Shirley returned to San Antonio and began their life together. They emailed their photos from Hawaii to their friends and family members. Some of the photos were posted to the San Antonio Gorillas' website, as well as Frank's SpeakBook page. His fans were able to share in their honeymoon.

Frank met a message from Dr. Vanderhurst when they returned. He was cleared to play football again. For Frank and Jimmy, it was great news. Dr. Vanderhurst had already notified Jimmy about the clearance.

"Ma, I've been cleared to play." Frank told Amelia with excitement.

"Thank the Lord – praise God." Amelia responded. She knew how important her son's career was to him; she also knew how vital Frank's presence was with the Gorillas.

Shirley Opens Her Salon

Shirley busied herself with preparations for the grand opening of her salon in San Antonio. Nana and Amelia arrived in San Antonio a week prior to the opening to assist Shirley with last minute arrangements.

They planned to have a special presentation at the opening. Shirley selected male models to model her work as the opening presentation.

The eight male models presented haircuts from the most conservative cuts to the trendiest. They paraded on the runway, as they impressed the audience. The salon was decorated in a modern setting with lilac and green walls. The grand opening was well attended by all of Frank's friends, Shirley's former co-workers, Amelia, Shirley's parents, Jean-Claude, Kiddi, Diane Parsons, Jimmy Jeffries and his wife, Sean Jeffries and several others. Diane Parsons performed for the occasion.

Nana was seated with Dr. Alec Vanderhurst, Kiddi and her husband and Jean-Claude. Jean-Claude noticed that Alec paid an unusual amount of attention to his friend, Nana. He made a mental note to have a word with Nana about that.

During Nana's stay in San Antonio, she and Alec went out every evening. He took her to the movie, to dinner and to a physicians' dinner party. He took her on a boat ride and a tour of the city. They ate breakfast at the old flour mill restaurant, where the best pancakes were known to be served. At the end of her stay, Nana and Alec had become close. She opened up to him about FGM and how it was done to her.

Alec told Nana about his own life. He was born in Barbados to English parents. His father was in the Foreign Service at the time of his birth. He spent the first ten years of his life in Barbados until his father was recalled home. He did his undergraduate studies at Princeton in the States and his medical degree at Johns Hopkins University. He did his residency at Mount Sinai Hospital in New York.

"So you see we have a lot in common." Alec told her. "We both came from another place. We both have no blood relatives in America."

"I guess we do." She smiled with a bashful expression on her face.

"I read a great deal on female genital cutting before I even met you. So I set out to study possibilities on how to help victims of it on the physical level." Alec told her.

"What do you mean by physical?" Nana's cautious button sounded.

"You see, FAFGM support centers are going to help the girls on a mental and emotional scale. The procedure cannot be reversed but it can be corrected. When I was in New York at Sinai, a young lady in her early twenties went to the emergency room; she was pregnant but was on the verge of a miscarriage. I examined her and discovered something I had never seen in my life. Her vagina was disfigured; she had no clitoris and no labia at all. We were amazed that she was able to become pregnant." He sighed. "We were able to save her fetus, but we also performed corrective surgery on her, against her husband's protests." He sighed. "I guess it was destined for me to be exposed to it early in my career."

"Those little girls cannot afford such a surgery." She felt uneasy to discuss it with him. "Kiddi had the surgery, so I suppose it works."

"I thought that I could persuade some of my colleagues to join me – we could work with your foundation to provide the medical services at your centers."

"You would do that?" Nana was excited.

"I understand that FAFGM advocates for the eradication of FGM, but the girls need medical care until we can get their parents to stop the practice." She liked the fact that he used the word 'we'.

"Well, let's pose this idea to the rest of the foundation to hear how they feel about it." Nana did not think that her friends would have any objection to the idea.

Training Camp

Shirley said goodbye to Frank as he left for training camp. Since their marriage, they had not been apart. She became accustomed to Frank's presence in the bed every night; she did not know what she would do without her husband.

"I am happy for you sweetheart, but I'll miss you a lot."

"I know – I'll miss you more. I'll call every break I have." He kissed her as he held her close. "I love you babe."

"I love you more."

Shirley's salon did exceptionally in the first two quarters; her clientele soared since opening night. There were thirty workstations in her salon, and each was occupied by a barber or stylist. Her barbers and stylists paid her forty percent of what they made to occupy a workstation in her salon. To have a workstation at Shirley's salon was considered elegant and honorable. Men vied for an appointment on Shirley's book. She knew all of the players on the San Antonio Gorillas; all of the players got their haircuts at Shirley's; all the doctors from the hospital where Alec worked became clients at Shirley's.

Frank worked hard at training camp; he was up every morning to do his usual laps around the practice field. He had sessions with the quarterback coach, where he went over films, plays and strategies. He felt odd without Tommie at camp, but he knew that he needed to get past his feelings about that. He missed his brother; but he promised Tommie each time he visited his grave site in Washington that he would play football for both of them. He figured that there was a reason why Tommie was taken, and he was spared. The authorities had not yet solved the case of the stadium attack. They ruled it an act of terrorism, but they still did not bring anyone to justice for killing his brother and hundreds of others.

Chapter Ten

NANA RETURNS TO THE JOB FORCE

I will praise the Lord at all times. I will constantly speak his praises. – Psalm 34:1 (NLT)

Nana found herself alone in the Herndon townhouse and her only excitement she looked forward to were her phone calls from her newfound friend, Alec Vanderhurst. She busied herself with the plans for the foundation's trip to Africa. She received a surprise phone call from an old friend on a Sunday afternoon, as she worked on the sketch of another play. She still waited to hear from Diane Parson's producer friend in Atlanta about her play. She felt that no news was supposed to be good news.

Nana answered the phone on the desk in her bedroom without taking her eyes off her computer screen. She hoped it was Alec. "Hello, this is Nana."

"Well, hello Nana. How are you doing?" The voice at the other end said with a smile.

"Oh my goodness, I hope nothing is going to happen to me." She exclaimed in the phone, as she recognized the male voice. "James Dunn, what is going on?" James was Nana's former co-worker at Proficiency Travel at the IFT. They ate lunch together every day in the cafeteria, but they lost close touch after James was fired from Proficiency, long before Nana resigned.

"I am doing well, now that I have a great job." He paused. "I have not called because I went through a tough time there after Proficiency, but I just found a job."

"That is great news, James." Nana knew how long he was without a job. He had worked for Proficiency for fifteen years before they fired him. "Where is the job?"

"It is downtown in the city at a client site. The client is a government agency that has a travel office on its premises." James explained with excitement.

"I'm excited for you, James." Nana told him but she knew that he had something else to tell her but seemed to be holding back. "So what else is going on with you? How is life treating you otherwise?"

"Not as good as it's been for you though." He smiled. "I have been reading about the good things you and your foundation are doing against female genital mutilation. I am glad that it is working out for you." He turned serious. "I'm also sorry about the tragedy with your friend Paula Braun and your friend Tommie Thurston."

"Thanks, things have been both good and trying for us, but we continue to persevere." Nana told him.

"I was wondering if you are interested in going back to the work force, Nana." He held his breath. "There is a job offer that came to me, but I cannot accept the offer because I just got a new job. I did some temp work at this place for a couple of weeks while I was looking for a permanent job. When I turned her down, she asked if I knew someone who is good with international travel. I thought of you."

"Hmmm, James – I was not really planning on going to someone's job, but it might not be a bad idea while I wait to hear about my play." She did not believe that she was actually entertaining the idea of going back to work in the travel industry, which she had already left.

"Well good, let me give you the owner's name and number but she will be calling you this afternoon. She's on her way to Florida but said she will call you from the airport after I speak with you."

"Okay, I will expect her call." Nana told James. "What is that noise? Where are you?"

"I'm at the airport myself, on my way to Charlotte for two weeks of training before I begin the new job."

"That is good, James." She moved her attention from her computer and wrote down the phone number and the name of the lady James said would call her. "Thanks for thinking of me. I will expect Valerie Penney's call." She smiled in the phone. "I wish you all the best with training and your new job. Keep in touch."

"You bet I will. I wish you all the best too."

An hour after James and Nana ended their conversation, her phone rang and it was Valerie Penney, as James had predicted. "Hello, is this Nana Nkuku?" Nana acknowledged that she was indeed that person. "Hi, this is Valerie Penney. James Dunn referred me to you."

"Hello Ms. Penney. Yes, he did tell me to expect your call." Nana told Valerie.

"So, are you coming to work for me or not?" Nana was lost for words by Valerie's direct question.

"Well, perhaps we should begin by setting an appointment for an interview first." She was unsure if she wanted to work for the character that was on the other end of the phone.

"Listen, I'm on my way to Florida today." Valerie told her. "I'll be back on Monday so why don't we plan to meet at my office on Tuesday at 3:30pm?"

"I will be there at 3:30 on Tuesday then." Nana wondered what she was getting herself in but she thought it would be fun to go on a job interview when she did not really need to get a job.

"Here's what you can do for me. Email me your resume and I'll send you the address to the office. If you take the metro, Dupont Circle is the station." Valerie and Nana ended their call on a positive note.

Since Nana was already in front of her computer, she pulled up her resume, updated it and sent it to the email address Valerie Penney had given her. She wondered why she was about to put herself through the stressful job force, which she had already left. She called Shirley to discuss it with her, even though she dreaded listening to the lecture from her best friend.

"Have you lost your mind?" Shirley thought it was a joke at first until Nana convinced her that she was not joking about it. "Is it what happens when I get married and leave you in the world by yourself?"

"No, I am not crazy, but it will keep me busy while I wait to hear from the producers about my play." Nana massaged her forehead. "The wait is getting to me, my friend."

"I should tell Frank to have Alec step up his chase on you." She chuckled. "That should keep you busy."

Alec's chase on me will keep me occupied enough to forget about my play?" Nana laughed. "I really like Alec, but I don't think his presence will matter in this case."

"When you begin to complain about the travel industry and the stress, I promise not to remind you about this conversation."

"Thanks for being so considerate, Mrs. Thurston." They both laughed at themselves.

Nana sent an email to both Jean-Claude and Kiddi to tell them that she planned to return to the work force. "I want to let the foundation know that I will return to working part time for it again. The foundation is now at the place where we do not need to tour and work 24/7 any longer." She wrote in the email.

Kiddi's response to Nana's email was supportive. She wrote, "I trust your judgment and know that whatever decision you make will be a wise one. My prayers are with you and please do be careful."

Jean-Claude was as baffled as Shirley was. He called his friend and was candid with her. "What is going on over there in the States, my sister?"

Nana laughed at the tone of his voice. "You sound like you are about to cry, my brother." She sighed. "I just think that I need something to occupy my time while I wait to hear from the producers about the play."

"There is a lot to keep you occupied – there is the foundation- I suggest you go and spend some time in San Antonio with Shirley and Frank." He paused. "From what I heard, there is a certain doctor down there who might not mind you being down there. I know what you went through at Proficiency Travel – I do not wish to see you go through that again."

"This is not Proficiency Travel; this is Eastern Travel." Nana defended her decision.

"Well, I will try not to remind you of this conversation later." There was a brief silence.

"Shirley said the same thing so I will hold both of you to your promise not to remind me." She smiled. "That is, if the situation arises at all." They laughed and ended their conversation after he wished her the best.

Nana stepped off the Washington, D.C. Metro train at the Dupont Circle station. She stopped at the kiosk and asked the attendant which exit would place her closer to the store, "Multiple Books". The attendant directed her to the exit. She was surprised to see the height of the escalator;

it was like coming through a tunnel. The wind was so brisk, she braced herself as she walked against it and slowly stepped onto the moving steep stairs. Nana felt as though her escalator ride was at least 5 minutes. She was glad that she gave herself ample time before her impending interview. She was relieved to see the sign on the Multiple Books building. Valerie told her that the office was located on the third floor of the Multiple Books building. The bookstore was located on the ground level, where many authors held their book signings and appearances.

Nana was instructed by Valerie in her email to go in the bookstore and take a seat at one of the tables in the coffee shop, and then call her on her cell phone. She did not understand why Valerie did not want her to go up to the office. A few minutes after Nana called Valerie, a young, short African American woman appeared in the bookstore and made her way toward Nana's table. She flashed a smile and greeted Nana. "Hi, I'm Teah. Val will be down in a few minutes, but she wants you to complete these forms." She handed Nana the forms and indicated a separate sheet of paper. "This is geography and airline test that she wants you to take." She smiled again. "If you need anything, please give me a call. Would you like something to drink?"

Nana shook her head. "No thank you, I am fine. It is a pleasure to meet you, Teah." She turned to walk away, and Nana noticed how large Teah's hips were. She did not make it a habit of noticing such things on women, but a two-year-old child would not have missed it. Her hips extended so far from her back, that it appeared not to be a part of her body. She moved slowly, and Nana thought, "What a load to carry around with you." She turned her focus on the forms and test before her. She wanted to have everything completed before Valerie appeared. She was grateful that the bookstore was quiet at that time of the afternoon.

Nana completed the application form, which consisted of three pages. She listed her former employer, which was only Proficiency Travel. In order to account for the time of unemployment, she listed the foundation and described the work she did for the foundation. She began the test, which she found to be quite simple, at least for her. Most of the geography portion of the questions asked for the major destinations to countries in Europe, Asia, Latin America, and Africa. Nana was confident that she had all of those questions answered correctly. The other half of the test was to match those same cities to their airport codes, such as BKO for Bamako, Mali, CAI for Cairo, Egypt, CDG for Paris Charles de Gaulle and several others. Just as she completed the test, another short lady, but Caucasian appeared at Nana's table. She was dressed casually and appeared to be in her mid-fifties. She extended her hand to Nana and introduced herself.

"Hi, I'm Valerie, good to meet you." She smiled but her eyes told Nana otherwise. Nana returned her greeting with a handshake and handed her the test and application forms she had already completed. Valerie proceeded to ask her a number of questions about her background. Since she came highly recommended by James, it helped ease things during the interview. "So tell me a little about yourself."

Nana disliked that question. She always thought, "I am not going to say anything ill about myself anyway." She figured she would respond as sincerely as she could. "I was born in Accra, Ghana, where I spent all of childhood. Then I came to the States to attend university and just never returned to live." She wondered if Valerie watched television, and if she would make the connection with Nana and the mention of the foundation on her application, but she did not mention it at all. Nana was grateful for that because she did not want her to think that she was a celebrity with a lot of money, and not offer her the job.

"My concern is where you live." Valerie told her. "You live in Herndon – how do you plan on getting here every day? I need you here every day for my clients." She stared at Nana with a questionable look. "I am thinking about bad weather, the metro problems and any other thing that could go wrong on any given day in the life of a commuter."

Nana wondered if she was fishing for a reason not to offer her the job. James had told her that Valerie was in dire need for a well experienced international agent, and she was everything she needed. "I think, instead of us anticipating problems before we even finalize our decisions, let us look at the bright side and deal with the weather and metro when the occasion arises."

Valerie looked at her in surprise by her statement. "I like your positive attitude." She smiled. "Maybe I should employ the same attitude." She explained about the position. "I have two new accounts coming on board in less than a month. I need an experienced international agent because these people go to places like Africa, Asia, the Middle East and Latin

America. I just don't want an agent who will freak out when a client calls and asks to go to Ouagadougou, and the agent doesn't even know how to spell it." She and Nana laughed at the thought of that. "You would be surprised how many have crossed my path that did not know geography."

"Well, my father was a stickler for spelling, history and geography. I had to learn such things from an early age. He made sure that I retained it as well." Valerie regarded Nana with a smile.

"Thanks for seeing me – I know you traveled a good distance." She extended her hand to Nana. "I will be in touch with you within the next couple of days. I need to check your references. Please do understand because I have been burned too many times for hiring people without checking references. I have had people even steal from me."

Nana was taken aback by her last statement. "I fully understand - I would not want it any other way." She looked Valerie directly in the eye. "I know that my references will give you a clean account of my time with them." They wished each other well and parted company. Nana hung around in the bookstore for an additional fifteen minutes to look at books and magazines. She was unable to resist a bookstore therefore the venue for her interview met her approval.

Nana traveled back to Herndon with a lot on her mind. She wondered why she really considered returning to the work force. She was not sure about the result of the submission of her play, and where it would take her. Though she had the support of Diane Parsons but it was not Diane's decision, it was the decision of Diane's producer friend in Atlanta. She had bills to pay. She had lost Shirley's contribution to the mortgage of the townhouse, though Jean-Claude continued to pay his share of rent. She was accustomed to having the household bills split in three, and now they were split in two. She and Jean-Claude had willingly adjusted their individual budgets to accommodate the recent increase in their expenses. The foundation was responsible to pay Cynthia of Don & Day, Chuck of the lobbying firm, Rich, their Webmaster and Eugenia, the Administrator of the foundation. The Friends did not put themselves on the payroll of the foundation. The other friends urged Nana to put herself on the payroll but she did not want to do so unless all of the Friends were on the payroll. Frank and Shirley did not need to be on the payroll, and neither did Jean-Claude and Kiddi. Nana was a starving Playwright and Travel Agent.

Her colleagues realized that but she wanted to be fair, without any special treatments. Now here she was, anticipating a return to the workforce.

"So how did your interview go?" Shirley was eager to know. She called shortly after Nana walked in the door.

"It went well." She walked toward the kitchen to get a drink. "I met with the owner, who seems nice." She chuckled, as she filled a glass with carrot juice. "They had me take a geography test."

Shirley laughed, "Wow, they just did not know what a history and geography buff you are. I'm sure you aced it."

"I know I did but it is a long commute from Herndon to Dupont Circle, should I be offered the job." Nana told her friend.

"Are you sure you want to do this?" Shirley sighed, "I can send you money every month to help with the bills."

"I did not realize that I am a charity case." The two women laughed at Nana's statement. "If it ever comes to that, I will let you know, but thanks anyway. That is the end of discussion."

"I hear you, but you cannot prevent your best friend from sending you a gift – can you?" Shirley pushed.

"If you do that, I will return it to the sender." They laughed into the phone and ended the conversation.

Two days after Nana's job interview, she received an email from Valerie Penney with an offer. She was not too pleased with the salary. She communicated the same to Valerie in her email response. Valerie assured her that they would revisit an increase after her probationary period, which was three months. With that explanation, Nana accepted the position of International Travel Consultant. She agreed to begin her position the following Monday, though she had mixed feelings about it.

Nana's First Day at Eastern Travel

Nana's morning commute from Herndon to Dupont Circle took two hours. She drove from her house to West Falls Church Metro station, parked her car there and boarded the train from there to Metro Center station, where she connected to the Red Line that took her to Dupont Circle. She walked in the lobby of the building for the first time. The building entrance to offices was in the rear, and the front of the building was the bookstore. Nana was somewhat disappointed by the lobby; it was a bit shabby compared to the lobby of the International Finance Trust. She walked up to the reception desk.

"Good Morning, can I help you?" The plump uniformed lady behind the desk displayed tobacco stained teeth. Nana wondered why some people insist on saying, "Can I help you" instead of "May I help you" but she knew better than to go around correcting people.

"Good morning, today is my first day at Eastern Travel." Nana told the guard at the desk with enthusiasm.

"How are you today?" The guard asked with a smile. "Good morning and I wish you all the luck with your new job. Eastern is located on the 3rd floor."

"Thank you very much." Nana smiled at the guard and entered the elevator. Within a few minutes, she found herself standing in front of the door with the sign, 'Eastern Travel'. She took a deep breath and gently turned the knob on the door. She walked in quietly and took in the room. She recognized Teah whom she had met on the day of her interview. Five desks occupied the room but only three of them had people at them.

"Hi Nana, it's good to see you again and welcome to our office." Valerie's sudden appearance startled her, as she made her way to where Nana stood. Valerie, a relatively short woman wore a red sweat suit with matching red sneakers. Nana wore a navy pinstriped pant suit, which offset her pale blue shirt and navy two-inch heel pumps. Small pearl studs adorned her ears, and she wore a matching single string of pearls on her neck. She looked impressive but Valerie was not pleased with what Nana wore. She busied her thoughts by introducing her staff to Nana. "This is Janet." Valerie pointed to an overweight Caucasian woman, who suffered from heavy asthmatic breathing. "You remembered Teah, and this is Amber, our receptionist." Amber was a tall young black girl, who would have been a lovely attractive young woman without the many tattoos and piercings on her body. As Nana exchanged handshakes with Teah, Amber and Janet, a tall man appeared from the back of the suite. "Oh, I forgot, this is Antomeyer, our accountant." Nana extended her hand to Antomeyer. "Antomeyer is from Ethiopia…"

"I am from Eritrea, not Ethiopia." Antomeyer corrected Valerie.

Valerie showed Nana to her desk, which was directly behind a vacant desk and just in the front of Amber's desk. She wondered why the receptionist's desk was the third in the room. Nana took her seat at the desk, and got comfortable. Valerie assigned Janet to get Nana acclimated to their accounts and the office, while she quickly placed a stack of papers on Nana's desk.

Nana's first day moved rapidly, as she worked with Janet and learned about the policies and procedures of Eastern Travel. She was glad when the day ended and she traveled back to Herndon. All of her friends called that night to find out how her first day went, and she told them the truth. "I am not so impressed by the place and my new co-workers but I will give it a try anyway."

"Well if you don't like it there, you should make a move now before you are there too long, honey." Shirley urged her.

"They just seem strange, all of them." Nana said thoughtfully. "There is just something about them and the place that I cannot pinpoint but I will stick it out at the moment."

On her second day at Eastern Travel, Nana got a taste of her suspicions. She walked in, dressed in another stunning suit, and Valerie attacked her on sight. "Nana, why are you all dressed up? I thought I.told you during the interview that this office is a casual office?" Valerie stood with hands on her hips as she addressed Nana about her attire.

"I'm sorry but I do not recall you telling me that." Nana continued to her desk and began to get settled. "I don't have that many casual business clothes anyway. I came from an office at the IFT where we had to dress up every day with the exception of Fridays."

"Well then I suggest you go out shopping and purchase some jeans and t-shirts because I will not allow you to continue to come in here like you're going to a convention." Valerie's voice carried force, which surprised Nana but she remained quiet. In spite of how her second day began, Nana made it through the day and was glad to leave that place.

Nana exhausted the few items of casual clothes she already had in her closet for the rest of the week, just to please Valerie. That ended the issue about her attires. She went shopping that weekend and purchased four pairs of jeans, two in black and 2 in blue denim.

"That Valerie lady sounds like bad news to me, Nana." Shirley expressed after Nana told her about Valerie's outburst over her business attire on her second day. "She has no right to demand that her employees wear casual clothes to work, if they do not have it."

"I absolutely concur but if an employer has the right to set business dress code, then I suppose they also have the right to set casual dress code." Nana explained to Shirley. "Her ex-husband is an attorney in Washington; so she has a great deal of clout. I have to tread carefully with Valerie Penney."

"Has she mentioned your involvement with FAFGM?"

"I have it listed on my resume so she asked me about it during the interview but she did not make a big deal of it." Nana thought for a moment. "Why?"

"You know the same old jealousy that tends to follow you with some females."

Nana laughed at Shirley's suggestion. "Why would she be jealous of me? She is a successful business woman with her own travel agency – she drives a brand new BMW sedan, and has everything she wants. Her son, an only child attends a prestigious university in Washington."

"You have told me so many times that those very things do not guarantee happiness." Shirley reminded her.

Shirley was right. Valerie lacked inner peace; she controlled her son, Josh and all of her employees. It was little wonder that her marriage ended. "I know that I still believe that no wealth and success in the world can guarantee happiness." Nana told Shirley. "I still don't feel that her behavior has anything to do with jealousy."

"Well, just be careful, that's all." Shirley was not convinced. She knew that her friend was equally modest and humble, but she also knew that some women tended to get intimidated by Nana's presence, knowledge and good looks. Nana had encountered problems with female superiors in the past, and she shuddered each time she thought about Valerie's behavior toward her.

Nana smiled at the phone. "You worry too much, Mrs. Thurston. Of course I will be careful." Both girls laughed and ended their call.

Valerie was generally nice to Nana for the next two weeks. One morning she surprised the staff Nana included, and brought in organic muffins for them. She walked in the office with a large flat box, straight to the little kitchen in the office suite. "I even got a lactose-free and gluten-free muffin for Nana." Valerie's comment took Nana by surprise – she did not realize that Valerie remembered that she was a vegetarian and was lactose intolerant.

Nana wanted to rethink her earlier opinion of Valerie. She figured that the two of them would get along after all. Perhaps she was not really the unkind person Nana saw a couple of weeks before. "Thank you, Valerie. I appreciate the thought." Valerie walked out of the kitchen to her office and did not respond to Nana.

Nana quickly became acquainted with her assigned clients. She even received some compliments from them. However nothing she did for the clients was enough for Valerie. She constantly complained about the manner in which Nana communicated with the clients, or something she should have done or should not have done. Nana became frustrated but she was not one to walk away from a job. She was dependable, reliable and loyal to her employers but she had never before encountered an employer like Valerie.

Valerie was unpredictable and never ceased to surprise Nana. She went to her Florida weekend home every weekend. She left on Thursdays and returned on Monday afternoons. Valerie owned a weekend home in Colorado in addition to the one in Florida; during the winter months she went to Florida, and in the summer, she went to Colorado. Every free ticket that Eastern Travel earned from high productivity, she used to take her weekend trips. She never offered any of them to her employees, even though it was the hard work and smart performance of the employees of travel agencies that credited the agencies with complimentary travel perks. Nana was accustomed to such opportunities at Proficiency Travel at the IFT. She had traveled extensively to nearly every continent in the world, from being in the travel industry.

Whenever Valerie was out of the office, Teah took the liberty to order lunches for everyone in the office. The first time Nana was offered a free lunch, she declined. "I brought my lunch, Teah but I appreciate the offer."

"You could leave your lunch in the 'frig for another day but it is a free lunch." Teah assured her.

"I know but I will join you next time, today I will have the lunch that I brought. Thanks."

Valerie ran her business like a typical 'mom and pop' operation, and at times she exuded unprofessionalism. She sat in her executive office with her feet in the chair, not to mention her choice of attires she wore to the office. On any given day, Valerie walked in sporting a sweat suit with matching red sneakers or an extremely short skirt. She was fifty-seven years old but behaved as though she was a college student. She befriended the professional and college basketball players. The friends that visited her at the office were all half her age.

On one occasion, Valerie's boyfriend called the office and Nana answered the phone. She placed the caller on hold and told Valerie that a man was on hold for her, "His name was Tom Johnson."

"He's my boyfriend." Valerie snapped at Nana, rolled her eyes at her and picked up the call.

Nana was confused over Valerie's behavior about the phone call. She did not know that Valerie had a boyfriend; but she behaved as though Nana should have known that Tom Johnson was her boyfriend.

Two weeks after Tom Johnson's phone call, a tall black man with heavy facial hair and dark skin walked in the office and said he was there to see Valerie. Nana told him that Valerie was on the phone at the time but asked him to have a seat, which he did. Teah recognized him and spoke but no one else appeared to know who he was. Suddenly, there was an outburst from Valerie's office, as she ran out of her office toward the stranger and flung herself onto his lap. They proceeded to engage in the most passionate kiss Nana had ever witnessed in a place of business. Valerie assumed the attitude that it was her company and she could do whatever she felt, regardless of how unprofessional her behavior was. Nana wondered into what she had gotten herself, and she also wondered if she should be worried.

Nana was at Eastern Travel for six months. She found it difficult to believe that she had actually survived the scorn of Valerie. Whenever she thought she had seen it all from Valerie, she witnessed another shocking experience. She had absolutely no respect for her employees, and spoke to them in the most demeaning manner. When she needed to speak to them or needed to see someone in her office, Valerie shouted out the person's name. Nana wondered if Valerie thought that they all had hearing problems.

She shouted for Amber but she was on the phone with a client. Valerie barged out of her office, as she continued to shout Amber's name. "Amber, don't you hear me calling you?"

Amber hurried off the phone. "Yes Valerie." Her voice was full of annoyance.

"When I call you, I expect you to drop everything and come to me." Valerie shouted again.

"I was finishing a call with a client." Amber awkwardly explained.

"I am sick of you, I can't take you today. Just get out, go home now- get out now." Valerie shouted at Amber, while she took her bag and left the office.

Nana was speechless, as she struggled to comprehend what she had just witnessed. The office was quiet for a long time. Everyone was afraid to speak until the phone broke the silence. Nana was even more astonished when Valerie took a phone call only minutes after the incident with Amber. She behaved as though nothing had happened. She was certain that her new employer was a narcissistic control freak.

"Hi Sweetie – how are you?" Valarie put on her loving and caring voice for the caller, who happened to be the basketball star, Bakimbe Mobutu. Bakimbe was originally from the Congo; and Valerie was the oldest known groupie of basketball players in the United States. Her friends comprised of Bakimbe Mobutu, Peter Gwining and several players of the Washington, D.C. soccer team. At any given day or time, anyone from the sports arena was likely to walk through the door of Eastern Travel.

Nana became familiar with the clients' voices, and one day she had the pleasure of speaking to the popular Bakimbe Mobutu. She answered the phone and Nana recognized the voice. He needed airline tickets for not only himself, but for his wife and three children. He and Nana were on the phone for more than twenty minutes. "You are set, Mr. Mobutu. I will email you all of the tickets once I am done." Nana told Bakimbe at the end of their call. "Is there anything else I may do for you?"

"Your name and accent tell me that you are from the continent." He referred to the continent of Africa. "I would guess it is the western coast of the continent."

"You are correct on the first statement and on the second statement as well." Nana smiled in the phone. "Ghana it is and I know where you are from."

"Of course you know." Bakimbe told her in that familiar accent.

"I hope you don't mind my saying it but I am proud of what you've done with your fame and fortune for your country."

"Thank you my African sister, thank you." They had the opportunity to talk because Valerie was out of the office that day. When she was in the office, she did not allow anyone else to speak to Bakimbe and Peter.

Nana had the opportunity to speak with Peter Gwining on a couple of occasions but she did not care much about assisting him. Peter Gwining had a child in every city where there was a basketball team. Though he was already retired from playing, he appeared to have left a child in each city in which he played. He called to get airline tickets for all of his children to attend his induction into the Hall of the Sports; and Nana had the pleasure of assisting him. He had a child in Miami, New York, Boston, Chicago, Los Angeles, Washington, D.C., Detroit, Philadelphia, Dallas and San Antonio. He purchased a ticket for each child to fly to New York, and a limo for the child in New York. Nana arranged for a limo to take each child to the airport. She was in disbelief to discover the number of children Gwining had but she was impressed that he supported all of them, and wanted them to be present at his induction ceremony.

Nana told Shirley and Frank about her encounter with Valerie's athletic friends, including her boyfriend, Tom Johnson. "He never played in the professional basketball league but he played for his university in Washington, D.C." Nana explained to them.

"Oh I know all about Tom Johnson." Frank told Nana on the phone with Shirley next to him on the loveseat. "Johnson was playing for his Washington, D.C. University in the college league finals against the university team in North Carolina. The famous Mickey Jakesaw played in that same game for the North Carolina University team." Frank chuckled before he continued with the story about Valerie's boyfriend. "Tom Johnson had the opportunity to dribble the ball down the court and score, which would have given his team victory; but instead, he attempted to pass the ball to his teammate and threw it directly into the hands of Mickey Jakesaw. Mickey drove the ball down the court and for the first time, scored with a jump shot that became famous. The university in North Carolina defeated the university in Washington, D.C., and Jakesaw became a hero and was drafted to the pros while Johnson was never drafted to the pros."

"In other words, your boss' boyfriend is a flunkey." Shirley told Nana. "You can tell her that next time she tries to intimidate you."

"You know I will not do that but it is good to know the type of people I have around me." Nana told her friend.

Nana had many such conversations with Shirley and Frank. She was quite concerned about what she had gotten herself involved in. She also spoke to Alec about her new job and the problems she had with her employer. "The other day, Valerie shouted at me and I asked her not to speak to me in that manner." Nana explained to Alec. "She did the same thing to me that she did to Amber. She drove me out of the office and told me to leave for the day because she did not want to look at me that day."

"Why would she do something like that?" Alec wanted to know.

"She is crazy. You should see the hateful look in her eyes when she is doing these things."

"So what did you do, sweetheart?"

"I did not leave like Amber did. I ignored her and continued to do my work. She eventually calmed down and behaved as though nothing had ever happened that day."

"You should have left and not gone back."

"She did the same thing to me another time but I warned her that the next time she drives me out of the office, I will leave and not return."

"Good for you, Nana. Do not allow her to take advantage of you and abuse you. It sounds to me like this individual is an abusive employer, and her employees are abused victims."

"You are right about that because everyone is afraid of her and because she knows that I am not afraid of her, she does not like me at all. One day she shouted at Antomeyer, the accountant and he did not take it lightly. He shouted back at her and slammed his office door."

"It does not sound like he is afraid of her."

"No he isn't afraid of her because she does not drive him out of the office and she doesn't usually speak to him that way. He was leaving at 3:00 in the afternoon and she told him he couldn't leave. He is there every morning at 6:00 so he feels he should leave at 2:00 in the afternoon."

"This job is a distraction from your work with the foundation. You are allowing it to consume you. Do not do this to yourself."

"I know but this lady should not be allowed to treat her employees like that. Janet and Amber are treated like they are less than humans. She told Antomeyer to talk to Janet about her bad hygiene and he does not feel comfortable doing that. Teah seems to have something on her because she does not mess with Teah."

"What a crazy bunch you have there, sweetheart."

Nana was grateful that she had good friends to whom she could discuss her problems. Perhaps Alec was right, she thought. She allowed Valerie and her job to consume her. She made a mental note to get back to the business of ending female genital mutilation. After all, that was her mission, her passion and she did not want to have anything stop her from carrying out her mission.

Chapter Eleven

THE SAMARITAN

Have mercy on me, O God, because of your unfailing love. Because of your great compassion, blot out the stain of my sins. – Psalm 51:1 (NLT)

Nana stepped out of the shower as the phone began to ring. She took the phone in the bathroom with her that night because she was expecting a call from Alec and she did not want to miss his call. "Hello." She placed her full-length terrycloth bathrobe around her and placed the phone on speaker as she gently moisturized her face and neck. "James, how is it going?"

"It is not going well, my sister." James Dunn, her buddy from Proficiency told her.

"Why, what happened?" She was suddenly alarmed, James did not sound like his usual jovial self.

"I was evicted from my place this afternoon." He sighed. "The management locked me out and I cannot get to my belongings."

"Oh my, James – I am sorry to hear that. What are you going to do?"

"Well, I was wondering if you would let me stay at your place just for tonight until I can get my things tomorrow."

Nana knew that she could not let James spend the night on the streets that night. God had blessed her with a comfortable home so she decided to do him the favor. "Sure James – you know how to get here I assume."

"Yes I do and thanks so much for doing this for me. God bless you." Nana wondered if she should have conferred with Jean-Claude about having James spend the night at their house but it was late over in France. Furthermore, James needed a place to sleep that night and she was not going to have him stay on the street. James was from Georgia, where his father still resided. Nana remembered when he lost his mother several years before, when they both worked for Proficiency at the IFT. He was an only child and he did have a few cousins of whom he frequently spoke but they all lived in Georgia.

Nana busied herself and prepared their guest bedroom before James arrived. She had already eaten her dinner, but she checked in the pantry to see if there was anything she could offer him. She knew she would not extend herself for anyone she did not know well but she and James had a sister and brother relationship. Her thoughts were interrupted by the doorbell.

"Hi James, come on in." She held the front door open as James entered with an overnight bag and his briefcase. He looked sad but Nana tried to cheer him up. She had not seen him look like that since he lost his mother. "Nice shirt – I like the color."

"Thanks my sister for taking me in for the night." He gave her a quick hug.

"I know that you would do the same for me." She waved off his words of thanks. "I'll show you to your room and bathroom. James followed her up the stairs and to the third bedroom at the top of the stairs. "This is our guest bedroom." She stepped aside for him to enter the room. "Shirley's room is still set up for her if she ever comes to visit." She chuckled. "I guess I just don't want to let go." They both laughed. "The bathroom is down the hall and I have already equipped it with towels and wash cloths for your convenience." She turned back. "Have you eaten?"

"My sister, I cannot thank you enough for such kind hospitality." He seemed better. "Yes I went ahead and stopped on the way to eat something."

"We call it African Hospitality." They laughed again as she left him to be alone. "Good night."

The next day was Saturday and Nana usually slept in late. She took advantage of the days she did not go to her job. She was accustomed to walking around the house without being fully dressed since Shirley and Jean-Claude were no longer there but that morning she was reminded by the movement she heard out in the hall that she needed to shower and get dressed before leaving her room.

"Good morning, my sister." James greeted her with bright and wide eyes as she walked in the living room where he sat.

"Good morning. How are you this morning?" She sat in the large arm chair, across from the sofa where James sat. "Did you rest well?"

"Oh yes I did, very well too." He stood and picked up his briefcase. "I am going to the rental office to see if they will let me in to get some of my things or all of them."

"If they do, what are you going to do with your things?" Nana wondered if he had been evicted, she did not see how they would release his things until he paid what he owed them. "You might need to consult an attorney."

"If I get my things out, I will put them in storage, where my other belongings are."

"Why do you have some of your belongings in storage?" She was puzzled.

"The apartment where I was staying was fully furnished so I put my furniture in storage."

"Would you like something to eat before you leave?" Nana went to the kitchen while James followed her. She found a packet of instant oatmeal in the pantry. "This is the last packet but you are welcomed to it." She handed it to him but he refused to accept it.

"Wow, this African Hospitality is serious with you it seems." He laughed. "You would actually give me your last packet of oatmeal, and I know how much you like having oatmeal in the mornings."

She smiled. "We have been known to give up our only bed for a guest."

"That is so nice of you but I will stop on the way and get some coffee and doughnuts." He walked to the door and Nana let him out and wished him all the best with his rental office.

Later that afternoon, Nana received a call from James. He was successful in getting the rental office to release his things but he had no place to stay for the night. Nana's sympathy got the best of her again and she gave in and agreed for him to return to the Herndon townhouse for another night.

Nana was puzzled when James returned to her house and told her that his friends in Washington had invited him to attend a concert at the Kennedy Center with them. "They have an extra ticket and asked me if I wanted to join them."

Though she hoped that they would sit and talk about his plans and where he intended to live, she did not say anything. Instead, Nana told him to have a great time and enjoy the concert. She figured that since he already had a job and a car, he could stay there and share some of the expenses. "Tomorrow is Sunday so we can talk then."

She noticed that James brought a number of duffle bags with him, and she wondered how long he intended to stay. It was obvious that he did not plan on leaving the next day or the day after. She decided to wait until their talk on Sunday. He was spiffily dressed when he came downstairs to leave. After James left, Nana sat and thought about the situation in which she found herself. She wondered why his friends who invited him out to the Kennedy Center that night did not extend their generosity to accommodate him with a place to stay. Their invitation to him that night was totally impractical. When James desperately needed a place to stay, they took him to a concert instead of giving him a room to stay. She wondered why James did not call them that night when he called her. They lived in Washington, D.C. and it would have been much more convenient for James than Herndon.

It turns out that Nana never got the opportunity on that Sunday to discuss anything with James because he purposely made himself unavailable that day. He told her that he was invited by the same friends from the night before to have brunch with them. She bit her tongue to prevent her from asking him why he did not just go and stay with them. Her parents taught her never to extend a good deed and take it back so since she had already extended the good deed to James, she was stuck and was not going to take it back.

James drove every morning from Herndon to West Falls Church Metro station, parked his car and boarded the Metro to get to work. He encouraged Nana to ride with him instead of taking her car to the Metro. Nana was grateful for his offer since she did not like to drive in rush hour traffic. She became a regular rider with James every morning, and at times they planned to meet at the Metro station so that she would get a ride home with him. They never sat and discussed the duration of his stay, neither did they discuss the sharing of expenses.

James continued to stay with Nana, which seemed to be without end. Nana was awakened every Saturday morning to the sound of the vacuum cleaner. James vacuumed the entire house on Saturdays; he mopped the kitchen and foyer floors, cleaned the guest bathroom and powder room, dusted and watered the plants. Nana felt as though she had a live-in male maid, but she figured since James did not pay any expenses in the house, his willingness to keep the house clean was not a bad idea. In addition to cleaning, James also cooked a great southern breakfast on Saturday mornings, and cared for Nana's plants. He cooked a large pot of grits, soaked in butter and cheddar cheese, topped with smoked salmon. Shirley was the first to introduce grits to Nana, and though she ate no dairy products, she improvised with soy-based cheese and olive oil in place of butter and dairy cheese. James began to take out a portion of the grits for Nana before he added cheese and butter. Nana took a great likeness to southern grits.

Nana and James got along well. They were good friends when they worked together at the IFT but one never knows how living with a person will work out. She and James watched football, basketball and soccer games together. Although James did not understand soccer, Nana explained the game and the rules to him. Whenever Nana needed to be escorted to a party or another function, she was able to count on James as her escort. He liked to dance and get dressed up and be seen by people. He escorted Nana to the Ghanaian Embassy for dinner parties and other functions, and he also took delight in going on shopping sprees with her. She and Shirley in the past discussed James' sexuality but he never discussed it with her, as close as they were. He said nothing, though he never brought any women around. He never brought any men around either, and Nana preferred not to tread on sensitive waters.

Nana finally heard from Diane Parson's friends in Atlanta, when she did not expect it. "Nana darling, how are you?" Diane's charming deep southern accent bellowed in the phone, as though she was about to break out in a song. "It has been a long time."

"Diane, it is good to hear from you." Nana was pleasantly surprised as her heart palpitated much more rapidly than normal. "I am doing well." She displayed her white teeth against her dark beautiful skin. "I was just waiting to hear from you."

"I told you I would call." Diane was reclined on her settee recliner in her music room. "You know how those folks in theater and film are kept busy." Diane wiggled her bare toes as she spoke to Nana. "Well I have good news." Nana held her breath as she waited for Diane to slowly speak in the southern drawl, but she was patient. "They read your script and think that something can be done with it."

"Something like what?" She did not intend to sound ungrateful but she wanted to hear a more positive statement. "I'm just so excited that I am not sure what they are saying or what I am asking."

"Nana, they want to see you in Atlanta in three weeks to discuss the production of your script." Diane realized that Nana did not quite comprehend her show business lingo. "If you like what they offer and they like what is discussed, your play will be prepared for production." Nana's scream interrupted Diane. "I guess that scream means that you will see them in three weeks then". The ladies laughed in agreement.

"Yes Diane, I will be there in three weeks, ready for a deal." Nana was ecstatic. "Thank you Diane – I am forever grateful."

"I just want to explain how the things will work after the Atlanta trip." Nana listened intently. "They will want to prepare a contract for you to sign while you are in Atlanta. Do not sign anything until you return to Washington and seek out a lawyer. If you do not know a lawyer, I will help find one for you that specializes in intellectual property. You will need an agent or the lawyer might be all that you need at the time. Call your friends and share the news with them. Prepare for your trip and keep me informed on everything. Take care of yourself." Diane ended the phone call quickly, as she knew that Nana was eager to call Shirley and Frank.

James was downstairs watching television when she got off the phone. He was the first to hear the news. Nana raced down the stairs, shouting for James. "My play has been picked up by Diane Parsons' friends." Although she was in great shape, she paused to catch her breath. "They want to see me in Atlanta in three weeks.

James leaped out of his chair and gave Nana a huge hug. "Congratulations, my sister. I am happy for you.

She jumped around like a child. "I have waited for this moment for years." Her voice was shaky. "Now that the moment is here, I'm nervous."

"Sure you will be nervous, it is expected." He shrugged. "I like this kind of nervousness." They both laughed. "Well, I think this news calls for a toast." James walked to the kitchen and opened a bottle of Chardonnay and handed a glass of it to Nana. "Cheers my sister, I hope your play will be the most successful and make it to Broadway." They clicked glasses and sipped.

"Off Broadway would still work for me." She took another sip and they chuckled.

"I can help you plan your trip to ATL." James offered.

"You should be able to help because you are a product of Morehouse College."

"On second thought, Diane Parsons' folks might handle hotel, flight and ground transportation, so it's not much I need to do." James pondered after he took a sip from his glass. "I could come along in case you need me."

"Would you really do that?" Nana was touched.

"I have a free ticket from work, and I have a free-stay at a hotel in Atlanta so the trip would not cost me much other than my meals."

"Great, sounds like a plan then." She raised her glass. "Thanks my brother." Nana never had a brother in Ghana but she made James, Jean-Claude and the Thurston brothers her brothers in America.

Nana was excited as she called Shirley and Frank to share the news with them.

"I would meet you in Atlanta for support but I have a cosmetology conference scheduled in Houston that week." Shirley told her with regret.

"I never had any doubt in my mind that your play would be picked up someday." Frank told Nana. "I am really happy for you; let us know if there is anything we can do."

"Thanks guys, it is fine. Being happy for me is more than enough." Nana sighed. "James has also offered to accompany me at his own expense."

"Hmm, you know how I feel about James living there so don't get me started." Shirley told her as she had so often when they spoke. "I just don't like the fact that he has moved in there without making any contribution to the house. He must think that you are loaded with money."

"Even if you were loaded with millions of dollars, he is still using you by not making a contribution or at least offering to assist." Frank chimed in.

"I know – one night only has turned into four months." Nana concurred with her friends, and then she sighed. "I am being tolerant and accommodating because becoming homeless in this country is only a job removed. God blessed me with a nice home so I figured I would help out someone in need."

"I wonder would James feel the same if the situation was the reverse." Shirley asked.

"Well, I am doing it because my faith taught me to help others when we have what they need. If he would not do the same for me, then it is just his mindset." Nana clarified her action to her friends. Nana was a devout Christian. She gave herself to the Lord, and received him as her Savior a year before. She was serious about her newfound religion, and what it did for her life. She did not want to go back to her old life without God in it. She knew there had to be a God but she did not know him at all. She did not have a relationship with him. She attended church almost every Sunday. She became active in church activities. She volunteered for the church. Frank's mother helped her understand the Bible and how to use its contents in her daily life. She called it her walk with the Lord. She picked that phrase up from Amelia.

Nana called Alec, Jean-Claude and Kiddi with her good news. She took the time to explain the details of her phone conversation with Diane Parsons earlier that day to Alec, Jean-Claude and with Kiddi.

"Congratulations, I am delighted for you." Alec told her. "I think you should request the time off as early as Monday from your devious employer."

Nana laughed at his description of Valerie, though she could have come up with several other words to describe the woman. "Fortunately I do not need to ask her, they want to meet with me on a Saturday."

"Fantastic, that's a relief." Alec told her. "I hope this development will be your one way ticket out of there."

"I am certain that my days are numbered at Eastern Travel." They both laughed at the way she said it. He wanted to ask her if James still lived in her house but he decided against it. He was aware of the persistent objection from her other friends, Jean-Claude, Frank and Shirley. He did not want to add more pressure on her.

Nana expressed to Alec that she lived with the regret of doing James the favor. She did not regret the good deed but she wished that she had pressed James to tell her exactly how long he needed to stay at the house. He told her the first night that he only needed to be there that night. They were about to enter his fifth month of being in her house, with no sign of preparation to move out. James also made it difficult for Nana to say anything about making a contribution and when he planned to leave. He was helpful with housekeeping, and just being there as a friend and brother. Shirley reminded her whenever the topic came up, "No brother of yours would take advantage like that. You are not originally from here but he is, so he should be in the position to help you." Nana always quieted her and said, "It is fine, Shirl, it really is fine."

Nana was an even-tempered woman, and she did anything she could to maintain peace around her. She survived female genital mutilation at an early age – she would allow nothing to disturb her inner peace. That included Valerie's evil behavior towards her. She believed that if she took her problems to the Almighty, whom she had come to know, they would be solved one at a time, but only at the designated or appointed time by God.

Nana's parents never took her to church as a child in Ghana. They had no religious affiliation, instead they believed in the traditions of their tribe. When she came to the States, she became indoctrinated by Frank and Jean-Claude. Frank grew up in a Baptist home while Jean-Claude was Catholic. The two men often debated about Catholicism and Baptism, each one argued that his denomination was the better. What their religious debates did for Nana was more than they imagined. She was inspired to conduct her own research on Christianity. She read about John Wesley and his brother, and became inspired by their doctrine and methodical teachings.

Both Frank and Jean-Claude questioned her fascination for the Wesley brothers.

"John Wesley and his brother were known for their methodical teachings so much that their friends referred to them as the Methodists. The name stuck and their followers were also called Methodists." Nana explained to her friends. She quickly learned a great deal about Christianity and thought that Wesley's method was easy to apply to her daily life.

Nana purchased a copy of the Bible and read a little of it each day to see how it related to her own life. A lot of it made sense to her, though some of it confused her as well. Her favorite part became the Psalms of David. It was through David's Psalms that she developed an inner peace and felt compelled to give of herself to those in need.

While she agreed with her friends to ask James to leave, she knew within her heart that she was unable to bring herself to do it. She wrestled with the thought each night when she retired, but when morning came, James greeted her downstairs with a bubbly smile. She learned to communicate with God; something which Amelia taught her. Talking to God became her favorite thing to do at the end of the day. She retreated to her bedroom and with no formality she proceeded to talk to God, whom she could not see. She told him about the difficult decision she needed to make about James.

"God, I know you are listening and can see me even though I cannot see you or hear you. Please tell me what to do about James." Sometimes she felt silly talking to someone she was unable to see and received no readily response.

Amelia told her in one of their conversations, that God does indeed hear everything she said to him and to others. "You have to be alert when you ask him for things or you could very well miss his answers to you."

"Well, how alert do I need to be?" She appeared almost innocent. "He's not going to speak to me like he did to Moses and Aaron."

Amelia thought her biblical knowledge had improved a great deal, and she laughed at her statement. "No he will not do that but when you least expect it, his answers come to you; sometimes through someone else and at times he puts his answers in your mind."

"So when we have a problem and we ask him to solve the problem, if the solution comes to my mind later, does that mean he sent the solution to my mind?" She looked pensive and Amelia wondered what else was going through her mind. "Absolutely, that is how it works."

Atlanta, Georgia

Nana and James did not fly on the same flight. James had a free ticket from his job on a different airline, and Nana's ticket came from Zebra Productions in Atlanta. Upon her arrival, she saw James at the baggage claim area as he waited with patience for her. "You did not have to wait for me; you should have gone and checked into your hotel and relaxed." Zebra had Nana registered at a different hotel, which was about thirty minutes from where James was registered.

"No problem, my sister, I will have enough time to relax." James told her. "I just wanted to make sure that you arrived safely, and that Zebra Productions was here to meet you."

Nana boarded the black chauffeured sedan that was sent for her by Zebra Productions, and James got onto the shuttle to pick up his rental car. Nana offered him a ride in her car but he declined since he needed to get his rental.

They arrived on a Friday evening, and Nana just wanted to check in and get to bed. She wanted to be fresh and well rested for her appointment the next morning with the people at Zebra Productions. Her hotel room was exquisite with a large bouquet of flowers from Zebra, a welcome letter from the hotel management and a box of assorted chocolates. She smiled when she saw the chocolates and made a mental note to save them for James. Nana being a strict vegetarian, she did not eat dairy products, including all chocolates. She appreciated the gesture from both the hotel management and Zebra Productions.

James called her mobile phone and told her that he was comfortably settled in his hotel room. "I'm about to order dinner and call it a night."

"That sounds good." Nana sat in the arm chair in her room as her feet rested on the stool in the front of the chair. She kicked off her pumps and wiggled her bare toes. "I just did the same, I am quite hungry." She told James about the chocolates and flowers. He was delighted because chocolates were one of his favorite snack foods.

The next morning, Nana felt rested and ready for her appointment. The sedan and same driver met her in front of the hotel. She wore a peach skirt suit with a beige camisole blouse, off-white nylons that covered her shapely legs and a pair of beige pumps. Her hair was cut in a short afro with a part to the right side of her head. Heads turned in the lobby as she stepped off the elevator and walked out to the sedan.

James was not invited to sit in the meeting, and that is what Nana preferred. He sat in the reception lounge while she met with three men from Zebra Productions; Robert and Richard Gallagher and Stephen Green sat across the conference room table from Nana. The Gallagher brothers were the founders of Zebra, and later were joined by their college buddy, Stephen Green. The three men ran the business and had grown it to a successful production company. They produced movies, Broadway plays, television, Billboard and radio commercials and television dramas. Nana sat before them as they discussed her play.

"We are interested in staging your play." Robert told her. "We also want to offer you two options; we could either stage it or we could turn it into a movie."

Nana was expecting only the option of a stage play. "How much would you change the story line to turn it into a movie?" She was not expecting such a decision.

"You don't need to be concerned about us chopping up your play." Richard told her. "We intend to have you participate in the screenwriting as well as the casting."

"After all, you created the story." Stephen interjected. "Nobody else knows the story better than you."

"Do you have any questions?" Robert asked. "Bombard us with them."

Nana did not speak for a while. The men saw that she was taken by surprise. They did not want to pressure her. "Is it possible for me to sleep on this before I give you an answer?" She paused for a moment. "I need more than a night for this, if you don't mind." She placed her hand under her chin. "I should also confer with an attorney perhaps."

"We would not have it any other way, Ms. Nkuku." Robert was quick to clarify. "We expected you to be accompanied by an attorney."

"You may call me Nana." She gave him a broad smile.

"Diane advised me to get an attorney but everything happened so fast." She made a funny face. "I really appreciate you meeting with me on a Saturday." She gave them that broad smile again. "I understand how important weekends are to working people." The men laughed along with her. She felt comfortable with them. They were everything Diane had told her and even more.

"Weekend, what's that?" Robert joked and they laughed again. "Most times we are here on Saturdays."

"And especially when we're working on a special project." Richard offered.

She liked the camaraderie among the three men, and wondered how three young men became successful early in their lives. She made a mental note to ask them someday.

"Well Nana, here is what we should do." Robert seemed to be the most talkative. "You can take your time in making your decision." He paused for a moment. "Do you already have an attorney?"

"Yes, she is the attorney for our foundation but she will have no objection to represent me."

"You would be better off with a lawyer who specializes in intellectual property." Stephen mentioned. "They understand fully what we are offering you." He held his hands up as though he was about to surrender. "Don't get me wrong now, all lawyers can explain our contract and terms to you but a specialist is more familiar with intellectual property law than would, say an immigration lawyer."

"I understand, she is not an intellectual property attorney but she can refer me to one, I'm sure." Nana told them.

"Good, and if she doesn't know one, we can refer you to one in the Washington, D.C. area." Robert told her. "We will give you a tentative contract to take with you. Whatever you and your attorney request, we will work together to make amendments." Robert prepared a package while he spoke. "We will have many of such meetings before we get to the final stage." He indicated the folder in front of him on the table. "We have included two contracts, one is for a movie and the other is for a stage production. We will work with your choice." He handed Nana the stuffed folder across the large conference room table.

"Once you make your decision and give us your requests, we will sit down again for another meeting." Stephen said. "Your attorney will need to accompany you." Nana nodded and placed the folder before her. "Do you have any questions?"

She cupped her lips and shook her head. "Not at the moment but tonight I will go over the documents and if I have any questions, I will call or send you an email." She looked around the table at each of them. "Is that acceptable?"

"Absolutely, you may contact us anytime." Robert assured her. "Are you hungry? We would like to have you join us for lunch."

Nana smiled. "I would love to but I have my buddy waiting in the lounge for me. He was kind enough to accompany me."

"We have no problem with him joining us." Stephen was quick to speak, and his partners agreed.

They each had a handshake for Nana before they walked out of the conference room. In the lounge, they met James where he waited with patience. Nana introduced him to Robert, Stephen and Richard as they exchanged handshakes.

"So shall we go? I'm starving." Robert told them, and they concurred and walked out to the elevator.

Lunch was enjoyable and Nana learned a lot more about her prospective producers. The restaurant was a blend of Southern and French called Le Marchais. The owner was at the restaurant, and it was obvious that the three men frequented her restaurant. She gave more attention to them and their guests than she did to any of her other patrons. A mere hello or a smile and the nod of her head was what the others in the restaurant received. She spent a good deal of time at Nana's table. Her name was Anaïs Marchais, and she was well dressed with impeccably coiffed hair. She moved around her place of business with grace.

Anais wanted to know Nana's origin and how long she had lived in America. She felt a commonality since she too was an immigrant to the United States. She told Nana that she once visited the Eastern part of Africa but not the West. "I found the Safari to be quite fascinating." She explained with a slight French accent that reminded Nana of Jean-Claude.

"So did I when I went there as a child." Nana shared with her. "You should see more of the continent; you will like our beaches in West Africa."

"I know but I want to go for your lovely jewelry. You have such uniquely made pieces over there."

"Thank you." Nana blushed. "What part of France did you originally come from? My other roommate, Jean-Claude Girard is from Nice."

"Ah, Nice?" Anais seemed excited. "I am from Montpellier, also in the South."

"Great city, I want to vacation there next time I'm in the South of France." Stephen told them as their main course arrived.

"I will leave you now to enjoy your meal." Anais told them. "Bon appetite." She stopped by a couple of other tables to greet other patrons as she made her way across the room.

James later expressed how impressed he was with the production company and its owners, and Nana agreed with him.

She filled James in on her meeting with the three producers. "I need to engage an attorney who will review and advise me on this contract." She indicated the folder on her lap. "Then I guess it will be back here to Atlanta for signing and planning."

"You don't seem excited, my sister." James noticed that she was nonchalant about everything. "Are you okay?"

"I'm fine; I need to absorb all of this sudden eminent change, that's all." She chuckled. "I guess I have been slaving for Proficiency Travel and now Eastern Travel for so long that I will not know how to deal with fame and fortune." Both she and James laughed at her statement.

"You know, you are just so humble." James teased, but he really meant it. Nana never allowed the little bit of fame and attention she and her friends received from the success of the foundation to change her. Shirley was always somewhat snobbish; and the fame of the foundation and her marriage to the star quarterback, Frank Thurston made her worse. Jean-Claude was still his usual self, even with his job promotion to Chief

Purser. Frank did not behave differently because he was accustomed to the limelight. Kiddi was humble but not in the way that Nana exhibited. "You exude a certain personality that is one of a kind among the folks I know." James drove her back to her hotel after lunch, as they caught up. "You're beautiful inside and outside, yet you seem totally unaware of it."

She shrugged and gave him a half smile. "Thank you but how am I supposed to behave? My life has not been the easiest; there was FGM at an early age, which changed my happy childhood. My father was a disciplinarian, whose wife was equally as frightened of him as I was." She shrugged. "In certain ways, I'm thankful that he was strict because I excelled in my studies all through secondary school and college." She smiled. "Now thanks to you, Frank and Jean-Claude, I know that there is truly an Almighty God who hears me and responds to me."

"Amen." James shouted as they pulled up to her hotel front entrance. Being the gentleman he always was, he got out of the car, walked in swift strides to the passenger's door and helped her out of his rental sports car. "Well my sister, it has been quite a full and fun day."

"Yes it has." She had a grateful hug for him. "Thanks for being here, I appreciate it."

"I wanted to do it. Get some rest and I shall see you at the airport in the morning. At least we get to fly back together." She nodded and waved as he drove away and she walked into the hotel lobby. The rest of the afternoon and evening was spent making phone calls to her friends. She called Frank and Shirley first.

"So how is the Playwright?" Shirley was excited to hear her friend's voice. "I have you on speaker so Frank can hear everything I hear."

Nana laughed. "Good idea, then you will not need to explain to him later. Hi Frank"

"Hey, how's my girl?" Frank came over the speaker. "We have been waiting at the edge of our seats for the news from ATL."

"The meeting this morning went well." Nana told them everything about the meeting and lunch. She told them how she met the restaurant owner, Anais Marchais. "Frank, do you know any intellectual property attorneys?"

"Hmm, not off the top of my head but I can ask a couple of attorneys; hopefully they might recommend someone." Frank promised.

"Thanks, I will also check in Washington myself." Nana told them.

Nana called Kiddi and then she called Jean-Claude; she told them about her trip to Atlanta and how the meeting and lunch went. The more she told the story to each friend, the more she began to see the reality of what was about to happen to her life.

She saved Alec for last, and when she called him he was excited to hear her voice as usual. "How are you dearest?" Alec inquired. "I have been thinking about you."

"You have?" Nana smiled. "I hope they were good thoughts."

"When I think about you, it is only good thoughts, my dear." He was stretched out on the sofa in his recreation room. When he was not busy with his patients, Alec enjoyed physical workouts and listening to classical music. Reading was his other pastime.

"Am I interrupting anything?" Nana was always mindful and respectful of other people's time.

"Not at all, I came home and decided to catch up on my reading." He chuckled. "I think the book was reading me."

"So I did interrupt your well-deserved nap then." She made a funny face. "I'm sorry about that. Go back to sleep and we can talk later."

"I'm glad that you called, I have been waiting to hear from you." He propped an additional pillow under his head. "Please tell me all about your meeting with the producers."

She told him the same story she told her other friends, as she tried to paraphrase so that she would not sound redundant. He listened without interruption as she left out nothing. "So, I am in search of an attorney to explain this complicated contract to me."

"I'm sure you're quite capable of understanding the contract. You only need someone to answer questions if you have any."

"Thanks for the compliment but I don't have a legal mind, and I do have questions." They laughed at her response.

"I know a couple of attorneys but they don't specialize in that type of law." He scratched his head for a moment as he thought. "I can check with them and see if they can refer you."

"I would be much appreciative."

"Not a problem; it is better to have a referral than to find one off the internet." They laughed together. "Well, some folks resort to that when they have no other way."

"I suppose they do."

Alec had some questions for her about the meeting, and she answered them readily. They were some of the same questions Frank asked her. "Well, I'm really happy for you," Alec told her. "Have you been to church lately?" It was one of the things they had in common. Although Alec was a physician, he was spiritually connected with the Almighty. He and Nana often discussed the Bible and shared some of their most intimate encounters with God. Alec told her how he always prayed prior to surgery.

"I have not gone recently." She suddenly realized that she had not been to church for a long time. "I have been busy and tired lately." She attended services at a small neighborhood Methodist Church but she did not commit herself to membership. Nana had come a long way from not knowing anything about faith but she was not positive if she wanted to commit to that kind of connectivity to a particular church.

"You don't really need church to have a relationship with God." Alec assured her. "With my schedule at the hospital, I am not in the position to attend church services." Alec made it a habit of stopping in the little chapel at the hospital. He always lit a candle and said a quiet prayer. He did that especially when he had critical cases. He believed that God led him through surgeries and critical cases. Frank was one of those critical cases that caused him to frequent the little chapel.

"I fully agree. Some people feel that if they don't go to church every Sunday, they are not good Christians."

"Take it from me, I know several that attend church every Sunday and some other days of the week but you would not know from their behavior." They laughed.

"I will get off this phone now and leave you to carry on with your reading." She smiled into the phone. "I appreciate you taking the time to talk."

"I enjoyed every minute of it. Travel back safely tomorrow."

"Thanks." She held the phone to her chest and smiled before she placed it back on the cradle. Alec was likable, and he won her trust and attention a long time before. She fell asleep with a smile on her face, thinking about Alec and all that he had said to her.

Nana knew that the Atlanta Airport was a large one but she was not prepared for what she faced. She overslept and arrived at the airport only less than an hour prior to her flight. She tried to check in her bag but the attendant at the check-in desk declined. Nana missed the deadline to check-in her bag.

"If you plan to get on that flight lady, you will have to move fast." The check-in attendant told Nana as she handed her a boarding pass. "Good luck."

"Thank you." Nana barely responded as she raced away to the nearest escalator that pointed toward her gate. She wished she had worn her walking shoes but she was in three-inch heels. She also wished she had packed her Pullman luggage but instead, she had a small shoulder garment bag. She could do nothing about her regrets at the time. She only concentrated on making her way to the gate. She finally made it to the tram that she hoped would take her directly to the gate. It was minutes later that Nana discovered she was on the wrong tram.

She hurried off that tram and waited for the correct tram, which arrived not long after the previous one. Nana had no room for error, and inquired from an airport employee if that tram was going to her gate. She was in disbelief that it was only going as far as ten gates down from hers. She got off and began to walk as swiftly as she could. She was glad that she was in good shape. As she walked, she prayed for God to get her to the gate in time. Nana knew that James was already at the gate. He was a stickler for time, and his hotel was much closer to the airport than hers was. She continued to strut in her heels and pray in her mind.

Meanwhile, James was at the gate, and refused to board the flight, though every passenger was already boarded. He pleaded with and begged the gate attendant to wait a few more minutes before he closed the gate. "I know she is in the airport, and making her way to the gate now." He told the attendant, while he engaged and distracted him with small talk. "You know, she came here to arrange for a movie on a play she wrote." He bragged to the attendant.

Nana turned the last corner before she saw her gate in full view. She saw James as he stood with a man in the airline uniform, engaged in conversation. He looked down the hall and spotted her.

"There she is." James told the attendant. "I told you." He ran toward her and relieved her of her garment bag.

"Did we miss the flight?" Nana's face was moist with perspiration and she appeared disheveled.

"What happened to you, you had me nervous." He walked in swift strides with Nana in tow. "The flight is being held for you." He glanced at Nana and smiled as they walked up to the door of the gate, where the attendant waited.

Nana handed her wrinkled boarding pass to the attendant. "Thank you for waiting for me, I really appreciate it."

"I'm sorry ma'am but I cannot accept this boarding pass in this condition." The attendant told her with a serious expression, and Nana was distraught and speechless. Then the attendant burst into laughter and confessed that he was joking, as James joined in the laughter but Nana was not amused.

Nana was grateful that God had answered her prayer to enable her to make the flight, as she and James waved to the attendant and made their way down the ramp toward the waiting plane. As they walked through the first class cabin to their economy seats, everyone shot them curious and nasty looks. They wondered who the couple was that the flight was held up for them. It did not make sense that they were in economy class, yet they were important enough to keep plane load of passengers waiting. Nana did not look at anyone as she took her seat in the window, while James took the aisle. The fight was not full so the middle seat was vacant. As they settled in, Nana shared her experience in the Atlanta airport with James, and how she ran through the terminal. James told her how he convinced the gate attendant to hold up the flight for her. She reclined her seat after take-off, closed her eyes and thanked God.

Nana and James were back in Herndon, and back to their jobs. Nana found it difficult to return to Eastern Travel after her meeting with her prospective producers. She returned to the office that Monday to find Valerie with a bad case of the shingles. Valerie's face and arms were covered with red pimples, and she appeared to have some sort of white paste rubbed on her. She already was not the best looking woman, and she should not have been in public by the way she looked. She wasted no time telling Nana how painful it was, and she would not be able to stay the full day in the office.

Nana was sympathetic. "Are you going to be okay, Val? I'm really sorry."

Her sympathy was short lived after Valerie snapped back at her. "How do I know if I'm going to be okay? All I know is that I'm in a lot of pain, and I'm depending on you to be here in the office so I can stay at home."

Nana said no more to Valerie for the rest of the morning until she left the office at noon. Nana was somewhat relieved to see Valerie leave the office. She was mean spirited when she was well and she was just as awful even when she was ill. Nana thought that the shingles could not have happened to a better person.

Later that evening while speaking with Alec, she had reason to panic. "She should not be in the office because shingles can be contagious. Have you ever had chickenpox?" Alec asked Nana.

"No, I don't believe so." Nana was alarmed. "So Valerie knew that she was contagious and she went in to the office. That woman cares about no one; she is wicked and evil."

"She exposed all of you to who have not had the chickenpox virus to shingles." Alec was concerned for Nana. "If you have not had chickenpox and you are exposed to shingles, you will not contract shingles but you will get chickenpox."

"If she comes in to that office with chalk all over her this week, I will walk out of there."

"You should not return at all, if you ask me but I cannot tell you what to do." Alec tried to be diplomatic.

"You are right, and I know that you are but I have a plan and I need to follow my plan." Nana was worried but she remained calm because she did not want Alec to know how worried she was about the possibility of contracting that disease from Valerie.

Valerie did not return to the office after that Monday; she became very ill and was taken to the emergency room several times.

Nana continued to report to work at Eastern Travel, while she searched for an Intellectual Property attorney. Valerie returned to the office when she was healed from her attack of shingles. Her attitude toward her employees did not improve, especially toward Nana. Nana caught her looking at her with disdain several times in the office. She felt uncomfortable and unprotected when Valerie was near her. She did not want to resign her job until she signed the contract with Zebra Productions. She was afraid that Valerie might attempt to hurt her physically during one of her tantrum episodes.

A Test of Friendship

James had lived with Nana for a little more than seven months. He showed no signs of any intention of moving out. He was comfortable, and never offered to assist with any bills during his entire stay. Her water quarterly bill jumped from $25.00 to $45.00. Her electric bill increased to double of what it was prior to James' stay. In spite of Nana's humanitarian heart, James overstayed his welcome, and she continued to pray and ask God to give James a reason to leave. She wondered how long he planned to stay with her without making a contribution to the household expenses.

James was so comfortable in the house that every Friday night he sat in the living room of the townhouse as he watched television and sipped on a couple of martinis. Since he was meticulous about everything he did, he took care with the preparation of his martinis. He had the proper shaker, gin and liqueur mixer, along with green olives. He usually put the olives on toothpicks and placed it in the martini glass. He was the only person in the house that used toothpicks on a regular basis.

Nana finished cooking her meal on a Saturday afternoon and proceeded to clean up the kitchen. After she loaded the dishwasher, she turned on the garbage disposal and it did not work. She was astonished that the disposal did not come on but only made a low humming sound. When James returned from his Saturday outing that evening, she shared with him that the garbage disposal was not working. She did not suspect him of breaking it but she only shared the information to alert him not to use the disposal.

Nana called a repair company and asked them to check her garbage disposal. The repairman told her that the disposal was damaged and it had to be replaced. Nana held her breath until he told her the cost of replacing the garbage disposal. He was prepared to replace it that afternoon but it would cost her $250.00. She was distraught for someone on a budget to pay that unexpected amount. She had no choice but to have him replace the disposal. She did not want to let it go unattended until the damage became worse. He opened the disposal to replace it and informed Nana that he pulled a few pieces of toothpicks from inside the garbage disposal. She knew without a doubt that it was James' toothpicks from his martinis that had most likely mistakenly fallen in the disposal. She knew that James would not intentionally drop toothpicks in the disposal, and that it was an accident.

James was out that afternoon when the repairman diagnosed and replaced the garbage disposal. Nana approached him about the toothpicks in the disposal but he denied having anything to do with that.

"I saw the pieces of toothpicks he pulled out from under there, James." Nana wished he did not lie about something like that.

"I usually put all of my toothpicks in the trash." He defended.

"Well I suppose a ghost put them down in there because I don't use toothpicks." Though Nana's remark was sarcastic, her voice did not exhibit anger. James did not take her remark well because he kept quiet after that and retreated to his room upstairs.

In the weeks that followed, James was not his usual bubbly self around the house. He spoke to Nana but it was clear that the garbage disposal issue had put a strain on their friendship. Nana felt betrayed; she had defended him to her friends and against protest, she had welcomed him into her home. She had never asked him to contribute anything toward household expenses. She at least expected him to offer to share the $250.00 cost to replace the garbage disposal. She felt embarrassed to mention this issue to her friends. She did not want to hear the obvious, 'I told you so'. Instead, she continued to pray for God to step in and have James move out.

Nana was introduced to several intellectual property attorneys in the weeks that followed. She was most impressed by the husband and wife team of attorneys in downtown Washington, D.C. She was referred to them by Frank's attorney in Dallas. She had a brief phone conversation with Sara and Elliott Wilcox. They extended a lunch invitation to Nana to give them time to get to know her. She sent them a copy of her play and a copy of the contract by email two days prior to her conversation with them. They had already read the script and expressed how impressed they were by the story line.

A week later, Nana requested the afternoon off from work. She did not want to use her one hour lunch break to meet the Wilcox's, and rush through lunch with them to hurry back to work. Valerie granted her the afternoon, for which she was grateful.

Nana stepped out of the taxi and checked the number on the canopy of the building entrance to make sure that she stood before the correct building on Vermont Avenue, Northwest. The lobby was plush with a large oval glass desk in the center of the room. She walked up to the desk and greeted the guard behind it.

"Sign in, take the elevator to the 4th floor and make a right down the hall, suite 420." The guard instructed, as Nana obeyed.

She stepped out of the elevator and followed the guard's direction down the long hall. She was dressed in a navy pant suit with a burgundy cotton French cuffed shirt. As she entered the reception area of the Wilcox Law Firm, she was greeted by a smiling young blond. "Hello, are you Ms. Nkuku?"

Nana walked up to the desk. "Hello, yes I am but you may call me Nana." She flashed the receptionist a smile. "I'm a bit early for my appointment."

"Please have a seat. I will tell Mr. and Mrs. Wilcox that you are here."

"Thank you." Nana took her seat to wait for her prospective attorneys to appear. She picked up the latest issue of World Magazine. As she leafed through the magazine, she noticed a story that caught her attention. It was about a woman who had died at the hands of her abusive husband in Uganda. Nana read part of the story before the attorneys came out to greet her. The man had beaten his wife until she lay lifeless on the ground. According to the story, their five year old son and 7 year old daughter had witnessed their father kill their mother. She made a mental note to remember to purchase a copy of her own. She wanted to finish reading the story and share it with her friends. The story made her think about abused women in the world, and how many more women had died at their spouses' or boyfriends' weaponry hands. Her thought was interrupted when the two attorneys and their paralegal entered the reception area.

"Hello Nana, it is a great pleasure to meet you." Mr. Wilcox was the first to make his appearance.

Nana stood and extended her hand to Mr. Wilcox. "It is my pleasure likewise." She noticed Sara Wilcox directly behind her husband. "You must be Mrs. Wilcox." She extended her hand as Sara offered her own hand to Nana. "I am very pleased to meet you."

"Please call me Sara." Sara shook Nana's hand and held onto it for a moment. "I hope you are hungry. We are taking you to a nice little restaurant."

"We heard you like Thai food." Elliott Wilcox told her as he led the way through the door of their office, after he had introduced their paralegal, Ginny Hall.

"I do like Thai food very much." Nana blushed. She knew that Frank must have told his attorney, who told them. She wondered how much they already knew about her.

Lunch was more enjoyable than she imagined it would be. She ordered from their vegetarian menu. It was one of the reasons why she liked Thai food;

the many spices they used, similar to West African cuisine and they catered to vegetarians.

The attorneys wanted to know about Nana's childhood and Ghana. She told them about female genital mutilation but she also shared the proud history of her native home. "I've always dreamed about becoming a playwright, even when I was a child."

"You turned out to be a really good one too." Sara told her. She was able to envision Nana's play on stage or on the screen when she read it a few days before their lunch date.

"We reviewed the contract from the producers and it is in good order." Elliott Wilcox told Nana. "We do not see anything in that we would want to change but with your approval, we could add a few clauses to it."

"What are the clauses?" Nana was curious. So far she was impressed by the Wilcox's knowledge of intellectual property law. They left no eyes not dotted and no T's uncrossed. She liked the legal advice they gave her.

"We want to make sure that you receive compensation percentage in the future each time the television movie is shown." Sara explained to her. "We want the movie to be produced and released first. With the success of the movie, we want them to stage the play in New York on Broadway."

"And with the production of both movie and stage, we want you to sit in on the castings and be a part of the decision makers in casting." Elliott added. "After all, you created these characters in the script and only you know exactly what they should sound and look like."

"What do you think?" Sara asked her. She noticed that Nana was quiet as they spoke and she wanted to make sure that she agreed with what they proposed before they moved forward.

"Oh I most certainly agree with everything you are saying." Nana assured them. "What is the next step now?"

"Would you like us to represent you?" Elliott asked her with a smile.

"Absolutely but I need to know your terms and what my obligations are." Nana was concerned about legal fees and they were affordable.

"We will draw up a contract between you and our firm." Sara told her. "We will go over our contract with you in a follow up meeting. Then we will contact the attorneys of the production company to arrange the meeting in Atlanta."

Nana smiled at Sara. "I'm glad I have you to handle things from here."

"After our next meeting, we will handle all phone calls and arrange all trips, etc. for you."

They finished their meal on a pleasant note. She chatted a little with Ginny and got to know her while they ate. They parted company outside the restaurant as Nana took her time in her walk to the nearest Metro station. She was excited and looked forward to sharing her day with Frank and Shirley. She wanted to tell James about her lunch with the Wilcox attorneys. After all, he had been so kind by accompanying her to Atlanta. She will never forget how he had the gate agent hold up the flight for her in Atlanta. She felt sad that she had offended him over the garbage disposal but she just wished he had owned up to it.

Chapter Twelve

A TWIST OF LIFE

Search me, O God, and know my heart; test me and know my anxious thoughts. – Psalm 139:23 (NLT)

Nana left the house with James for her job at Eastern Travel. Though she was on the verge of great success, she continued to remain humble and report to her job each day. She always knew that God had great plans for her future. That same knowledge helped her get through turbulent times in America. She was able to get through each day at Eastern Travel under the wrath of Valerie because she knew that there was something to which she looked forward.

James parked his car as he did each day and they took the Metro to their respective jobs. Nana was settled in for the morning. She usually ate her breakfast at her desk as she prepared to commence her work before the phones began to ring.

Nana kept her mobile phone on 'silent' when she was in the office. It was 11:00 that morning when her mobile phone began to hum. She looked at the caller's ID and recognized the number. It was the number of Ghanaian Embassy. Her cousin at the Embassy never called her while she was at work so she knew that it was an emergency. She answered, "Hello."

"Nana, how are you?" The voice was that of her cousin at the Embassy.

"Adjoa this is a surprise." She did not like the sound of her cousin's voice. "Is everything ok?"

"Nana, I have very bad news." Adjoa's voice cracked as Nana remained quiet. "Aunty Keekee dropped dead this morning in her house." Adjoa was not merely a cousin of Nana's, she was her first cousin. Adjoa was the only child of Keekee's sister who preceded her in death several years before. She and Nana had a close relationship until Nana's public appearances against female genital mutilation. The girls continued to talk on occasions but not often enough. Adjoa came to the States more recently.

Nana screamed, "What are you saying?" She ran out of the office as she said, "No, no."

"Nana what happened?" Amber followed her out of the office but Nana was still talking to Adjoa. "Are you okay?"

"My mother passed away." Nana told Amber. "I am speaking to my cousin; I will be back in when I'm done." She was still crying as she spoke.

"I'm so sorry, I'm really sorry." Amber told her as she hurried back to the office. Valerie had sent her to find out what had happened to Nana.

Adjoa explained to Nana that her mother was in the kitchen preparing breakfast when she collapsed and suffered a heart attack. She died instantly. Her neighbor was there to have breakfast with her and witnessed the incident. She called for help but by the time they arrived at the hospital, Keekee was dead.

Nana had lost her father a few years before but the impact was not as grave as the idea of losing her mother. She ended her conversation with Adjoa and returned to the office. She sat at her desk and continued her work like a robot. Valerie came out of her office, and it was the most humane behavior she ever showed to Nana.

"I'm sorry to hear about your mother." Valerie gave Nana a pat on the back. "You need to go home to absorb the news. Please do not stay here."

"Thank you but my ride is not available to get me home until after working hours anyway." She knew that James was at work and she had ridden in with him that morning.

"I can arrange to have a sedan drive you home or take you to wherever you care to go." She was shocked to hear Valerie make an offer like that.

"Thank you." Nana was grateful for the offer from Valerie. She began to gather her things to leave.

The other co-workers then gathered around her desk one at a time to express their condolences. Teah embraced Nana as tears escaped her eyes.

Antomeyer gave her shoulder a slight touch, and told her how sorry he was. Amber told her again how sorry she was and embraced her that time. Then Janet walked over, rocking from side to side as she did when she walked. She told Nana to have her sympathy and wished her well, and she rocked back to her desk.

Valerie instructed Teah to call the limo company and ask for a car to come and take Nana where she needed to go. Teah asked Nana for her address and within half an hour, the sedan was in front of the building. Nana thanked Valerie again and bid goodbye to everyone and left the building.

She got in the sedan as the driver held the door and helped her in. Teah had already informed him that Nana lost her mother. He extended his sympathy as he got back in the driver's seat. He was from Ethiopia, held a brief conversation with Nana as he drove through Washington toward Route I-66.

Nana called James from the sedan. "My mother passed away this morning." She told him how it happened, and that she was already on her way home. She told him about Valerie's kind gesture. She did not want him to wait for her at the Metro station that evening.

"I'm so sorry, my sister." James was shocked by the news. "Is there anything I can do for you or pick up on my way home?"

"No not at this time." She sighed. "I just want to go home, have some quiet time. I have to make a few calls."

"Take it easy, and I will see you this evening."

"Thanks." She hung up and closed her eyes as the shocking news sank in her mind. She knew she would have to make the trip home to Ghana for the funeral. She was looking forward to the trip to Africa which their foundation planned to make the following year.

Nana continued to keep her eyes closed as she slipped into the memory of her childhood with her mother. She recalled being angry for many years with her mother for taking her to the bush that day and allowed the Medicine Woman to mutilate her. She was glad that she had forgiven her mother so long ago. She and her mother mended their relationship over the years, especially after her father passed away. She remembered how her mother combed her hair as a child. Her hair was kept short when she was a child with a part at the side. Her mother's friends always commented on how cute she looked with her hair cut short. Her mother confessed that she was grateful that she did not need to braid her daughter's hair. She remembered the time that Kiddi came over to her house to play; it was April 1st that day. They gave a note to a man whom they knew was illiterate. The note read, "Keep this fool going around." The poor man took the note to several houses, and when people read the note, they sent him to the next house until someone pitied him and told him to go home. The person told him that he had been a victim of April's Fool Day. The man complained to Nana's parents and she and Kiddi got into trouble that day. She never played April's Fool again. She shook her head at the thought of her childhood.

It was a long ride to Herndon from Dupont Circle. She thought she was in Ghana for a while during the drive, until the driver stopped before her house.

"Miss Nkuku, we are here at your house." Her eyes were still closed when she heard the driver's voice.

"Oh I'm sorry." She grabbed her brief case and handbag while he walked around to help her out of the car. "Thank you very much." She handed him a $10.00 tip from her wallet. "I really appreciate it."

"Thank you." He was back to the driver's side of the car. "I wish you all the best in your loss."

"Thanks again." She walked up the stairs as he drove away from their driveway.

Nana dropped her briefcase and handbag on the sofa and headed for her bedroom. She fell across the bed and allowed the tears to flow. She curled up in a fetal position like she did when her mother held her as a child. She cried until she drifted off to sleep.

When she awoke, Nana called Shirley and Frank; she called Kiddi and Jean-Claude, Alec and Cynthia at the public relations firm. She called and left a message for Sara and Elliott Wilcox, but spoke with Ginny Hall. She was not in the mood for much talking so she kept her phone calls and conversations brief.

Nana knew what her next move was. She needed to begin preparations for her trip to Ghana. Adjoa had already told her that she planned to make the trip to her aunt's funeral. Nana called Ghana and spoke with her mother's neighbor and a couple of other people in their neighborhood. It was a long time since she lived in Ghana. She did not know how to make funeral arrangements more than 10 thousand miles away. She asked her mother's neighbor, Mrs. Nkrumah to make the arrangements on her behalf. Nana promised her that she would take care of the cost when she arrived in Ghana.

"I will purchase the burial attire from here." Nana told Mrs. Nkrumah. "I will also bring anything else we will need for the funeral and the repast." She was not sure what would be needed. "Why don't you make a list of what will be needed for the repast and the funeral?"

"I think that is a good idea." Mrs. Nkrumah agreed. "I will make one list for the repast and one for the funeral itself. The items to be purchased here in Ghana, I will inquire about the prices."

"Thank you. Do you have email or access to it?"

"I do not use emails myself but I can have my son send you an email with the costs." She gave Nana her son's email address.

"Thanks again. I will email your son my flight itinerary once I have it confirmed. Nana ended the call. She was grateful for Mrs. Nkrumah and her willingness to handle everything in Ghana.

Nana returned to work the following day, even though her mother had just passed away the day before. She wanted to prepare her airline ticket, speak to Valerie about her time off and finalize loose ends prior to her departure. In addition, she preferred not to sit around the house alone. She was quick to regret that she went in that day. Valerie's kind gesture from the day before was short lived. She got into a fight with Nana and shouted at her several times.

"Please be mindful that my mother just died yesterday." Nana reminded her.

"Then you should have stayed home." Valerie snapped back after Nana's mild reaction to her shouts.

"Perhaps I should not have come in." Nana ignored her the rest of the day, as she booked her flight to Accra to leave the Friday of that week. Her mother's funeral was scheduled for the following weekend. She coordinated her flight with Adjoa so that they traveled together. But just before Nana and Adjoa purchased their tickets, she received a surprise call from her dear brother, Jean-Claude.

"I hope you have not purchased your ticket yet." Jean-Claude told her after she returned home from work that night.

"No I have not purchased it yet but Adjoa and I plan to do that tomorrow when I go to work."

"I will take care of your ticket. I have so many airline passes that I must use before an expiration date." He explained. "No need for you to spend your money on air fare when you need it for other things."

"Oh my brother, you are really awesome." She wiped a tear as it escaped from her eye and she sniffed. "I just don't know what to say." She was touched by his gesture.

"Say nothing my dear, just show up at Dulles Airport. Your pass will be there waiting for you." He thought for a moment. "I will have two sets of passes there for both you and Adjoa so that she will accompany you on the same flight."

"She will be grateful. Thank you Jean-Claude."

"It is my pleasure my sister. I will meet you at Charles de Gaulle Airport; I will join you on the flight. I spoke with Frank yesterday and he told me that Shirley intends to attend the funeral. They will call you later tonight but she is booked on a different carrier and will arrive a day after we do."

Nana was in tears. She did not expect any of them to attend the funeral except Kiddi. She was appreciative that three of her dearest friends would be there with her when she put her mother to rest. Frank was unable to make the trip with them; training camp started the following week but Nana fully understood.

Though it was far from a fun trip she was about to take, Nana felt a pang of excitement. It was home going for her mother but it was homecoming for Kiddi and her. While she had mixed feelings about going back to Ghana after many years, she also looked forward to it.

Nana went to the mall the next evening after work. Shopping was one of her least favorite things to do. She only went to the mall when she had the need to purchase a piece of garment. She purchased 3 black dresses, 2 black skirts and 2 white blouses. She purchased a dress for Mrs. Nkrumah as a gift for all that she did with the preparations of the funeral.

The following day, Nana took off from work and met Adjoa in Silver Spring, Maryland where Adjoa lived. She told Nana about a funeral home that sold burial dresses. Nana did not feel comfortable going to a funeral home but she had no choice.

The undertaker expected them when they arrived because Adjoa had called him and set up an appointment. He led them to the elevator as Nana walked with reluctance. As they stepped off the elevator, he led the way to the room with the dresses. The doors to other rooms were open and Nana had an eye view of corpses in caskets. She was taken aback and did not appreciate seeing corpses to whom she had no connection. The undertaker showed them several dresses. There were many from which to choose but Nana just wanted to select one and get out of there.

"I have another closet with more selections." He began to show them additional dresses when Nana interrupted him.

"That is okay, I have already decided on the one I like." She wondered if the undertaker thought they were at the mall on a shopping spree. She held up a dress with sequence down the front. "My mother's favorite color was pink so this is perfect for her. She would have liked this." Nana held up the dress while Adjoa agreed.

They followed the undertaker closely as they boarded the elevator, trying not to look in the other rooms with the corpses. They paid for the dress, thanked him and left the funeral home. Nana did not tell Mrs. Nkrumah that she had purchased a burial dress for her mother. She wanted to surprise her.

Nana's Prayer is Answered

Nana was in the kitchen. She was exhausted but she needed to eat before she went upstairs to retire. James joined her in the kitchen but declined her invitation to join her at the table.

"How are things going in preparation of your trip?" James inquired.

"I'm making great progress." She bit on a carrot. "Thanks for asking." Things were polite between them since the incident over the garbage disposal. Nana moved on and forgot about it. James was the kind that held grudges, and she disliked that about him. She did not like to sit in judgment over anyone; she only wondered how some people practiced such habits, yet claimed to be Christians.

"When are you leaving?" She thought she had already told him but he probably forgot.

"Adjoa and I leave on Sunday. Our flight is at 3:00 in the afternoon."

"Well, I'm glad that you don't leave until Sunday. I wanted to let you know that I'm moving out on Saturday." He looked for a reaction from Nana.

"Oh, may I ask where you will be living?" She was surprised but it was what she had prayed to God for many months. She did not believe that it took her mother's death to prompt his move.

"I found an apartment in Southeast Washington." He shrugged his shoulders. "It's a one bedroom but it is all I need. I will leave you my telephone number at the apartment and the address. My mobile will remain the same."

"I am happy for you." She became emotional for a moment. "I will miss you but I am still happy for you to accomplish this. I know how much you have been through in the past months."

"I will miss you too, my sister." He hung his head in thought. "I appreciate all that you did for me. Many people would never have extended such gesture."

"Well you know what they say about us." She smiled. "It is that African hospitality." She made a funny face and they laughed. "You better keep in touch. I will give you a call when I get back."

"Sure I will." The ice between them broke and he sat across from her at the breakfast bar in the kitchen. "So are you ready for this homecoming?"

She smiled and nodded. "I suppose I am, though I must be honest." Nana pushed her empty salad bowl aside. "I'm a little scared but it is something I have to do. At least I have enough support from my friends."

James was up early on Saturday morning, ready to move his belongings out of the house. Nana wanted to see him off. She was dressed early, and ate breakfast with James before he loaded the last of his things in his car. He moved his belongings out a little at a time.

"Well, this is it my sister." He had a big hug for her. "Again, I thank you for that African hospitality." They laughed.

"It was my pleasure." She stood at the door as he walked out onto the steps. "I wish you all the best in your new home." She waved as he returned her wave and walked down the steps.

Return to the Homeland

Nana and Adjoa stood in the long security line that reminded Nana of an endless funeral procession. She felt that it was a bad time to get such a reminder. She held her Ghanaian passport in her hand, along with her driver's license. Her carry-on bag was suspended from her right shoulder.

She chatted with Adjoa as they made their way through the line. Nana wore a pair of black jeans and a matching black short sleeved shirt. She still believed in dress-up travel but she also wanted to be comfortable since they had a long journey ahead of them. Adjoa wore a white blouse with black slacks. Due to their tradition, they were expected to arrive in mourning attire.

The two young ladies arrived at the security checkpoint where they removed their shoes, watches and other items. They made it through security without incident and headed for their departure gate. Adjoa released a long sigh of relief. "I thought we would never get to the gate." The gate was located in the international terminal with several corners to turn and moving stairs.

"I know what you mean." Nana concurred as they took their seats in the waiting area. "Traveling is not what it used to be." She chuckled. "I had so much fun traveling around the world to various countries on familiarization trips. It is no longer the fun we had back then."

"I feel like I'm listening to an old woman." Adjoa turned to face her cousin. "What happened to you?" She shook her head in disbelief. "This is not the Nana with whom I grew up."

"What do you mean?" Nana placed her right hand over her chest. "I am the same Nana Nkuku, only older and wiser." Her face took on a more serious appearance. "Have you ever thought about what happens after death?"

"No and I don't want to think about it either. Do you? Adjoa wondered what Nana had in mind.

"You have to think about it and accept the fact that we all must leave this world someday." Nana wanted to share her experience with her cousin but fumbled somewhat. "I have indeed changed but nothing like you think. I now have a relationship with God, and it is the best relationship I have ever had in my entire life." Adjoa was speechless as her eyes widened in an indescribable fashion. Nana continued with her revelation to her baffled cousin. "When I discovered Christianity and the being that is responsible for all of us and the universe, I realized that I could not be the person I was."

"How did you discover all of that?" Adjoa was finally out of her shock, and her speech was restored. "I am confused. When did all of this happen to you?"

"My roommates, Frank, Shirley and Jean-Claude are Christians but you see, they were born into Christianity." Nana smiled. "They told me the little that they knew from their childhood, and Shirley gave me a copy of the Christian Holy Book, called the Bible. I began to read that book, and discovered that it is the greatest book that was ever written."

"Wow, I don't know anything about that sort of thing, and I have heard that religion can be scary." Both girls laughed at Adjoa's statement.

The announcement came over the intercom that their flight began to board. "Hold that thought, we will pick up where we left off." Nana told her as they picked up their carry-on bags and joined the line to make their way to the plane. Unlike Nana, Adjoa went to Ghana every other year on her bi-annual vacation. She kept closer ties to the country and their culture than Nana and Kiddi. Although Adjoa was also a victim of female genital mutilation, she held no hard feelings about it. She regarded it as a part of their culture and felt that it was a society initiation into womanhood that should not be discussed. She did not fault Nana and Kiddi for exposing the secrets of their culture but she refused to participate in the exposure. That was the reason why Nana did not keep in close touch with her cousin. They were separated only by the American Legion Bridge, which is the state line between Maryland and Virginia but Nana realized that the bridge was only the physical structure of the separation. There was a much deeper separation between them, and she did not know how she would close that gap.

They were seated in the mid-section of the plane. Nana was in the window seat and Adjoa was in the aisle. Nana liked the window because she enjoyed sleeping while inflight. As the flight lifted off the tarmac, Nana continued her conversation with Adjoa about her new life as a Christian.

"I see that you are really serious about this new life of yours, cousin." Adjoa was still in disbelief. "Was that your Christian book you read before we took off?"

"I am more serious than I have ever been about anything in my life." She looked her cousin in the eye. "It is called a Bible, the Holy book of Christians." Nana looked out of the window. "You should try reading it someday."

"I cannot make any promises but if this book helps you have the kind of success you are having at this point in your life, then I will not rule it out completely." The girls exchanged smiles.

Sweet Home

Nana and Adjoa had a safe landing at Charles de Gaulle Airport in Paris, France. As they approached their connecting gate, they spotted Jean-Claude. He waved and hurried over to them, where he picked Nana up off the floor in a warm embrace. They held onto each other for what seemed longer than it really was.

"I am so happy to see you, my sister." He told Nana while he still held her. "It is a pity that we have to reunite under such sad circumstance." He finally released her from their embrace.

"The feeling is mutual, my brother." She ruffled his hair as she always did to tease him. "I missed you so much."

"I missed you guys too." He looked her over. "You look great – still looking the same as always."

"Look at you – as handsome as ever." They found three vacant seats in the gate area and rested from carrying their overnight bags. "So tell me all about your new position." Nana was happy to be reunited with Jean-Claude. It was a long time since they saw each other.

"Before I get into that, let me acknowledge Adjoa." The two were wrapped in each other's presence, that Adjoa was nearly invisible. The three laughed. "How are you, dear?" Jean-Claude asked Adjoa. "I think the last time I saw you was several years ago at a party at the Ghanaian Embassy."

"You are correct – it was the last time I saw you." Adjoa exchanged kisses on each cheek. "I'm doing fine, except for the loss of my aunt."

Jean-Claude became serious. "I know – I am really sorry. Please have my deepest sympathy, both of you." He never had the opportunity of meeting Nana's mother. She did not attend their graduation ceremonies from college. Nana's father came alone for her graduation. He wished he had had the pleasure of meeting the woman responsible for giving birth to one of the nicest people he knew in his life. "I know what it is like to lose a parent, but to lose both parents is still beyond my mindset." Though young at the time, he still had the memory of losing his father. "I just do not want to think about what I would do if I lost my mother."

"Let's change the subject." Nana interrupted. She did not want to be saddened again. She knew that once they arrived in Ghana, there would be a great deal of weeping and mourning. "Let's get back to catching up."

"I like my new post a lot." Jean-Claude told her. Being Purser, I get to call the shots in flight." He made a funny face and the girls laughed along with him.

"So are you a passenger today or a Purser?" Nana teased.

"I am a passenger – I will be right there in the cabin with you two ladies."

"Great, I'm glad – we can chat, sleep, eat and chat some more." She wanted to hear everything about him, and he was eager to hear about her movie deal. She updated him on the status of her contract. "Everything is on hold now with the contract until I return. They understood."

"I wonder what your boss Valerie will say when she finds out that you have a movie." Jean-Claude shook his head in disbelief as he remembered Valerie's behavior to Nana. "Let's board ladies." He stood and waited while the girls took their bags and started toward the gate. The three boarded the flight and found their seats. The configuration of the aircraft was two-seven-two. Nana was seated in the aisle with Adjoa in the window, while Jean-Claude was in the aisle across from Nana.

Nana took out her Bible and began to read the twenty-third Psalm. She always read from the Book of Psalms just before she boarded a flight or prior to take-off, since she became a Christian. The twenty-third Psalm was one of her favorite Psalms. Nana looked over at Adjoa and smiled. "This verse makes me feel fearless; it says, 'Yea though I walk through the valley of the shadow of death, I will fear no evil for you are with me. Your rod and staff, they comfort me.' Those words are the most comforting words I have ever heard."

Adjoa only returned Nana's smile and wondered if she would ever understand what her cousin had become. She decided to remain quiet since she was confused about this Christianity thing that had taken control of Nana.

The flight attendants served dinner, and Jean-Claude was grateful that he no longer did that for a living. He was also grateful that he was a passenger on that flight instead of an employee. He fell asleep shortly after dinner, and so did Adjoa. Nana tried to sleep but her mind played tricks with her; she thought about her mother and if she would ever become a mother. She knew that she would not have a child because of the female genital mutilation she suffered so many years before. Nana closed her eyes and vowed that she would never subject her little girl to that dreadful act, if

God would bless her with a child. She finally drifted off to sleep and slept in peace for the rest of the night, as the aircraft crossed the Atlantic Ocean.

The flight attendants turned on the lights in the cabin as the flight made its way over the Sahara. The passengers on board felt the heat enter the cabin. "We are home." Adjoa turned to Nana with excitement and anticipation. "Do you feel it?"

"I smell it as well." Nana returned the excited feeling.

"It is all the usual for me, ladies." Jean-Claude offered. "I fly this route so often that I never notice the difference."

"I know- you are coming to your second home continent, Jean-Claude." Nana told him.

Jean-Claude chuckled and shook his head. "Actually, I am the man of three continents." He adjusted his view of Nana and Adjoa across the aisle from him as a flight attendant walked by. "I was born in Europe – I spent most of my adult life in the United States – I travel to West and North Africa more than I travel to anywhere else in the world."

"Wait until I tell Shirley what your new name is – the man of three continents." Nana teased as she got laughs from both Jean-Claude and Adjoa.

As Nana and Adjoa continued to experience the Sahara Desert warmth, the excitement built even more. Nana's heart beat rapidly, as her palms moistened. She felt faint but she decided not to worry Adjoa and Jean-Claude. She figured the feeling would pass.

"Are you okay?" Jean-Claude was not easily fooled.

"I'm fine." Nana pretended but she did not look well.

"Well you do not look fine." Jean-Claude studied her closely. "You are perspiring profusely." He frowned, as a flight attendant walked by their seats. "Excusez moi." He spoke in French to the flight attendant.

She stopped and looked at Nana with concern. "Oui?" She turned to Jean-Claude. "Vous vous sentez bien?" She asked Nana in French at first, and she realized that the passenger was English-speaking. "Are you feeling okay? I am sorry." She looked more concerned upon seeing Nana's condition. "I'll get her something to drink." She hurried toward the back and returned with a can of ginger ale and a cup of ice.

Nana released the tray in front of her, and the flight attendant placed the ginger ale and ice on it. "Thank you." Nana managed a slight smile, and she was grateful for the cold drink.

Jean-Claude was quiet but he was confused about Nana's sudden attack of perspiration and weakness. He had never seen her in that state. He wondered if her mother's death was just catching up with her. He hoped that whatever the problem, it was only something temporary. He went to the lavatory and he returned to find both Adjoa and Nana asleep. He decided to take a nap while the ladies slept.

The announcement on the intercom woke them. "Good Morning passengers – this is your captain. We are only fifteen minutes from Accra. We ask you to remain seated and keep your seat belts fastened."

The flight landed in Accra, with Kiddi and Mrs. Nkrumah at the airport to meet them. Kiddi arrived a day earlier. She was glad to see the new arrivals again. She and Nana held their embrace for a long time as they wept. "Thanks for coming." Nana whispered to her childhood friend.

"I would not miss it." Kiddi whispered back to her.

Nana fell into the open arms of Mrs. Nkrumah as she wept with bitter emotions. "Thank you for being the friend you were to Mama."

The older lady comforted her through her own tears. "She did not suffer."

Nana stepped out of Mrs. Nkrumah's arms to mind her manners. "Mrs. Nkrumah, this is my roommate, Jean-Claude Girard."

"It is my pleasure to meet you, Madam." Jean-Claude exchanged handshakes with Mrs. Nkrumah. "Please accept my sympathy."

Jean-Claude greeted Kiddi with a big hug and Adjoa and Kiddi greeted as they reunited after a long time. Kiddi hired a large Mercedes sports utility vehicle to accommodate everyone. They piled in the vehicle and headed for the hotel.

Adjoa shared Nana's hotel room. Nana did not want to stay at her mother's home since she had not lived there for many years. Adjoa's mother and father were already deceased, and their home was occupied by renters. Kiddi was in a separate room and so was Jean-Claude. Shirley was expected the following day, and her room was reserved.

Shirley arrived in Accra, and she was ecstatic about being on African soil for the first time in her life. Her excitement caused her to ignore the excessive heat. "I am so happy to see my dearest friends after so long." Shirley exclaimed as she embraced each of her friends. She and Nana held each other and cried.

The friends left from the airport and went directly to the funeral home for the viewing of the body of Nana's mother. Nana cried harder when she saw her mother's corpse. Everyone present at the viewing was touched by Nana's mournful reaction. Adjoa cried nearly as hard as Nana for her dear aunt. Kiddi was seen wiping the corners of her eyes on a couple of occasion.

Mrs. Nkuku was put to rest the next morning in a traditional ceremony, with the beating of drums, singing and dancing around the grave site. They moved the body from the funeral home to the cemetery. The deceased was not affiliated with any religion. She only believed in tradition customs. Nana did not participate in the dancing and singing at the grave. She stood beside a tree and prayed in silence for the soul of her mother. She asked God to save her mother's soul, so that she would be reunited with her someday. She believed in the after-life.

With Mrs. Nkuku in the grave, Nana was faced with the task of going through her mother's belongings. She did not look forward to it but she had Mrs. Nkrumah, Adjoa, Kiddi and Shirley to assist her with that. Nana's mother did not leave much but she did leave her daughter a few pieces of 18-karat gold jewelry. Her mother had a closet full of custom made traditional attires. Since her mother was much larger in size than Nana, most of the clothes were given to Mrs. Nkrumah. Nana only took a sash of their traditional cloth, the Kente. Her mother's authentic Kente held sentimental value. Most Ghanaians save their money for many years to be able to afford to purchase an authentic piece of Kente. Nana knew how proud her mother was of the Kente. She held the kente sash to her chest as the tears streamed down her cheeks.

"It is okay to cry it out, Nana." Kiddi put her arm around her shoulders to comfort her. "I know how it feels but I found that you cannot cry it all out at once."

"I know but you know how the mixed emotions are." Nana looked at her childhood friend through tears. "I remained angry at my mother for so many years for allowing that woman to perform FGM on me." She was hysterical. "Now I wish I had not wasted so much time being angry at her."

"You know that the same thing happened to me when my own mother passed away." Kiddi reassured her. "I was never given the opportunity to make up with my mother but you were able to do that with yours."

"I suppose we must count our blessings and be thankful for them." Nana stopped crying and returned to her mother's belongings.

The four women finished packing everything that was being picked up the next morning by a thrift store. Nana told Mrs. Nkrumah to help herself to whatever she wanted from her mother's clothes.

"Nana, look at what I found." Adjoa held up an envelope. "It is a letter from Aunty to you."

Adjoa handed the envelope to Nana. "Well, let's see what Mama wrote." She opened the envelope with haste. Everyone took a seat to hear what was in the letter as Nana read. "My Dearest Daughter, when you read this letter, I will be dead but I want you to know that I loved you. You will never know how I felt the day you were cut – I relived the pain that I felt on the day of my own cutting. I cannot tell you that I am sorry about the cutting but I am sorry for the pain you felt. I know that you and your friends started that organization to tell people to hate our tradition, but it is our tradition. I am sorry that I will die and we will not agree on this. You just do not disrespect a tradition that is more than two thousand years old. That is what you and your fancy friends did to our tradition. For that, I will take this hurt to my death. Goodbye Nana. ~ Your Mother ~

"Would you believe this?" Nana held up the letter with tears in her eyes. "She died without making peace." She shook her head in disbelief. "It is a pity that Mama did not know God because she would have found it in her heart to make peace not only with me but with God."

"It is the past, Nana." Kiddi walked over to where Nana sat and placed her hand on her shoulder. "Let's move forward." She looked her friend in the eye. "You know that I went through the same situation." She shrugged her shoulders. "I moved on and tried to forget. You do forget in time, my friend."

"Kiddi is absolutely correct, Nana." Shirley spoke for the first time since Nana read the letter. "Just think about the impact we have made on the lives of girls in the world." Shirley waved her hands in the air as she spoke. "We are only about peace, love and concern for the girls. We are not about spreading hatred."

"I don't know what to say about the letter Aunty left." Adjoa sympathized with Nana but she did not want to dishonor her dear aunt. "I think you should listen to your friends and put this thing behind you."

Mrs. Nkrumah did not offer any advice at that time. "Well ladies, the driver is here for you."

"Are you ready ladies?" Jean-Claude walked in with a big smile on his face. "I had a great day sightseeing around the city." He smiled. "The driver will take us to dinner tonight. I hope you ladies are in the mood for traditional food."

"I am hungry so anything will do me good." Shirley made a funny face at Jean-Claude.

"Good. Mrs. Nkrumah, will you join us for dinner?" Jean-Claude asked.

"I had a long day, Jean-Claude but thank you for the invitation." Mrs. Nkrumah responded. She was not in the mood to socialize. She was saddened by the letter that her neighbor and friend left for Nana. She only wished that there was something she could do to ease Nana's hurt. She was glad that Nana had good and loyal friends to support her.

Nana locked her mother's house and handed the keys to Mrs. Nkrumah. "Get some rest – you did really well." Nana had a kiss on the cheek for her mother's neighbor. "I appreciate everything you did." She knew that it would be the last time she walked out of her mother's house. She had already made arrangements for the house to be sold.

The friends returned to the hotel in their hired vehicle to freshen up before dinner. The driver drove them to a restaurant in Greater Accra. Kiddi, Nana and Adjoa assisted Jean-Claude and Shirley with the menu, since the restaurant had no American or European items on the menu.

"This groundnut soup sounds really good. What is in it?" Shirley stared at the menu. She was thankful to see something on it that she once witnessed Nana prepare.

"The obvious is in it – peanuts, spices, fish and some okra." Adjoa explained. "It is really good but I'm having the palm soup with fufu."

"You know that I'm going to have fufu, my favorite." Nana told them as she continued to regard the menu. "I called ahead and asked them to prepare a special palm soup without meat or fish."

"Are you only going to have the plain palm soup, Nana?" Kiddi asked. "I will have jollof rice, which is my favorite."

"I asked them to put mushroom and okra in my palm soup." Nana explained.

"I will have jollof rice but I will order a large order of fried plantain for everyone to have as a side dish." Jean-Claude studied the menu. "If anyone wants to try the palm wine, I will order a bottle."

"I will try the palm wine- that sounds good." Shirley told him. "Does it have alcohol?"

"Oh yes it does my dear." Kiddi told her. "I will order enough Omo Tuo for everyone to taste."

"What is Omo Tuo?" Shirley asked.

"Omo Tuo is rice balls." Nana told her American friend. "You like rice so you will like that, Shirley." She looked over at Jean-Claude. "Please order a bottle of coconut juice and a bottle of palm wine. I no longer drink alcohol due to my faith."

"I think it is great how you went from knowing nothing about the Bible and Christianity to being the most devout Christian at this table." Jean-Claude told Nana.

"I applaud you, Nana for taking such a big step toward a great belief." Kiddi told her childhood friend. "I am rather proud of you."

"I have Mrs. Thurston, Jean-Claude, Shirley and Frank to thank for indoctrinating me to Christianity." Nana smiled. "I am enjoying this journey of developing a relationship with my heavenly father."

"Amen." Shirley said in agreement.

The waiter arrived with their drinks and served each person with what he or she wanted. "Your meal will be out in a few minutes." He told them with a slight bow and walked away.

Jean-Claude raised his glass of palm wine. "I want to propose a toast to the future playwright and film writer among us." Everyone clicked their glasses in agreement with Jean-Claude's toast.

"Thank you – all of you for coming to my mother's funeral. I appreciate your kindness, and most importantly, your undying friendship to me." She raised her glass of coconut juice. "Join me as I drink to ending female genital mutilation."

Everyone joined her in toasting to the primary goal of Friends against Female Genital Mutilation (FAFGM) as the waiter arrived with their main course. Nana had them bow their heads as she blessed the meal. "We thank you Lord for this meal we are about to receive. Make it nourish and strengthen our bodies and make us always mindful of those in the world without food. Amen"

They enjoyed their meal and left the restaurant for their hotel. They had another long day the following day. Jean-Claude had a full day of sightseeing of the countryside planned for them.

The friends set out in the morning on their sightseeing tour. Their driver was also a tour guide. He drove to the most visited water falls in Ghana, situated in the Eastern Region in a village called Boti. "That water fall is called the Boti Falls." The tour guide told them.

Shirley was speechless as they got out of the car and began to walk the Boti Falls. "I have not seen anything like this in my life." She was like a child at an amusement park for the first time. "I only wish I could share this with Frank."

"Perhaps you can take a vacation together and come back here." Adjoa suggested.

"That is a good idea. I will talk to Frank about it. Thanks Adjoa."

They left the water falls and went to the Kakum Forest Reserve. They walked down the Canopy Walkway to get the best view of the Rainforest. At first Shirley was afraid to walk on the Canopy Walk because it was shaky. She held onto Jean-Claude until she felt comfortable to let go of his arm.

"I've never been in a rainforest before." Shirley confessed. "I love it."

The friends enjoyed their sightseeing tour. They returned to the hotel to pack and rest before their trip the following day.

The next morning the friends checked out of the hotel and rode to the airport in Kiddi's hired car. Mrs. Nkrumah was at the airport to say her goodbye.

"Well Nana, I do not know when I will see you again." Mrs. Nkrumah held her embrace and fought back the tears. She suspected that Nana might not ever return to Ghana. She said goodbye to the rest of the friends as they joined the security line in the terminal.

The sun rays shone on the tarmac until it glittered. Both Shirley and Kiddi had purchased return tickets on the same flight as Jean-Claude, Nana and Adjoa. They wanted to fly back together as far as Paris. Nana was grateful to have her friends with her. She only wished that Frank was able to make the trip.

"So how is my other brother?" Nana asked Shirley while they waited in the terminal for their flight.

"He is back to the old Frank, only older and more mature." Shirley told her. "He told me last night that training camp is serious this year. The have rookies to indoctrinate before the season." She sighed. "The pressure is on – the Gorillas have not been to the Big Bowl since I moved to San Antonio."

"They will be back, Shirl." Jean-Claude joined in the conversation when he heard football. "Frank has two Big Bowl rings already. He has to get another one before he retires."

"I agree – he needs three." Nana said. "I have no doubt that he will lead the Gorillas to another Big Bowl."

Kiddi and Adjoa chatted with Mrs. Nkrumah while the three football fans discussed the state of the Gorillas. They did not understand the game, and had no interest whatsoever. Kiddi was a soccer fan, and Adjoa had no interest in sports.

The announcement came across the intercom that their flight was ready to board. The friends boarded with delight, but Nana felt a pang of sadness in her heart as she took one look back. She inhaled the smell of the Ghanaian heat one more time before she disappeared through the door of the plane. She said a quiet farewell to her mother as she fought back tears.

The flight to Paris was not smooth. They encountered turbulence and a thunderstorm but the friends made the best of it. Shirley and Nana were seated together at the window and aisle. Kiddi and Adjoa sat together in the row directly behind Shirley and Nana, and Jean-Claude was across the aisle from Shirley and Nana. The passengers knew that the flight was in a bad situation when they heard the Captain announce that everyone should remain seated with seat belts, when he asked the flight attendants to take their seats. The flight attendants were still serving lunch when they were ordered to take their seats. Jean-Claude was more concerned about Nana. They never figured out why Nana became sick during the flight from Paris to Ghana. They did not encounter any turbulence on that flight. He figured that it might have been the heat from the Sahara.

"Are you ladies doing well?" Jean-Claude checked with his friends. He was accustomed to flying in thunderstorms and turbulence while he worked.

"I will be honest I am scared out of my mind." Shirley told him.

"Shirl, everything will be fine." Nana assured Shirley and her other friends. "There is no need to be afraid. Remember when Jesus calmed the waves when he was with his disciples?"

"I remember but we don't have Jesus here and we need him to calm this plane from jumping up and down in the air." Shirley responded as the others laughed.

"Shirley of little faith, just pray and all will be well." Nana told her.

Everyone was terrified during the turbulence in the cabin, but Nana remained unmoved. "And why are you so calm while everyone else holds onto their seats?" Shirley teased her friend.

"Because since I became a Christian, I never board a plane without reading my Bible." Nana told her. "Remember what David said in the twenty-third Psalm, 'Yea though I walk through the valley of the shadow of death, I will fear no evil for thou art with me.'"

"Amen." Shirley responded in an accommodating fashion but Nana ignored her.

After the turbulence and thunderstorm passed, the rest of the flight was smooth into Paris. Shirley's nerves calmed and she chatted with Nana until they arrived in Paris. They had a great deal of catching up to do. "I had to get used to having a maid." Shirley told Nana. "I didn't want a maid but Frank would not hear of it." She made a funny face as Nana laughed. "He didn't want me to break my nails."

"So what does your maid do for you?" Nana inquired. She looked across the aisle and noticed that Jean-Claude was asleep and so were Adjoa and Kiddi behind them. She wished she too was asleep but she wanted to listen to her friend. They had been apart for a long time.

"She cleans the house, does the laundry and she does most of the cooking unless I want to prepare something special for Frank." Shirley explained.

"So what do you do in your house if the maid does all of that?" Nana raised an eyebrow and they both laughed.

"I run my salon and keep my husband happy." Shirley flashed the usual bright smile, as she displayed her even white teeth.

"That sounds like a full time job." Nana smiled at her. Her friend seemed happy, but she was not surprised. She always knew that Frank would take care of Shirley. "I'm happy for you and Frank, Shirl." She patted the back of Shirley's hand. They were interrupted by the Captain's announcement for the flight attendants to prepare for landing. Nana did not believe that they were already in Paris.

Charles de Gaulle International Airport

The friends had teary eyes when Shirley and Kiddi said their goodbyes and left for their departure gates. Kiddi was scheduled to continue to London Heathrow Airport and Shirley's continuing flight was headed to Dallas/Fort Worth. Shirley was in for a long journey home to San Antonio.

"Okay ladies let's have a group hug before I head to baggage claim for my luggage." Jean-Claude suggested. He was the only one already at his final destination. They made a circle and hugged in a group, with Adjoa included. "I wish each of you a safe trip." He wagged his finger at them with tease in his voice. "I expect an email from each of you when you arrive so I know that you made it home safely."

"Yes Papa." Shirley teased him back as she always did.

Nana and Adjoa waved and walked toward their gate for the flight to Washington's Dulles International Airport. It was a sad moment when they separated, each in a different direction. They enjoyed being together, even though it was sadness that reunited them.

Unlike the flight from Accra to Paris, Nana slept during the entire flight from Paris to Washington, D.C. Adjoa attempted to get her to wake up for dinner and breakfast during the flight but she waved her off. "I just want to sleep, I don't want to eat." She yawned. "I'm really exhausted, Adjoa." Adjoa saw how tired her cousin was so she left her to sleep.

Nana was glad to be back in her little Herndon townhouse. Adjoa offered to spend some time with her in Herndon to keep her mind off her loss but Nana declined with gratitude. "I need to be alone – furthermore I have a lot of calls to make in the next few days before I return to that ghastly job." They both laughed as she gave Adjoa a hug for her kind gesture. "Take good care of yourself and let's keep in touch always." They shared car service from Dulles Airport. Nana's house was only five minutes from the airport. Adjoa continued in the town car to her apartment in Silver Spring, Maryland.

Her phone chimed to tell her that she had incoming email messages. Kiddi sent her an email message to let her know that she was safely home and was glad to be back with her husband and son. She responded and told Kiddi that she and Adjoa were home safely. She later received an email from Shirley and from Jean-Claude. Nana was relieved that all of her friends were safe.

The following day after her return to the States, Nana called Alec to let him know that she was back from her mother's funeral. "Welcome back, my dear." Alec was excited to hear from her.

"Thank you – it is good to be back, and to hear your voice."

"So how did it go over there?" He was anxious to hear about her trip.

"Once we buried my mother, the trip became fun." She told him all about their sightseeing tours, and about the letter her mother left her. She told him about the flight over and the flight back home.

"I am really sorry, dear that your mother felt that way even up to her death." He wished he was there in Virginia to take her in his arms and console her. "I know that it is a difficult time for you but you have a lot going on in your life at the moment."

"I know- I need to make several calls before I return to my job in two days." She told him.

"Do you seriously intend to return to that place?" Alec was surprised to hear that she was actually going back to her job. "I guess I just assumed that you were going to focus on your movie, casting sessions, the foundation and other things that are waiting for you."

"Well until I sign the contract for the show and receive my advance, I have to continue to bring in the pay check every two weeks." She chuckled at the thought of no longer commuting to Washington. "Valerie might surprise me – she might no longer behave in her usual manner." They both laughed at her hopeful analogy of Valerie.

"Changing the subject a bit, I know that you are busy now." He exhaled before speaking again. "You will become even busier once you sign the contract and the project begins."

"Yes?" She wondered where exactly was he taking their conversation.

"I would like to see you again but you have been really busy so I have not troubled you." He bit his bottom lip, a habit he did when he was nervous. "I want to build a relationship with you but I want to take things at your pace, not mine."

"I too want to see you." She liked the fact that he wanted to build a relationship but she had that scared feeling in her stomach again. It was that same feeling she got whenever a man wanted to take the next step from being just friends to a relationship. "You never trouble me – never think that way." She did not believe that she actually told him that. She really liked him a great deal but she did not want to take their relationship further unless it would be successful. She valued their friendship, and did not want anything to change that. "We will plan to meet once I get through all that's facing me at the moment."

"It sounds like a plan." He smiled into the phone and they ended their conversation on a pleasant note.

Nana called the Wilcox law firm to get an update on the movie. "Hi Ginny – how are things going with the Atlanta contract?"

"Welcome back. I hope everything went as expected in Ghana." Ginny did not want to hope that things had gone well, under the circumstances.

"Everything went well, thank you." She was anxious to hear what was going on with her contract. She had signed the contract with Wilcox law firm prior to her trip but she did not get to sign the contract with the producers.

"I'm glad you called." Ginny told her. "We have been waiting for you to come back. The producers decided to push back the plans for the movie."

"What do you mean?" Her heart sank. "Did they change their minds?" Nana's hands shook as she held the phone.

"No they have not changed their minds about the movie." Ginny explained to her with care. "It has something to do with the scheduling of their budget."

"Did they say how long we will wait for their budget to be scheduled correctly?" Nana was in disbelief. She wished she had not called the law firm. She did not need to hear bad news at the time. She knew better than to sulk or worry about it. Where her life was in faith, she never worried. She said a prayer and left her decision in God's care. Nana believed that the Lord intended for her movie to materialize – therefore she saw no need to dwell on a slight disappointment. She was glad that she still had her income at Eastern Travel.

Nana turned her focus to the preparation of returning to her job. Although she did not enjoy working with Valerie, she actually looked forward to returning to Eastern. She felt that it was not as bad as long as she knew it was only temporary.

Nana called her next door neighbor to let her know that she had returned. Everyone felt that she had the best neighbor in the world. Betty Sue McLean checked and held her mail while she was in Ghana. Ever since Shirley and Jean-Claude left the townhouse, Betty Sue and Nana had developed a much closer relationship. Betty Sue was a special neighbor to the three friends, from the day they moved into the townhouse.

The day Nana and Jean-Claude moved in, Betty Sue went over to welcome them to the neighborhood. She took a cake and home baked cookies to them. She thought that the two were a couple until they quickly explained their history of friendship. Two months later when Shirley moved in, Nana took Shirley to Betty Sue's house and introduced her. Betty Sue had lived there since the inception of the development. The townhouses were built in 1985, and she was one of the first buyers. She knew nearly everyone in the neighborhood. She was a second mother to the three friends. They exchanged phone numbers; in addition, Betty Sue gave her son's phone number to them in the event of an emergency. Each Mother's Day, the friends bought her flowers and a card. They exchanged Christmas gifts every year; she had learned what each person's favorite drink, nuts, dessert, etc. were. She surprised them from time to time with such things.

Betty Sue insisted on helping Nana with grocery money and the cost of lawn mowing while she was unemployed. Betty Sue suggested to Nana that she discontinued her newspaper subscription to the *Washington Insider*. She offered to share her daily newspaper with Nana, which would save her money. Betty Sue left her paper on Nana's steps each day after she read it. Nana was grateful to her for the help. Nana felt badly each time Betty Sue offered her money to assist. Betty Sue would place money in the center of the newspaper to surprise Nana. When Nana opened the paper to read, three or four Twenty Dollar bills fell out. She knew that Betty Sue was up to her surprises again. She was a mother to Nana, and she was one of the kindest and most caring people Nana knew. She always told Nana that she was praying for her. She provided Nana with little prayer books to help along in her Christianity. Nana was not Catholic like Betty Sue was but she believed in the power of prayer; whether it was from a little prayer book or from someone's mind, she liked prayer.

"Thank you so much for taking care of my mail while I was gone." Nana told Betty Sue as she stood in her foyer.

"Come on in and have a seat." She ushered Nana to a seat in her living room. "Tell me all about the trip." She wore that comforting and motherly look on her face. "How did you hold up?"

"I am grateful that my friends and cousin were there with me." She sat back on the sofa. "My mother's neighbor was a mother to me over there." She smiled as she spoke. "I am blessed to have Mrs. Nkrumah in Ghana, and have you and Mrs. Thurston here in the States." She smiled at her gracious neighbor. "What more could I ask for?"

They chatted about her conversation with the law office and with Alec. Betty Sue assured her that her movie would materialize because she was in her prayers. "I have seen other movies that I wonder how they even made it that far, so I know yours will be a great hit." The two women laughed at Betty Sue's statement. "I wish you did not have to return to your job." She shook her head with concern. "Going back to that awful boss of yours just worries me."

"I will go back and make the best of it." Nana made a face. "I pray that my tenure there will not be long." She said goodbye and Betty Sue wished her well on her return to work.

As Nana prepared to return to Eastern Travel the next day, she thought about her plan to become a U.S. citizen. She received two letters from the United States Immigration to let her know that she was eligible for citizenship. It was already seven years since she obtained her permanent residence status. While Nana was in Ghana, she received a vision from God to become a citizen of the United States of America. She prayed over her vision and made her final decision to follow the Lord's instruction. She did not want to give up her citizenship as a Ghanaian until she made the trip back to Ghana to put her mother to rest. She saw that there was not a future for her in Ghana, however she still wanted to keep close ties with not only Ghana but with the Continent of Africa. She wanted to make a difference in that beautiful continent where her roots were but she waited for instructions from God.

Chapter Thirteen

A STEP TOWARD THE STARS AND STRIPES

It is better to take refuge in the Lord than to trust in people. – Psalm 118:8 (NLT)

Nana stood before the U.S. Immigration building in Arlington, Virginia. She was told that it was where all Northern Virginia residents went to apply for either green cards or citizenship. She recalled her first visit to that building when she applied for her permanent residency. She remembered how afraid she was the day she applied for her green card. Her student visa on which she came to the States did not allow her to enter the work force after graduation. Nana took advantage of a special legal program in Northern Virginia for immigrants. They provided free immigration legal counsel for those who needed that service. She was fresh out of college and was not in the position to hire an attorney to help her obtain her green card. She remembered when she was granted her permanent residency; she did not stop looking at the card. "I can get a real job now, not just volunteer work." She told Shirley and Jean-Claude. They celebrated over dinner at a Thai restaurant, which was Jean-Claude's treat. Nana enjoyed Thai food since they catered to vegetarians on their menus.

Nana pushed the past out of her mind to focus on her application to become a citizen of the United States. She completed the long application form and all other required paperwork. She was glad that the process was over. Nana was given a hundred American civic questions to study and prepare for the test to become a citizen. She took the large brown envelope with the questions and other information and went back to Herndon.

Nana returned to her job at Eastern Travel to a rousing welcome from Valerie and her staff. She gave Valerie a wooden cup with a lid that displayed Ghanaian art. She gave Janet, Tammy and Amber each a souvenir key chain. She gave Antomeyer a Ghanaian hat made of traditional fabric. Everyone was grateful to her for the thoughtful gesture from Nana, including Valerie.

Nana wasted no time getting back to her clients. It did not take her long to get on the phone and began to take reservations. Valerie was pleased when she heard Nana on the phone; she sounded as though she had never left. The clients were happy to hear from her. They trusted Nana, and some of them really missed her during her absence.

The great welcome at the office for Nana was short lived. Three weeks after she returned to her job at Eastern Travel, Valerie began to show her old self. She drove Amber out of the office, and told her not to return. Amber did not take Valerie's threat and action to be serious. She knew that Valerie always told her to leave, and not to return; but when Amber returned the next morning, Valerie accepted her back. Amber happily picked up her bag and left the office. She whispered to her co-workers that she would see them the next morning.

Amber met the surprise of her life when she reported to work the next morning. Valerie had Tammy pack all of Amber's belongings from her desk in a large shopping bag. She handed the bag to Amber, and told her to vacate her premises, never to return. She informed the security guard down at the front desk to not allow Amber in the building.

The office was quiet the rest of the day. Antomeyer was ordered to issue a final payroll check for Amber. The atmosphere in the office was somber. Though Amber had an unconventional style of dressing and a body full of provocative tattoos, she was pleasant and got her work done.

Nana felt sympathy for Amber as she said goodbye to her coworkers and left with her belongings. Nana wondered what would happen to Amber, with a baby on the way. Amber announced that she was expecting a baby when Nana returned. Though she was not married, she knew that Amber lived with her male companion. "I wish you all the best with the baby." Nana told her with sincere wishes.

Valerie had no empathy whatsoever for Amber. She used the most vulgar words to communicate with Amber that day. Nana said quiet prayers for both women as Valerie continued to bellow out swear words in the office. Nana felt regretful that she decided to return to that office.

Two weeks after the Amber episode, Nana encountered a problem with the metro. The train on which she traveled to work that morning off-loaded at a station stop away. She walked six long blocks to the office to avoid getting to work late. As she made her way toward Dupont Circle along Farragut North, she was grateful for the cool morning breeze.

Nana arrived at the office with a few minutes to spare. She settled in at her desk, and placed a call to a hotel in London on behalf of her client. The client had sent her a complaint in an email, that the hotel accommodations were not what he expected. Nana was in the process of investigating before she responded to the client.

"Nana, get in here." Valerie shouted from her office. "Get in here I said."

Nana asked the hotel manager to hold a moment. "I'm on the phone."

"Nana, I said to get in here." Valerie ignored Nana's response that she was on the phone.

"I'll be right there. I'm on with a hotel manager in London."

Valerie barged out of her office and over to Nana's desk. She shouted even louder at Nana, as she picked up Nana's keyboard and slammed it back down on the desk. It was her way of getting Nana's attention.

The hotel manager on the phone asked in his authentic English accent, "Who is that discourteous character?"

"It is really nobody of significance." Nana told him. "I apologize but may I call you back?" She ended the call before Valerie embarrassed both of them any further.

Valerie was still enraged beside Nana's desk. "Just leave – I want you to leave now."

"Are you sure you want me to do that?" Nana wanted to be sure. She had warned Valerie the last time that if she asked her to leave the office again, she would not ever return.

"Yes I am sure because I just can't stand to look at you today." She actually drove Nana out of the office.

Nana got up from her desk, packed her bag, put on her coat and began to leave. "Goodbye everyone – it has been a pleasure working with you." She walked toward the door.

Valerie suddenly had a change of heart. "If you leave, what should I do about your clients?"

"I really don't care." Nana told her as she slowly turned away from Valerie.

"Are you coming back tomorrow?"

"The last time you did this to me, I told you that if you drove me out of your office again, I will not come back." Nana spoke to Valerie as she walked closer toward the door. "You asked me to leave and I am obliging." With that said, she walked out, not to return to Eastern Travel.

Nana was without a job for more than six months. She continued to wait for Zebra Productions to contact her attorneys with the contract for the movie. The time seemed like eternity to her but she had faith that it would work out for the better. Not having an income took a toll on her finances. She did not enjoy getting up in the morning with nowhere to go. She placed her resume on several travel sites but she did not hear anything from them. She saw in the newspaper that Alpha Travel Agency had an opening for a senior international agent. Nana was familiar with Alpha but she never had any desire to work for them in the past. She knew her situation and decided to send in her resume to the email address that was listed in the advertisement. Within two days, Polly contacted her from Alpha. She conducted a brief phone interview with Nana. Polly liked Nana's background and invited her to the office for an in-person interview.

Nana's schedule was free since she had no job. She set up the appointment to meet with Polly the next day. Although she had a job prospect, Nana set up appointments with several non-profit organizations to meet with them. She wanted to set up partnerships with them to work with FAFGM. Those were organizations that supported and addressed the FGM issue. She met with two organizations that agreed to a possible partnership by staging events in raising awareness about FGM. She was excited about that accomplishment.

"I wish Alec would stop wasting time, and just marry you. Then you will not need to worry about money." Shirley told her one evening as they chatted.

Nana chuckled. "Shirl, you and Frank saw each other for years before he popped the question to you."

"You and Alec have known each other for a few years now."

"Knowing each other and dating are two different things."

"I know but if you would allow him to go up there and visit you, things would move a little faster."

"Well, he told me already that he wants our friendship to move to the next level."

"Why am I just hearing about this?" Shirley was gleeful.

"I just heard about it since we came back from Ghana." They laughed at themselves. "I have been so busy since we returned that I forgot."

"I think he is a great guy."

"I know, Shirl but I cannot marry him for his money." She stood before her closet as she selected an outfit for her interview the following day. "I have to love him and it has to be mutual."

"Are you sure it is not the old fear raising his ugly head again?" Shirley pushed.

"It has nothing to do with fear." She frowned at the thought of her fear of men getting close to her. "Alec is a different kind of man." She paused. "He is a Christian and I don't need to be concerned about such things."

"Well, excuse me, Miss Nkuku." They laughed. "I like that."

They discussed the foundation and its newly acquired partnerships. "I think these partnerships will benefit us, Shirl."

"Agreed but we need to resume our annual benefit dinner. We have not held one in years." Shirley reminded her.

"So much has happened over the years." She knew that they had slacked in their drive to make the foundation successful. "Perhaps we should hold a conference call through Globe." Globe was the new technology of which everyone took advantage for long distance and international calls. With a camera on a computer, they would be able to have Kiddi and Jean-Claude join the call, and they would see each other on the screen. Globe was a great way to communicate with friends and relatives internationally.

"It sounds like a plan. Frank has two more weeks in training camp. I can't wait."

"We might not be able to host a dinner this year but we can begin to plan for next year."

"We need to get Frank and the Football Association back in the swing of public service announcements again. We lost our drive – we can get it back, Nana."

"I know what you mean, Shirl." She thought about how things had died down with FAFGM. "Once we pick up again, I will run the foundation full time, just like you wanted me to do before." They ended their conversation on a positive tempo, as Shirley wished Nana the best with her interview the next day.

Nana's interview went well with Polly at Alpha Travel. She was pleased to drive to her interview in Sterling. She knew that if she got the job at Alpha, she would not have a long commute to Washington, D.C. The thought made her excited. Alpha's headquarters was located about three miles from Dulles Airport, off on Frying Pan Road, off Route 28. Polly had an extensive chat with her about her resume and background. She was impressed by Nana's international knowledge. Unlike Eastern Travel, Alpha did not administer an exam but she was prepared if she had been required to take a test. Polly invited the woman to whom Nana's prospective immediate boss reported. Indira was a short Indian woman with jet black cropped hair. She had a pleasant smile, and asked Nana several questions. Nana did not list Eastern Travel on her resume. She knew that Valerie would give her a bad reference if she gave her as reference. She called Antomeyer and asked him if she could list him as a personal reference.

"Don't give Valerie as reference." Antomeyer told her. "She told us that she will never give you a good reference if she is ever called."

"I would be insane to list her as reference." Nana laughed.

"She told us yesterday that you had applied for unemployment." He hesitated then continued. "She was furious and she does not feel that you should receive unemployment."

"Why shouldn't I apply?" Nana wondered if Antomeyer agreed with Valerie about the unemployment benefits.

"She is claiming that you abandoned the job."

"She told me to leave." Nana paused to think for a moment. "In fact, she did not ask me to leave – she ordered me to leave and actually drove me out of the office."

"I know how that woman is – I have worked with her for more than twenty years. I don't know how I have done it." He grunted. "This woman is dangerous so be careful. Give my name as reference and I will make sure to tell them how good you are."

"Thanks – I really appreciate it, Antomeyer." They wished each other a great day and concluded their call.

Indira and Polly completed the interview on a pleasant note. They told Nana that they would be in touch with her. "We are still interviewing – we still have a couple of people to see but we will be in touch with you, regardless." Polly told Nana as she shook her hand. Polly and Indira walked Nana out to the door.

Nana did not sit and wait to hear from Alpha Travel or any other company she had sent her resume. She busied herself with FAFGM affairs. She wanted to get the foundation back in circulation so that she would someday work full time for it. She attended a luncheon benefit, held by National Circulation. Nana exchanged business cards with a number of people, whom she met at the luncheon.

National Circulation was a company that published a magazine based on photographs their explorers took on their journeys. The magazine was renowned around the world. The luncheon benefit was held at National Circulation's headquarters in Washington. Nana was seated next to an attractive black woman who introduced herself as Bridgette Umo. Although Bridgette used the surname Umo, she was an American by birth from Arkansas. She articulated without the southern accent. Bridgette told Nana a little about her background. She legally changed her real surname to Umo because she liked the name, but she did not like her real name. Bridgette was self-employed with her own marketing company. She was at the luncheon to meet people and offer her services to them. Bridgette saw Nana's business card for the foundation and became interested in FAFGM.

"I've heard of your organization." Bridgette told Nana. "Do you need a Public Relations rep?"

"We already work with Don& Day Public Relations here in Washington." Nana told her. "Have you heard of them?"

"Yes I have." She raised her eyebrow. "You're running with big boys now." The two women laughed at Bridgette's comment.

"Not really – Cynthia, our rep was a friend of a friend." She shrugged. "You know how it works."

"How does that female genitalia thing work?" She noticed Nana's startling expression. "I mean, what is the reason for doing it?"

"It depends on who you are asking. You might get an answer that says it is for cleanliness or marriageability or a number of other reasons."

"Your organization is against the practice of it, I understand."

"That is correct – we are one hundred percent against it."

"Was it done to you?" Again she observed Nana's look of surprise. "I hope you don't mind my asking."

"I do not mind." She shrugged. "I have told the world that it was done to me. I am not ashamed – I did not will it on myself."

"I'm sorry." Bridgette wanted to crawl under the table and remain there.

"If you're sorry that it was done to me, so am I. If you're sorry for asking, I'm not."

"Do you get questions about it a lot?" Bridgette pushed.

"Not really." Nana wanted to let her inquisitive table mate know that she did not think of herself as a victim. "You see, when I first came out to the public about FGM, I thought of myself as a victim. Now that I found the Lord, I am no longer a victim."

"Were you a Christian in Ghana?"

"I was not a Christian – I knew nothing about that. I lived from day to day without acknowledging who was responsible for my very existence."

"What caused you to become a Christian?"

"Are you conducting an interview?" Bridgette laughed at Nana's candor.

"No, I am just fascinated by you, your cause and your survival."

"I appreciate it but the little girls that are cut every day in the world are the true survivors. They are the victims."

"I applaud you for your efforts to end this thing." She shook Nana's hand. "If there is anything that I can do to help, let me know." They exchanged business cards.

Nana turned her attention to her meal before her. She took out her miniature bottle of hand sanitizer and prepared her hands to eat. She graced her food as Bridgette regarded her. Nana was particular about her hands. She told Shirley and Jean-Claude often when they lived together, that one of the dirtiest parts of a person's body were the hands. She did not like to exchange handshakes because of her serious germ phobia. Nana never touched anything when she rode the metro. She thought the metro was filthy and full of germs. She did not touch common areas. Whenever she used public facilities, Nana opened the doors with a paper towel. She always took paper towels, hand sanitizer and a pen. She did not use common pens and other office supplies such as staplers, staple removers, scissors, keyboards, mouse, phones, etc.

The lunch was appetizing. The meal options were roasted chicken or beef. She asked the waiter if the chef would prepare a vegetable plate for her, and the chef obliged. They served her a plate of steamed broccoli, green beans, carrot, cauliflower and red pepper. She was grateful that Bridgette did not continue her interrogation during the meal.

Shirley advised Nana to apply for unemployment. "Just go to the Virginia Employment Website and submit the application."

"I walked out – she didn't fire me." Nana remembered her conversation with Antomeyer.

"She told you to leave – it is the same as being fired."

"I know Shirl but I just don't feel like fighting with Valerie Penney."

"It's your money you worked for. Go claim it."

"I will." She updated Shirley about her interview with Alpha Travel, and told her all about Bridgette Umo.

"Is she African?"

"She's from Alabama – born and raised."

"With a name like Umo in Alabama, how did she survive?" Nana laughed at Shirley's remark until tears filled her eyes.

"She was not born with Umo – she took the name and changed her birth name legally."

Nana followed Shirley's advice and applied for unemployment online. The form was long and tiring but she continued from one page to the next until she completed it.

Two weeks later, Nana received a call from Polly at Alpha Travel. "I want to let you know that we checked all of your references. Everyone had great things to say about you."

"Thanks."

Polly continued. "We would like to offer the position to you."

"Thank you." Nana did not expect to get the job. She felt that after two weeks, Alpha had offered it to another candidate.

"Are you interested?" Polly broke the silence.

"Yes I am interested."

"When will you be able to begin?"

"Is it the same salary we discussed during the interview?"

"Yes it is – I will send you the offer letter via email this afternoon."

"I accept the offer." She wondered why she felt apprehensive but she needed the job. "When I receive the letter, I will respond in writing with my acceptance."

"So when can you start?"

"How about in two weeks?" Nana had some things she needed to conclude before tying up her time with the job.

"Two weeks it is then." Polly agreed. "Thanks and we look forward to seeing you in a couple of weeks.'

Nana sat still with the handset on her lap long after she ended her call with Polly. She wanted to be still to listen for God's response. She had a habit of praying in solitude then she would listen for the answer. She wanted to be sure that her decision to accept the position at Alpha Travel was wise. Alpha was not her ideal travel company but it sufficed at that time.

Later that afternoon Nana went to a neighborhood Thai restaurant and treated herself to an early dinner. She often had an appreciation for Thai cuisine – they catered to vegetarians so she was assured to have a good selection on their menu.

Nana sat in the restaurant that evening and reflected on her trip to Bangkok when she worked at Proficiency Travel at the IFT. She traveled with a group of travel agents from both the IFT and the Universal Bank. They were a total of twelve in the group. They stopped in Tokyo for three days. Nana barely ate during their stay in Tokyo. She did not enjoy Japanese food, especially sushi. She enjoyed the sights in Tokyo more than anything else. She was eager to arrive in Bangkok – Nana made up for her sparse diet when she got to Thailand. She ate heartily during every meal. Their hotel was one of the best in Bangkok. They each occupied a plush room on the Executive Floors. The hotel served a fabulous complimentary buffet breakfast every morning for their VIP guests on the Executive Floors. Nana appreciated the fresh warm soy they served with a variety of whole grain cereals. The buffet had an assortment of fresh fruits and juices from which to choose. Nana and her colleagues had a great familiarization trip, both in Japan as well as in Thailand. In Japan they had the pleasure of witnessing a formal Japanese traditional wedding. In Thailand they experienced visits to the many Buddhist temples around Bangkok. Nana wore socks each time they entered a temple since they were required to remove their shoes. The trip was long but Nana fell in love with Thai food. The flight from Washington Dulles Airport to Tokyo Narita Airport was fourteen hours non-stop. The three day break in Tokyo was needed before they continued to Bangkok on the seven hour flight. They flew a total of twenty-one hours each way. She sat in the Thai restaurant and took in the décor as she reflected on that memorable trip.

Nana made her selection on the menu and chatted with the waitress. They knew her in that restaurant due to her frequency. The waitress and waiters knew her by name and they even knew her favorite items on the menu. That night she chose to have Ka Pow Jae – a dish that consist of string beans, zucchini, mushroom and fried tofu sautéed with ground fresh chili pepper, garlic and Thai sweet basil leaves.

The ambiance and peaceful atmosphere also attracted Nana to enjoy her visits and meals there. That particular night an older couple sat across from her table. Nana noticed that the woman tried not to stare at her but she looked at Nana as though she recognized her from somewhere. She wondered if the lady thought she reminded her of someone.

Nana's meal came just as her stomach began to tell her that it was her dinner hour. She graced her meal and ate at a pace of comfort and peace. The only distraction was the woman across from her table. The woman must have said something to her husband because he turned to look at Nana a couple of times during theirs and her meal. She was curious why they gave her attention. She finished her meal and sat in her own thoughts. The woman went over to Nana's table. Nana welcomed her because she wanted to know why she sought her.

"I am sorry for intruding on your private dinner time." The woman said with a smile. She had a pleasant face.

"Please don't apologize – it is quite okay." Nana assured her.

"My husband and I were wondering if you are who we think you are." She looked at Nana without turning her gaze away.

"Who do you think I am?" Nana returned her smile. "Do I have a double that I don't know about?" The two women laughed.

"You're Nana Nkuku – I recognized your face but I was not sure. Your voice just revealed your identity."

"Yes I am." Nana thought that the encounter became stranger.

"I recognized you from the time you spoke at Warner University a couple of years ago."

"Ah, that was a while ago." Nana hoped that the lady was a supporter of FAFGM. "Did you get anything from my message that night?"

"Absolutely – you won my interest on female genital mutilation." The lady sat in the other chair at Nana's table. "I did research on the topic after that night. I continue to follow your cause."

"Thank you." Nana was complimented and moved by what the woman said. "Have you finished your dinner?"

"We're finished but I told my husband that it was you. He didn't believe me." The two women laughed as Nana blushed.

"Would you like to join me in a cup of tea or coffee?" She wanted to find out more about the woman.

"Sure – I'll ask my husband." She excused herself and walked back to their table. They had already paid their bill to the waiter. They moved to Nana's table.

"Nana, my name is Martha Reynolds – this is my husband Peter."

"It's a pleasure to meet you both." Nana signaled to the waiter who hurried to her table. "I would like a teapot of ginger and cinnamon tea. Kindly take Mr. and Mrs. Reynolds' order. Add it to my bill, please." The Reynolds ordered a cup of coffee each. "Is that all you will have?"

"That is enough – we appreciate the invitation and the company." Peter told Nana. "My wife is a big advocate of your cause. She had never heard of it until a colleague invited her to hear you speak. Since then, she supports your cause." He did not bring himself to say female genital mutilation.

"Well, I could not conceive of the dreadful act on little girls." Martha told Nana. "I thought I had heard it all until I listened to you that night. I applaud you for sharing your story with us that night."

"Thank you." Nana was in awe as she blushed. She went out to celebrate her new job and found an adversary.

"What can we do to help?" Martha asked as she placed her hand over her heart area. "Do you have volunteers working with you?"

"Not at the moment, but we will soon be organizing a volunteer program. The organization has been quiet lately." She told them how Jean-Claude got a promotion and moved back to Europe – that Shirley got married and moved to San Antonio. "When we were all here in the area, we did not find the need for volunteers but now that I'm alone, we will organize a volunteer program." Nana said a quiet prayer of appreciation to God for sending her to that restaurant that night. They sipped tea and coffee as Martha and Peter told her stories about their own trips to places in the world. Nana acknowledged that she too had visited Hawaii, Saint Thomas and Barbados. They discovered that they had commonalities such as travel, foods, Christianity, and the appreciation for culture and history. They talked until all of the other patrons had left the restaurant. The staff had begun to clean up when they realized how late it was. Nana and Martha exchanged business cards.

Peter revealed that he was a retired Marine Colonel. He enjoyed his retirement through trips to destinations he did not get to see while he was in the Marines. When he was not traveling, he volunteered at their church in Herndon and mentored teenage boys. He taught them self-discipline and how to become gentlemen. Nana was impressed and touched by Peter's own cause and efforts. Martha was a retired Psychology Professor. She traveled with Peter around the world, taught Sunday school at their church and volunteered at a hospital in Fairfax County. She visited cancer patients at the hospital, read the Bible to them and spent time with them to encourage the patients in their pain.

"I think you two are awesome." Nana exclaimed.

"Do you already have the 501c3 status for your organization?" Martha inquired.

"Yes we filed almost ten years ago. We received it a year later." Nana told her. "We have a board of directors – we're only a few but the members do a lot of work. The members are committed and passionate about our cause."

"Great – I'm glad to hear that." Martha said. "Whatever you need me to do, just let me know."

"Thank you." Nana was grateful. "I think we had better be going before they throw us out of here." The three laughed and got up to leave. Nana took care of the check. The waiters and waitresses like to serve her table because she was a generous tipper.

The three walked out together to the parking lot. Nana felt fortunate that her car was parked in the same area of where the Reynolds' was parked. They saw that Nana was in her car before they said goodnight and walked to their car.

Nana drove home in silence. She did not turn on the radio in her car – she wanted to think and communicate with God in silence. She had survived a busy and eventful day. Nana decided she would not make any phone calls that night – she wanted to be alone in her thoughts.

The next day after her encounter with the Reynolds, Nana called Shirley and Frank and told them about the previous day. She shared with them her job offer and about the Reynolds. They were excited about the Reynolds. Nana's friends never liked the fact that she no longer had them with her in Virginia. They were pleased to hear of the Reynolds' willingness to assist with FAFGM. Frank was at home from training camp.

"I have the break until preseason begins in two weeks." Frank told Nana. "Let's get J.C. on the phone so we can discuss the volunteer idea." He referred to Jean-Claude at time as J.C. He and Shirley had Nana on speaker, as he placed her on hold and dialed Jean-Claude's number. He clicked over to bring Nana into the conference as Jean-Claude's phone began to ring.

"Hallo." They heard the French accent join the conference.

"Hey J.C. – so you're back to that French accent?" Frank bellowed into the phone.

"Hey, my man, what is going on?" They laughed at how quickly Jean-Claude's accent switched to American when he heard Frank's voice. "What is going on in State side?" He was happy to hear from his friends – he missed them a lot. "Are you ready for the season?" He still followed American football from Europe.

"Yes I'm as ready as I will ever be." Frank grinned. "I thank God that I'm healthy – Doc Alec gave me a clean bill of health during training camp."

"That's important – you can't win games if you're unhealthy. You need to get another ring before you retire."

"You got that right, Papa." Shirley chimed in and they laughed at her special name for Jean-Claude. "We have Nana here with us."

"Hey – how are my girls?" He was really excited then. "So what is the purpose of this call – is Nana announcing her engagement to Doc Alec?" He teased.

"You have an amazing imagination, my brother." Nana told him. "Sorry to disappoint you."

"We thought to call and bring you up to date on FAFGM." Frank told him. "Nana called us with information and ideas. We think that we have taken a long enough hiatus from the organization. It's time to rekindle the flame with our crusade against FGM."

Nana shared with Jean-Claude about the Reynolds, the idea of getting help from volunteers, and the possibility of expanding their board of directors. "We need to plan for next year – draft a calendar with the events we intend to have and begin spreading the word."

"I like that very much." Jean-Claude exclaimed. "You beat me to it – I was intending to ask when you thought we should restart our campaign against FGM."

"We all had a lot going on, especially Nana." Shirley said. "I think we're ready to get things going again."

"This is great timing to start the media campaign with football season upon us." Frank reminded them. "I'll speak to some of the players and coaches to see who is interested in doing public service announcements."

"I think Mrs. Reynolds would be a good person to ask to head the volunteers." Nana told them. "She seems to be an expert in volunteering."

"I know we only have Doc Alec, Diane Parsons and Mr. Jeffries on our board." Jean-Claude said. "How many members did our bylaws dictate?"

"It says a minimum of five and maximum of nine – so we have an uneven number." Shirley said. She had her laptop in front of her with the bylaws on the screen. "So with the four of us and Kiddi, we can only add one more."

"In that case, we should leave the board as it is." Nana suggested. "We can solicit as many volunteers as we can since they do not have voting rights."

"It sounds good to me – let's do it." Jean-Claude said.

"Okay, so we move forward with the volunteers and get in touch with Cynthia at Don and Day about reviving our media campaign." Frank recounted what they had discussed and their plans. He was the President of FAFGM; Nana was the Vice President. Shirley was Recording Secretary and Jean-Claude was the Treasurer. Kiddi was the Financial Secretary and Jimmy Jeffries was the Financial Advisor. Alec was the Medical advisor.

Shirley promised to send the minutes from the conference call to all board members, and Jean-Claude offered to call Kiddi and brief her. With that, they ended their call.

Nana felt better that she had the support of FAFGM, and they were in agreement with her. She was relaxed as she read her Psalm of inspiration for the evening. She enjoyed the Psalms that David wrote. She thought that he was an intellectual, and that Paul was a great philosopher. She wished such men walked the earth during her time. Nana made one observation in her studies of the Bible; the people in biblical times were not perfect, just like the world during her time. They seemed to have set the stage for what was happening in current times. They seemed to have more wars – there were evil men and women – there was deception, adultery, idolatry, theft, murders, cheating, unfairness, lies, envy, etc. Then she also observed the kindness, joy, peace, harmony, love, compassion, sharing, giving, fairness, honesty, loyalty, faithfulness, God-fearing, etc. She realized that the stage was set from the beginning of time for what went on during her lifetime. It was the world in which she lived. She noticed one difference – God spoke to Abraham, David, Peter, Paul, Samuel, Elijah and many others in his voice, according to the Bible; and they actually heard him speak to them. She once asked her Bible study teacher why God did not speak to people in her time like he did centuries before.

"We live after the new covenant. Jesus Christ is the new covenant, and he speaks to us through the Holy Spirit." Rachel, her Bible study teacher explained to her at the time.

Nana remembered how complicated it all sounded and how confused she was in her first four weeks of Bible study. "How do I know that it is the Holy Spirit speaking to me and not my own thoughts?" She asked Rachel.

"When you have that spiritual connection with the Lord, you just know when he instructs you or speaks to you." Rachel explained. "You feel it in your soul. That's why when we pray, we ask God to let us know when his answer will come and to know that it will come so we can recognize it."

"Is it the same as people say, that you feel it in your gut?" Nana wanted to make that comparison. "Sometimes I feel things deep from inside of me – as though a voice is coming from in me."

"It is very similar." Rachel told her. "You just know – take this example. I was driving to Haymarket recently and I could not decide which route I wanted to take. While I wanted to get there faster and the best way was to take I-66, a voice spoke inside of me and told me to take route 29. I really did not want to do that because of the many lights but I followed the suggestion of that voice inside and drove to route 29. When I arrived at my mother's home in Haymarket, she was watching a six-car accident that had shut down I-66. The accident resulted in four deaths and serious injuries. My mother was relieved when I rang the bell and walked in." Rachel smiled. "Mom and I hugged and prayed for those souls in the accident but we also praised God for saving me from it." She regarded Nana as she spoke. "Some would say that it was their gut feeling that kept them from

I-66, and others might call it luck. I called it the power of the Holy Spirit guided me away from I-66."

That day, Nana had a much clearer understanding of how the Holy Spirit worked. She was a Christian for about four years. She came to know the Bible well during those years. Nana believed in doing nothing halfway. When she decided to become a Christian, she knew that her commitment would be all or not at all. She noticed that some Christians attended church every Sunday, yet they harbored malice, while others were prejudiced toward others. She knew Christians who smoked and consumed alcohol. Nana refused to judge others; she learned from the Bible that only God could judge and she was not positioned to pass judgment. She also learned that if someone wronged or hurt her, it was not in her power to take revenge on that individual. She left that person in the hands of God, and actually prayed for that person.

A Second Time Samaritan

She was buried in her thoughts and the Bible when the ringing of the phone startled her. She answered on the third ring. "Hello." She did not recognize the number displayed on her caller's ID. She figured it was a telemarketer.

"Hello – this is Bridgette." She and Bridgette spoke several times after they met at the function. She was interested in doing PR work for FAFGM; but Nana made it clear that they did not have the budget to accommodate Don and Day Public Relations as well as her firm.

"Bridgette – how are you?"

"I am not doing well at all." Bridgette's voice sounded as though she was close to tears.

"Are you ill?" Nana was concerned. "What may I do to help you feel better?"

"I'm not sick – I just need someone to listen – someone with a caring heart." She began to sob.

Nana was uneasy – she had heard of suicidal people but she never encountered one. Bridgette sounded depressed. "I am all ears – please stop crying and tell me what the matter is." She wondered how she would talk Bridgette out of suicide, if it was what she had in mind.

"I am homeless – I lost my condo." She continued to sob.

"Where are you at the moment?" Nana had a flash back of James Dunn. He was in desperate need of a place to stay, and she took him in with the understanding that he needed a place only for the night. James stayed with her for seven months.

"I'm at the condo packing my things – the Marshals will be here tomorrow morning to clear the condo." She sobbed harder. "I thought I would be able to save it – I went to court, and even filed bankruptcy a couple of months before." More sobs poured out. "My business has struggled for some time now and I was under water, and I just could not make my mortgage payments."

Nana's sympathy went out to Bridgette. "I'm so very sorry – it is difficult to lose your home." She came close to losing the townhouse in Herndon after Jean-Claude and Shirley left. During her unemployment, she fell behind in her payments. The house was in her name, and her roommates paid rent to her. Nana recalled having to file bankruptcy, just as Bridgette had done. The legal and filing fees amounted to Seven Hundred Dollars ($700). Her mortgage company refused to take her out of foreclosure unless she paid all of the back payments. The total amount of back payments was far more than Seven Hundred Dollars. She offered the bank that amount but they declined. She fought to keep her home. She fasted and prayed many days for God to keep her in her home. Nana recalled that the times that the Sheriff banged on her door to serve her notice from ForeContrust. She cried for hours at a time, as she prayed to the Lord to keep her from being homeless. She never told her friends about her situation. She did not want anyone to give her handouts. She believed that God would rescue her and save her home. One night Nana dreamed that Tommie and Paula were in a boat, and she stood on the shore all alone. They waved to her and told her to hang in there – that help was on the way. Both Paula and Tommie were dead but they looked alive and well. She awoke in sweat, but she was not afraid. She told Frank, Mrs. Thurston, Shirley and Jean-Claude about her dream. Mrs. Thurston told her that it meant that Tommie and Paula were resting in peace with God. She asked Nana if she had any problems at that time. Mrs. Thurston said that since they told her to hang in there, they were the bearers of a message she was about to receive something. Nana only smiled but did not admit to Mrs. Thurston that she was on the verge of foreclosure. Paula and Tommie brought her the message from God to let her know that he would send her help with her home. She knew that if the bank had foreclosed on her, she would not be homeless. Her friends would take her in – even Mrs. Thurston would offer her a room in her home. She did not want it to get to that. She knew that her home would be saved from foreclosure.

Nana went through a great test of faith during that period. She was afraid to answer her phone or her door for fear that it was a bill collector or the Sheriff with a notice to vacate. She turned to no one else but her newly discovered friend at that time – her Lord and Savior Jesus Christ. Nana fell in love with God and the Holy book, the Bible. She studied the book as she did her text books during her school years. She wanted to get a full understanding of what her discovery was about. Although her roommates introduced her to Christianity, they were never where Nana was in her walk with God. Frank, Tommie, Shirley, Jean-Claude and Paula were Christians by birth. Their parents were Christians – they grew up in Christian homes, and were taught the Bible from early childhood. Amelia Thurston was a devout Baptis – Shirley's parents were also Baptists – Paula's parents were Lutherans, and Jean-Claude's parents were Catholics. Nana had options to listen to her friends' debate about denominations, faith and religions. When she made her decision to walk with God and become a Christian, she was led to the Methodist church. She was invited to join a couple of committees at the church. Nana felt a sense of contentment when she served her church. It was how she showed her gratitude to God for deliverance from the blade of the Medicine Woman so many decades before. She liked the work that the Methodist church did around the world. They built and operated schools and churches all over the world, which included her beloved continent of Africa. She met a student from Liberia at the university many years before. The girl told her that she was a graduate from Monrovia Methodist Secondary School in Liberia. The name of the school did not register to her at the time; not until she embraced Christianity, and discovered John Wesley and his brother.

"I was wondering if I could come and stay with you until I am back on my feet." Bridgette stopped her sobs long enough to bring Nana back to the present.

Nana was hesitant at first. She had opened her home to James Dunn when he called distressed and homeless one night. She was accommodating to James when he needed her. He only moved out when she lost her mother, and Nana never heard from him again. She was grateful that she had the night to pray and sleep over Bridgette's request. She wanted the Lord to tell her that it was okay to take in this stranger, whom she only knew for a few months. After all, she had known James for many years while they both worked at Proficiency Travel at the IFT. He still showed no gratitude after he left her home. The Holy Spirit led her to what she said next. "Bridgette, I need to sleep on this and take it to the Lord in prayer." She chose her words with care but she knew who was in control of everything. "I'm not sure when the Marshals are scheduled to come to your condo tomorrow. In any case, I will let you know my answer before they get there." Her heart went out to Bridgette. She remembered one of her friends telling her that they were all a paycheck away from homelessness.

"They're scheduled to come late morning." Bridgette told her. "I've been packing all day."

"If I agree to this, I can only accommodate you with a suitcase. My guest bedroom and bathroom are already fully furnished." Nana did not want her to bring a lot of things with her. She did not want to get stuck with Bridgette like it was with James.

"Oh I understand. I have arranged for a storage place."

Nana knew that it meant nothing; James also had a storage facility and when he moved, he needed to make four trips with his car. Within seven months, James had accumulated a lot of stuff. Nana ended the call and promised to call her in the morning.

When Nana hung up, she wondered why James and Bridgette both needed her in their time of distress. She wondered why they reached out to her and not a relative or close friend. She certainly did not consider herself a friend of Bridgette's. She thought at the time that James had been a friend but after his ungrateful behavior, she knew that he was only a user. She told herself that Africans were different in that sense. They would give up their beds for a guest. She knew that before Adjoa saw her homeless, she would take her in to share the one bedroom apartment in which she lived. She would take Adjoa in before she saw her cousin on the street with no place to go.

Nana prayed and wrestled with her decision the entire night and the wee hours of the morning. She wanted God to speak to her through the Holy Spirit and tell her not to take in Bridgette. The more she prayed, the more the answer came to her in the same message; she was supposed to take in Bridgette and help her in her distress. She made the much dreaded phone call at 8:30 that morning to Bridgette. "I've made my decision – I might be crazy for doing this but I will allow you to stay here for a little bit until you get on your feet." She did not believe that she was actually going to take another person in her home that did not have a job.

"You will not regret, I promise." Bridgette's voice trembled. "I was only waiting for your call before leaving for the storage place. Thank you."

"What time do you suppose you will be coming to Herndon?"

"I would say about 2:30 this afternoon."

"I need to run my errands, which is why I need an exact time." Nana felt a problem already, if Bridgette was vague about her arrival. "I cannot have you move in here after dark. I live in a quiet neighborhood."

"I understand."

"I'm glad you do understand because I have rules in my home, and I expect you to adhere to them."

"I will see you this afternoon. Thanks."

Nana wondered about what she had just agreed to do. She did not know Bridgette, and she knew nothing about the woman. She called Shirley as she braced herself for a lecture about why she should not have Bridgette move in with her.

"Have you lost your mind?" Shirley was in disbelief. "What do you know about this woman?"

"Quite frankly, Shirl, I know nothing about her except what she told me. Her business card shows that she has her own public relations firm." Nana said. "She has no website, and her email address on the business card is a Mymail address."

"Do not take that woman in your home." Shirley was adamant. "For all we know, she could be a criminal."

Nana laughed. "I would not go that far. She's just in a bad way at the time, and she needs assistance."

"Let her go find assistance elsewhere." Shirley was troubled. "Does she not have relatives? She's an American so she should have relatives somewhere in the country. Why did she choose you?"

"I am wondering about the very same thing. I would not seek this type of assistance from someone I just met less than five months ago."

"This is exactly why I can't believe you agreed for her to move in with you."

"Well, she has nowhere else to go. She could be on her way here already. If it doesn't work out, I will ask her to leave."

"After that James character, you said you would not take anyone like that in your home again."

"I know that but she won my sympathy. It could happen to me or anyone else, Shirl."

"I strongly disagree about that." Shirley shook her head as she held the phone. "If that woman steps out of line, call me and I'll be on the first available flight." The two women laughed and ended their conversation on a note of mixed feelings.

Bridgette arrived at the Herndon townhouse at 3:30 that afternoon. Nana welcomed her and showed her to Shirley's former room. She showed her the to the hall bathroom which Shirley used when she lived there. The two women went back downstairs to the living room to chat. "I hope you brought your own linen." Nana told her, which was more of a question than a statement. "You are welcomed to use my everyday dishes but the dishes in the dining room are off limits to you. I'm very particular about my surroundings and things. I would appreciate it if you clean up after yourself. Let me know when you need the vacuum cleaner, and I will show you where to find it."

"I got it, and I thank you for the hospitality. I did bring some linen with me. I don't do much cooking so I will not need to use the kitchen much." Bridgette's eyes were full of tears. "I am grateful to you for taking me, a stranger into your home."

"I'm a vegetarian so I have separate pots if you ever want to cook meat kinds."

"What a coincidence – so am I. I have not eaten meat for more than ten years now." Bridgette told Nana. "We do have something in common after all."

"I'm glad to hear that. Do you consume dairy?"

"I'm not a vegan; I just don't eat red meat, poultry and seafood."

"Well I am a vegan – no dairy, or any type of meat do I eat." Nana told her. "Do you eat tofu?"

"I've had it before but I don't make it a habit of eating it. I guess I just never acquired the taste for it."

"Then how do you get your protein?"

"I eat lots of nuts and I also like lentils, collards and spinach."

"I like the red lentils; they're easier to cook than the green lentils." It did not take the two women long before they began to laugh and exchange jokes. Nana told Bridgette about life when she grew up in Ghana.

Bridgette shared with her about life in Alabama. She told stories about the civil rights movement. "I sat at the lunch counter when only whites were allowed to sit there."

"Were you old enough to participate in such things?" Nana wondered how old Bridgette was. She looked younger than civil rights era.

"I was a little girl about nine years old when I sat at the counter with my father and others from our church."

That made Bridgette about sixty years old but she did not look like it. "Were you afraid? Have you ever seen a live Do Dragons Die?" Nana was curious. "I've heard stories about them but I hope I will never have the opportunity of seeing one." She shrugged. "Of course, I've seen them in movies from the 1960's."

"Yes I saw the DDD whenever they marched with their hoods and robes." Bridgette told Nana. "But I never had any close encounters with them."

"Why do they disguise themselves?" Nana wondered aloud. "I thought a person disguises himself either when he's afraid of something or when he doesn't want to be identified. I did not think that either of those was a problem for the DDD."

Bridgette laughed at Nana's analogy. "Some of them don't want to be identified and some of them don't really care. I doubt whether fear has anything to do with their choice of attire."

"It's sad that some people have such problems with other human beings."

Bridgette and Nana had a good start. Nana was relieved, and she felt more comfortable with Bridgette being in her home. She figured that they would get along well, and that she and Shirley were worried for nothing.

A U.S. Citizen is Welcomed

A week after Bridgette moved in, Nana received good news from the United States Immigration. She needed to report to the Immigration office in Arlington, Virginia the next day. She was prepared for the citizenship test. Nana had studied the one hundred questions the Immigration gave her to study. She had Bridgette test her on the questions, and she knew all of the answers by memory. The questions were based on United States civic. "You are really fortunate that you were born here and do not have to earn your citizenship like we do." Nana told Bridgette as she tested her.

"I guess we are fortunate in a way but it is also nice to be born in Africa."

"I am proud of my birthplace but where one was born is not as important as what one makes of oneself after he or she is born." Nana wanted to make her point. "I once attended a memorial service for a friend's mother. The Bishop that delivered the eulogy spoke about the 'dash' in a person's life. He said, when a person dies, they publish the date that person was born, a dash and the date the person died. He went on to say that the dash represents that person's life here on earth. He said that all the things that the person did from birth until his or her demise is within that dash. He asked us how short or how long would our dashes be. It gave me something to think about that day. Our legacies consist of what we do here on earth. I always search myself and my actions for the difference that I am making here on earth." She had a serious look on her face. "I would like to think that my legacy will be significant enough to be shared with others at my own life celebration."

"I like the way you put that." Bridgette smiled in admiration. "How do you remember all of the first thirteen states of the union? You name them as though you studied them in grade school."

"As you well know, I did not attend grade school in the States. I only attended university here. We learned about Ghanaian civic in Ghana when I was in grade school there." Nana used her hands when she spoke. "Since I have the map of the U.S. in my mind, I count them from the south and I work my way upward along the east coast until I get to the upper part of New England."

"I never thought about it that way. What time is your test tomorrow?"

"They want me there at noon. After I pass my test tomorrow, I will be sworn in with the 3:00 o'clock group."

"You sound really sure about passing."

"I don't like to say the word 'if' – it makes me sound as though I'm doubtful or I don't have faith."

"I see – it is also a positive outlook."

"Absolutely, it is." Nana agreed with Bridgette. "Did you study any of these civic questions in your grade school?"

"Oh yes, I think we all had to study that." Bridgette chuckled. "Don't ask me if I remembered all of the answers because I do not recall all of this stuff." She indicated the two sheets of paper of questions in her hand.

"I had to retain everything I learned back then. My father tested me at the dinner table at night on Ghana civics. He told me that knowing such things exhibited your patriotism." She shook her head as she thought about her father's beliefs and opinions. "As of tomorrow, I will have two countries to exhibit my patriotism, I suppose."

Nana's test results proved her correct. Although she did not expect the test to comprise of ten essay questions, she still scored one hundred percent. Two months before her test, a friend took her citizenship test in Texas. She told her that it was too simple to fail it, and that a person had to be a moron to fail it. She told Nana that they asked her only three questions in Texas, and one of them was who the first President of the United States was. Another question was the number of states in the U.S. Virginia's test was far from simple if the person did not study.

Nana's first question was to list the first thirteen colonies of the union. She smiled and listed them from Georgia, the Carolinas, as she worked her way up to the New England states. Another question was the number of Senators in the U.S. Senate and another was the number of Congressmen or Congresswomen were in the House of Representatives. The simplest question on Nana's test was the date of when the U.S. declared independence. The tester checked Nana's answers on her test while she sat there across from her. Nana was certain that she had passed the test but she was not sure that she had scored 100% until the lady told her.

"This is very good." The lady smiled at Nana over her glasses which rested on her nose. "You got all of your answers correct." She extended her hand to Nana for a handshake. "Congratulations – the ceremony will begin in half an hour. You may wait in the reception room until you are called. Your friend is eagerly waiting out there for you." She referred to Bridgette who had offered to accompany Nana.

"Thank you – it is an honor to know that I am only half an hour from becoming a citizen of the United States."

"You deserve it – I can tell that you paid attention to what it means to become an American citizen." She saw Nana out to the reception room, and called in the next candidate.

"What are you doing here, Adjoa?" Nana hurried over to her cousin who decided to surprise her, and witness her swearing in ceremony.

"I would not miss this – I had to come and support you." Adjoa told her cousin. "So how was the test?"

"The test was perfect." Nana was excited. "I scored 100%. There were ten questions and I got all of them correct."

"Congratulations – you predicted it." Bridgette told her.

"Thank you." She smiled. "I thank the Lord for being with me today in a way that I did not expect."

The three women sat and chatted until they announced that the ceremony was about to begin. An Immigration officer escorted them to the room where the ceremony was to be held. Nana was nervous because she was about to swear to honor another country's patriotic laws. The consolation was that Ghana and the United States had a dual citizenship agreement. The Immigration tester advised Nana that her Ghanaian passport would be returned to her. She did not feel as though she had traded off her country.

An officer advised the audience of their rights as citizens of the United States, and what it meant to be an American. She instructed the candidates to raise their right hands and take the oath of citizenship. All fifty-six candidates, who included Nana, repeated the oath after the officer. Nana's hand shook as she repeated the oath. They were asked to say the pledge of allegiance, while they faced a large American flag that stood tall on a stand. Nana took the entire process to be a serious action. They were allowed to read the pledge of allegiance if they did not know it by memory. Nana did not know it by memory therefore she used the paper that was provided them. The officer congratulated the candidates, and welcomed them to the United States as Americans. The United States had just added fifty-six Americans to its population, and that was only in Northern Virginia. That year happened to be a presidential election year. Nana was excited that she would have the opportunity to vote in three months.

Adjoa and Bridgette fussed over Nana, as they snapped photographs of her beside the large flag. They took additional photos of Nana with some of her citizenship counterparts and with the officer that swore them in. The new citizens were each given a package. The contents of the package were the voter's registration application, the passport application, words to the national anthem, (the Star Spangled Banner) a welcome letter from the current President of the United States and the words to the pledge of allegiance.

Adjoa and Bridgette took Nana out for a late lunch at a restaurant near the Immigration building. Bridgette was familiar with the area because it was where her former condo was located.

Nana whispered to Bridgette. "Are you sure being in this area does not bother you?"

Bridgette whispered back to her. "I'm positive about it." She smiled at Nana.

Nana and Adjoa caught up on their lives, but Adjoa was cautious of Bridgette. There was something about Bridgette that Adjoa did not like but she was unable to single it out. She told the same to Nana when Bridgette visited the restroom at the restaurant.

"Shirl and I had bad intuitions about her but since she moved in, I've changed my mind about her."

"I just cannot put my finger on it, but there is something that bothers me about her." Adjoa leaned closer to Nana. "Watch her closely, cousin."

The three women enjoyed their meal as Nana shared her test experience with Adjoa and Bridgette. Adjoa needed to leave for a doctor's appointment in the city. Bridgette and Nana took the Metro in the opposite direction to pick up Nana's car which was parked at the West Falls Church Metro Station.

"If you don't like to ride the metro, why do you do it?" Bridgette asked Nana when she noticed how Nana touched nothing during her ride in the train.

"It's convenient and I don't have to sit in traffic." Nana thought Bridgette asked too many questions.

"Why do you have part of the newspaper under your feet?" Bridgette indicated the paper under Nana's feet. "Is it because you don't want your feet to touch the floor?"

"Are you conducting an interview again?" Nana laughed with Bridgette. "I don't understand why they don't just remove the filthy carpet from the floors of the trains. If they replaced the carpet with linoleum, it would be a lot easier to keep clean."

"I guess you're right about that." Bridgette agreed. "I try not to pay any attention to it."

"I'm too particular about what I touch and what touches me not to pay attention."

"Do you realize that you have a germ phobia?" Bridgette grinned and displayed teeth that needed major dental care.

"Are you also a shrink?" Nana asked God to grant her patience with Bridgette so that she would not lose her patience.

"Are you upset?" Bridgette realized that she had just hit a nerve. "I'm sorry for probing so much."

"It is no problem. Here we are." The train pulled into West Falls Church. "Let's get out of here." The women left the train and the station. They found Nana's car and drove to Herndon. "I need to make a quick stop at the ATM." Nana drove up to the drive through window and made her withdrawal, but she was shocked when she noticed her account balance on her receipt. "Something strange has happened." Nana told Bridgette as she drove home. "There is at least more than a Thousand Dollars in my account that I did not put there."

"Don't complain just take it as a gift for becoming a citizen." Bridgette told her as a joke.

"No I think I know what it is." Nana said as an afterthought. "I applied for unemployment a while ago but I totally forgot about it." She smiled. "I like being an American."

Nana was bombarded with phone calls of congratulations for the rest of that day. Shirley called from her salon, and Frank called from New York where the Gorillas played their third preseason game that night. Nana looked forward to watching that game. Jean-Claude and Kiddi sent her text messages from Paris and London. Alec called her and put her in an even better mood.

"You are now officially one of us." Alec said when she answered the phone.

"Hi there – it's good to hear from you." She smiled and blushed into the phone. "You ought to know how it feels." Alec was also a naturalized citizen of the United States.

"Yes but mine was so long ago, I'm an old American now." They laughed.

"Okay, old American – do you have any advice for this young American?" They laughed harder at Nana's smart response.

"Well, with elections right around the corner, you need to scrutinize the candidates and decide which candidate you will support."

"I filled out my voter's registration application this afternoon, and dropped it in the mail already."

"That is a really good citizen. You're not wasting any time I see."

"I need some time to let my citizenship set in first." She smiled. "Politics have never been my forte but I do take this citizenship thing seriously. I will exercise my right to vote because I never voted in Ghana."

"Some of the Americans that were born here take their citizenship for granted because they do not have to study for and take a test." Alec shared with her. "When I raised my right hand and took that oath to be a law-abiding citizen of the United States and to uphold the clauses in the constitution, it is a feeling that I take seriously, and I never take it for granted.

"That's what we have in common." Nana told him. "You were born in a different country to diverse parents, and became a U.S. citizen. I was born in Ghana to cultural parents, and just became a U.S. citizen today."

"Is that all we have in common?" He teased her. "I thought we had a lot more than that in common."

"You know what I mean."

"Anyway, I hate to break up our conversation but I have a patient waiting for me. Congratulations again on your accomplishment today. I'm very proud of you." They ended their conversation, and Alec promised to call her another day.

The Reynolds also called later that afternoon. Nana had told them about her scheduled test, and they anticipated that she would pass the test. "When you have the time, Peter and I would like to take you to the restaurant where we met." Martha told Nana. "We can go someplace else if you prefer; it is your choice."

"I would like that." Nana was touched by the invitation. "You know how much I like Thai food so that would be great to go back there." She smiled. "Plus, that is where we met so it makes it more significant."

"Then it is a plan." Martha told her. "Let's try to do it before you begin your new job."

"It will have to be next week, which is my last week before I begin the job." They agreed on Thursday evening the following week and ended their call.

Nana was in a celebratory mood that she did not bother to check her mail until the next day. She received a letter from an attorney in Washington, D.C. The letter informed Nana that she was being sued by Eastern Travel for job negligence. Nana was baffled, and wasted no time before she called Sara and Elliott Wilcox to seek legal advice.

"What are my chances in this case – can she do this?" Nana asked Sara Wilcox.

"Unfortunately she can, otherwise she would not be suing you." Sara told Nana. "You will need an attorney that specializes in human resources. I know someone to refer you to because we do not handle such cases."

"I appreciate it. What kind of money will this attorney expect me to pay?" Nana was concerned. She was scheduled to begin a new job the following week. She did not want any publicity with the case. Her reputation was at stake. "Sara I am not in the position to pay a lot of legal fees at this time."

"Stop worrying so much. I will speak to Jacob myself, and ask him to give you a payment plan and a discount."

"Thanks – I really appreciate your favor."

"I will email you the details of the attorney. His name is Jacob Cohen. He and Elliott attended law school together. He is very good and will provide you with the right legal advice. You need someone who knows what he's doing because your former employer sounds like she knows what she's doing."

"Thanks again, Sara. I will wait to receive your email with his information."

"It is not a problem. By the time you receive my email, I will have already spoken with Jacob so he will be expecting your call."

Nana called Jacob Cohen after she received Sara's email with his phone number, email and the name of his law firm.

"I don't want you to contact anyone from Eastern Travel, even if you had a good relationship when you worked there." Jacob told Nana. "Sara tells me that you're a playwright so I'm sure you write well. I want you to write out everything you can remember from the first day you began working at Eastern Travel until the day you left." Nana listened intently and took notes as Jacob instructed her. "Do not leave out anything."

"It should be easy. I kept notes from my employment there. I kept a journal so I can just send you my journal. I printed so it will be clear enough for you to read."

"Good, that will save time then. Do you have my address?"

"Yes, Sara provided your information. I will send it to you this afternoon by Primary Mail. You should have it tomorrow."

"Okay, that sounds good. We have to build a firm case against this lady, Valerie at Eastern. She accuses you of employment negligence. Did you sign an agreement with Eastern?"

"No, I never did sign anything with her."

"So you were employed at will." He wondered why she felt she had the right to sue Nana for negligence if she was hired at will.

"I was hired by Eastern just the same as I have been hired in the past by any other employer." Nana explained but she too was puzzled. "I did apply for unemployment some weeks ago. I never heard anything from them until I noticed that they were depositing money to my account. I have not used any of the funds. I only discovered that yesterday."

"When you send me the journal tomorrow, I want you to include the date you applied for unemployment and the date you discovered the money in your account. Let me know the amount that was deposited to your account." Jacob continued his instructions to Nana. "Oh, make sure you let me know the date you started the job and the day you left as well."

"I will provide everything you need to help me." Nana was troubled but she had the confidence that Valerie Penney did not have the power to hurt her. She knew that only one person had that kind of power and she knew that the Lord would never hurt her. "Thank you Mr. Cohen."

"Sara said you're worried but there is no need to worry. You have not broken the law in anyway. I look forward to reading your journal and notes." He also looked forward to facing Valerie Penney and her attorney. "By the way, congratulations are in order on your accomplishment yesterday. Sara told me about the citizenship. It is a big step you took and that gives you just as much equal rights to this country as Valerie Penney has."

"Thank you." She had tears in her eyes. Jacob Cohen was an angel from God.

Later that day, Nana called Shirley and Frank and shared everything with them about the case.

"That woman is a degenerate that has no business being among decent human beings." Frank spat out the angry words into the phone. "How dare she pull this?"

"It is not enough that she put me out of her office and out of a job, she wants to make sure that I am not happy."

"It will back fire on her, Nana." Shirley was furious. "I bet it is all because she was made to pay unemployment."

"That is why I didn't want to apply for the unemployment in the first place." Nana told her friends.

"You cannot always roll over to keep peace, Nana." Shirley told her. "I know you believe in turning the other cheek but I prefer what the Old Testament said about eye for an eye."

Nana laughed. "Shirl, the Lord also promised to take vengeance for us."

"You did the right thing by contacting an attorney, Nana." Frank told her. "Please don't worry about the cost of the lawyer and all that. Just let him get you out of this nonsense and send me his bill. I will not take no for an answer."

"I appreciate your offer but the lawyer said he will set up a payment plan for me if I cannot afford his legal fees."

"Nana, this case is closed about the legal fees." Frank told her with persistence in his voice. "This one is on Shirl and me."

Nana sighed. "I should not be your responsibility. I should be able to handle my situations myself."

"Shirl and I have the money, and those legal fees are not going to break us." Frank placed his arm around Shirley's shoulders. "Now I know that if the situation was reversed, you would be happy to oblige."

"I would do so without a twitch in my eye." Nana assured him.

"Then it is settled." Shirley said. "Please email the lawyer's information to me, Nana. We will let him know to do everything he can to get you out of this situation and send us the bill."

Nana sighed and shook her head in disbelief. She wished she had not told them but it was too late to have regrets. She agreed with them but she decided that she would not send them Jacob's contact information. Even though she had regrets about her call to them, she had to admit to herself that she felt better after she spoke with them. She told herself how blessed she was to have friends like Frank and Shirley, Jean-Claude and Kiddi. They never had their hands out to her for assistance so she did not intend to have them pay her bills.

The next day Jacob called Nana to let her know that he had received her journal and other information she sent him. "I've read your journal. You really kept good notes." Jacob told her. "It was smart of you to do that."

"So do we have a good case then?" Nana wanted him to get to the point.

"Oh yes we do have a good case. The fact that she told you to leave her office because she didn't want to see you, that alone is a case. According to your journal, it was not the first time she put you out of the office."

"That is correct."

"Then negligence is not a case. You also had the right to apply for unemployment based on the fact that she drove you out of her office. You took that to mean dismissal." Jacob sipped his coffee. "This will be a slam dunk."

Nana smiled at Jacob's description of the case. "I'm glad to hear that, Mr. Cohen."

"Call me Jacob – no need to be so formal."

"Whatever you want me to call you." Nana liked his demeanor.

"Be ready to appear in court two weeks from now. Meanwhile if you have any questions or concerns, do not hesitate to contact me. If I have any further questions, I'll give you a call."

"Thank you, Jacob."

"Thank me in two weeks after we win this case."

Nana thought about everything that had happened to her that year. Her mother passed away and James Dunn cut off all communications with her, after she had aided him for seven months. She found a new job, she took in another stranger, and she became a U.S. citizen. Now she faced a lawsuit for job negligence. She wondered what else would happen in her life.

The Shocking Unexpected

Nana did not wonder for a long time about what else could happen in her life. It was only a week later when she was on her way to a meeting; she had an appointment with a woman who owned an organization that was interested in partnership with FAFGM. She sat at the corner of Elden Street and Herndon Parkway in her car as she waited for the light to change. There was a car ahead of her at the light. As they waited for the light to change, Nana's car was shoved into the car ahead of her without her control of it. She was in shock as she tried to control the car but it was shoved again into the back of the car ahead of her. It did not register to her at first what had happened until she realized that she was in an accident. Her knees hurt and her hands trembled, she wept and she prayed in solitude. She sat still without attempting to move. She noticed that the car ahead of her was also still.

A man with long braids in his hair came up to her window. "I'm really sorry but it looked to me like y'all were moving."

She regarded the man at her window and pulled herself together before she addressed him. "How could we have been moving, when the light was still red, Sir?" She wondered if he was intoxicated. In anyone's right frame of mind, he would not have thought that the cars ahead of him were in motion, since the traffic light was red.

"Are you okay?" The man asked Nana. "I was just taking my two boys to soccer practice and we were running late."

"Well, now you will not get there at all." Nana retorted. She had always been concerned about a head on collision on highways such as the Capital Beltway and I-66 but she never anticipated being shoved into one car by another car. It was her first accident and she was scared. Nana did not like to drive. She learned to drive as an adult in the U.S., unlike her American and European counterparts. Driving was something that very few women in Africa made their priority or a necessity. She forced herself to learn how to drive, only because it was difficult to get around the suburbs of Washington, D.C. without a car. She drove only when it was absolutely necessary.

"I have already called the police." The man said to her. "If you are injured, the ambulance will be here to take you to the hospital."

"I see you thought of everything. Thank you." She noticed that he walked over to the car that was ahead of her, and said something to the woman in the car. Nana thought to herself that he felt guilty so he reported himself to the police.

The police did not take long to arrive. Nana heard the sirens as they got closer to the scene of the accident. There were spectators standing around as well as from the vehicles in traffic.

A police officer walked up to her car and introduced himself. "Ma'am, are you hurt? Do you need to go to the hospital? The ambulance is here and can take you. Here's the paramedic now but first I need to take your statement." Nana noticed that another officer and paramedic were at the car ahead of her. "Can you tell me what happened here?"

"It all happened so fast that I was in shock, Officer." Nana was still shaken up and the officer noticed that. "I was waiting for the light to change, and the car in front of me was also waiting." She began to sweat. "I suddenly felt my car moving without my control. My car and I were shoved into the car ahead of me." She wiped her face with a napkin from her bag. "The man behind me said that he thought we were moving and that he was running late for his sons' soccer practice."

"Thank you. I will leave you now with the paramedics. You will need to provide your information to the driver that caused this wreck before you leave." The officer told Nana.

"Thanks officer." She turned to the paramedic, who spoke to her with a nod and a look of concern. "Hello."

The paramedic opened the driver's door of her car. "How do you feel?"

"My knees hurt, and the back of my neck hurts somewhat." Nana told the paramedic.

"You must have hit your knees on the steering as the car hit the other car." He told her. "I see that you drive with your steering close up to you."

"I feel comfortable driving that way." Nana explained to him. She always drove close to the steering from the time she learned to drive. Her friends teased her about it.

The paramedic checked her knees and asked her if certain areas of them hurt as he pressed on them. "Do you think you can walk?"

"I think I can walk." Nana got out of the car with the aid of the paramedic. He wanted to see if she could stand on the knees and walk on them. She was able to stand with very little pain. She took a few steps only with a slight limp.

"Your knees are not swollen, so that tells me that they're not broken or fractured. You might have a sprain in the right knee. I would recommend that we take you to the emergency room and have them do x-rays on your knees and your neck." He saw that Nana was reluctant to go to the hospital. "I know you don't want to spend the rest of your afternoon in the emergency but you don't want to take accidents and injuries lightly."

"Okay, you have convinced me. I will go with you." Nana knew that she should go and get checked out by the doctors but she did not like hospitals and needles. When she was a child, she cried at the sight of a doctor or nurse. She associated them with needles, and she despised needles. She prepared to get in the ambulance, but she called Bridgette to let her know what had happened. She did not own a vehicle but she had a rental. Bridgette offered to meet her at the hospital.

Nana walked around her car to see if any damage was done to it. No damage was done to the car ahead of her, and no damage was done to the front of her car. She screamed when she saw the rear of her car. The trunk of her car looked like an accordion. It was totally gone. She saw the vehicle that had hit her, and she knew that he was in the wrong. Nana's car was a Toyota Echo and his vehicle was a large Chevy Tahoe. No damage was done to his truck. Nana stood and wept as she examined her car. She had paid off her car only six months before. Her car only had twenty-nine thousand miles on it at the time, and it was in pristine condition. She was thankful to God that her life was spared, as well as the lives of others but she was angry at the driver of the Tahoe for the damage to her car and the inconvenience. She called the woman with whom she had the appointment and told her about the accident. They agreed to reschedule for a later date, after Nana recuperated.

"I'm sorry – I was trying to tell my dad that you were stopped but he wasn't paying attention." The voice of the eleven-year old son of the Tahoe driver told Nana as she looked at her car.

"You did?" Nana saw that the police who stood nearby heard the boy's apology to her, and she knew that the boy had just dug a deeper hole for his father. The child did not realize what he did. She saw the police take notes on his pad. "It was not your fault, my dear so no need to apologize." She rubbed his head. "At least we are all alive – God spared us, and that is the important thing here. I can get another vehicle but I cannot get another life."

"You're a nice lady. Thanks." The eleven-year old told her. He was about to say more to her when his father interrupted him with a raised voice and ordered him to get back in the vehicle.

Nana was taken to the hospital in the ambulance. The lady in the car ahead of her opted not to be taken to the hospital. She did not complain about pain therefore the paramedics checked her and released her to leave. Her car was not damaged but she still provided her information to both the police and the Tahoe driver. It turned out that the Tahoe driver and his family lived in the same development as Nana. They owned a townhouse on the other side of where Nana lived. Nana exchanged information with the driver before she boarded the ambulance. The police assured her that they would have her car towed to where she wanted it towed. She asked them to have it towed to her home.

The paramedic that checked Nana at the scene of the accident was right. Her x-rays showed no fracture or brake in her knees. However her right knee was bruised. Her neck suffered a strain but it was not serious. The doctor at the emergency room advised Nana to seek physical therapy. She smiled to herself, and knew the best person to consult before she did anything else. Her friend, Alec specialized in sports medicine and reconstructive surgery. He would know how to steer her in the right direction.

Bridgette met her at the hospital as she had promised, and drove her home in her rental car. Nana filled her in on the accident and her experience while they drove back to Herndon. Bridgette drove by the scene of the accident to make sure that Nana's car was towed. Nana's car was parked in the driveway of her home when they pulled up in front of the house. Bridgette gasped when she saw the damage to the rear of Nana's car.

"I'm sorry about your car." Bridgette turned to look at Nana. "Are you going to get a rental?"

"I cannot think at the moment." Nana told her. "I just want to make a couple of phone calls this evening. The man's insurance company will contact me in the morning." She let them in the house as she spoke to Bridgette. "I will pray on this tonight and make my decisions in the morning. I do need a car – I start my new job next week."

Nana called Alec for medical advice after she was settled for the evening. She took a warm bath, and rubbed her knees with what they gave her at the emergency room. She also took a pain killer, which she did not like to take. Nana was a health fanatic, and she did not believe in the consumption of medications. She believed in preventive care.

"Are you okay? What did they say at the hospital? What did they give you?" Alec was troubled and concerned over the news of her accident.

"I'm fine." She wanted him to calm down. "I need you to give me medical advice. What do you think I should do?" She gave him the details of her accident, what the paramedics said, and what she was told at the hospital.

"I know a good physical therapist in Alexandria, Virginia whom you can see. I will give him a call and let him know that you will be calling to set up an appointment. If it is okay with you, I will ask him to share with me the results of your x-rays and tests."

"It is fine with me. I can sign whatever papers he requires." Nana agreed.

"Meanwhile, I think you should rest until your appointment with the therapist. You need to stay off your knee as much as you can."

"Thanks, Doctor." They laughed and wished each other a good night.

Nana sat in the waiting room of Dr. Rob Gamble, the physical therapist that Alec recommended to her. The events of two days before when she met up with the accident filled her thoughts. The Tahoe driver's insurance company did contact her and informed her that they would declare her car totaled.

"No, you cannot do that." Nana told the insurance woman. "My car is drivable, and there was no damage done to the engine. I started it yesterday morning and the engine sounds fine to me. I want my car repaired."

"We have looked at the car and we have declared it totaled, ma'am." The insurance woman told her.

"If you total my car, what are you offering for it? I need enough money to purchase a new car. My car was all paid for, and I would prefer not to have a car note."

"We will give you what the blue book shows that it is worth."

"And may I ask what that blue book value is?" Nana did not appreciate what the insurance company did.

"We will offer you Seven Thousand Dollars for your car. That is what the blue book value is."

"That is totally absurd." Her hands trembled as she held the phone. "Your client rammed his big old truck into my car, and you want to pay me off with $7000? I do not think so."

"That is our offer, ma'am."

"My car is all paid up – I had no car note. My car is in good condition. All you're going to do is have it repaired and sell it for far more than $7000."

"That is your opinion, and I don't know where you got that idea."

"It is also my car, and I want to have my car repaired. I can accept the $7000 only if I get to keep my car and have it repaired on my own."

"I will have to advise my boss of what you are asking before we can come to a conclusion."

"Then you do just that." Nana told her. "Thank you."

While she waited for Dr. Gamble to call her in to his office, she thought about the injustice people suffer in the world by others. Her life was interrupted by an irresponsible driver, and his insurance company wanted to take advantage of her. She decided that she was tired of being a victim; she was no longer going to be a victim. She was going to be the victor. The Medicine Woman made her a victim of female genital mutilation so many decades before. Valerie Penney made her a victim on the job, and sued her. Her mother's letter to her after her death made her feel like a victim. She thought to herself that the victimization was going to stop there. She was not going to allow this insurance company to bully her. She was going to stand up to them. After all, that was how a victor reacted. A victim felt sorry for herself; she rolled over and gave in to disadvantages. A victor stood firm and did not allow bullies such as Valerie Penney and the insurance company to dictate her fate.

"Nana Nkuku?" The announcement of Nana's name startled her and brought her back to the doctor's waiting room.

"Yes, I am Nana." She gathered her bag and shawl and followed the nurse to the doctor's examining room.

"The doctor will be right with you. Please have a seat." The nurse told her with a pleasant smile.

"Thank you." Nana returned her smile.

Nana was glad to meet Dr. Gamble. He had great bedside manners and was gentle when he checked her knee and asked her questions about the accident. Alec had already provided him with the initial information he needed. Nana gave him the rest of what he needed to assist her. He took additional x-rays to make sure that the knee did not worsen after she saw the doctor at the emergency room.

"The emergency room was correct about your knee, it is badly bruised." Dr. Gamble told her. "I will suggest that we wait until the bruising subsides before we begin physical therapy."

"Is there anything I need to do in the mean time?" Nana asked him.

"I will prescribe a rub and I will give you a cold pact to apply to the knee after the rub. When you are not using the pact, keep it in the freezer. Now about your neck, you did suffer a minor strain. You do not need a brace on it but you do need to be careful when you move about and sleep."

Nana told him about the insurance company, and asked him if he thought she needed a lawyer.

"Our practice has a law firm with which we deal on behalf of our patients. If you feel that the insurance company is not being cooperative, I would suggest that you speak with one of the attorneys at that firm."

"I would like to do that." She did not believe how many attorneys she was made to engage in such short a time. She wanted all of it behind her so she could move on with her life.

"As for the injury, we will have our attorneys work with the insurance company on your behalf. The car is a different case." He gave her the name and number to the lawyer he wanted her to contact about her car situation. "It is better to have the attorney handle the case about the car as well as the injury. You will not need to speak with the insurance company directly, moving forward."

"Thanks Dr. Gamble. I really appreciate it." She left the doctor's office and Bridgette drove her back to Herndon from Alexandria.

Nana followed the doctor's advice about her neck and her knee. She began to feel better; she only felt pain in her knee when she stood for long periods of time. The pain in her neck was gone. Nana began to look forward to the start of her new job at Alpha Travel. She spoke with the lawyer that Dr. Gamble recommended, and she gave that lawyer the contact information to the insurance company. Meanwhile her damaged car remained in the driveway of her townhouse. As the news about her accident spread, Nana began to receive phone calls from Jean-Claude, Shirley and Frank, Kiddi, Adjoa, the Reynolds, the Wilcox's, etc. Alec called her every day to check on her. She appreciated the attention but she assured them that she was fine, and there was no need to fuss over her.

Each time that Shirley called, she grilled Nana about Bridgette and how her behavior was. "I hope that woman is not taking advantage of you since you have been distracted with the accident and lawsuit." Shirley told Nana in one of their phone conversations.

"Actually Shirl, she has been really nice to me." Nana told her. "She drives me to my appointments. She makes the best herbal teas for me and keeps me company at times."

"She still needs to be watched." Shirley was not convinced. "I just do not trust her for some reason."

"You don't know her and have not met her." Nana told her. "Give her the benefit of the doubt, Shirl."

"Whatever." The two friends laughed. "Ok, I'm going to change the subject then. "Frank wants you to know that he's praying for you and have you in his thoughts. He's busy at the conclusion of preseason."

"I saw that they won all of their preseason games. I was glad to see that."

"It's an indication of the kind of season they will have." Shirley bragged.

"Go Gorillas." Nana shouted. "By the way, if it makes you feel better about Bridgette, she is a big fan of the Gorillas." Nana smiled.

"She probably told you that because of your relationship to the Quarterback." Shirley was still not softened by that.

"Now it is my time to say, 'whatever'." They laughed again. "I want to tell you something that happened to me since the accident."

"What is it?" Shirley's voice took on a serious tune.

"I have developed a fear of the road. I'm not only afraid to drive but I'm afraid of being in a car." It was something that was on Nana's mind but she did not disclose it to anyone else. She prayed about it, and asked God to remove the fear from her.

"It's probably normal. It was your first accident. You have always been a careful driver. Then this happened to you. The impact of it all is a lot to swallow. I think it is only a phase. You will get over it once you get back on the road."

Nana hoped that Shirley was right but she did not think that it was only a phase. Something happened to her confidence as a driver that day. "You're probably right." She decided to leave the rest in the Lord's hands.

Nana reported for her first day of work at Alpha Travel at 8:00 that morning. She was not expected to begin work until 9:00 in the morning but she wanted to be prompt on her first day. She waited in the reception area until Polly came out of the Managers' meeting that morning.

Her first day at Alpha Travel went well. There she was with a new group of coworkers. She thought about her first day at Eastern Travel, when she was introduced to Antomeyer, Tammie, Amber and Janet. She found herself with new names to remember and new personalities with which to work.

Polly took Nana to the floor of the building where she would work. She introduced her to Rene, the woman who was Nana's manager. Polly wished Nana a great day and left her in the care of Rene. Rene showed Nana around the office and introduced her to Donald, Tom and Trudy. Donald was the assistant manager of the office. Tom was the senior agent, and Trudy and Sootha were international agents there. Alpha Travel was founded by a lady called Rose, who still went to the office when she was in Virginia. Rose traveled a great deal, especially since her husband's death. Rose and her late husband ran the agency together until he died from cancer a year before Nana went to work there. Rose was a good businesswoman, and she surrounded herself with experienced staff. Her Vice-President, Leonard was a strewed salesman. Leonard handled all sales transactions of new and prospective clients. He was a favorite of Rose's.

Nana informed Rene and Polly on her first day about her upcoming court appearance. She also advised them of her recent accident, and her physical therapy sessions. They assured her that it was not a problem with them. Rene told her to give her the exact dates and she would mark them on her calendar.

Tom was assigned to train Nana and familiarize her with the systems and the various international accounts she was expected to service. Nana worked at Proficiency for such a long time; she became accustomed to only one client to service. The IFT was hardly an easy client to keep happy but she knew them, and she felt comfortable with them. She still had regrets of leaving there. Eastern Travel reminded her of a general market. She serviced everyone, which included walk-ins off the street. Valerie did not want to lose a possible dime.

Nana looked around the office at Alpha, and she did not like the environment. It was not clean; the carpet full of stains, which reminded her of the carpet in the metro trains. She made it a point to take disinfecting spray and sanitizing wipes on her second day to clean the desk and computer that were assigned to her. She was shocked by the grime and dirt that came off the keyboard and mouse of her computer. The armrests of her chair disgusted her when she cleaned them. Nana wondered who occupied the desk before she came there. The dust and dirt that came off the desk were enough to fill a large paper cup. She took a handheld vacuum and cleaned the carpet under her desk and around her cubicle. Everyone made hilarious comments and jokes about how she was particular and clean. Her manager, Rene teased her and said, "When you're finished with your cubicle, you can come and do mine." Nana was accustomed to the jokes and comments from coworkers wherever she worked. The comments did not bother her. She regarded them as compliments about her character. She once told one of her coworkers at Proficiency Travel that he should be so fortunate to be as particular as she was. He called her a 'neat freak'. Some of the other names Nana was called in previous jobs were 'health freak', 'miss too organized', 'miss perfect', miss OCD, (obsessive compulsive disorder), and many more.

Donald, Tom, Sootha and Trudy were all from Vietnam. They spoke their native language throughout the day. They did not care whether or not there were others in their midst who did not understand it. Donald was the only one who felt that they should not speak their language in the office during business hours. Rene did not appreciate it but she seemed too afraid to offend anyone. Sootha and Trudy were the biggest violators of that. Nana's cubicle was in the middle of Trudy's and Sootha's cubicles. She teased them and said, "By the time I leave here, I will know how to speak Vietnamese." They laughed at Nana's remark but continued to speak their language. Tom was not much better than Trudy and Sootha. He spoke it to them whenever they spoke it to him. Nana did not allow their language bother her. After all she was from a different country herself; had a couple of Ghanaians from the Ashanti region and the Fanti tribe were in the employ of Alpha, they might be tempted to speak in their language as well.

At the end of Nana's first week at Alpha Travel, she knew everyone's name. She formulated an opinion in her mind of everyone's character. Polly was an inquisitive red haired attractive woman. She was a big fan of the local football team in the Washington, D.C. area. Nana found out that Rose owned a suite at the local football stadium. Tom, Donald, Rene and Leonard were also fans of the local football team. While Trudy was a football fan, she was not a fan of the local team. She was an ardent fan of one of the football teams in New York. Trudy held a grudge against the San Antonio Gorillas from the time they defeated her favorite team in the Big Bowl four years before. Her team was the only team in the Association that had maintained a perfect record throughout the season four years before. They made it to the Big Bowl without a problem. The Gorillas were not a favorite team to even make it through the playoffs that year. However they made it to the Big Bowl, and defeated Trudy's undefeated team.

Nana listened to all the football rhetoric that was discussed in the office. She kept quiet in her first week. She did not want Trudy to know that her favorite team was the Gorillas, and that the quarterback was a close friend. She was afraid that she might be carried out of the office on a stretcher if she disclosed such information to her coworkers. She enjoyed a good laugh with Frank and Shirley that weekend after her first week. Frank was at home for an early bi-week in the season. The Gorillas had their bi-week after the second week of the season. He took advantage to spend some quality time with Shirley.

"You need to be careful with your new coworkers, Nana." Frank teased her. "The hatred will only intensify when we meet the Washington local team in two weeks. That is an important division game for us."

"You mean when you whip them in two weeks." Nana said as they laughed.

"I would not be doing that kind of trash-talking there at your job now." Frank warned her.

"I know better than that." Nana told them. "These people are football fanatics. I thought we were the worse fanatics but my new coworkers make us look like we don't even like the game." They laughed at her analogy of her coworkers. "Trudy hates you, Frank – she despises the Gorillas."

"It was four years ago when we messed up their perfect record." Frank said. "They lost – they need to get over it."

"I haven't seen them going to another Big Bowl since four years ago so they do need to get over it." Shirley added.

Whenever Trudy found the time to speak English, she interrogated Nana about her background. Nana was hesitant to warm up to Trudy. She was afraid to get comfortable with her for fear that Trudy would discover her knowledge of football.

"I notice you know your international stuff." Trudy said to Nana one day. "Where did you work before?"

"I worked for Proficiency Travel at the International Finance Trust."

"So you were on site there?" It was more of a statement than a question.

"Yes. I learned a lot about international travel from there."

"Where are you from?" Trudy was curious. She was unable to guess by Nana's accent.

"You ask a lot of questions." Trudy and Nana laughed at her statement. "I'm originally from Ghana. And you're from Vietnam."

"Actually, I was born here in the States. My parents came from Vietnam."

"That's nice." Nana understood the English names that her Vietnamese coworkers had. They were all first or second generation born in America. "I was not born here but I'm an American now. I was sworn in as a citizen only a few weeks ago."

"That's nice – congratulations." Trudy flashed a broad smile at Nana. "My parents had to go through that a long time ago. Does Ghana have one language or do they have multiple languages?"

"English is the official language that is spoken in Ghana." Nana wondered where the line of questioning was headed. "We don't have one common language in Ghana. Ghana is not ethnically homogeneous. We have several ethnic groups, such as Ewe, Akan, Guan and several others."

"What kind of sports do you play in Ghana?"

Nana cringed by that question. She did not want to engage in the subject of sports. "They play mostly soccer, also rugby."

"Rugby is something like football, right?"

"Hmm, I guess it's somewhat like it but not entirely."

"They don't wear as much padding in rugby like they do in football." Trudy pointed out.

"You seem to know all about it." Nana wanted the conversation to end right at that moment.

"Do you like sports at all?" Trudy pushed forward.

"Somewhat." Nana tried to change the subject. "Is there a special queue for us to place our PNR's (personal name records)?"

"Did Tom give you the list of queues?"

"No I don't think he did." Nana knew that she had everything Tom gave her during his training sessions with her.

"No worries, I will forward the list to you. What is your email address?"

"My email address is nnkuku@at.com." Nana was relieved that she had escaped from the football conversation.

"So what kind of sports do you like?" Trudy did not abandon the conversation.

"I like all of them." Nana wanted the phone to ring and interrupt them but that day was a slow one. They did not have many phone calls. "They're all competitive."

"Don't be so boring, girl." Trudy teased her. "We are huge football fans in this office."

Nana smiled at Trudy. "I've noticed. That's nice."

"Every year during football season, the employees are treated to a football game. We get to watch the game from Rose's suite at the stadium." Trudy explained to Nana with excitement in her eyes. "I will remind you to sign up for the game when the list comes around."

Nana wondered why Trudy tried so hard to befriend her. She thought it was nice of her to talk but she just did not want to disclose too much of her background to Trudy or anyone there. "Thanks."

"We will make a football fan out of you yet." Trudy told her.

Nana smiled back at her and turned her attention to her computer.

Nana still was unable to bring herself to drive again. She had a rental car, which the insurance company provided her. She did not have the confidence to drive her rental car. She asked Bridgette to drive the car. Bridgette was more than pleased to drive the car since she did not have her own transportation. She drove Nana to her job in Reston every morning, and picked her up from Reston in the evening. Bridgette had full use of the car throughout the day.

Inquisitive Trudy asked Nana once, "Is that your mother that brings you to work and picks you up"

Nana laughed. "She's not old enough to be my mother. She is a friend of mine." She did not offer any additional information to Trudy.

Nana's new coworkers engaged in conversations in the office about certain football players. One day while they had one of those discussions, Frank Thurston's name managed to get in the conversation. Nana's heart beat rapidly as she listened to them talk about the players whom they did not know.

"That Gorillas quarterback is hot." Polly said when she was downstairs in the International Department.

"Yuck." Trudy said. "He has a big nose." She made a face of disgust.

"I heard that he's a flirt." Rene said.

Nana did not believe what she heard. "Do you know these players at all?" Everyone was quiet. "Does anyone in here really knows Frank Thurston?"

"We know what we read in the papers – we know what we hear about them." Trudy said.

"Perhaps it is unfair to say these things about them if you don't know them personally." Nana did not want them to know that she was a close friend of Frank. "Sometimes it is good to get our facts straight before we pass judgment."

"Well excuse me." Trudy said as she rolled her eyes. She wondered why Nana defended those players whom none of them knew.

Nana hoped that such conversations would be kept at a minimal in the future, if she was going to survive at Alpha Travel.

Chapter Fourteen

NANA'S ADVENTURES

> *O Lord, rescue me from evil people. Protect me from those who are violent, those who plot evil in their hearts and stir up trouble all day long. – Psalm 140:1-2 (NLT)*

Friends Against Female Genital Mutilation was back in business. The organization had been on a hiatus for years. Although the organization had a sizable bank account, Nana refused to live off the organization. Her friends told her that it was acceptable to all of them, if she took out a salary for herself from the funds of the organization. Nana would not hear of it. She argued that FAFGM still paid the legal fees to the attorney, and they still paid Don and Day Public Relations.

Frank recuperated from his injuries in the stadium attack. Shirley got married to Frank and moved to San Antonio. Jean-Claude was promoted to Chief Purser of the airline, and moved to Paris. Kiddi was busy in England with her son and husband. Nana was left to run the foundation in Washington. She resigned from her job at Proficiency Travel at the IFT to run the foundation. She fell on financial hard times, and almost lost her home to foreclosure. She went back to the work force, and landed in the abusive employ of Valerie Penney.

The founders of FAFGM were ready to restart their organization. Frank solicited several players on his team, and coaches from other teams to accept the invitation to appear in public service announcements. Cynthia from Don and Day worked on the special media campaign against female genital mutilation. Shirley spoke to her clients about the campaign, and she solicited their support. Kiddi contacted her former supporters from years before, and renewed their support. Jean-Claude solicited a few flight attendants and pilots to participate in public service announcements. Nana was not comfortable to ask her new coworkers for support of her organization. They still did not know who she was. She knew that her identity would be disclosed once the campaign began. Cynthia started to set up interviews and public appearances for Nana and some of the other founders of the organization.

"How are you going to manage it when someone from Alpha Travel sees you on TV or in the newspapers?" Bridgette asked Nana one evening when she expressed her concern to her.

"When I get to that bridge, I will cross it." She told Bridgette. "I will say nothing to them until they discover me." She shrugged. "Then I will give them an explanation."

"Let me know what I can do to assist with the campaign." Bridgette told Nana. "The other day I was at an event. I asked a few women there if they had ever heard of female genital mutilation."

"What kind of response did you get from them?" Nana was anxious.

"A woman from Ghana denied that it exists there. She said it didn't happen to her."

"Then I suppose Kiddi and I made up our stories." Nana was sarcastic.

"Six of the women I asked had never heard of FGM."

"I'm not surprised at all."

"One woman had heard about it." Bridgette smiled and shook her head. "She insisted on referring to it as female genitalia. I was just glad that she had heard of it."

"That's an improvement." Nana pushed back her recliner. "What kind of help do you want to render to the foundation?"

"No commitment – I can just help when I can." Bridgette was noncommittal.

"What kind of help are we talking about?" Nana wanted her to define her help.

"I can make phone calls, run errands while you're at work, just admin kind of work." She was still not entirely specific but Nana understood what she had in mind.

"Okay, that sounds good enough." Nana figured it would be a good way for Bridgette to help her in exchange for free lodging.

"What time is your court appearance tomorrow?" Bridgette knew that she needed to take Nana to the courthouse the next morning.

"Mr. Cohen wants me there at 8:00 in the morning." Nana did not look forward to the encounter with Valerie Penney again.

"I will take you in the morning." Bridgette looked at Nana. "I will not just drive you there. I will park the car and come in for support."

"Thanks, I appreciate it. Betty Sue said she too will be there for support."

"That is really nice of her. She seems like a nice lady."

"She is the best neighbor anyone could have. I'm blessed to have her as my neighbor."

"Are you ready for the case?" Bridgette knew that Nana was nervous about being in a courtroom.

"I've never stepped foot in a courtroom – not in Ghana and not in the U.S. This is my first."

"I understand how you feel."

"Have you been in court before in your lifetime?"

"I've been there only once when I fought a speeding ticket."

"Did you beat the charge?"

"Oh yes I did." Bridgette smiled. "I think the Judge knew that I was not exceeding the speed limit but the cop was out to get me."

"Well, let's pray that the Judge will see what your Judge saw." Nana got up and stretched her body. "On that note, I will take myself to bed so I will be fully alert tomorrow morning when I look Valerie Penney in the eye."

"I will find my bed as well." Bridgette followed Nana up the stairs. "Goodnight and have a good rest."

Fairfax Courthouse

Nana and Bridgette met Jacob Cohen in the lobby of the courthouse. She introduced Bridgette to him.

"Nana, there you are." Betty Sue spotted Nana, Jacob and Bridgette. She made her way to where they stood. She walked with the aid of a cane but she was there to support her neighbor.

Nana introduced Betty Sue to Jacob. "I really appreciate you being here but you did not have to come. You should have gotten a ride with us."

"That's fine with me. I wanted to be here for you. I need my car here with me. I'm not going straight home after here."

Nana was called to the stand to testify on her behalf against Valerie. Jacob asked her why she left Eastern Travel. Nana explained in detail what happened the morning that Valerie drove her out of the office the first time. She told the story about the second time Valerie told her to leave.

"The day that Ms. Penney drove you out of the office, did she give you any indication that she did not intend for you to leave?" Jacob asked Nana.

"No she did not give that indication. She told me that she did not want to see me or look at me again." Nana responded.

Jacob called Amber to the stand. "Were you ever driven out of the office by Valerie Penney during your employment at Eastern Travel?"

"Yes I was driven out many times by Valerie." Amber responded. "She told me she didn't want to see my face again."

Valerie did not have any witnesses with her. She did not have an attorney with her. Antomeyer was in the courtroom but he did not testify on her behalf. She told the Judge that she represented herself. She opted not to cross examine Nana or Amber.

She took stand in her own defense. "I am a great employer. I treat the employees to lunch all the time. Sometimes I even bring in donuts and cupcakes for my employees. When I found out that Nana was a vegetarian and did not eat dairy, I accommodated her by bringing in dairy free muffins. When her mother died, I sent her home in a sedan with a driver." She patted her chest. "I paid for the car service. I told the driver to take her anywhere she wanted to go." She looked over to where Nana sat with her attorney. "Does that sound like a bad and abusive employer to you?"

"You cannot ask the questions, Ms. Penney. You are allowed to make your statement." The Judge told her.

"Okay then – I am not a bad and abusive employer."

"I have listened to the testimonies here today against Ms. Penney." The Judge said. "I have also listened to the testimony of Ms. Penney." He turned his attention to Valerie. "Ms. Penney, I did not hear you once deny that you drove either of your employees out of the office. I'm sorry but the fact that you treated them to lunch and breakfast, does not prove that you did not ask Ms. Nkuku to leave the office. Therefore I rule in favor of the defendant, Ms. Nkuku. She is not guilty of deserting her job. I also rule that Ms. Nkuku does not have to return the unemployment money." He slammed his gavel down on the desk. "Case is dismissed."

Valerie was furious. She flashed an evil glare at Nana, as Nana hugged Bridgette and Betty Sue. Nana watched Valerie storm out of the courtroom. Antomeyer looked at Nana and waved at her. He was too afraid to approach Nana for fear of being fired by Valerie.

Nana shook Jacob's hand. "Thank you. Now I can put this behind me and get on with my life." She turned to Amber. "Thank you for coming in and testifying on my behalf. I appreciate it." They walked out of the courtroom to the parking garage to find their respective cars.

Nana checked her mailbox. She separated the junk mail from her actual mail. She saw an envelope from the Virginia Voter's Registration. "I've got it." She jumped up and down in her kitchen, as Bridgette looked at her in confusion.

"What did you get?"

"I have my voter's registration card." She waved it at Bridgette.

"Wow, I thought you had just won the lottery."

"Please don't burst my bubbles." Nana told Bridgette. "I just received my first voter's registration card. I am excited. I can vote next month."

"Sorry, I didn't mean to burst your bubble at all. I just haven't seen anybody get that excited over a voter's registration card before."

"I don't suppose so. How many Ghanaians turned American have you witnessed get a voter's registration card?" They laughed.

"I haven't seen any until now." They laughed again.

"How do I vote next month?" Nana was curious. "What is it like to vote?"

"I'm not sure how the voting booths are here in Fairfax County. In Arlington, we go in the booth and make our selections. When you're done, then you push the green button to solidify your selected votes."

"You make it sound so simple."

"Well, it's not difficult."

"When you cast your vote, you are selecting the person or persons that will run the country. It is a big decision in my mind. We should not take that seriously."

"If you put it that way, I guess."

Nana enjoyed Bridgette's company. She appreciated her assistance in driving her around in her rental car. She was not too pleased with how Bridgette kept her surroundings. She never washed dishes after she used them. She never changed the sheets on her bed. Bridgette slept on the same set of sheets that Nana had on the bed when she moved in. What were once pink sheets resembled brown sheets and pillow cases. Nana had a reason to visit Bridgette's room and she observed the untidy conditions in which she kept the room. Nana was appalled but she decided to keep peace and not say anything to Bridgette.

One night, Bridgette brought the floor mats from her bathroom to Nana. "These need to be replaced. They're ruined."

"How did they get ruined? When you moved in, they were not ruined."

"They're old, that's how they got ruined."

Nana was floored by her response. "They were not old when you moved in."

"I'm sorry I didn't mean to upset you. I just wanted you to know."

"I'm not going to replace those mats. The mats in my bathroom were purchased the same time as these. My mats are not ruined."

Nana saw the red warning flag flash in front of her. She recalled how everything went well during James' stay in her home until the tooth pick and garbage disposal incident. Shirley's words rang in her ears. What had she done again? Nana made a decision then that she was going to get back behind the steering wheel. She was going to end the fear of driving. Even if she needed to take driving lessons again, she was going to take back her independence to get around. She did not want to wake up one morning and find that Bridgette was gone, and she had no way to get around.

Nana had a gruesome schedule for six weeks after her accident. She went to all of her physical therapy sessions. She hardly missed a day at work since she started her job at Alpha Travel. She scheduled meetings with local volunteers of FAFGM on weekends and evenings. She attended church services on Sunday mornings. She volunteered some Saturday mornings at her church, when they served food to the needy.

"How do you do it?" Martha Reynolds asked her once when they finished one of their meetings. Martha was the leader of the FAFGM volunteers. She did a great job with the volunteers. She solicited volunteers from all over the Washington, D.C. metro area.

"How do I do what?" Nana smiled.

"How do you juggle such a tight schedule?"

"The Lord gives me the strength." She patted Martha's shoulder. "He also gives me perseverance to carry on."

"We need you here with us. We have a lot of work to do. We don't want anything to happen to you." She gave Nana a look of concern.

"Nothing will happen to me. Remember he doesn't place us in positions that we can't handle."

"Just take good care of yourself, kiddo." Martha smiled at her. "You've been through a lot lately. You need a break."

"You're so kind but I'll be fine."

"How's the job going?"

"It's going well even though they hate one of my best friends, Frank Thurston."

"Do they still not know that he's your friend?"

Nana shook her head. "They still don't know anything. I dread the time when they find out what I do when I'm not a travel agent."

The two women laughed at the thought. "You just might win some fans there."

"I doubt it. They will not like me when they find out that Frank Thurston is not only a close friend but he's also the President of FAFGM."

"They'll get over it."

Nana received a call from the lawyer in her accident case. "Can you come to my office tomorrow?" The lawyer asked.

"Sure, I can make it during my lunch hour." Nana told him. "I've taken too time off from the office lately. I would rather not ask for more time off."

"My office is in Reston Town Center. Don't you work in Reston?"

"I work about five minutes from the Town Center. My office is off Reston Parkway."

"Good then I'll see you around noon tomorrow."

"Thanks."

Nana walked in the house in a great mood. She looked forward to her meeting with the lawyer the next day. She hoped that it meant great news from the insurance company. They took so long to get back to the lawyer that she almost gave up on them. She did not like what she saw in her living room. Bridgette sat in the living room on the sofa as she put curlers in her hair.

"What happened to your bedroom?" Nana asked Bridgette.

"The lamp in my room is broken. It's not working. I can't see in there to curl my hair."

"How did the lamp get broken?"

"I switched on the light and it didn't come on."

"It means that you need to change the light bulb." Nana was surprised that Bridgette did not figure that out. "I keep the bulbs in the utility closet, next to the powder room."

"I tried to change the bulb but it still didn't work. I think something is wrong with the lamp, not the bulb."

"Is the light fixture in your bathroom broken as well?"

"No but I would have to stand the entire time while I curl my hair. There is no chair in the bathroom."

"I don't have a seat in my bathroom either, Bridgette." She took off her coat and hung it in the closet. "Had I brought a guest home, it would not have been a pleasant sight to meet you in your bathrobe with your curlers, combs and brush all over the place."

Nana went to her room without dinner that night. She had second thoughts about being a Good Samaritan for the second time. The months slipped by so she lost track of the time. She realized then that it was seven months already since Bridgette moved in. Nana did not expect her to stay with her as long as she had.

The next day Nana took a taxi from her job to the lawyer's office in Reston Town Center. The lawyer welcomed her to his office. His office was plush with eighteenth century décor. He enjoyed the plush appearance of a Washington, D.C. downtown law office, and the rent of Northern Virginia.

"The insurance company went back and forth with me on the settlement." He removed some papers from a folder as he spoke. "This is their final offer. Believe me they started at half of this at first." He showed Nana the check of $15,000. "I need you to sign here." He indicated where she needed to sign. "I have cut a check for you of $5,000 as your share." He handed her the check made out to her for $5,000.

"What happens to the $15,000 check?" Nana was confused. She actually thought that the $15,000 check was for her only.

"The total amount paid by the insurance company is $15,000. $5,000 goes to you; $5,000 goes to the doctor and $5,000 to me." He smiled at her with pride.

She wanted to storm out of his office but she smiled back. "What about my car?"

"The good news is that I got them to have your car repaired and returned to you." He smiled at her again. "They will pay for your rental car until your car is returned to you."

"Since they're having my car repaired by their mechanic, I want to have one year warranty on all repairs."

"That is no problem. I've already included that in the agreement for the car." He took out more papers for her to sign. "I need to get your signature here. This says you agree to the repairs of the car, and you can see right here that all repairs will have a year's warranty."

Nana signed all of the papers. She wished the settlement had been more but it was better than nothing. She would get her car back, and she had $5,000, after expenses. "Thank you for the settlement." She handed the last set of signed papers to him. "I appreciate it."

"It's my pleasure to be of service to you." He shook her hand, and saw her to the door. "Let me know if you have any questions later on."

Nana called for another taxi to take her back to her office at Alpha Travel. While she waited for the taxi to arrive, she stopped in Tosi, her favorite salad and sandwich chain and ordered their signature salad. She liked their signature salad, which contained spinach, lettuce, pine nuts, grapes, berries and cherries. It was a complete meal for her. She did not take her lunch to work that day, and she was hungry by the time she left the lawyer's office. She ate her salad at her desk while she worked that afternoon. It was common for everyone in the office to eat in the cubicles. She understood why the carpet and cubicles were so dirty. Everyone was not careful with food droppings. Her office mates teased her about how she spread paper towels on her desk before she ate in her cubicle. She did not let it bother her.

The regular football season started with great success for Frank and his team. They won the first three games. Their fourth game was in Washington, D.C. against the local team, the Washington Grizzlies. Nana was excited. She was going to see Frank after a long time. Though she did not expect to attend the game, she knew that Frank would find a way to see her. She had double unexpected surprise that came her way.

"I'm coming to D.C." Shirley revealed to her the week before the game. "Do you want to see the game in person?"

"Of course but I can't afford the ticket." Nana told her.

"We don't expect you to pay for any ticket." Shirley laughed. "I will be sitting in Jimmy Jeffries' box with him and his family. I can have a guest with me."

"Are you asking me to be your guest in the booth with Jimmy Jeffries and his family?" Nana was excited.

"Yes I am. What kind of friend do you think I would be if I didn't invite you?"

"Well I never assume anything." They laughed. "It's not the first time we will be in the box with Mr. Jeffries anyway."

"No it's not the first time but this time we will be in D.C."

"Thank you and I'll feel safe enough to wear my Gorillas sweatshirt and baseball cap."

"Just don't let any of your coworkers see you."

"I doubt if they can afford tickets to the game."

"Then you're safe." Shirley chuckled. "I will see you soon."

Nana had a shock when she went to work the Monday before the game. She received an email from Polly in her Alpha inbox that read, "We are offering free admission to the first 25 people who respond to this email to the game on Sunday between our own Grizzlies and the visiting San Antonio Gorillas. Each Alpha employee is allowed to bring a guest. We will provide free hand towels to wave and free baseball caps. Salads, sandwiches, chips and drinks will be served in the Alpha suite at the stadium. If you get your name in on time, your tickets will be given out on Friday before the close of the day."

Nana read the email about three times. She did not believe the opportunities to see the game. She still was not about to pass up the opportunity to sit in Jimmy Jeffries' box with Shirley and the Jeffries family. She did not want to wear a Grizzlies cap and cheer for them. She knew that she would get slaughtered or thrown out of the Alpha suite if she cheered for the Gorillas. Since she had a great option, she was going to pass up the offer from Alpha. She smiled when she recalled Shirley's statement that she was safe to wear her Gorilla's cap and sweatshirt to the game. She shook her head in disbelief.

Nana hired a car service to take her to the stadium the Sunday of the game. She did not tell Trudy or anyone in her office that she had plans to attend the game. She did know that Trudy, Polly, Donald, Tom, Leonard and Rene were on the list of attendees from the office. They assumed that Nana passed up the offer to attend the game with them because she did not care much for football.

Nana was instructed to let the security at the entrance know when she arrived that she was a guest of Jimmy Jeffries. As she was escorted upstairs to the Jeffries suite, Nana was surprised by someone who shouted her name, "Nana Nkuku, I thought you didn't want to come to the game."

She came face to face with Trudy. "I got an invitation from a friend after I made my decision which I could not refuse."

"So you're not going to sit with us in the suite?" Trudy glared at her outfit. "What are you doing dressed in the enemy's uniform?"

"They're not my enemy. They have done nothing to me."

Trudy then noticed that Nana was escorted by a security guard on the floor of the suites. "Where are you going now?"

"I'm escorting Ms. Nkuku to the suite of Mr. Jeffries, ma'am." The security guard told inquisitive Trudy. "Are you ready, Ms. Nkuku?"

Nana nodded and waved to a confused Trudy as she stood with her mouth open. The secret was out in the open. Nana knew that Trudy was going to the Alpha suite to tell them what she had just seen and heard. She had no intention to ruin her excitement. She was not going to worry about what her coworkers were going to say about her or to her that Monday.

She arrived at the Jeffries suite and greeted Shirley who waited with eager. Shirley introduced her to Mrs. Jeffries and the wives of two of the wide receivers who were also guests of Jimmy Jeffries. Mr. Jeffries and his son told Nana that they remembered her. They welcomed her to the game and told her to enjoy the game.

"I like your outfit, Nana." Jimmy Jeffries told her when he saw her sweatshirt and baseball cap.

"Thank you, Mr. Jeffries. It is an honor to wear it." Nana responded.

The Gorillas scored on their first drive. Frank threw his fifth touchdown pass since the season began. "He gets better with each game, Shirl."

"I think it's because he truly loves this team. He really cares about the team. He cares for the Jeffries." Shirley told Nana.

Nana enjoyed the game. She was comfortable where she was. She cheered without any reservations. She and Shirley jumped up and hugged each time the Gorillas scored. The game was close. In the last five minutes of the game, the score was 14 Grizzlies, 17 Gorillas. The Grizzlies had possession of the ball. The mood was intense that everyone in the Jeffries' box was on his or her feet. The game was resumed after the two-minute warning. The Grizzlies still possessed the ball on the 20-yard line of the Gorillas. The Grizzlies threatened to score, take the lead and defeat the Gorillas. The Grizzlies' quarterback leaned back to throw the touchdown pass, which would defeat the Gorillas. The Jeffries' suite was quiet. The ball left the hand of the Grizzlies' quarterback. It suspended in the air for what seemed to them as hours. The ball was headed straight for the end zone. The Grizzlies' wide receiver braced himself to receive the ball, when one of the Gorillas' defenders stepped in at the exact time and intercepted the ball in the end zone. The box was still quiet. Everyone wanted to be sure that no penalty flags were thrown. They saw no flag. The referee announced, "The ruling on the field is that the ball was intercepted. It is San Antonio ball – first down." He pointed in the direction of the Grizzlies' end zone. The mood in the Jeffries' box was jubilant. Everyone embraced as Shirley and Nana wiped the corners of their eyes in victory. Since the Grizzlies had no more time-outs left, the Gorillas took their final time-out in the game. There was only less than a minute left in regulation. Frank and his team took a knee to end the game.

Nana wondered what the mood was like in the Alpha Travel suite. She knew that it was different from the mood in their suite. Mr. Jeffries was not in the suite for the final 5 minutes of the game. It was a habit of his to leave his suite and go to the sideline in the final minutes of the game.

The Monday after the game was an eventful day for Nana. Trudy did not speak to her that morning. Donald and Rene had many questions her.

"I heard you were at the game yesterday." Rene asked.

"Yes I was."

"How do you know the owner of the Gorillas?" Rene continued.

"I know him through a mutual friend."

"That is impressive."

"Who is the mutual friend?" Donald chimed in the conversation.

Nana was in an awful position. Rene was her manager and Donald was her assistant manager. She hoped Polly did not come downstairs to their office that day. "Frank Thurston."

"Frank Thurston is your friend?" Rene asked with widened eyes. Nana figured that she was already exposed, and she was not about to tell them lies. It was one thing to keep information from them if they never asked. It was another thing to lie to them when they asked.

"Yes he is."

"But he's married." Rene said.

"Yes he is married – his wife is beautiful." Donald interjected.

"I know he's married." Nana chuckled. "He's happily married to my best friend, Shirley." There was silence in the office for a couple of minutes.

"You were on the big screen after the interception in the game." Donald told Nana. "They showed you celebrating with them."

"I think it's neat that you're friends with them." Rene said.

"This is a Grizzlies office in here." Tom said. "I just want to warn you that it didn't sit well with the higher ups yesterday."

"When I was hired for the job, I was not told that cheering for the Washington Grizzlies was one of the job requirements." Nana told Tom.

"I hate those Gorillas." Trudy joined the conversation, and she was mean.

"It's not a healthy thing to hate, Trudy." Nana said with a smile.

"I just wish it was not the Gorillas you were friends with." Trudy responded.

"Sorry but that part of my life happened long before I came to work here." Nana told her.

"We will excuse you since you're friends with Gorillas." Everyone in the office laughed at Trudy's statement. "At least you don't just like those Gorillas because of the team."

Nana thought she had seen fanatics but her coworkers at Alpha Travel took the prize. "Thank you for being so considerate." They knew that Nana's response was with sarcasm so nobody laughed.

Trudy was far from done with Nana. "So tell us how you became friends with Frank Thurston."

"We were classmates in college."

"Was his wife your classmate too?" Trudy continued her interrogation.

"No, I met her after college. I was looking for a roommate. She became my roommate and best friend in America."

"Why didn't you grab Frank Thurston for yourself?" Donald wanted to know.

"Frank was like a brother to me. He looked out for me at school. I didn't like him in that manner. So I introduced him to Shirley."

"You're really a good friend." Donald told her. "You would not be working now if you had taken him for yourself." Everyone in the office echoed Donald in agreement.

"That guy is cute." Rene added. "He sounds smart too. Whenever he's interviewed, his diction is so precise."

"You're correct." Nana told Rene. "Frank is handsome. He was one of the brightest in the classes we took together."

"And you took him for your brother instead of your boyfriend." It was more of a statement from Donald than a question.

"Yes. God did not intend for our relationship to turn into a romantic one." Her coworkers exchanged glances when she mentioned God. She had become accustomed to the reaction. Her faith was another thing that her coworkers did not know about her.

"I see you're really into God, huh?" Tom asked Nana.

"Yes I am very much so."

"I noticed you the other day at lunch. You graced your food before eating." Tom pointed out.

"One must always give thanks to the Lord for the provisions."

"Amen." Rene said. Nana did not know if her remark was a joke or not.

Nana did not spend a day after that game without being interrogated about Frank and Shirley. Polly visited their office often to ask Nana about her relationship with the Jeffries and the Gorillas. She wondered why some people were so star struck.

The Day the Bathroom Tiles Moved

It was a beautiful October afternoon. The sun shone bright onto the buildings in Reston. Nana took her lunch as she did every day. She ate at her desk and she read the newspaper. She went out for a walk, just to get away from the noise of the office. Her coworkers spoke excessive Vietnamese that day. She did not want to hear it during her lunch time. She walked around what her coworkers referred to as 'The Campus'. Alpha Travel owned two 2-storied buildings with clusters of trees and benches. The grounds were paved with brushes of greenery alongside the driveways. The buildings had bright green rooftops that glittered in the sun. Nana walked and stopped to sit on one of the benches. She noticed that her weatherman had not mentioned anything about rain. She was thankful that she remembered to put a small umbrella in her briefcase. The clouds appeared to turn to dark gray. She walked back to the building. She swiped her electronic security key to let herself in the building. The travel office was on the ground floor.

Nana put her bag, cell phone and keys on her desk. She still had a few minutes to spare before lunch was over. She decided to visit the restroom before she resumed work. Alpha did not have special ladies and men's rooms. Their restrooms were unisex. It was common to hear the women in the office scold the men whenever they left the toilet seats up. As long as the bathroom was kept clean, and did not smell like a public toilet, Nana was not bothered by it.

While Nana was in the bathroom, she heard a loud and strange noise. The noise resembled a plane or a truck. It sounded to her as though a truck drove through the building. She was on her feet with her pants down. Nana screamed when the floor beneath her feet began to rock back and forth. The tiny tiles on the bathroom floor appeared to move as the building rocked. She had no idea what she had just experienced. She wondered if her coworkers heard the disturbance. She hurried and washed her hands to leave the bathroom. Nana rushed out of the bathroom as she forgot to zip her pants all the way. She noticed that the entire office was empty. She hurried to the door, where she saw everyone from both buildings out in the yard. She wondered if the rocking noise was the reason for the evacuation. As she ran out, Nana asked her coworkers, "What happened? What is going on?"

To her surprise, they laughed at her. Trudy told her, "There's been an earthquake."

"We were banging on the bathroom door but you didn't answer." Donald told her. "We didn't want to leave you in there."

"I was unable to hear anything except for that loud sound." Nana told them. "We had an earthquake on the east coast of America?" She was in disbelief. "I thought they only happened on the west coast."

"Well today disproved that theory." Trudy said.

They were cleared to return to the buildings; everyone shared his or her experience of the previous half hour. Trudy mocked everyone's reaction and action at the time of the quake. Although Nana was glad that Trudy did not get to see her reaction in the bathroom, Trudy still managed to mock her when she ran out of the building. She showed how Nana ran out as she held up her pants, and asked, 'what is going on?' Trudy reenacted every movement of everyone in such a hilarious way, that everyone was in hysterics.

Sootha said that she was familiar with the sound of earthquake. She grew up in California, where she often experienced them. Trudy reenacted how Sootha stood up as soon as she heard the noise. She put on her sunglasses and alerted them when she yelled, "Earthquake."

Joyce had just moved from California to the area. She worked in the other wing of the office. Nana was not acquainted with her. Joyce told them that she stayed under her desk until the quake was over. She said, "We never run out of the building during a quake. We take shelter in an enclosed room without windows. The basement and a closet are ideal places."

"I guess I was safer than all of you then." Nana told them." The bathroom has no windows."

The office phones did not work for about half an hour after they returned to their cubicles. Nana used her mobile phone to call Adjoa. She was not at work that day. Adjoa told her that she took off from work to visit the new memorial that was just unveiled on the Mall in Washington. It was the first memorial of a black man to be built on the Mall. Beside the Washington Monument, the only other memorials on the Mall were of late Presidents of the United States.

"You took off from work just to do that?" Nana was surprised.

"Yes. This man was the reason for many changes in this country today."

"I know that. I plan to visit the memorial during the weekend." Nana told her after her brief history lesson. "I just wanted to make sure you survived the quake."

"It was scary – we didn't know what was going on at first. You should see the many people out here. These are the downtown workers that were evacuated."

Nana called to check on Betty Sue, her neighbor. "Did you feel the earthquake?" She asked Betty Sue.

"I was in my car at the drive through window of the bank. I couldn't understand why my car was rocking back and forth. It went on like that for a few minutes, and it stopped. Then I heard the radio announce that it was an earthquake." Betty Sue shared her experience with Nana. "I'm glad you're okay. Thanks for checking on me."

Nana told her what they experienced at the office. She checked on the Reynolds and a couple of people from her church. Other than the shock of the earthquake, everyone she knew was safe. Her cell phone went off every five minutes with text messages from Alec, Shirley, Frank, Cynthia, and Mrs. Wilcox. They busied themselves to check in and make sure that their loved ones were safe.

When Nana got home, she noticed some of her wall hangings in the house were disturbed. Bridgette was not at home during the quake. She was where Adjoa had been. Bridgette was a civil rights activist, so Nana was not surprised that she was at the new memorial on the Mall.

The earthquake was felt throughout the Washington, D.C. metro area. Those closest to western and central Virginia felt a greater impact. People as far as Frederick and Hagerstown in Maryland felt the impact of the earthquake that measured 7 on the Richter scale.

Virginia Makes History

With the earthquake behind them, Washingtonians focused their attention to the presidential elections. Beside sport fanatics, Nana's coworkers were also big debaters of politics. Donald was well read and he kept himself up to date on the latest news on Capitol Hill. He was not only well informed on American politics, but he was a political machine on world politics as well. He was heard on any given day, discussing African politics with Nana. He and Tom debated about what was going in North Korea or Venezuela and Haiti. Donald took pride in his political knowledge. He looked forward to the elections, which were only two days away.

"Are you a U.S. citizen?" Donald asked Nana the day before the election.

"Yes I am." Nana replied with glee. "This is my first election."

"So you're a new kid on the block." Donald said.

"Do you know who you will be voting for tomorrow?" He figured he could indoctrinate her into his political party of choice.

"Yes I know. I'm not a swing voter so there is no need to campaign me." Everyone in the office laughed at her statement.

"Well excuse me, Miss Nana." Donald said. "Just make sure you vote for the right person."

"You can bet on that." She assured him. The race was a heated one. The campaign was muddy from the start. The two major presidential candidates represented the two major parties. However there was a third candidate from the Independent Party. While he was not a threat, his supporters were essential to the final decision. They were almost like the swing voters. As the hours diminished, the media tried to outdo each other on the most updated reports. The polls were not decisive. The results depended on the network which one watched.

"For the first time in American history, a woman could be elected President of the United States." The news anchor reported on television that night, as Nana and Bridgette watched. Like Donald, Bridgette supported the woman candidate, Christine Eleanor Richardson. Nana refused to disclose her choice of candidate.

Bridgette tried to force her to reveal her choice. "You have to vote for Richardson. Your organization supports the female gender. It is no way you can vote for Johnson."

"My organization supports victims of female genital mutilation, who just happen to be of the female gender." Nana corrected her. "How do you know that Johnson will not sympathize with our cause?"

Nana joined Bridgette and laughed at her own question. Charles William Johnson, the major male candidate was a far right wing conservative.

"Johnson probably doesn't even know what female genital mutilation is." Bridgette told Nana.

"One never knows." She told her. "I know many conservatives who support our cause. You'll be surprise."

"Tell me, are you on the fence about who to support?"

"I'm not on the fence. I am reviewing all of the debate results and interviews."

"I can respect that."

"This is a crucial time, not only in the U.S. but in the world. The person that becomes president of the most powerful country in the world must understand what is happening out there."

"I fully agree with you, Nana. We can't miss this golden opportunity."

"The world has changed." She took a sip of her green tea. "We're seeing a shift in leadership around the world. Whoever gets in tomorrow will need to recognize that. The old order is obsolete now."

"I absolutely agree that it is essential for Virginians to make the right decision tomorrow."

"I can't believe that we're only less than 24 hours from the polls." Bridgette was excited. "I'm not going anywhere tomorrow when I get back from the poll." She needed to travel back to Arlington where she used to live to cast her vote. Her voter's registration card and driver's license still had her former address on them.

The next morning Bridgette drove Nana to the elementary school in Herndon. Nana's polling place was located there. The school was in walking distance. "You can take the car to Arlington." Nana told her. "I will walk back home."

"Are you sure about that?" Bridgette asked. "I can wait. The polls don't close until 7:00 tonight. You have to go to work – I don't need to."

"I'm sure about that. Take a look at that queue." The line extended from the parking lot.

"Good luck on your first time voting." Bridgette wished her as she got out of the car.

Nana saw Richardson's supporters with signs and Johnson's supporters with their signs. Some of them handed out sample ballots with Johnson and his running mate on them. Others handed out sample ballots with Mrs. Richardson and her running mate on them. Nana was grateful for the sample ballots. She felt a rush of excitement flow through her as she joined the line.

The line moved at quick intervals. It stopped for two minutes, it moved for five minutes at that same pace. Everyone seemed tense over the magnitude of the elections. Nana prayed earlier that morning for God to select the candidate of his choice. It did not matter for whom she voted; she asked God to put who he felt was the better candidate. There were a couple of things she liked about Senator Johnson; his racist remarks during the campaign made her doubtful. Both times he was caught in such remarks he did not realize that his microphone was still on. She wondered what he said about people who looked like her when the microphones were turned off. Mrs. Richardson's son was married to a beautiful Asian young lady. One of Senator Johnson's remarks was in reference to that. He said, "If that woman wins, there will be Chinese takeout being delivered to the White House." That remark only showed Senator Johnson's ignorance.

Burt Richardson's wife was of Japanese descent, not Chinese. Her father fought in the Vietnam War and her brother was a decorated Sargent from the Iraqi war. She was the second generation born in the United States. Mia Richardson earned just as much right to the country as any other American. Senator Johnson lost the Asian support after that story was released.

Nana stood in that line and wondered why some people utter the things they say. She felt that America was a great country with unlimited opportunities. She had met some wonderful people, who respected others, regardless of race or religion. She felt that such people should never be exposed to the prejudice and racism of the world. Nana thought that it was unhealthy and toxic to be in the company of racist people, even when it was not directed at her. She survived in America because she kept her distance when she suspected that type of behavior in people.

"Ma'am, you're up next." The lady at the election poll brought Nana back to the present. She was deep in her own thoughts that she did not notice that she was at the front of the line. "Go over to the table and give your ID to one of the clerks." The long table extended halfway across the large room. There were several clerks seated behind the table. "What is the first letter of your last name?"

"My last name begins with 'N'. Nana told the lady. She went to the clerk that had the sign before her that read, 'M to S'. Nana was nervous. "Good morning." She spoke to the clerk with a smile.

"Good morning." The clerk returned her smile. "May I have your voter's registration card or your driver's license please?"

Nana handed her the voter's registration card. The clerk had a long list of names and addresses in front of her on the table. She found Nana's name on the list. She handed her back the card, along with a 5x7 card that had 210 on it. Nana wondered if that number meant that she was the 210th voter that morning. She joined another line with her number in hand. She observed the people ahead of her as they handed their cards to another set of ladies. The ladies directed them to booths that were enclosed. That time, Nana was in line not long before her turn came. She handed her card to one of the ladies and whispered, "This is my first time doing this. I'm nervous."

"There's nothing to be nervous about." The lady assured her as they walked to the available booth. "I'm going to switch the light on in the booth. When the light goes off, make your selections. When you're sure of your selections, hit this green button that says 'VOTE'. Nothing goes through until you hit VOTE."

"Thank you." Nana entered the booth. Her hands shook as the light went on. Nana saw the list of presidential candidates and below was the list of gubernatorial candidates. Below were 3 issues on which to vote for or against. One was something about the parks in Virginia. She decided to vote for the presidential candidate first. Her hands shook to the extent where her finger slipped and pushed the button next to Rhino Pellam, the independent candidate. "Ahhhhhhhhhhhhh." Nana screamed from the booth as though she had just seen something frightful.

The lady made her way in quick strides to the booth. "Did you make a mistake?" She was accustomed to such occurrences, though not the type of scream she heard from Nana's booth.

"I voted for the wrong person." A disheveled Nana told her. Her brow was wet from perspiration. "What do I do now?"

The lady was tickled but she dared not laugh at a time like that. She did something in the booth to cancel what Nana had done. "I will turn on the light again, and then I will turn it off. Don't worry I have cleared it so you can begin over. Take your time – don't feel you need to rush."

"Thank you for being helpful." Nana was embarrassed. She made a mental note not to let her coworkers at Alpha hear of that. She took her time and made her selections with care; the president, vice president, governor and then she voted on the last 3 items. She proofread her selections again. She was pleased with her choices. Then she pushed the big green button marked VOTE. "Whew." She was relieved. She felt proud that she had just voted in such an important and historical election as an American citizen. She walked out of the booth with a broad smile on her face.

The same lady greeted her with a sticker that said, 'I voted.' "Congratulations, you did it." The lady said to her with a smile.

"Thank you for your help. This is such an honor for me." She was relaxed. "Have a blessed day."

"You do the same."

Nana left the elementary school in a great mood. The line appeared to be worse than before. She was glad that she decided to arrive early. The polls in Virginia opened at 6:00 in the morning and closed at 7:00 in the evening. Those in Maryland and the District of Columbia opened an hour later than Virginia and closed an hour later. She wished she had taken the day off from work. She and Bridgette would watch the entire day's events on television. She strolled home in the cool early November breeze. She wore a navy sweater with navy matching slacks and a tan shirt. She wore a navy felt hat, which was appropriate for autumn. Nana called Jean-Claude from her mobile phone as she walked to her house.

"Hallo." "Bonjour." Jean-Claude answered the phone.

"Bonjour Monsieur Girard." Nana laughed into the phone.

"Mademoiselle Nana. What is happening over in State side?" He always changed his accent to that of an American when he spoke to his friends in the States. "Have you cast your vote yet?"

Nana beamed as she recounted her morning at the elementary school. "I am a proud voter."

"I sent in my absentee ballot a month ago so I hope my vote will help the lady."

"You just told me who you voted for, Jean-Claude Girard."

"I thought it was a known fact that I was supporting Mrs. Richardson." He chuckled. "Don't you tell me that you voted for that racist?"

"Jean-Claude, behave yourself." She did not believe how blatant he was about the candidates. "He made a costly mistake when he said those remarks."

"So you did vote for him?" There was a brief silence between them. "Did you really vote for Johnson, Nana? When he puts on his hood and burns a cross on your lawn, you will regret that you voted for him."

"Jean-Claude, listen to me. I did not want to reveal my vote but since you're so out of control, I voted for Mrs. Richardson." She was in disbelief of his behavior. "I assure you that Senator Johnson will not be in a hood and he will not be burning anything on mine or anyone's lawn." The both laughed. "I am on my way to work now. We will be in touch after the results come in tonight." They ended their call in good spirits.

The day did not go fast enough at work for Nana. It was not a busy day for them. They chatted about their experiences at their respective polls. They each had their predictions about the results. It was evident that most of her coworkers voted for Mrs. Richardson. Most of the travel agents in her department were fans of the Richardson family. They had

Asian backgrounds, and they hailed the fact that Burt Richardson married to an Asian girl.

Her coworkers congratulated her on her first vote as an American. She shared with them her experience at the poll that morning. Nana expected their jokes and laughter. She joined them and laughed at herself. "It was not funny at the time, I assure you."

"That is scary – voting for Rhino Pellam." Trudy told her.

Donald offered to give Nana a ride home that evening. They had just discovered that he only lived ten minutes from her. "Until you get back on the road, I can take you home every day unless I have somewhere to go after work."

"Thank you, I really appreciate it." She figured that she was now accepted by them. She knew that Donald was married so it was safe for her to accept the ride from him.

He knew where she lived when Nana gave him her address to enter in his GPS. "A friend of mine used live in one of those houses. He lost his home to foreclosure."

"I'm sorry to hear that." She was reminded of how close she came to being a victim of foreclosure. Whenever Nana heard such stories, she realized how blessed she was.

Bridgette was at home when Nana got home. She was glued in the living room before the television, with an update on the elections for Nana. "It's too soon to call but I feel optimistic for our girl."

Nana did not realize that Mrs. Richardson belonged to them. "I want her to win but I don't want to be disappointed if it doesn't happen."

"Don't be so uptight. She will win." Bridgette went to the kitchen. "I hope you like what you smell."

"What is it?" Nana had not eaten anything cooked by Bridgette. "You cooked?" She was shocked. Bridgette never went in the kitchen; only to get something to drink or to eat something that Nana offered her. "Is it safe for me to eat?" Nana joked and they laughed.

"Yes it's safe. I'm baking a vegan cake for us to celebrate tonight when Christine wins."

"What did you put in the vegan cake?"

"I used almond meal instead of flour, brown raw sugar, aluminum-free baking powder, pure vanilla, almond milk, coconut oil, apple sauce, cinnamon and salt."

"It smells delicious. I had no idea you have domestic attributes." She went to the kitchen. "I take back what I just said." The kitchen was in disarray.

"Don't worry; I will clean up my mess." She saw the look on Nana's face. "I'm sorry I've been watching the polls come in."

"As long as you clean it up, it's fine with me." Nana settled in to watch the results.

The networks reported the results as they came in to them. The eastern states came in first. Their polls closed between 7:00 and 8:00. Then the Midwestern states began to report their results. Nana and Bridgette did their own calculations, as the results were reported. The race was close. The political analyst on the international network explained his chart on the map of the U.S. He showed the states that Mrs. Richardson needed to win and what Senator Johnson needed to win. The projections continued to be announced. Mrs. Richardson won all of the New England states. She won New York, New Jersey, Pennsylvania, Delaware, Maryland and Michigan. Michigan was her home state.

"How long will it take them to call Virginia? Our polls closed since 7:00." Nana said with anxiety.

"Wait a minute, she just won Illinois." Bridgette interrupted.

Senator Johnson picked up many of the southern states such as Kentucky, Tennessee, Georgia, Alabama, Mississippi and South Carolina. Illinois was a battleground state, and so was Pennsylvania.

"Everyone is waiting for Virginia. No liberal candidate has ever won Virginia since the 1960's." Bridgette gave Nan a history lesson.

"So I guess history could be made tonight." Nana chuckled. "Imagine that my vote helped to make history in the great United States of America."

"You're really funny." Bridgette stopped and glared at the television. She did a victory dance in the center of the floor. Nana was distracted by the victory dance, that she did not notice the TV screen. "She just took Ohio." She continued the dance.

"Is that another battleground state?"

"Of course it is. No conservative candidate has ever won the presidency without winning Ohio." Bridgette offered another history lesson. "Didn't they teach you that on your citizenship test?" She teased.

"Obviously they did not." Nana knew that Bridgette enjoyed it when she was teased. "Based on what you just said, we can rightfully begin the victory celebration since we can assume that Johnson is defeated."

"It's not over until the networks project her as the winner. Our state has not come in yet. There are still California, Washington State, Oregon and those other west coast states. The night is still young."

"Should they have also included that on my citizenship test?" Nana sought the opportunity to get back at her with a joke. They laughed. "What confuses me is this electoral college thing. Why not just tally the popular votes and go by that? Wouldn't it make more sense?"

"The reason for the electoral college is because of the size of certain states versus others." Bridgette enjoyed politics, and she was at her best when she discussed or debated it. "Take for example; New York has 31 electoral votes, while Delaware has 3. California has 55, Texas 34 and Pennsylvania has 21. If they went by the popular votes, some small states would not have a chance against the large states."

"The inequity is with the electoral college then, not with the popular votes." Nana was more confused.

"I think they created the electoral to make it fair so that all of the states can contribute to the elections."

"Wait a minute, Bridgette." Nana jumped up from her chair and began to jump up and down. "She won, she won." The networks had all declared Christine Eleanor Richardson the next President of the United States of America. "Our state was the deciding state. As soon as they called Virginia for her, they declared her the winner." Nana was beside herself. Her phone began to ring. It was a little past eleven at night in Virginia.

Shirley and Frank called her and they celebrated together on the phone. "She didn't win in our state but we're just glad that she won, thanks to my old state." Shirley told Nana.

Jean-Claude sent her a text to say that he had not slept the entire night. He stayed up and watched the election process from Nice, France. Alec sent her a text about the result of the elections.

Fireworks began to go off in Herndon. "Virginians have spoken tonight, and in a big way too." Bridgette shouted. "Go Virginia – we just made history tonight." The Commonwealth of Virginia also elected a liberal governor that night.

"We will be telling our grandchildren about this night." Nana shouted back.

They ate their vegan cake and sipped on green tea into the night. They were too excited to sleep. The news showed the scene around the country of how Americans celebrated. They showed scenes of people around the world. They embraced the new American President. "Americans finally came to their senses and elected a woman to lead them." One woman said in England.

"The United States now joins those countries in history that have or have had women leaders; Liberia, India, Pakistan, Great Britain, Denmark, Thailand, Germany, Argentina, Brazil, Australia, Bangladesh, Iceland, Costa Rica, Finland, Malawi, Lithuania and Trinidad and Tobago." The news anchor announced.

Nana smiled with pride. "Africa has two already. Not bad for such a male dominated continent."

The celebrations continued the next day when Nana went to work. Donald was late for work. He said he stayed up the entire night to watch the elections. He only had two hours of sleep. Everyone in the office was in a jovial mood for a change. The elections were the main discussion in the office that day.

Nana had more to celebrate that day when she went home from work. She met an overnight delivery package inside her storm door. She opened the package to find her contract from Zebra Productions for her movie. She jumped around and waved the contract in the air in celebration. She was so excited that she did not notice that Bridgette was in the kitchen.

"Did Ghana just elect a woman leader as well?" Bridgette walked out of the kitchen as she jumped around in the living room. "What's going on?"

"No this is much better." She showed Bridgette the contract. "I finally got it from the producers."

"What do you do now?"

"I'll send my attorneys an email tonight. I'll try to set up an appointment with them to review the contract." She read the cover letter. "The Wilcox's already have their copy of the contract."

"I meant what happens when you sign it?" Bridgette did not seem happy for her. Her voice had negative connotations. "What will you do about your job at Alpha?"

"Well, it depends on what kind of schedule the producers expect me to keep. Also how much they will pay me during the making of the movie." Nana wished Bridgette had not been at home when she got home with her contract. She was too inquisitive but her faith told her to behave nicely to Bridgette.

In her celebration, she had not thought about her job at Alpha at all. She wondered what she needed to do. She decided to go upstairs to her room for privacy. She planned to read the contract by paragraph before she came to any conclusions. Her first thing she did after she had read the contract was to take it to the Lord in prayer. She asked him to direct her and guide her in the right decision, even if it caused disappointment for her.

Nana set an appointment to meet with the attorneys two days after she received the contract. She was pleased with the terms of her contract. Zebra Productions wanted her as an active participant in the preparation of the movie. They wanted her to be a part of the cast selection. She needed to be on the set while they filmed. She was named an honorary director. It only meant that she would sit in a director's chair, and observe the performance. They wanted her to be present since she developed all of the characters. She knew how she wanted them to look and behave. She had breathed life into her characters. The two main characters were key characters to Nana. They were two of the little girls that were genitally cut in her stage play. Nana pulled some of hers and Kiddi's experiences into the script.

Her meeting with Sara and Elliott Wilcox went well. They told her how hard they worked to get the contract to her satisfaction. "Are you happy with your role?" Sara asked her.

She smiled. "Yes I am."

"How do you like being honorary director?" Elliott asked. They wanted to be sure that she was pleased with their work.

"Thank you for everything." She told them. "Honorary director is awesome. It will look nice on my CV."

"All of your travel and lodging expenses will be covered by Zebra Productions." Elliott explained as they went over the contract. "This clause right here says that you hold the stage rights and literary publishing rights. Zebra Productions will share the movie rights with you. That share is 50 – 50 of all royalties."

"How are the royalties paid out?" Nana wanted to ensure that nothing was left unanswered.

"We've arranged for you to receive an advance of $250,000 plus your travel expenses prior to filming." Elliott told her. "Our 30% comes out of that amount. You will receive a check of $175,000 for your advance. After the release of the movie, your royalties will be paid on a quarterly schedule. You will get paid your 50% on the box office sales. In addition, you will get paid your 50% of the DVD sales."

"That is a lot to absorb all at once." Nana told them with a smile on her face. "Do you know what that means to me?"

"It means, my dear Nana that you do not need to keep that 9 to 5 job any longer." Sara told her.

"Precisely so – I can finally do work that I enjoy and make a lot of money in doing so." Nana was happy with the arrangements. Sara and Elliott did a good job with their negotiations. "Thank you for looking out for me like you did. I am quite pleased with what you did."

"Zebra Productions will be in touch with you to give you the casting schedule and when the shoot will begin." Sara told her. "Begin to pack your bags. Be ready when they call. They will send your ticket and your hotel confirmation."

"It all sounds good to me." She took the contract and affixed her signature to it. They shook hands across the table and they saw her to the door.

"Let's have lunch before you leave for casting- our treat." Sara suggested.

"I would love to have lunch. It will give me an excuse to come to the city for a change."

Nana had a lot to take care of before the selection of the cast. Her mind was crowded with her thoughts. She knew what she wanted to do before anything else. She registered with a driving school. She came to the realization that she needed to regain her confidence and independence on the road. She did not feel confident enough to get behind the wheel after so many months of being a passenger. Although she had her valid driver's license, Nana wanted the driving school to give her a few lessons. She felt that if she went through a few lessons with someone in the vehicle, she would regain her confidence. She had a fear that would not go away. Each time she attempted to drive, she relived the moment of her accident.

The owner of the driving school suggested that she attended 3 theoretical classes before she took the practical lessons. She agreed to the suggestion. Nana began her theoretical lessons without delay.

"How do you feel when you sit in the driver's seat?" The Driver's Psychologist asked Nana in her first session.

"My heart takes rapid beats. My palm becomes clammy. I look in the rearview mirror every 2 minutes. I tense up when a car is close behind me." Tears escaped from her eyes. The Psychologist handed her a tissue. She wiped the corner of her eyes. "Shortly after the accident, I was driving my rental car on I-66. Thank God it was a Saturday without much traffic on the road. I suddenly had a panic attack. I abruptly stopped the car until I smelled burned rubber from the tires. It was when I decided to stay off the road."

"So you have not driven since that day."

"That is correct. I just could not bring myself to drive again."

"So why do you want to drive now?"

"My career is about to take a great turn. I need my independence. The only way I can do that is to drive myself again."

"You will have enough money soon to pay someone to drive you around. Why don't you settle for that?"

"Because I need to drive again. Otherwise I will never get rid of the fear that I have. It is not only the driving. It is my confidence that I need to regain."

"I'm sorry if I seemed hard on you but I wanted you to tell me that you know what the problem is. I wanted you to tell me that you need to receive help."

"That is why I came to you. I know that I have a problem. I know what my problem is. I do want my problem remedied."

"You did well today for the first session. By the time we come to the end of our third session, you should be ready for the road lessons." He shook Nana's hand. "You will drive with confidence again, Ms. Nkuku."

The next 2 sessions went well for Nana. The Psychologist cleared her for her road lessons. She was excited. She felt more confident than before she began her theoretical sessions. She was glad that she went that route.

Nana had only 3 road lessons. Her instructor told her that she did not give herself enough credit. "You are a careful driver. You're an alert driver."

"I was a careful driver. I always drove not only for myself but for every other driver out there."

"I know you were. You still are that same driver. You will be an even better driver now."

❧

Nana drove her rental to the car rental company. She did not need Bridgette to drive her to return the car. Her car was delivered to her the next day from the repair shop. The warranty on all repairs was 1 full year. She was glad to see her car. She missed her car. Nana had no regrets for the decision to have her car repaired. She wasted no time to drive herself to the neighborhood store.

"I see you're back on the road again." Bridgette told her with sarcasm. "I guess you don't need me around here now."

"I don't need you to drive me anywhere anymore. You need to stay here though."

"Whatever, Nana."

"What is that about?" Bridgette did not respond. Nana went to her bedroom to avoid a debate. She noticed that Bridgette had assumed an attitude from the time she decided to do something about her driving problem. She thought that Bridgette would be happy for her. She thought she was tired of being her driver. Her real friends celebrated with her.

Nana received the casting schedule from Zebra Productions. She was expected in Atlanta for cast selection in a month. She also received her advance check of $175,000 in the same package as the schedule. She sent an email to Sara Wilcox to inform her that she had received the check and schedule. Sara reminded her that they needed to set up their promised lunch date. Nana wasted no time before she deposited her check. She had never held that much money in her hand. She thanked God for his goodness to her. Her dreams would finally be realized.

Bridgette told Nana that she had a job lead in San Francisco she wanted to pursue. "I feel good about this lead so I don't want to pass it up."

"I'm happy for you. When do you leave for San Fran?"

"I leave this Friday."

Nana thanked God that night in her evening prayer. She dreaded the thought of being forced to ask Bridgette to leave. She did not want to leave her in her home when she went to Atlanta. She pondered the thought and prayed over it. She felt that the Lord gave her the answer. Bridgette will get the job in San Francisco, and she would be rid of her. She liked her and gave her refuge for nine months. She did not offer any help with food or bills. Nana's household expenses doubled from the time Bridgette moved in. At least James had a job. He bought his own food. He had his own vehicle. He too never offered any assistance with bills. He also cleaned not only his area but the common areas. Bridgette was a total dependent.

Nana had some decisions to make as she prepared for her trip to Atlanta. Bridgette stayed in San Francisco for 2 weeks. She never called or sent an email to Nana in her absence.

"We need to talk." Nana told Bridgette when she returned. She hoped that Bridgette had the job that is why she stayed so long. Nana was in her home office at her desk. Bridgette stood at the door of the office. "I'm leaving for Atlanta in 2 weeks. I will be gone for at least 2 to 3 weeks."

"That's nice. What's going on down there?"

"I've signed the contract with Zebra Productions. We start casting in 2 weeks. How did it go in San Fran?"

"I didn't get the job but at least it's a start."

"I'm sorry to hear that. Have you done anything yet about finding a place of your own?" She had spoken to Bridgette 6 weeks before about what could happen in her life. She told her that once she signed her contract, things would happen without much notice. She told her that she will need to find another place to live. Bridgette began to limit her time she spent at Nana's home. She changed her routine. She came in late and left early to avoid Nana. When she left for San Francisco, Nana took the spare key which Bridgette used. After all, she did not pay rent therefore Nana was not obligated to give her a key.

"It's hard to find an apartment when you don't have a job, Nana."

"You should have been looking from the first week you moved in here."

"You don't know what I've been doing since I've been in here."

"What I do know is that you have been here for more than 10 months now. You have eaten heartily. You have made no contributions."

"What are you saying?"

"I'm giving you 2 week's notice to find a place. I will not carry you any further."

"What do you want me to do in such short a time?"

"I want you to find a place. I want you to move out of my home. I'm the immigrant, yet I've had to rescue 2 born Americans. I thought it should be the other way around." Nana needed to leave for work.

"You Miss big church-going Christian are asking me to leave? Isn't that hypocritical?"

Nana was in disbelief of what she heard. She spun around to face Bridgette. "Are you questioning my Christianity? It is because I am a Christian that I took you in and have practically supported you for almost a year." Nana picked up her briefcase and her keys from her desk. "I want you out of my home. I change my mind about 2 weeks. I want you out within 24 hours." Nana walked out of the house.

Nana sat in her car and said a prayer. She asked God to forgive Bridgette and to forgive her. She felt used and spent. She did not want to throw Bridgette out without a place to go. God knew that Nana believed in philanthropy, humanitarianism and generosity. She was willing to give of herself to assist others. She just did not want people to misread her generosity for weakness. Nana knew that both James and Bridgette took advantage of her kindness.

Nana requested the next day off from work. Rene approved her request. She wanted to be at home while Bridgette packed and moved out. Bridgette got home late that night. She made a lot of noise with her boxes up the stairs. Nana knew that the disturbance was on purpose. She ignored Bridgette's vindictive behavior. She read her Psalm 91 for comfort, had a quiet conversation with the Lord and fell asleep with a peaceful heart. Nana knew that she extended a helpful hand to Bridgette. Her help was abused therefore she was no longer going to be a victim.

The next morning Bridgette began to stack her boxes in the driveway. Nana was speechless when she saw how much Bridgette had accumulated in less than a year. She did not recall Bridgette having all of those things when she moved in 10 months before. Her things looked like a yard sale. Nana realized that Bridgette sneaked in things each time she went to her storage facility. She had no intention to move out. If Nana had allowed her to remain there without end, Bridgette would have stayed and never moved. She did not believe that Bridgette went to San Francisco for a job interview. She went on a fun trip.

Bridgette got all of her belongings out of the house by 2:00 that afternoon. Her friends brought a trailer truck and loaded her things on it. They were 2 women and 2 men. Nana wondered where they were when their friend, Bridgette was homeless the night she took her in.

Before Bridgette left, she gave Nana a hug and the 2 women held their embrace. Her face was wet with tears. "Thank you for everything. You came to my rescue when I was at my lowest. I will always appreciate it."

Nana wiped the corners of her own eyes. "It was my pleasure to do it. I could not see you homeless. I'm glad to see that you have friends to assist you. Will you be with them?"

"Yes, I'll be with them until I can get back on my feet."

"I pray that you will do that soon. I wish you only the best and God's blessings."

"I wish you luck with your movie. I'll look for it in theaters to go and see it." She managed a smile and made a quick exit through the front door. Nana walked with her down the walkway. She gave Bridgette one last wave before the truck rolled away, as Nana said a quiet prayer for Bridgette. She hoped that she would see Bridgette again. She also understood that it was America. People moved on and never looked back. Nana found it difficult to cut cords and burn bridges when she became acquainted with people.

Frank called a conference call meeting for FAFGM on Globe, where they were able to see each other. He had Kiddi, Jean-Claude, Shirley, Cynthia of Don and Day, Eugenia, Martha Reynolds, who agreed to organize and direct the volunteers, Alec and Jimmy Jeffries on the call. "We have a full house today. I thank everyone for joining the call on such short notice." Frank told them. He reminded them of the minutes they had received two months before from the call with Nana, Jean-Claude and Shirley. "I called this quick meeting to bring everyone up to date where we are with FAFGM."

Shirley read the minutes, and brought everyone up to date on the calendar of events for the next few months.

Frank continued. "We have been invited by the President of Senegal. He wants to meet with us to discuss the eradication of FGM. We're looking at some time in February after the Big Bowl. This trip is Jean-Claude's baby. He's been working on it for a year now. Please tell us where you are with it."

"We have the invitation now. I am working with the Senegalese President's office on the itinerary and the agenda. As things progress, I will update everyone. The entire trip will cost $2500 per person. I am working on hotel arrangements to be included in the $2500. If you want to go on the trip, please send an email to Shirley."

"I will break protocol here for a minute, if you don't mind, Frank." Jimmy Jeffries spoke in his Texan accent. "I don't know how many people will be in the party to Senegal. Shirley, you just let me know how many people and what the final cost is. I will donate the cost of the trip to FAFGM." Everyone marveled at Mr. Jeffries' generous donation.

"Jimmy, we thank you for the offer. We are fortunate to have you on our Board of Directors and a supporter of our cause." Frank told Mr. Jeffries. He welcomed Martha and her volunteers to FAFGM. "We look forward to working with you, Martha. You and the volunteers have already been a great help to us since you started." He moved to other business. "We all are proud to congratulate Nana on her movie contract with Zebra Productions. The movie, *Replace your Blades* is scheduled to be released in early February. We look forward to a sold out box office hit." Everyone applauded. "Mr. Jeffries' modesty prevented him from telling you that the opening night of *Replace your Blades* will have an exclusive showing at our own 'San Antonio Gorillas Stadium.'." They applauded again.

Mr. Jeffries had just built the stadium. There was a great deal of admiration for his new stadium. It was the latest talk of the Football Association. It was the largest stadium in the Association at that time. Jimmy told them that he wanted them to fill the stadium on opening night. He approached Zebra Productions, and made the offer, which they did not refuse, and neither did Nana. The Gorillas stadium hosted many events when football was out of season. It was a popular venue for events that required a lot of space.

"Cynthia, where are we with the Media Campaign?" Frank asked.

"The public service announcements are recorded. They're ready to be aired. Most of the networks have already agreed to run them. The airing begins next week." Cynthia paused. "Beside the public service announcements, we have full-page announcements to run in all major newspapers in the country. Those will also start next week."

"Cynthia said women's magazines in Europe, the Middle East, Latin America, South East Asia and the U.S. have committed to either run articles or public service announcements." Nana told them.

"The support is overwhelming." Cynthia said. "The video we ran on our website on FGM sparked outrage among women and men alike."

"We can talk all day long. People will not really get it until they see the actual procedure." Jean-Claude reminded them.

"I think the movie will have an even greater impact." Alec spoke. He was excited for Nana. It was good to hear her voice. They had not spoken for a while – she was busy.

"Martha, do you have anything for us before we sign off?" Frank checked.

"The volunteers are organizing a 5K Walk against FGM for next summer. We will have more for you in our next meeting." Martha updated them.

"While Nana is on location, Alec has agreed to sit in for her. I'll be busy during the end of the season and playoffs. Shirley will handle my duties." Frank told them. It was obvious that the Gorillas would make the playoffs. "With that, we will adjourn in prayer. Father we thank you for all your gifts. We thank you for each person on this call. We ask you to direct us in all our under takings to get this organization to where you intend it to be. We pray for our continued safety and great health. We ask for all of these blessings. Amen."

Chapter Fifteen

THE UNSPEAKABLE

In my distress I prayed to the Lord, and the Lord answered me and set me free. – Psalm 118:5 (NLT)

Nana arrived in Atlanta with a feeling of contentment. She no longer needed to deal with the lengthy commute to Washington, D.C. She no longer would need to drive to Reston to her job at Alpha. She did not have to be regimented in a job; where someone dictated when she took lunch – how long she took to eat lunch – when she began work – when she left work – when she took vacation or even when she could become ill. She was her own boss on earth with God as her only dictator. She did not mind that God was her boss. He steered her in the right direction. He would never fire her. He would never ask her to present a doctor's note if she visited the physician. He never deceived her. He would never throw her out of the office or sue her for job desertion.

Nana handed Alpha her resignation with confidence that she would not return. She had resigned her job at Proficiency Travel many years before. She had no doubt in her mind that her resignation from Alpha was God's doing. She was not going to look back, only ahead. She remembered that the scriptures told her to *'Trust in the Lord with all your heart; and lean not unto your own understanding. In all your ways acknowledge him, and he will direct your paths.' Proverbs 3:5-6 (KJV).* She knew that she did not fail to acknowledge him in everything she did.

The Lord delivered her from female genital mutilation. He saw her through her education in a foreign land. She had no family until Adjoa came to America years after Nana. He provided a family for her that gave her unconditional love; Shirley, Frank and Jean-Claude. She suffered the gruesome deaths of Tommie and Paula. Nana felt that her sacrifices were made. She paid some dues in profound ways. She was ready to spend the rest of her life the way God designed – not the way man had designed. The eradication of FGM was her priority. It was her job now. It was the reason she was in Atlanta.

Nana had never been to a casting before. Zebra Productions sent her a package of educational information. They wanted her to familiarize herself with terminologies to minimize intimidation on the set. They also sent her the final draft of the script. She read the entire script along with all other information she received. She did not realize all the work that went into a movie. She was amazed by how many people worked behind the scenes of a film.

Robert Gallagher took Nana around to the different departments, on the tour of the many studios. They had 4 theaters in Zebra Productions' complex. She smiled when she thought of how Alpha referred to their 2-building complex as a campus. Zebra had 4 buildings in their complex. She was able to get from one building to the other without going outside. She only knew that they had left one building when Robert needed to use his security card to enter the next one. Each building was 8 stories high with many offices and recording studios.

"We specifically chose this area for our complex." Robert told Nana as he gave her the tour. "There is a lot of room for expansion if we ever grow out of space. There is enough land to add another 2 buildings, if needed."

"It sounds like you planned ahead before you began to build." Nana said it as a compliment.

"We planned before we purchased the land." He held a door open for her. "We work the same way with our entire operation."

"It is undoubtedly apparent."

He introduced Nana to some of the people with whom she would work. She wondered how she would remember all of the names and titles. He took her through Production Design, Art, Sound, Visual Effects, Casting, Costume/Wardrobe, Music, Camera/Electrical, Cinematography and Film Editing. Then he introduced her to the Production Management team.

The casting process began the next morning. Nana sat poised between the Casting Director, Rex Kane and the Producer, Richard Gallagher. Also on the casting panel were the Cinematographer and the Creative

Consultant. They sat behind a large desk that was part of the sound and visual studio, where they conducted the casting auditions. The first day was dedicated to casting auditions only for the 3 roles. They auditioned 15 actresses for the lead role, which was the little girl that was genitally mutilated at 5 years old. They also auditioned for the little girl's friend who was also mutilated. The 3rd role that day was for the lead Medicine Woman who performed the mutilation on the girls. Nana was impressed by the African American actress that was selected for the lead Medicine Woman. Some of the other ladies that did not make the lead Medicine Woman role were assigned to play other medicine women. The script called for about 8 medicine women in all.

The story was about a 5-year old girl and her friend who were genitally cut at that age. Nana more or less replicated parts of her own life story but she heightened it for the story to have a greater impact on the minds of the audience. The 2 girls made a promise that they would always be friends. That they would grow up and become politicians to make it unlawful for parents to have their daughters genitally cut. Both girls grew up and remained in school. One girl (the lead role) became a high powered attorney in Ghana. She rose in her career and was appointed to the Ghanaian High Court. Her friend became an Obstetrician, and specialized in corrective genitalia. The 2 friends teamed up and pushed for the High Court to outlaw the practice they had suffered. It became unlawful for parents to have their daughters genitally cut. The Obstetrician had a successful practice. She performed corrective surgery on a total of 300 young women and girls within her 2nd year of practice. The High Court Judge (lead role) had a day of the year declared as *'Replace your Blades'* day in Ghana. Thus was the movie title. The High Court Judge and the Obstetrician opened a vocational center to teach alternative careers to the medicine women, and future medicine women. Some of the women learned to sew, others learned to tilt the soil and farm, while others learned hair design, manicure and pedicure. The vocational career center also taught self-esteem and compassion to the women. According to Nana's script, the center was so successful that subsequent centers were built in each region of Ghana.

Casting auditions took only 2 weeks. Nana expected to stay in Atlanta for at least a month. She was surprised how smoothly it went and how quickly the time expired. She was glad to return to her own bed and house. Although the accommodations in Atlanta were great, she was ready to return to Virginia. She did not stay in a hotel; the production company put her up in one of their business condos, where she had a full kitchen and living room with daily maid service. She preferred that to a conventional hotel. The nights that she did not join some of the casting crew for dinner, Nana cooked a nice vegetarian meal for herself. She had a sedan assigned to her with a driver during her entire stay in Atlanta. She had no complaints with the hospitality from Zebra Productions. She enjoyed her work with them. She did not consider it 'work' because she had so much fun. Nana was pleased with the casting selections. Majority of the selected cast were well known actors. She knew that such names on the bill would make for great box office results.

Betty Sue was glad to see Nana back. She was excited and wanted to hear all about the casting selections. Nana shared stories of her experiences with her. She wanted to know which movie stars Nana met and what they were like in person. "I had dinner one night with the cast after we finalized the selections. Sophie Behan is really nice in person. I enjoyed talking with Cindy Roller." Sophie Behan was popular among both young and old fans, and so was Cindy Roller. Sophie and Cindy were selected to play the 2 girls after they became women.

"I have prayed for you for so many years." Betty Sue told her with a delightful smile. "I'm so glad that you finally made it, Nana. It just proves that when we set our minds to our goals, and leave the rest with God, we can accomplish anything."

"This is what I find so amazing about the God we serve." She sat in Betty Sue's living room with her. "You were born into a Catholic home so you always knew God in this manner." Nana hung her head for a moment. "I discovered him late in my life, and I only wish I had grown up in a Christian home like you and my other friends did."

"It's never too late. The important thing is that you know him now."

"Yes, I'm enjoying my relationship with him as well as this special 'walk' I'm taking with him."

Nana began to sound like a broken record to her friends. Everyone asked similar questions about the actors and actresses she met in Atlanta. Her American friends always tickled her with their star-struck behavior. It was the culture, and even she had conformed to that culture. It took her the first 2 days before she relaxed and did not pay attention to the movie stars. She told herself that they went to the bathroom just as she did. They needed to please her because it was her script.

Replace your Blades

The filming of *Replace your Blades* was fun for Nana. She invited Shirley and Alec to join her on the set but they were busy with FAFGM in hers and Frank's absence. It killed Shirley to turn down such an offer. "No worries, you will meet the cast when we have the premiere in San Antonio." She assured Shirley and Alec.

Nana was surprised how early the cast and crew began work on a movie set. She set her alarm every night to ensure that she did not oversleep. They were on the set every morning at 6:00. The crew members were in place and the actors were in their places for shoot. Most of the scenes were set in Ghana or other parts in Africa. The production team was brilliant. They sent a delegation to the places in Ghana which Nana had described in her script. They took stills and videotaped scenes and used them to replicate what they saw. "Even I could be fooled by those scenes." She told the Cinematographer when she first saw the set. They built Ghana in parts of Georgia. Where the script called for rural Ghana, they used parts of rural Georgia. They had palm trees and other tropical trees, such as mango and coconut trees. The money they saved from airfare and accommodations for each crew and cast member, they spent on remarkable and believable scenes.

Nana learned the lingo on the set, and before long, she too joined in the usage of it. She heard names such as Call Sheet, Wrap Party, Clapper, Clap Board, Places, Clean Speech and Change Pages. They referred to the Casting Director as 'CD'. She mistook that at first for a music CD. She liked the fact that the Production Management said a prayer every morning before they began to film.

She told Stephen Green once, "It is no wonder that this film is moving without problems. We've had clean speech 2 days in a row." Clean speech was when all dialogue in a scene was performed without any errors.

The wrap party was different from Nana's conservative type of parties to which she was accustomed. Everyone had worked hard with brilliance and excellence. They wanted to let everything go by the time the Director yelled, "It's a wrap." The reaction of the cast and crew reminded Nana of the end of her college graduation. They all threw their caps in the air.

At the sound of 'it's a wrap', everyone threw baseball caps and paper cups in the air. They embraced one another and shouted, "We did it." She received so many hugs that day, she lost count. They were in a joyous mood. They were a group of individuals who had worked together for four months. They felt like family. Nana wondered what she would do now that the movie was finished. She then realized that she had not seen her home for months. When the crew took hiatus, she took the opportunity to see Georgia instead of going home. Her driver took her to the border of Georgia and Florida. It was beautiful there. She spent 3 days on that island. She was ready to go home.

Nana was glad to be back in Virginia. She wished she had the time to spare. She wanted to visit her friends in San Antonio. She had work to do in Virginia. She spoke with Cynthia for an update on the media campaign. "Great things are going on in Africa." Cynthia told her. Certain countries are working toward outlawing the practice of FGM."

"Which countries are they?" Nana was elated.

"We knew that Egypt passed their bill into law some years ago."

"They did since 2007."

"The reports said that some of them are considering it."

"Well, that is hopeful."

"The bad news is that the Republic of Geddeh supports the practice of FGM. In that country, it is some sort of a secret society that practices it."

"That is absurd. I hope they know that sanctions could be imposed on them.

"Does FAFGM want to issue a press release about it? Shirley and Alec felt that we should make a statement."

"I agree that we should issue a statement."

"Jean-Claude said he will be happy to release a statement to the European Media."

"Unless Shirley or Alec is willing to make the statement here in the States, I'll be happy to do so."

"Then I'll prepare yours and Jean-Claude's. We will arrange an appearance for both of you."

"Thanks, Cynthia for the great work. I wonder what the President of Geddeh is thinking. As a woman, you think she would be the first to outlaw FGM."

"A lot of women in Africa are in denial, I've observed. Maybe it was done to her."

"That is more reason for her to oppose it now."

Nana went on both radio and television two days later to denounce the stand that the Republic of Geddeh had taken in support of FGM. Jean-Claude went on television in France and Italy with the same message as Nana's. He delivered his message in English, French and Italian. Kiddi went on the international television station in London to denounce Geddeh's decision. The messages were full of passion and emotion. In their messages, FAFGM also applauded those countries that had joined in the campaign against FGM and had already outlawed the practice.

As the media campaign continued to run on television, radio and in the print media, the momentum began to heighten. Zebra Productions was in the process of edits. They advised Nana that the movie would be ready for the premier before FAFGM for their African tour. The volunteers work on the 5K Walk was close to completion. Frank and the Gorillas had only lost 1 game in the season. They held the best record in the Association. It was evident that they were headed for the playoffs. The question remained, would they make it all the way to the Big Bowl.

Nana was much more relaxed with her life as it was. She slept in every morning. She did not need to rush through her morning devotions and meditations. She went for power walks in the mornings after devotions. She ate breakfast on her deck, as she watched the squirrels and rabbits jump about her back yard. She never knew that it was possible for life to be so easy. There were days when she had a meeting with Sara Wilcox. Other times she met with organizations of similar interest as FAFGM's. She prayed for the Gorillas to make it to the Big Bowl. Nana had never been to the Big Bowl. She wanted to go but only if her favorite team was a contender.

She heard from Kiddi and Jean-Claude more often since the campaign began. She sat on her deck when the phone rang, just before noon on the east coast. "Hey my sister, what are you up to?"

"What happened to the French accent, Jean-Claude?" Nana teased him.

"I saved it for the French." They laughed. "I am bursting with excitement. I just could not wait to call you."

"What is it – tell me." Nana liked to receive good news.

"I was offered another promotion with the airline. I have accepted it."

"What is the new post?" Nana heard the glee in his voice.

"You are speaking to the new Managing Director of Operations for Europe."

"Congrats are most certainly in order." She beamed as the cool November breeze brushed against her face. "I am delighted for you, my brother. Cheers to the new Managing Director of Operations." She held up her cup of tea to toast. "Wait until Frank and Shirl hear."

"I already sent a text to Frank this morning. I know he's busy with practice for the playoffs. He forwarded my text to Shirl."

"So when do you begin the new post?"

"I begin after we return from our tour. I will take a month off for my vacation before I begin the big shot job." They laughed. "I have something to tell you."

"Aren't we full of news today? Tell me."

"I met someone."

"Hallelujah, praise the Lord. Tell me about her."

"She is from Cote d'Ivoire. I met her in flight. She was on her way to visit her parents in Abidjan. She lives here in Marseilles."

"How serious is this relationship?"

"I really like her, my sister. You know I have had no interest in anyone since we lost Paula. Fatima captured my heart."

"I'm getting two huge pieces of good news in one call. You're full of surprises. Do Shirl and Frank know this?"

"Yes I told Frank this morning. We could not stop texting. He's already getting us married."

"I'm right with him on the marriage part."

Jean-Claude laughed. "Perhaps we can have a double wedding. You and Doc Alec can join us." He just could not resist.

"Oh dear, here we go again."

"Don't dish it if you can't take it."

"O, you sounded too American just then."

"Look who's calling the fish a swimmer."

"I've never heard that one before." They laughed and ended their call.

A few days later, shocking news came out of Africa. The news hit the founders of FAFGM with mixed emotions. Sanctions were imposed on two countries in Africa for the continuation of the practice of female genital mutilation in those countries. One country was in East Africa and the other in West Africa.

FAFGM issued a statement to the press through Don& Day Public Relations. "The blatant defiance exhibited by the people of these two countries is totally outrageous. They have spoken loudly to the world that they do not intend to spare the little helpless girls. However FAFGM will continue to work until every little girl in the world is spared."

Every major newspaper and broadcast network ran that statement from FAFGM by the next day.

Another Big Bowl

Autumn came and slipped by like a quick wind. Nana's favorite season in America was the fall. She appreciated the vegetation when the leaves changed from green to orange and brown. She was amazed how they knew when to change colors and when to fall off the trees. She remembered how baffled she was at her first snow storm. She took off her shoes to have the bottom of her feet touch it. Nana told herself that it was all God's amazing work. She was confused about the creation before she knew him. She told herself that it was impossible for the creation to have happened all by itself. She thought of the mountains' formation, the depth of the valleys and the slope of the hills; the rivers, snow, rain, sun. How did unbelievers in God think that they just happened to be here? She too once took all of those things for granted. She once took the breath she was given each day for granted. She now saw life through a different set of eyes. Nana was thankful for her accomplishments; but she was also thankful for her spiritual growth. She had a beautiful relationship with someone whom she did not see with her naked eyes. She knew he was always there. She asked him for things and he gave them to her. He made the impossibilities possible for her. He did not expect anything from her except her trust and obedience.

The Gorillas swept through the playoffs. Nana had learned one thing about the football playoffs; there were no second chances. If a team lost a playoff game, that team was eliminated. She always thought that basketball teams were given far too many chances in their playoffs, compared to the football and soccer teams. She did not assume that because the Gorillas held the best record in the association that they were destined to win the Big Bowl. She had seen a team with a perfect record throughout the regular season and post season lose the Big Bowl to a team which no one expected to even go to the Big Bowl. Frank had told her, "I'm nervous about this upcoming Big Bowl."

"You only feel that way because it is your last game." She told him. "If you had plans to return to football next season, you would have so much confidence."

"That's just it, Nana. If I don't win this one, I will have to return. I've already told Jimmy that. I will not go out on a loss."

"First of all, you will not lose. You have to remove the word, 'losses' from your vocabulary. Secondly, do you see in football history how many great players who never played in the Big Bowl or won it? Frank Thurston, you have been blessed with 2 Big Bowl rings. You're on the verge of the third one. I wonder how many players in the association would like to trade places with you right now."

"Thanks Coach Nkuku. I get it. That's why I can depend on your little pep talks. Shirl and I love you."

"I love you both back. Now go win this one for Tommie – not just for you."

The Big Bowl was held in Tempe, Arizona that year. Nana was happy about the location. She had never been to Arizona. The late January weather was magnificent. It was in the mid 70's to low 80's every day. She needed a light jacket or sweater at night. She fell in love with the desert and no humidity. She did not miss the cold January days in Washington, D.C. She had seen such large cactus trees in her life. They were everywhere she looked. She and Shirley stayed together most of the time. Frank was busy with his teammates. His itinerary was hectic. He had Media Day, where they interviewed the players almost every hour. Although he had not released a formal announcement about his retirement, the news was leaked. He was upset about that. He did not want any distractions for his teammates. He told the Media, "At this time, I am here to win the Big Bowl with my team. I am focused on nothing else but that. I will address anything else after the Big Bowl." The Media even speculated that Jimmy Jeffries wanted Frank out. Jimmy loved Frank like a son. Frank was a three-time Big Bowl quarterback. There was no reason for him to get rid of a winner. Frank wanted to start a family with his wife. Jimmy supported him in his decision. He and Shirley had agreed that they would not begin a family while he played ball.

Alec was scheduled to arrive in Arizona the night before the game. He was unable to clear his schedule until then. He was eager to see nana again. It had been a long time. He wondered if she had given his statement to her any thought. He found it difficult to not think about her. He wanted to get close to her but she always managed to hold him off. He was like a school boy as he packed and prepared for his trip. He went to the barber and got a great haircut. He took care in his selection of attires he packed. He wanted to look his best when Nana saw him again.

Jean-Claude told Frank that he would make the Big Bowl. Everyone knew that it was possibly Frank's final game. Everyone close to him wanted to be there to support him and his team. Amelia was already in Arizona. She stayed at the same hotel as nana and Shirley. Nana kept in touch with Amelia by telephone most times. Whenever her schedule permitted, she drove to Potomac, Maryland to visit Amelia. Amelia had aged a great deal since Tommie's death and Frank's injuries. She was a woman of faith therefore she never complained of her loss. She said that we cannot question God's will. She considered herself blessed that he took one son and not both on that dreadful day.

Nana, Shirley, Amelia and Alec sat in the lobby restaurant of their hotel. They waited for Frank to join them for an early dinner. It was the evening before the Big Bowl game. The coach had granted Frank only a couple of hours to dine with his wife and family. It was not long before Frank joined them. Amelia beamed when she saw her son walk in. He had a kiss and a hug for Shirley, a hug for his mother and a hug for Nana. He exchanged handshakes with Alec. They had just ordered their selections when the Concierge of the hotel approached their table. "Mr. Thurston, there's a gentleman in the lobby asking for you. He just checked in."

"Does he have a name?" Frank figured it was a fan or a member of the media.

"His name is Mr. Girard." Jean-Claude walked up to the table before the Concierge was able to respond.

Frank bounced up and embraced his friend. "Look at you. What are you doing here? I thought you couldn't make it?" They hugged again.

Jean-Claude greeted everyone at the table, as Nana's and Shirley's mouths remained open and speechless. "Did you really believe that I would miss your big day?"

"Why didn't you tell us?" Shirley asked after the initial shock.

"Then I would have ruined the pleasure of seeing the look on your faces."

Nana ruffled his hair, as she did when she wanted to get back at him. "Why didn't you bring Fatima?"

"She was not able to get away soon enough for the game. She will join me in a couple of weeks."

"Does that mean you will be here that long?" Frank asked. He was still in disbelief of his friend's surprise.

"Yes, I will be here for the movie premiere as well."

"Jean-Claude, God bless you for being here." Amelia placed her hand on his shoulder. He was seated between Amelia and Nana. Alec sat on the other side of Nana. "We love you."

"Thank you, Mrs. Thurston." Jean-Claude patted Amelia's hand. "I love you all too." He recalled the many weekends he stayed with Frank at Amelia's former home in Northeast Washington. She fed them more than they were able to eat. He, Frank and Tommie had memorable times with Amelia. Nana became one of the boys when she hung out with them. She always wished Amelia had a daughter to hand out with her. Amelia always told her, that she was adopted daughter. Amelia introduced Nana and Jean-Claude to her neighbors as her foreign student children. Both Nana and Jean-Claude never forgot how Amelia had been to them as a mother.

"So what does Fatima do, Jean-Claude?" Alec asked.

"She's a geek." They laughed. "Don't tell her I said that. She has her Masters in Information Technology. She works for Cooper's Industries as their IT Manager."

"Great, we need a techy in this family." Shirley teased.

"About tomorrow, where do you guys prefer to sit at the game?" Frank checked with his friends. "You have the choice of being in the stands with all of the fans or in the box with Jimmy and his family."

"I will be on the side line in case of injuries." Alec told them. "I pray there will be none."

"That's a prayer to send up for sure." Frank said. "Jimmy said I can have up to five seats in his box. Since Doc Alec will be down there with us, Mom, Nana, Shirl and JC will be in the box. That is, unless you guys want to be out there with the noise. In the box, you will have enough food and refreshments throughout the game. Nana, they will have salads and nuts. He ensured that his family was taken care of for the game.

The momentum at the game grew more in favor of the Gorillas as the 1st half came to an end. The Gorillas led 14 to 3 when Frank and his team returned to the locker room at half time. The Jeffries' box was on fire. Shirley, Nana and Jean-Claude joined Jimmy's son in the celebration. They barely sat in their seats until half time. Frank was one half away from his 3rd Big Bowl victory, and possibly his retirement. Amelia sat next to Mrs. Jeffries as poised as she was in church on Sundays. She had told Jimmy when the games began, "Victory is the only word we will utter in this stadium today. This is what the Lord told me this morning."

The second half of the game took a turn against the Gorillas. Frank was sacked a couple of times but the fans did not give up. They continued the momentum as they did in the 1st half. The 3rd quarter belonged to the Leopards. The Gorillas only scored a field goal in that quarter. The Leopards came from behind and tied the game. The Jeffries' box was quiet. Jimmy appeared uneasy but the rest of the box kept faith. The 4th quarter began with a great play from Special Teams. The return receiver ran 98 yards with the ball and returned it for a touchdown. The stadium was on fire again and so was the Jeffries' box. Amelia reminded them, "He always saves the best for last." She even did a high five with Jimmy after the touchdown. The Offensive Line stepped up and Frank was not sacked for the rest of the game. The Defense also came to their senses, and the Leopards did not score in the last quarter. They had several 3 strike outs and punted the ball back to the Gorillas. The Leopards' coach told their punter not to kick the ball directly to the returner for fear that he would do a repeat of the 98-yard touchdown.

It was only 3 minutes left in the game. The score was 21 to 17. The Leopards drove down the field as the Gorillas' fans shouted. "Defense! Defense!" They were on the 3-yard line. It was 1st and goal. The Leopards' quarterback reared back and threw the ball into the end zone for a touchdown. The stadium was quiet as the ball circled the air and made its way into the arms of a Gorillas defender. The interception was caught in the end zone. Everyone in the box was out of his or her seat as they watched the ball circle the air. They jumped up and down. Jimmy was already down on the side lines, as he always did at the end of the games. He grabbed Frank on the side line as they held their embrace. Frank had not played for any other team but the Gorillas. He was part of Jimmy's family.

Amelia wiped the corners of her eyes, as she watched her son hug Jimmy. She thought of Tommie and wished that he had played in that game. Tommie was her baby; but he was gone from them. Frankie had done well for her. He took care of his mother and Shirley's parents. He always said, "It's in the laws of God. We must respect our parents – we must take care of them. We will get our reward." He believed that God had blessed him with a successful career because of his mother's prayers and his respect for her.

Everyone left the box and went down to the field for the ceremony and celebration. The reporter asked Frank, "Frank Thurston, what will you do with your third Big Bowl win?"

"I'm going to live." He had answered that question three times in his career. He hugged his mother, as she wept. He whispered to her, "This win is for Tommie, Mom."

"Thank you, son. I like the man you've become."

Frank held onto Shirley. "Thanks for putting up with my schedule, sweetheart."

He and Jean-Claude embraced. "My brother, thanks for coming to see me win the last one."

"Nana my sister, thank you for making me and JC pay attention to our studies in school."

"You need to get to the podium." Nana told him. "They're calling you."

Frank raised the trophy and handed it to Jimmy, as he shared the victory with his teammates. He knew he would miss them. He promised to stay in touch with them. It was rumored that Jimmy wanted him to work in the executive office with his son.

That night, Jimmy threw a party in one of the ballrooms at the hotel for members of the team and their families. Nana, Shirley, Jean-Claude and Alec attended the party with Frank as his guests.

"I've been attending more parties lately than I have in years." Nana whispered to Shirley.

"Well my dear, be prepared." Shirley whispered back. "If you will hang out with the Hollywood crowd, you will find yourself in many parties from now on."

"I do not intend to indulge in that lifestyle. This is a onetime thing for me."

"What happens if Zebra Productions approach you to write another script?"

"I will cross that bridge when I get to it."

"For now, let's just enjoy this party. Take it one party at a time."

The party was a nice decent and private one. The Media was not there. Jimmy wanted to just have the team socialize with their families and friends without the intrusion of interviews. It was an evening of relaxation and celebration. They had a band that played classical and jazz music with a soft tune. Some of the players danced with their wives and girlfriends. There was more food and drinks than the guests could consume.

Jean-Claude excused himself from their table, and went to chat with Jimmy and Sean Jeffries at their table. "Mr. Jeffries, I wanted to come over and congratulate you. I'm in awe of the kind of owner you are. Each player on your team I spoke to told me that you are the best in the Association. I applaud you for that."

"Thank you, Jean-Claude." Jimmy was surprised by the compliment. "Frankie can tell you that I don't just recruit these kids to play ball for me. I shape them into responsible men. I help them with their lives after they retire from playing ball."

Jean-Claude understood why Frank thought highly of the Jeffries family. He enjoyed his conversation with Jimmy, Mrs. Jeffries and their son, Sean. He had come to know Sean from when they both stood in Frank's wedding.

While Shirley and Frank were on the dance floor and Jean-Claude was at the Jeffries' table, Alec and Nana had privacy. "So how do you feel being a lady of leisure?" Alec asked Nana.

She laughed. "It is absolutely divine."

"So where do you go from here? You no longer need a job. FAFGM is doing well now. This movie is going to make you a wealthy woman."

"I'm not as concerned about the wealth as I am the cause. You know that already."

"What I'm getting at, Nana is our relationship." He took her hand in his. "You know how I feel about you. When are we going to be a couple?"

"We have this distance between us. It takes a toll on a relationship."

"It worked just fine for Frank and Shirley. Why wouldn't it work for us?"

"Do you think you're ready for a relationship with me?"

"Why wouldn't I be ready for a relationship with you, Nana?"

"You know the problem I have, Doc. Beside, how many interracial relationships have you had?

"I have had no interracial relationships before you. What does that have to do with anything at all? When I see you, I see a lovely woman on the inside and the exterior. I see Nana Nkuku, not a Ghanaian woman, not an African woman and not a black woman. I certainly hope you see more in me than my ethnicity."

She smiled. "I just want to make sure."

"You can be sure about that. As far as your other situation, I have a solution to that. I told you that I can perform the corrective surgery. What you wrote in your movie script, we can do it in real life."

"I have given the surgery a great deal of thought since we first discussed it. I just had so much on my mind at the time. I will talk further with you about the surgery after the release of the movie and the trip to Africa."

"When will you make a decision about our relationship?"

"Let's take it one day at a time. I agree to us being a couple."

Alec sighed and took Nana's hand in his again. "I am excited. I will be the best to you, Nana. I promise from the depth of my heart."

"Thank you and likewise me to you."

Nana did not have much time in Virginia when she returned from Arizona. She wasted no time with her preparations to fly to San Antonio. She was excited at the prospect of being reunited with Alec, Shirley and Frank. Jean-Claude flew to San Antonio with Frank, Alec and Shirley. He stayed at their home with them. He looked forward to seeing Fatima again. Alec could hardly wait for Nana to arrive in San Antonio. Although Zebra Productions offered a hotel room in San Antonio to Nana, she declined the hotel room. "I will stay with my friends. They have enough room to accommodate me at their home." She knew that they would have a lot of fun at Shirley's and Frank's with Jean-Claude there as well. It would be like the old days when they were roommates, and Frank came to visit them in Virginia. She was anxious to get down to San Antonio.

Nana collected her mail from Betty Sue. She told her neighbor all about the Big Bowl. Betty Sue told her that she saw her on television during the game. "They showed Jimmy Jeffries' box when the player caught the interception. I saw you and Shirley celebrating with the others. Why didn't you tell me that Jean-Claude was going to be at the game?"

"I didn't know myself. He surprised us."

"That was nice of him to do that."

"You will get to see him. He will return from San Antonio with me after the movie premiere. I wish you would come to the premiere with me. I'll pay your airfare. Shirley and Frank would be happy to give you a room in their home." Nana really meant what she said to Betty Sue.

"That is so kind of you kids but I will not be able to make the trip. I will go to the theater here in Herndon to see it. Thanks for the offer."

Movie Premiere

Nana arrived in San Antonio two days before the big day. She was ecstatic to see her friends again. She met Fatima who had arrived the day before she did. Fatima got along well with Nana and Shirley. Jean-Claude had talked so much about his friends, Fatima was nervous. She wondered if they would like her. Shirley and Nana developed an immediate likeness for Fatima. Jean-Claude was grateful for that. It was important to him for his mother, Nana, Shirley and Mrs. Thurston to like Fatima. He figured if she passed the Shirley and Nana test, she would pass Mrs. Thurston's test. His mother had already met Fatima, and she liked her. Fatima Diallo was a charming lady. Nana saw why Jean-Claude was crazy about her. She spoke proper French with a Southern French accent. Jean-Claude had already given Fatima the details of his relationship with Paula, and the plane crash. He told her about Tommie's death and the attack on the stadium. Her mother was originally from Marseille and her father was from Cote d'Ivoire. Her parents still resided in Cote d'Ivoire. Her father was a retired politician.

Alec spent a lot of time with Nana during her stay in San Antonio. He took her on a boat ride along the River Walk. They had a candlelight dinner at a restaurant along the River Walk. Nana was happy with Alec. He only held her hand. He never tried anything else with her, and she appreciated him for that. Alec showed a great time before the night of the movie.

The promotion of the movie ran nationwide. The movie was scheduled to be released the Friday after the premiere. The premiere was that Thursday, and the next day was the release nationwide. Everyone talked about the movie. It was something different from the movie types to which Americans were accustomed. They wanted to know about this female genital cutting. Rumors had it that it was a true story, that it was Nana's own story. Nana was interviewed several times. She and a couple of the cast members made television appearances to talk about the movie. Nana did not conceal the fact that she was a victim of female genital cutting. She did admit that she used some of her own experiences. She assured them that it was not her personal story entirely.

The big night arrived. Nana had opted not to see the film until the night that everyone else at the premiere saw it. She regretted her decision as the time drew closer. She was curious. Robert Gallagher has assured her that she had nothing to be nervous about. He told her that she would be pleased when she saw the film. She accepted his word for it. Nana wore a red and black taffeta evening gown. The top of the gown was black and from the waistline down was red. The neckline was V cut, and the skirt was bouffant. Shirley wore a lovely green gown. Fatima wore gorgeous African hot pink formal attire with matching head dress. Kiddi, who arrived the morning of the movie, wore a black silk gown. Her husband accompanied her on that trip. The men wore tuxedo attires, since the dress code was black tie. The Media was on the red carpet to greet and interview the arrivals. They mentioned Nana's escort. "Who is the handsome gentleman with you?" A reporter asked Nana as she and Alec stepped out of the limo.

"I'm her better half, thank you very much." Alec did not wait for Nana to respond to the reporter.

Shirley's parents and Amelia were in attendance of the premiere. Wayne Marshall, Shirley's older brother and his wife attended the show. The entire Gorillas football team and their wives or girlfriends attended the premiere at their stadium. Sara and Elliott Wilcox were at the showing. Adjoa made it down to the showing. Nana was surprised to see Anais Marchais, the restaurant owner in Atlanta. Diane Parsons made her appearance. There were coaches and players from other teams in attendance. The stadium was as full as it was on game day Sundays. Jimmy was pleased that he had filled the stadium, and so were Nana and Zebra Productions.

The film was believable on the screen. Nana was happy with the performance and the manner in which the practice was portrayed. A few drops of tears escaped from Nana's eyes as she watched the movie. It brought back memories which she did not particularly care to relive. She wondered how Kiddi felt at that moment. She looked over to where Kiddi and her husband sat. She saw Kiddi wipe the corners of her eyes, and she understood. She was grateful that Alec sat with her. He held her hand during the entire show.

At the end of the movie, everyone in the audience stood and applauded for five minutes. Nana was surprised to see her name in the credits as Honorary Director. She did not realize that the title was also in the credits. She thought it was only for the casting and production only.

Nana was eager to see the newspapers the next morning for the reviews from the Media. She knew that the movie release to the public was that afternoon. The reviews from the premiere played an important part to the turnout of the box office on opening day. Frank went out and picked up both of the major papers in San Antonio. The reviews were fabulous. They called the movie, 'The most imaginative, fascinating and believable plot in years." They raved about the performance, and the cinematography received high marks. They placed *Replace your Blades* on the list of awards contention. Nana was beside herself. Everyone at the Thurston house was in a great mood.

Richard and Robert Gallagher called Nana to ask her if she was satisfied with the reviews and the overall film. "Are you happy?

"I am ecstatic. Thanks for making my script look so great."

"Thanks for giving us such a fabulous script." Robert told her.

The opening of the movie nationwide was just as successful as the premiere night. The box office results around the nation were positive. Nana went online to check reviews from various cities. The reviews were all positive. Female genital cutting became a household name across America.

Nana, Jean-Claude and Fatima arrived in Virginia. Jean-Claude took Fatima on a sightseeing tour of the Washington, D.C. metro area. They visited the museums, the memorials, the monument and they saw the White House from a distance. Fatima was impressed by the architecture of some of the buildings in Washington. He drove her to the Skyline area of Virginia. They went to the Caverns, and had a picnic in the woods. He introduced Fatima to Betty Sue. Betty Sue gave Fatima a souvenir of the White House to remember her visit to America. They visited Amelia's home, and she cooked a scrumptious meal for them. They drove to the Harbor across the Woodrow Wilson Bridge, and had lunch in a quaint restaurant on the water. Fatima took a lot of pictures as they visited landmarks.

The day arrived for Nana, Fatima and Jean-Claude to leave for Senegal. The flight from Washington Dulles Airport landed at Paris Charles de Gaulle Airport at 7:30 in the morning. The flight from Dallas/ Fort Worth arrived in Paris at 7:45 in the morning. Jean-Claude, Fatima and Nana were there to greet Shirley and Frank. "Hey buddy, this marriage and retirement life seem to be good to you." Jean-Claude told Frank.

"You're right about that." Frank smiled and put his arm around Shirley's waist as she blushed. "I enjoy being married- especially when I have a wife like this."

"So what has Papa been up to?" Shirley always teased Jean-Claude and called him Papa. She and Nana were happy that he was involved with Fatima. He worked without end when they first lost Paula.

"Papa has been busy with Ms. Diallo." He smiled at Fatima as she returned his smile. They walked through the vast terminal. "Kiddi's flight arrives from London at 8:00. While we wait for Kiddi, we can relax in the VIP lounge. I arranged for a private section in the First Class lounge for us." Jean-Claude explained.

"I knew we could depend on you to take care of everything." Shirley told him.

"The trip is historical for everyone." Jean-Claude told them as they walked toward the area near Kiddi's gate. "It is home coming for Nana and Kiddi again – Shirl has already been once. Frank, you're on your way to the continent for the first time."

FAFGM were on their way to West Africa to break ground for their first support center for women. The first center was earmarked for Senegal. Jean-Claude arranged the trip; he arranged for everyone to gather in Paris to fly together to Dakar.

The foundation had done well; the controversy of little Thimbi in Tulsa, her death and her father's conviction brought a great deal of awareness to what FAFGM represented. The big victory was the bill which was passed against FGM. Thanks to the release of the movie, female genital cutting was no longer an unfamiliar name; American households were well educated on the practice. Donations were close to countless. The friends purchased some acres of land in Senegal. The architects completed the blue print of the design. The friends liked what was proposed by the builders and they approved the final blue print. They were on their way to Senegal to break ground in a formal ceremony for the structure. The centers were planned to provide emotional, medical and rehabilitation support to the victims of FGM. In addition, the centers were intended to create business and job opportunities for the Medicine Women, to replace their career in the practice of FGM. Some of the Medicine Women had argued that the practice of FGM was their only mean of making a living; they claimed that it was the only type of work they had done in their adult lives.

Kiddi's flight arrived to five eager friends. Shirley and Nana almost knocked Kiddi down to the floor while they greeted her.

"Has it been that long ladies?" Jean-Claude teased them.

"Yes it has been, Papa." Shirley shot back at him, as Kiddi grabbed him and gave him a big hug.

"I missed all of you – we had such a great time at the movie premiere." Kiddi told them. "I really miss our get-togethers at the townhouse in Virginia."

"Those were the good old days before weddings and movies." Jean-Claude said. "We did bring some life to Herndon in that townhouse." They all laughed.

They settled in their private area of the VIP lounge, as Jean-Claude and Frank brought the ladies their drinks.

The friends discussed with anticipation, the mission ahead of them. The years had accumulated between them and a great deal had happened during those years. Nana felt that her emotions were strong enough to revisit the past. She and Kiddi had discussed it at length; they had both accepted what happened to them a long time ago. This was their second visit to the continent. Her only regret was that Tommie and Paula were not there. At least Jean-Claude had Fatima now. When the friends first talked about a visit to Africa, Paula and Tommie was with them. She remembered how enthusiastic Tommie was about Africa. Nana found it hard to believe that Paula and Tommie were both gone from them in such tragic ways.

The time escaped them; it was time to board. They were scheduled to board from the lounge since they held first class tickets. Jean-Claude briefed them on the itinerary once they arrived in Dakar.

"We have a lunch meeting with the Commissioner tomorrow. We will arrive early morning – then we will proceed to the hotel to rest until lunch." Jean-Claude told them. "Cynthia is already there on the ground – she will take over once we arrive." Cynthia, their P.R. agent arrived in Dakar a week earlier to prepare ahead of the friends.

The flight from Paris to Dakar was turbulent, yet it did not interfere with the friends' anticipation. Jean-Claude did not have to work the flight as Purser; He was now an executive of the airline. His vacation was already effective.

The captain announced that they would land in half an hour. The girls took turns to visit the lavatory in preparation for landing. The flight attendants busied themselves, as they collected items from the passengers. Jean-Claude watched them rush around the cabin. He thought about the days when he flew in uniform and worked that same cabin. He had paid his time as a Flight Attendant and Purser. He no longer did that. He was finally an executive.

The landing cards were passed out to all passengers, scheduled to disembark at Dakar; the flight was scheduled to continue to Abidjan. Kiddi and Nana completed their landing cards with an odd feeling; they were about to land on African soil as foreign nationals. Nana was now an American citizen and Kiddi, a British citizen.

The Sahara Desert heat was intense when they landed in Dakar.

"My man, no wonder you're always tanned when you return from here." Frank told Jean-Claude, as he observed the sun rays.

"You've got that right, buddy." Jean-Claude agreed. "Nobody needs to sun bathe here – you only need to walk around."

"Look at Cynthia." Shirley exclaimed as she approached them. "She looks like she's been barbecued." Cynthia's skin was a red tan.

Both Nana and Kiddi suffered the shock of the sun rays as much as Frank and Shirley did. Kiddi was fourteen when she first left Africa for school in England and Nana was eighteen when she first left for America.

The luncheon with the Commissioner was a great success. He welcomed them to Senegal but he cautioned them that not everyone agreed with what FAFGM was about to do.

Jean-Claude translated from French to English as the Commissioner addressed them. "You must remember that this is an old tradition. Old habits are difficult to let go."

"But what are we going to do about the little girls?" Frank asked and Jean-Claude translated.

"All citizens are important to us – whether they are little girls or adults. We protect all of our citizens." The Commissioner was diplomatic in his response.

"FAFGM considers the entire human race important as well – however our focal point is the little girls who are being cut." Frank was determined to make it clear why they were there.

"I understand – I want you to realize that it will be a slow process."

"We do know that the process is slow – we just want your cooperation." Frank did not relent. He was told by Cynthia to hold most of the conversations along with Jean-Claude, since Senegal was a Muslim predominant country.

The Commissioner seemed somewhat uneasy but Frank was persistent. They ended their lunch meeting and the Commissioner was relieved. He took the friends to Goree Island to see where slaves were held in the 1700's before they were taken to America. The scene at Goree Island in the small rooms where they held hundreds of slaves was grim for the friends.

"It felt as though we heard the cries of the slaves." Shirley said with emotion.

They took photographs with the Commissioner, videotaped the island and returned to their hotel.

The following afternoon the friends gathered at the site of their future center to break ground. Jimmy Jeffries flew over to cut the ribbon. The Commissioner shoveled the ground to make it official. The land was already surveyed in the name of Friends against Female Genital Mutilation.

The ceremony was poorly attended by the locals; but the protesters attended in numbers. Majority of the protesters were men. The only women among them were some of the Medicine Women who performed FGM on girls, prior to the outlaw of FGM in Senegal. The police contained the crowd and kept them away from the friends and guests.

"I guess this is what the Commissioner warned us about." Jean-Claude pointed out as they drove to their hotel in the limo.

The friends left Dakar that afternoon for Lagos. Jimmy returned to the States. The news media in the States mentioned the protests and showed a clip of the ceremony.

Kiddi's and Nana's friend, Abisola Eze was at the airport to meet them. The reunion was tearful, yet joyful. Africa had changed a great deal since the girls lived there. Abisola was one of the little girls so many years ago that were cut by the Medicine Woman. Abisola left Ghana when she was a young teenager. She attended a school in Nigeria, where she met her husband. Although her husband passed away years before, she never moved back to Ghana. She remained in Nigeria with her son, who was now himself a teenager.

The next day Abisola invited the friends to lunch at her home. She still lived in the same house in which she and her husband shared. She served a traditional West African dish of steamed plantain, yam, fried fish with imported tomato sauce and an assortment of locally grown vegetables. Nana and Kiddi shared with Abisola their accomplishments with the foundation. Abisola brought them up to date about their friends and where they were. One of them lived in Kenya and another lived in Tanzania. house.

Abisola told Nana and Kiddi that they all supported FAFGM and the work they did. She also told of the difficult birth she experienced during child birth.

The next day the friends flew back to Paris; Jean-Claude and Fatima remained in France and Kiddi continued to London. Nana and Cynthia returned to Washington-Dulles Airport, while Shirley and Frank took a flight to San Antonio via Dallas.

Nana was back at the townhouse. She found herself alone once again. She really missed her friends. She met two phone messages from Alec. He wanted to know that she returned safely. She smiled as she listened to his messages; he sounded concerned about her safety. She decided to return his calls.

"Hello there…" Nana said with enthusiasm in her voice.

"Hey you." Alec interrupted in excitement. "How are you?"

Nana's smile was bright. "I'm doing well."

"Good to hear your voice – I miss you, dear."

She raised an eyebrow at the fact that he actually missed her. He wanted to know about the trip and she told him everything – about the sale of her mother's house, their friends in Africa, the ground breaking, Goree Island, the protests, etc. She enjoyed their conversations but she knew that their relationship would go no further since he lived in San Antonio. He talked about going to Virginia to visit but she did not encourage it.

The Surgery

Alec convinced the friends for his group of physicians to partner with the foundation. They would be known as Physicians against FGM.

Dr. Vanderhurst also convinced Nana to undergo corrective surgery. He and a couple of his colleagues were scheduled to perform the surgery. Nana was hesitant at first.

"Are you kidding me?" Nana did not believe what she heard.

"No I am not kidding – you became the poster face to the world against FGM. So if you want the little girls to trust us, you and Kiddi can become the faces for corrective surgery." Alec pleaded with her.

"What is the point for me? I am too old to have anything corrected." Her voice trembled.

Alec took her hand and kissed the back if it. He never made further advances than a kiss on the hand, on the cheek and a hug. "For one, you will experience comfortable menstruation and urination." He breathed in and exhaled. "Should you ever decide to bear a child, you would have an easier childbirth."

"I know all of that already." She sighed. "Kiddi explained it but I never considered it. The opportunity never presented itself."

"The opportunity is here now. Nana, do it for yourself – do it for the little girls in the world who look up to you now."

She agreed to take it under consideration but she asked for time to think about it. She prayed and meditated on it for several days.

Nana was in surgery for six hours. She had some of the best surgeons in the operating room. Alec ensured that she received the best care. Her recovery went as was expected.

Frank visited Nana at the hospital. Jean-Claude took some days off to see that his dear friend fared well. Kiddi made it in to offer support to her childhood friend. Shirley was at the hospital everyday beside Nana's bed.

"Okay, I promise I will be one of the godfathers to your first child when you do have one." Frank told Nana.

"What an honor." She blew him a kiss. "Thank you my friend – all the best in your retirement."

"So changing the subject for a minute – I want to hear about Doc. Alec and you." Jean-Claude teased Nana.

"What about him?" Nana asked with a smirk on her face.

"Well, a little birdie told me that you two have become an item." Jean-Claude added.

"That little birdie should have told you all about Dr. Vanderhurst then." Nana wore a devilish smirk.

"Papa here needs to have a serious talk with the doctor if this is serious." She knew he was not serious.

Nana laughed. "Okay Papa – we have enjoyed each other's company for years now." She winked at her friends and smiled. "I really like him – he is a good man. He asked me to take our relationship to the next level."

"Did you agree to that without Frank's and my approval?" Jean-Claude continued to tease.

"I made the introduction so I approve." Frank told him. "Nana is right – Doc is a great guy."

"Dr. V is really cool. He has my approval." Shirley wagged her finger at Nana. "Please don't dump him – this one is a keeper."

"As long as he is good to my friend, he has my vote." Kiddi added her take on the subject.

Nana recovered from surgery and convalesced at Frank's and Shirley's home. During that period, she and Alec became closer. He was at Frank's house everyday to visit Nana. He took her out to dinner, to the movie and on picnics, while he read passages from Shakespeare to her. Nana had never been happier.

Two Years Later

The friends accomplished a great deal since they began their work together. Frank was retired with three Big Bowl victories. Jimmy Jeffries appointed Frank as Executive Quarterback Coordinator. He was in charge of the quarterbacks. Shirley built a successful salon business. Her salon was written up in several style magazines in Texas. Kiddi announced that she and her husband were expected parents with their second child. Jean-Claude's new executive position was on an upward climb. He and Fatima were engaged. They set their wedding date for a year from their engagement.

Nana's movie was released in fifty countries and in ten different languages. It was a hit wherever it was released. She began work on another script titled, *Girls are the Winners*. Zebra Productions liked Nana's work. They asked her to write another script for them to produce. The movie had such influence on girls around the world. African girls protested against FGM and refused for it to be done to them. Girls in Southeast Asia joined the movement against the practice. They began to reach out through the internet to girls in Africa to let them know that they supported them.

Replace your Blades had set the stage for the success for Nana's next movie, *Girls are the Winners*. Nana put her townhouse in Herndon, Virginia on the market for sale. She made the decision to move to San Antonio. She wanted to be near her friends. She purchased 3-bedroom condo in San Antonio. Betty Sue was sad to lose Nana as a neighbor. The day that Nana moved, both she and Betty Sue cried as they said goodbye. "I will fly back to visit you and Mrs. Thurston. My attorneys are here in Washington. The Reynolds are here. I have all of you so I have to visit now and then."

"It will not be the same." Betty Sue told her and Nana knew that it would not be the same.

Jean-Claude purchased a flat in Paris and spent some weekends in Nice with his mother or in Marseille with Fatima. Madam Girard was happy with her son's life. She liked Fatima for her son.

Nana converted one bedroom to an office and the other spare bedroom for guests such as Kiddi and Jean-Claude. She wanted to be close to her friends as well as to Alec.

The foundation continued to host its benefit dinner every year; they moved it to San Antonio. Jean-Claude and Kiddi continued to travel to San Antonio to attend the benefit dinner. The first support center was successful in helping little girls. The center in Senegal was the flagship center. Alec and his team were effective at the center. The foundation opened three more centers in Africa. Jean-Claude and Kiddi offered to check on the centers every three months since they were closest to Africa.

FAFGM held their first 5K Walk in the state of Texas. Martha Reynolds and the volunteers organized a simultaneous Walk in San Antonio, Dallas, Fort Worth, El Paso and Houston. The Walk extended for many blocks in each of those cities.

Alec invited Nana to another picnic. He read a passage from a book of Christian love poetry. Nana closed her eyes as she listened to the words of the poem. She wore a fixed smile.

Alec took out a little box from his shirt pocket and opened it. "I would like you to be my wife Nana." She opened her eyes in amazement. "Would you marry me?"

She was shocked. "Yes – yes darling." He kissed her on the lips for the first time. "I am ready to be your wife – I know that you are the right man for me."

"I knew you were the woman for me when I saw you walk down the aisle at Frank's wedding." He kissed her again and held her close. They left the picnic and hurried to break the news to their friends.

Two Weeks Later

The friends had not heard from Jean-Claude for two weeks. He phoned at least twice a week since Nana's surgery. Nana called him to give him her happy news but she did not hear from him. They left several voice messages and emailed and sent text messages.

Kiddi called Madam Girard in Nice to ask if she had heard from her son. His mother had not heard from him either and she was concerned. His mother called his office in Paris and spoke with his boss. He told her that Jean-Claude was not there. They had not seen him for more than a week. They assumed that he was in the south of France.

Everyone became alarmed about Jean-Claude's sudden disappearance. The police was notified, and filed a missing person's report. The news of Jean-Claude's disappearance spread far and wide across the globe. Every news channel posted his photo on their news screen. The friends became somber once again – they did not want to think the worse. The foundation offered a reward of $100,000 to anyone who found their friend. Frank alone offered to pay the reward and so did Jimmy Jeffries.

The International Police called Nana at her apartment. "Is this Ms. Nkuku?"

"Yes it is Nana Nkuku. How may I help you?"

"I am Inspector Dumfries. We have discovered what happened to your friend, Mr. Girard…"

"You have – where is he?" Nana became ecstatic.

"Unfortunately Ms. Nkuku – he is still not in our possession. Mr. Girard was abducted by a group that is against what your foundation stands for."

Nana heard a sound in her ears like the sound of a bell – she no longer heard the Inspector; she was in a daze. Jean-Claude was kidnapped from off the street at night by a group that called themselves, "Men for FGC."

They took responsibility for the abduction of Jean-Claude as well as Paula's plane explosion and the stadium attack. Their demand was that FAFGM seize to exist and shut down all of its centers in Africa. Without their demands being met, Jean-Claude would die.

It all was clear to the friends and the authorities. Nana and the other friends were worried and distraught. Jean-Claude's mother cried to them. Paula's parents called Nana after they heard the revelation of their daughter's murder and Jean-Claude's abduction.

The kidnappers sent a video tape of Jean-Claude; he begged his friends not to comply with his abductors' demands. He looked like they had abused him; his friends observed the scars on his face and the black eye. The friends made the decision to dissolve the foundation in return for Jean-Claude's life, but Jean-Claude did not want them to conform to the kidnappers' demands.

It was three weeks since his disappearance in the video tape; the kidnappers sent a second tape recording of Jean-Claude after three weeks. He looked tired, frail and beaten. He read from a script.

"Dear Friends,

My name is Jean-Claude Girard. I am one of the founders of FAFGM. The men that have me in captive are demanding that FAFGM ceases to do business. They have demanded that the foundation closes all of its support centers in Africa. If we do not comply with their demands, I will be killed. Please do not do what they want. If they must kill me, then I will join Paula and Tommie and die for all the little girls. If I never see you again, please continue to fight for the little girls. I love you my dear friends. I love you Mama. I love you with all my heart, Fatima. Please join my friends in the fight for the little girls." The tape went to black.

Nana and Shirley wept as they watched the tape.

"I don't care what Jean-Claude says – we need to save him." Frank said as he spun around with clenched fists. "Those men are serious – they are not playing."

"You cannot bargain with terrorists." Inspector Griffin told them. He came to the States to deliver the tape and message from Europe. "They have already killed hundreds of people to make their point. If you comply with their demands, where does it stop?"

"They might continue to kill all of us if we don't meet their demands." Shirley pointed out.

"They killed Paula and Tommie – in order to get to one member of our foundation, they will sacrifice hundreds or thousands." Frank shrugged his shoulders. "At least that has been the case so far. They blew up a jet of people, only to kill Paula". He paced the floor. "They bombed a stadium of thousands just to kill me, my brother and perhaps Jimmy. Jimmy has been one of our biggest supporters."

"Leave the work to us. We will get those men." Inspector Griffin requested. "You are not quitters – none of you." He bit hard on his bottom lip. "Today it is FAFGM – tomorrow it could be something else."

"I wish they only wanted money for ransom – we would pay them for Jean-Claude's return." Nana said through sobs.

"These men do not need money – they already have a lot of it." The Inspector told them.

"Their ransom is priceless." Alec added, as he placed his arm around Nana to comfort her.

The friends agreed to leave the work with the authorities, after their meeting with the Inspector. Fatima called every day to the friends to beg them for their decision. "Please do not listen to what Jean-Claude said. We can always restart the organization after they release him."

A month later, the authorities still had not rescued Jean-Claude. They did not catch his abductors. They discovered that the group had members in most countries in which FGM was practiced.

The phone rang in Nana's condo. Shirley went to visit her. They sat and reminisced about Jean-Claude. Nana answered, "Inspector Griffin – do you have news for us?" She saw his number on her caller's identification.

"I have news – good but bad as well." The Inspector told her. "The good news is that we have arrested the leaders of that group. We have about fifty men in custody from various countries."

"It is great news – did they deliver Jean-Claude?"

"The bad news is that the arrests were made too late." He paused. "I'm sorry but your friend, Mr. Girard died today from starvation."

Nana placed the inspector on speaker phone in order for Shirley to participate in the call. She was certain that the news was all good. The two women screamed as their voices echoed through the speaker of the phone.

Jean-Claude was put to rest a week later in Nice, where his father and grandparents were buried. His funeral was attended by all of the surviving friends of FAFGM; Alec Vanderhurst; Jimmy Jeffries; Sean Jeffries; Shirley's mother; Paula's parents, the Brauns; Diane Parsons; Amelia Thurston, Fatima and her parents, and many flight attendants and pilots. Madam Girard looked frail but she held her head high. She said that her son gave his life for a great cause.

Nana, Frank, Shirley and Kiddi stood before his casket with locked arms; they promised Jean-Claude that they would never renege on what he believed. They would never forget the reason why he gave his life.

Fatima sat between her parents. She was unable to speak at the funeral. She wept during the entire service and at the grave site. She said in French how she did not want to live any longer. She said she did not know love until she met Jean-Claude. She thanked him for the time she knew him and what he was to her. She held onto Mrs. Girard as the two of them cried. Fatima told the Brauns how much Jean-Claude talked about them and about Paula. She wished she had met them under better circumstances.

Fatima's cry won sympathy from those in the Cathedral, at the cemetery and at the luncheon. She cried in French and in English. In her cries she said, "I will never love again, Jean-Claude. I will remember you forever. You brought joy to my life. You showed me what true love really is. Rest in peace my love. Wait for me in heaven. I know you are there. God made you so perfect for me. Only he would take you from me. The people who did this to you, God will punish them. Their punishment will be worse than what men on earth can do to them." As Fatima mixed French and English in her final words to her fiancé, it was difficult to find a dry eye in the room.

Mrs. Girard said, "The men who are responsible for my only child's death have not begun to feel the wrath of God. As sure as I stand here today in this house of God, they will burn. My good and loving son was all I had. God blessed me with him. He never did anything to cause me to hold my head in shame. He was a happy child. He made me laugh all the time. If Jean-Claude said you were his friend, you did not need to worry about his sincerity to you. Nana, Frank Shirley, Kiddi, Tommie, Paula were all he talked about when he came home." She paused to wipe her eyes. "He mourned Paula as though she was his wife. He did not show interest in any other girl for many years. I worried about him. The he came home one day. He looked radiant. He told me that he was in love. He said he had finally found someone to love again. He said Fatima would not replace Paula because they both held special places in his heart." She turned to her son's friends. "I want you all to continue the cause for the little girls. My son gave his life for the little girls. Do not become discourage. Honor him by building more centers. Honor him and save the little girls from female genital cutting." She took her seat.

Jean-Claude's boss delivered a tribute that left everyone with a thought to ponder. "Jean-Claude Girard was the epitome of dedication. Mrs. Girard made reference to her son's sincerity to his friends. He treated his job as though it was his own airline. He respected his passengers. He cared about his coworkers. He did not believe in absence from work unless it was planned." He smiled and shook his head. "I recall when he approached me about the support to FAFGM. He talked to me about the little girls until his eyes had tears in them. I agreed to participate after I saw how sincere he was about the injustices to the little girls." He wiped his face. "He earned more of my respect that day." He addressed Mrs. Girard. "Even if we could clone your son, we would never be able to duplicate him. He was one of a kind at our airline. He is already missed. Heaven just gained an angel."

The friends used a conference room at the hotel where they stayed for a post burial luncheon in honor of Jean-Claude. The hotel catered the lunch with a variety of French cuisine. Although Nana had not eaten the entire day, she had no appetite for anything served.

Frank seemed to take Jean-Claude's death much harder than Tommie's. He did not learn of Tommie's death until at least a month later when he came out of his coma. He sat in quiet and reflected on his years with Jean-Claude. He was the popular football player on campus. His coach was strict, and did not allow players to even practice if their grades were under the expected score. Frank was serious about his classes and studies. He was an average student in math and English Literature. He wanted high grades. He had two foreign students in his math and English classes. Nana Nkuku was brilliant when it came to English Literature. Jean-Claude

Girard was a math genius. Frank befriended them so they would study with him to help improve his grades. The three began to study together. Frank's grades showed tremendous improvement. They became friends. Nana and Jean-Claude went to watch him practice. They did not miss any of his home games. Frank took Jean-Claude and Nana home one weekend to meet his mother brother. Amelia fed them so much that they always wanted to go home with Frank. Amelia wanted Frank to date Nana when she discovered that Nana was not Jean-Claude's girlfriend. Both Frank and Jean-Claude like Nana at first. She would not date them because of her secret. She liked their company so she stuck with them. They were her protection on campus, and she liked that. Jean-Claude and Frank never had an argument in all their years of friendship. Jean-Claude liked to tease so he rarely got angry. He and Frank held no secrets from each other. They trusted each other without conditions. They promised that if one of them died before his mother, the other would take care of the other's mother.

Frank reflected on their junior year in college. He slacked off a bit in his studies. He and Jean-Claude partied a great deal. Nana scolded them as though she was their mother. "I want the three of us to walk across that stage next year. I want us to receive our degrees together. I want us to throw out caps in the air like I see them do on TV." She kept them in line when they stepped out of it. He remembered that Jean-Claude would not date a girl if he had interest in her. Frank returned the favor, and did not date a girl if Jean-Claude expressed interest. He hoped that the international police would bring the men responsible to justice.

Nana sat and took in the day they put Jean-Claude to rest. She recalled the day she found the Lord. Jean-Claude was on one of his breaks from a flight. He suggested that they visit Amelia to check on her. They called to ask Amelia when she would be home. She told them to go over and attend church service with her. Nana already was in study of the Bible and the Wesley doctrine. She was not yet a true believer. She was on the fence about her beliefs. She did not know if she wanted to really do it. She was indecisive.

She and Jean-Claude got dressed up. He told her, "I've been to Mrs. Thurston's church with Frank and Tommie. You would think it is a fashion show, for the way the people there dress."

Nana laughed. "Is that part of their faith? I don't want to be religiously incorrect."

Jean-Claude found her statement innocent and hilarious. "I have never heard that one before; religiously incorrect." He inspected her attire. "Believe me; you are most definitely correct for that church."

The only other time Nana was in Amelia's church was to attend Tommie's funeral. In fact, prior to Paula's funeral in Minnesota, Nana had not entered a church. She and Jean-Claude sat in the pew with Amelia. Jean-Claude was in the middle of the two women. Amelia wore a royal blue dress, black pumps to match her black purse and a royal blue hat to match her dress. All of the older women in the Washington Northeast Baptist Church dressed in that fashion. Jean-Claude was right, Nana thought. They were all high fashioned.

The choir sang gospel selections, as everyone rocked from side to side. When the music got to someone, she either stood or raised her hands in praise to God. Nana was baffled. She had not seen anything like it. As the clergyman delivered his message of the day, he was interrupted by a lot of "Amen". Jean-Claude was accustomed to that type of worship because of his weekends at the Thurstons' home during his college years. It was a far cry from his Catholic upbringing and mass on Sundays with his mother. He looked at Nana and saw the same expression on her face which he wore on his first visit to that church. He was teased by Tommie and Frank. They said he looked confused and afraid.

Nana saw that Jean-Claude was involved with the music and the service. He rocked from side to side like everyone else in the church. He clapped his hands and seemed to have a great time. She decided to join the party. She rocked from side to side and clapped her hands. She even raised her hand in the air when she saw Amelia do it at one time. Jean-Claude was tickled but he watched his friend have a good time. After the Pastor's message, he put out an Alter Call. "If you are touched today by the Holy Spirit; if you need prayer; if you want to give yourself to the Lord today; whatever your need may be; come to this alter." The choir began a gospel song as people walked up to the Alter for prayer. Nana wanted to go up but she was shy. Jean-Claude saw that and beckoned to her to follow him. They left the pew and walked up to the Alter. She found herself face to face with the Pastor. He shook her hand. "What is your name, young lady?" She told him her name. "What would you like us to do for you today?" She told him she wanted prayer. Jean-Claude asked for prayer as well.

During the prayer, Nana felt sorrow; she felt joyful. She felt an inner peace about herself. She felt a certain contentment that she had not felt in her life. She began to cry. Jean-Claude was concerned. He thought her tears were for Tommie. Then Nana fell on her knees and allowed her tears to flow. She folded her hands to pray. Jean-Claude was shocked. He knew what had happened to her. She was converted right there to Christianity. When Nana got up off her knees, she and Jean-Claude embraced. Jean-Claude cried with Nana. Amelia walked over to where they were. She embraced the two of them in a group hug. She cried along with them. Nana remembered how proud Jean-Claude was that day to be with her when she gave her life to Christ. He told everyone about the experience and what it meant to him. Nana smiled at the thought and wiped her eyes. She thought to herself, "Jean-Claude left a lifetime of memories with his friends. We will never cease to remember his laughter and charm.

Frank delivered the eulogy. "We were only five friends who were inspired to help needy families at Thanksgiving. Then we discovered something called female genital mutilation." He paused for composure. "We invited Kiddi to join us. FAFGM became powerful enough to threaten individuals to the extent of the loss of countless of lives." His voice trembled as he continued. "We lost Paula – then Tommie along with hundreds of innocent people, due to those men's senseless behavior. Now we put our dear friend Jean-Claude to rest." His voice became firm. "How many more must die – how many more little girls must be cut before something is done? FAFGM appeals to the world – help us find a solution – a few men cannot win over the rest of the world- write to us and tell us your suggestions – we must work together for the eradication of FGM - please help us save the little girls from female genital mutilation. Rest in peace our dear friend."